PRAISE

"As one of our nation's valiant soldiers who fought in Vietnam and served the U.S., and then continued his outstanding service with a long stint as my Congressional and Governor's aide on behalf of and-for the citizens of New Mexico and the country, Butch Maki has written an inspiring, fact-based story that tells of his real-life experiences that everyone should read and thank him for."

~ Bill Richardson, an American politician, author and diplomat, who served as the 30th governor of New Mexico from 2003 - 2011

"As a former slick and gunship pilot with the 170th Assault Helicopter Company, all of Butch Maki's stories ring true. Apparently, the names have been changed to protect the 'innocent.' Bikini Beach gives an authentic feel to the experiences of the pilots, crew chiefs and door gunners. It contains fun and real stories of the Army Aviation men of the Vietnam War."

~ Roger "Fuzzy" Weaver, Bikini 19/Buccaneer 3

"Bikini Beach is a compelling story of our young soldiers as they faced combat in Vietnam. Many of these young men were away from home for the first time in a conflict that was very controversial. Butch Maki brings out how these soldiers grew from boys to men. You are drawn into their lives as they face combat for the first time. The story is captivating – a must-read for what these soldiers experienced."

~ Bill Kangas, U.S. Army - 1968-1970

"An innocently told tale of how war 'happens' to someone, and what war is guilty of doing to them."

~ Tom Avitabile, Bestselling Author

MORE PRAISE FOR *BIKINI BEACH*

"This book is a great read. It starts out slow but quickly picks up the pace and maintains that cadence throughout. It is the story of a helicopter crew chief during the Vietnam War and his experiences while riding in the back of a Huey. When he wasn't twisting wrenches, he was sitting as an M-60 door gunner in that very same helicopter. This is more than a war story because it dredges up the reader's own memories of the conflict. The war's participants got very good at putting their own experiences into mental compartments. Throughout their working life, they were too busy slaying dragons to remember what they did and saw. Later, after they retired, they had time to recall events long since forgotten. This book will unleash some of those memories, but this is not all bad because some of the monsters are funny as well as evil. Butch Maki writes a real and readable story."

~ CWO Jon Landstrum, Veteran of Vietnam and Iraq wars

"Events of the late 1960s and early 1970s tested the resolve of the U.S. like no period since the Civil War. I was too young for the draft but had a heightened awareness of the drama playing out on our national stage. One window to the world was the daily headline on The Boston Globe newspapers I delivered to doorsteps across town. Another was through eyes of young boys, not much older than me, leaving for Vietnam and returning as men, forever changed. Butch Maki expertly tells their story. His story. Boys who had fathers that fought a clear and righteous WWII with a country united in support and sacrifice for whom the Vietnam experience provided neither. Men cast in the mold of a country at odds with itself. Butch does not preach, nor does he take sides. This is the essence of his message and storytelling style. Using actual events from combat and then the home front, he tells a compelling drama of innocence, conflict, growth, love, failure, and triumph. Loved this book. Could not put it down."

~ Bill Haigis, Senior Vice President, Retired, ABB

AWARD-WINNING SHORT STORIES / EXCERPTS FROM BIKINI BEACH INCLUDE:

"From a Chicken to an Eagle"

1st Place - Veterans Administration and the American Legion Auxiliary's National Award *presented at the April 2023 National Creative Arts Festival Ceremony for Winners for 2022-2023 Submissions*

Selected for the Military Writers Society Anthology [2023]

"Bob's Last Flight"

Selected for The New Mexico Arts Military Anthology [July 2023]

To my wife and muse, Patty Maki, who supported and encouraged me to embrace my Vietnam experience and then advised, encouraged, and supported me while I wrote it down in this novel.

To Thomas Gifford, who is the reason I'm here to write of the brave men of the Army Helicopter crews. He refused to change assignments for a combat assault mission to a safer one, even though I offered him $100. That day, he died in a helicopter crash, teaching me not to think someone has it better than me.

Bikini Beach

A Novel Based on True Events

Butch Maki

Cover composite image © Tom Avitable

Photo of Tiger Wagon with Jordan CE ©Mark Cullison

Layout & Design by SGW Design

Printed in the United States of America

First Printing, 2023

ISBN 979-8-218-14817-1

bikinibeach.info

PREFACE

There have been many books written about the "Vietnam Experience." Butch Maki's contribution to this non-fiction sub-genre, *Bikini Beach*, is a unique addition that should be read by anyone interested in not only the war in Vietnam, but also in the impact of trauma on young men and women who were sent into combat.

As with almost all those sent to Vietnam by the United States Government between 1961 and 1973, Butch Maki was an impressionable young person who may have received extensive military training but was in no way psychologically prepared to deal with what awaited him.

This fictionalized account of Maki's experiences is a poignant tale about innocence lost, the terror of combat, the courage of the 2.7 million Americans who served in Vietnam (including 514,000 who served offshore), and especially the 58,000 plus Americans who were killed there. It is a reminder of what happens when poor political leadership risks young lives with no real commitment to victory.

The characters in *Bikini Beach* are even more remarkable when one considers the lack of psychological support they received from their countrymen back home and the disdain for their service expressed by so many.

It is no wonder that PTSD was a rampant product of that war, affecting so many for years after their combat experiences, even for the rest of their lives for many of them. *Bikini Beach* introduces the reader to combat in Vietnam with its adrenaline-spurting periods of terror interspersed by periods of boredom and the PTSD experience that followed it.

Odds are that most Americans know one of the estimated 6.4 million Americans still living (median age today: 71) who served in

Vietnam: a friend, neighbor, relative, co-worker. The odds are even greater that they are not aware that someone they know served there, and the longest odds favor the possibility that they frequently interact with someone who served in Vietnam, has PTSD, and they are not aware of either fact.

Bikini Beach is an eye-opening story that deserves your read, as do all the men and women who served in Vietnam.

~ Joseph Badal,
Award-Winning Author of 18 Suspense Novels
...and a Vietnam Veteran

CHAPTER 1:
THANKS A LOT, MISSION PLANNERS!

June 1967

"Soldier Boy" by The Shirelles plays in the background as Susan and I spotted each other across the decorated gym. Bright-colored crepe paper and Christmas lights transform the cheesy sock-smelling, dreary, and darkened gym into a sunny spring-like garden. It is senior prom. Susan has been my longtime heartthrob; we have been inseparable since grade school. Tonight, she is wearing a strapless, low-cut ball gown and a big smile as she starts across the floor toward me. The reflections from the rotating mirror ball run across her bare shoulders and make her green eyes light up like emeralds. The pulsating light makes her appear as a ghost; there, then not. Susan is of French-Canadian descent with dark hair and light skin around a magnificent body, but it is just her smile that makes me, a small-town farm boy, tingle all over. As she comes closer, she bends over to lift the hem of her full-length gown. I guess it is so she can walk faster—towards me.

That move makes me giddy as it causes her top to open just enough to peek at where I wanted to be more than heaven itself. She

1

smiles and looks at me, then says through virginal lips, "Drop your cocks and grab your socks. It's time to wake up and become heroes."

The voice piercing my dream comes bellowing from the Charge of Quarters—or CQ—and the smell of fifty GIs housed in the same small hooch brings me back to reality.

I roll over and press the light button on my watch. It is three o'clock in the damn morning. I have gotten all of four and a half hours of sleep. It is nowhere near enough time to have recovered from yesterday, a day that consisted of ten hours of flying, a mission briefing, too much paperwork, an inspection of and repairs to my helicopter, followed by a night at the club.

Then, another unpleasant thought comes to me, like the slap that Susan would have given me if she had followed my eyes down during that dream. Last night's briefing hit me. It is the reason we are up so early—today's mission.

What was I thinking when I enlisted for this shit? Instead of cuddling with Susan back in New Hampshire while inhaling the sweet scent of her hair and skin and listening to the soft honey of her voice, I am in godforsaken, God-forgotten Vietnam. Here, I am surrounded by the ever-present stench of aviation fuel and fumes, the rank smell of my sweat, and the high-pitched fluttering sound of a helicopter off in the distance. I am not really sure how this happened, but I am now, incredibly, a UH-1 Huey helicopter crew chief. Me! Spec 5 Donald Makinen, or Mack to my friends. A few months earlier, I couldn't even spell helicopter, let alone be in charge of one. All just to keep this bullshit war going.

My company is the 170th Assault Helicopter Company. This particular day's assignment is to support a maximum combat offensive by the 4th Infantry Division into a North Vietnamese battalion's fortified bivouac area. There is only one word to describe my emotions at that moment, and I shout it, "FUCK!" I am not the only one cursing; the expletive echoed through the hooch like we are in a canyon.

I look around at the half wooden walls with studs showing and half screens in the hooch. I push up the mosquito net I had draped over the makeshift frame I slept on last night, and every night, courtesy of our slumlord of these fine accommodations—better known as the United States Army—that never quite keep all the little bloodsuckers out but does an excellent job this morning of keeping me in as I untangle myself from it.

I drag myself out of bed and stand up in my own tiny space defined by the tall lockers between me and my neighbors so as to wall off something akin to a small room. I don't bother to shower this morning. Who cares, I thought, I don't have a date today. At least, I hope not. The only date I will be likely to get would be an invitation to an all-expense-paid stay at the Hanoi Hilton, the infamous prisoner-of-war jail.

I do, however, put on clean underwear. I think this comes from my days playing high school sports when my mother would say, "Make sure you put on clean underwear in case you have to go to the hospital. I don't want anyone to think I'm not a good mother."

After putting my pants, boots, and shirt on, I stumble through the tropical night like a sleepwalker. The usual unpleasant aroma greets me as I approach the latrines. Our toilets are a half-dozen or more old-fashioned outhouse-style privies lined up side-by-side. Underneath each of these commodes is half of a 55-gallon barrel, strategically placed below the throne as a catch basin.

Screw up in your duties on base, and your assignment would be one of the most hated tasks imaginable. It is the "Shit Burning" detail. Shit burning is the Army's way of eliminating human waste. Detailees drag the barrels out from under the commode, douse it with diesel fuel, and set it on fire. No hot dogs, chestnuts, or marshmallows are found roasting over those open flames.

Unfortunately, you couldn't just hold your nose as you approach and use the latrines. You have to wait in a stinking line, literally! In the Army, everything you do has a line associated with it—from dumping to dining.

On this particular morning, my assigned gunner, Russ, is his usual hillbilly self. As he bangs on one of the latrine doors, he shouts, "Come on, man, I got to go! You can abuse yourself in the hooch while the rest of us are at breakfast." Russ, being from the wilds of Florida's Panhandle, has a particular backwoods approach to life. He is of average height and a little overweight with long blond hair, or at least as long as our platoon sergeant would allow. All the rest of us have short hair to minimize our grooming tasks, but not Russ. He always has to be different.

From the outside, our mess hall looks like our hooch. Sandbags were stacked against the outside plywood walls to stop shrapnel during mortar attacks. Solid wood shutters covered the weather screens and could be swung up in hot times to allow a breeze. On the inside, instead of bunks and wall lockers, there is a kitchen, a food serving line, and a 'dining area' with about twenty-five tables, each with four seats. The mess sergeant has his wife send him red and white checkered plastic table coverings. It is a nice touch, making things feel a little more like home.

The morning meal is nothing out of the ordinary and is certainly no gourmet treat. It consists of powdered eggs, deep-fried bacon, and cold toast with chipped beef and gravy. Since the Army served its first breakfast to Massachusetts Minutemen, that last delightful dish is referred to as "Shit on a Shingle." To wash it down, we have cowboy coffee with powdered milk and sugar. Cowboy coffee is made by adding coffee grounds to a kettle of boiling water. A real skill was the ability to dip your cup into that caldron and come away with no coffee grounds in your mug.

The food service line is staffed by the cooks who dish out the meal's offerings. On this particular morning, the cooks are none too pleased. Even my friend Josh doesn't have his usual big smile. When I get to him for my dry powdered eggs, I ask, "Why so glum this morning?"

"I was supposed to be off until second shift starting at eleven," Josh explains, "but they called everyone to work at one this morning to make sure we had enough cooks to get you guys out of here by four."

"Look at it this way," I assure him, "Between now and lunch, you'll have a chance to catch some rack. We may not be back in time to catch dinner."

Josh smiles and motions me to move on for my bacon.

There is always chatter in the food line. In front of me, Ron teasingly asks the cooks, "What is this called, you know, when they ask me at the hospital?"

Russ adds, "After the war, you guys have a future in Las Vegas as magicians. If you can turn good food into shit, just think what you could do with props on a stage."

Another cook tells Russ, "It's our job to keep you alive—not to fatten you up. That's your mother's job. Keep the line moving."

While eating breakfast, as the crews discuss what we heard in last night's brief about today's mission, a second lieutenant (or as the enlisted call them, "second lewys") from Brooklyn calls for everyone to "Shadup!"

We are all a little surprised to see our Commanding Officer (CO) Major Burk walk into the dining hall.

"What's this all about?" Vincent, another crew chief in my platoon, asks.

"Shit, if I know," Russ says. "The CO should be in the officer's mess hall."

Burk was in his mid-thirties. His brown hair was already infiltrated by enemy gray. Most surprising from this officer of the average build is the booming voice he possesses. He could bark out orders and get your attention at will. He did it often, and with great effect.

"Men," he starts, serious as a heart attack, "I just wanted to come down here and tell you to stay sharp today. This is the top mission on today's schedule for the entire Vietnam Theater of Operations. Last night, I covered the mission profile. One change though, General Ord—our 1st Aviation Brigade Commander—will now be in the Command-and-Control ship above us, along with the 4th Division Commander."

His demeanor relaxes. We think he is finished, until he adds, "And now boys, here's something I didn't tell you last night. Hell, why ruin a good night's sleep?"

To say that everyone in the mess hall is suddenly rapt would be an understatement.

Major Burk pauses as if to collect the right words, and then says flatly, "We plan to surprise them at breakfast. That means there will be no LZ prep until we're five minutes from landing."

The room erupts in murmurs, shocked expressions and questioning looks all around. Not prepping a landing zone (LZ) within a few hours of artillery bombardment was unheard of.

Someone is heard whispering, "Is he nuts?"

The second lewy yells, "Settle down, ya mutts. That means you, Kawalsky!"

He jutts his finger at 'Ski,' "Yeah, you!" He turns to the Major, "Sorry, sir."

"Look, men, I know this might seem unorthodox, but it's calculated that catching them with their pants down will result in a fifty to sixty percent increase in enemy losses than if they had the two-or-three-hour artillery 'alarm clock' to get them all ready to greet us. This is a new tactic, but we are confident it's the best approach and assures a decisive victory. Now, at five minutes out, two Air Force F-4 Fantoms will bring them hell with their bombs and Vulcan cannons. Captain Fisk's gunships will work the LZ, clearing potential booby traps and mines with miniguns and rockets."

I hadn't quite caught it last night when he mentioned that we will face heavy ground fire during our approach and departure but now, it scares the chipped beef out of me.

Burk makes eye contact with various men across the room. He continues, "If your ship can't make it out, stay with the grunts until we can get you. Those infantry boys know how to survive on the ground, and you don't! That's all I have to say, except, good luck. Send the bastards back to hell, and let's all make it back for a celebration tonight. I'm buying."

Everyone serving in 'Nam enjoyed the rare treat of cold beer, so that last line gets a big hurrah. As the Major leaves the mess, the second lewy barks, "Okay, guys, as you were. Ten minutes to the flight line."

"Thanks a lot, mission planners... the top mission in 'Nam today," I mumble under my breath.

"Five minutes! All those fly-boys will do is kick up a little dirt in five damn minutes. We're fucked. Ord is crazy. 'Calculated,' my ass!" Russ spits on the floor. "Those brainiacs will calculate us into body bags, and they won't feel a thing."

I like Major Burk, even though he had a Ph.D. in ass-chewing that came to him with ease and regularity. What I respected about him is that he isn't a West Point snob. He joined the Army as an enlisted man two years before deciding to go to Officer Candidate School. Those two years of eating chow, a culinary notch above pig slop, like the rest of us taught him how enlisted men lived and thought. That imprint forged the respect I have for him and, I believe, the trust he has in us. Like yin and yang, the bad part of his dog-face years is that he knows all our tricks on how we circumnavigate established procedures and have perfected screwing off.

The lieutenant enters again and orders, "I said ten minutes. Now move it!" and everyone stands up from the tables.

There isn't a word spoken as we leave. I could read their faces like the front page of my home paper and it is the same headline for me; Oh Shit, we are going in hot with no LZ prep.

Josh, the cook, breaks the silence, "We have an opening for a cook if someone wants it."

A chorus of, "Fuck you, Josh," answers his offer.

After breakfast, I go back to the hooch and arm myself with my regular assortment of weapons. I strap on my 45, pull the M79 grenade launcher over my shoulder, grab two LAW hand-held rockets, and my M16 with five double 30-round clips. Double clips consist of two 30-round clips taped together, so you just take the empty one out, turn it over, and reinsert it for another thirty rounds. Rambo would have been proud of my armament. I might even have won a gold star like my teacher gave out in grade school for being a good boy, if the NRA gave out gold stars, that is.

As I leave the hooch, I look left; Thomas Griffey, better known as Giff, is still in bed. I knock on his locker and say, "Giff, we have pitch pull in an hour. What the hell are you still doing in the rack?"

Giff is from Rifle, Colorado. The only bad thing anyone could say about Giff is he snored. If I landed late and had a '25-hour inspection' due, he would help me instead of going to the club like the rest of our merry band. It isn't only me. He helps out everywhere. Giff isn't a Saint but, in my opinion, he would do until a saint got drafted.

"Your take-off time is in an hour, but I'm flying C&C today," he says as he yawns and continues, "and I'm leaving after you guys."

I reply sheepishly, "So, you will be at 5,000 feet, all safe and cozy in your command-and-control 'copter, laughing your ass off at me getting mine shot off in the shit. I'll give you a hundred bucks to switch places."

"Nice try!" he smirks. "Let me get this straight, your ass will get shot off and mine laughed off, so both of us will be assless at the end of today."

I nod, not knowing where he was going with this.

He explains, "So, all we got to do tonight is go downtown and get a little ass back, if you know what I mean," he snorts.

"No thanks," I reply. "I got someone special expecting me to come home."

"…expecting me to come home," he blurts, talking in unison over the end of my answer which he has heard so many times before, "Yeah, I know."

I give him a middle finger salute and walk off to join Russ outside as we head for the flight line.

On the way, Russ and I meet the first gunner I flew with, Staff Sergeant Jefferson, a black man in his thirties who knows his way around guns. He taught me a lot about Hueys and duties while flying. He is a nice guy, keeps to himself, and is not real sociable with the rest of the crewmen. "Hey, Sarge, where have you been?" I ask as we get close. "I haven't seen you around for a while."

"Hi kid, I was on temporary duty with the 189th."

I notice he now has a Buccaneer patch, so he has transferred from my platoon to the gun platoon. "Are you in the guns now?"

"Yeah, kid," he quips. "Stay safe today. I hear the bad boys have 50-caliber machine guns and rocket-propelled grenades." With that said, he leaves us heading towards the gun platoon's parking.

"Ooooo, RPGs! Now, I feel all comfy." Russ sneers as he hitches his head towards Jefferson, shrugs and asks, "What's his story?"

"Jefferson was infantry in the 4th Division. Got a leg wound. Mucho problematic for a grunt humping in the bush all day, so the Army decided to send him to our company since we ain't got no E6 slots for infantry sergeants in an aviation unit. Their answer was to make him the gunner for the greenest mechanic entering the flight platoon, me."

"So, hold it. You were his boss? An E6, a platoon sarge, taking orders when you were a private first-class crew chief?"

"He's a good egg; he never let that get in the way."

"Rare."

"He did kinda piss me off in the beginning, though."

"Yeah, how?"

"On our first flights, he wouldn't load a round in my gun. He said it was to make sure I didn't shoot someone by accident."

"Ha! He made you, Barney Fife!" Russ looks puzzled when he asks, "How does he know there are 50-cals and RPGs in the LZ?"

"I don't know," I shake my head as I answer. "The Sarge has a sixth sense for shit like that, and he's usually right. I think it's because he rooms with the Senior NCOs and they tell him stuff."

"So, why would they send him to the 189th TDY when we're

short of gunners? There's got to be something strange about that there guy," Russ asks anxiously.

I elbow him, "It's your Southern roots, 'coloring' your opinion."

Russ says in a huff, "You know I ain't like that, you asshole."

CHAPTER 2:
FLIGHT LINE AT BIKINI BEACH

The flight line is alive with activity in the pre-dawn glow. Flashlights dance all over like a light show as crews are doing last-minute checks. Mechanics explain work done during the night to the crew chiefs and the fuelers add more fuel to the gunships. The extra JP-4 sacrifices the 'luxury' of short take-off runs for being able to spend more time protecting us on target. Buccaneer gunners load their weapons and extra ammo onto their ships.

Two enormous diesel generators run right behind the maintenance hangar that supplies power to the entire camp. That means for the next hour, I will be assaulted by their ever-present noise and exhaust smell. Still, that is more pleasant than the group of grumpy maintenance platoon members who worked on my bird through the night.

"What's up, guys?"

"They kept us on from the day shift to help the night crew get as many aircraft flyable as possible." He throws a wrench into his toolbox with extreme prejudice.

Another, walking like a zombie from exhaustion, tells me, "The lab reported that you have metal in your ship's transmission oil."

"Good! So, we're grounded and not flying today?"

"Not so lucky, Mack. You're good to go. We checked the magnetic plug and found no metal chips. Take another sample tonight and send it in," the mechanic instructs.

That brings me back to reality.

I am still involved in this monkey fuck.

Once the maintenance crew moves on to the next ship, I notice a wide-eyed PFC standing in front of me, looking lost.

"What's your problem, private?" I ask.

"I'm looking for aircraft six-three-four," he mutters.

"How long have you been here?"

"Three days, but it's my first night in maintenance. I'm looking for aircraft six-three-four," the bewildered kid repeats.

I realize he doesn't have a clue as to how things work, so I figure I will help him as some kindhearted crew member did for me when I was new. "I'm going to say this once, and you better get it. Okay?" I say with some persuasive authority and wait impatiently for his response.

Nervously, he shakes his head up and down.

"Every aviation company has two lift platoons, each consisting of troop and cargo haulers, called 'slicks.' Then there's one gun support platoon; their Hueys are equipped with armament. Now, here's how you know the difference: the slick helicopter's nose art is Little Annie Fanny."

He interrupts, "From the *Playboy* magazine? Is that why they call the flight line Bikini Beach?"

"Correct, and yes. Now, to help you determine which platoon the aircraft belongs in, look carefully at Little Annie Fanny's colored bikini painted on the aircraft's nose. See, ours is red as we're in the first flight platoon. The aircraft you're looking for is in the second platoon. Next line over, and her bikini will be blue."

"Blue. Got it ," he confirms.

"One last thing, the gun platoon's call sign is the Buccaneers. They're in the line behind us, and you'll see skull and crossbones for their nose art. Clear?"

He nods affirmatively.

"Now when you get to helicopter six-three-four, ask Jeffery— and make sure you call him Jeffery—for a bucket of rotor wash and bring it back here. Okay?" I instruct.

"Got it, rotor wash," he nods and scurries off in that direction.

Russ admonishes me, "You're cruel. You know he'll get his ass chewed; Jeff hates being called Jeffery, and I thought 'rotor wash' was what you called the turbulence coming from a helicopter in a hover? You sent him for a bucket of air?"

I shrug my shoulders and say, "Turbulent air. Hey, I was mostly nice to explain how to find the ship he is looking for. Besides, you don't want him to think flight crews are all together warm and fuzzy, do you? Let's get going on preflight."

I start my maintenance checks, keeping the cowling cover and the tail rotor drive shaft tunnel cover off until the pilots complete their preflight checks. At the same time, Russ mounts the two M60s and loads ammo into each machine gun.

"Put a couple of extra ammo cans on," I shout.

"Do I look stupid?" he replies and shrugs. "I already did."

I was about to say that he did look kind of ridiculous with the chaw of tobacco in his cheek at four in the morning, but instead, I ask, "How about extra barrels?"

"Yep, and one additional on one shot Charlie's side," he confirms as he snickers.

For me, extra barrels are a must because, on the left side of the ship where I sit, the wind from the aircraft's forward flight sometimes blows a spent round back into the ejector that causes two cartridges to jam in the barrel. The quickest way to fix this is to change the barrels and jack in another round, then continue. One time in the heat of battle, I changed a barrel and didn't lock the replacement one in properly. So, with the first shot fired, the barrel left with the bullet. Ever since, Russ has teased me by calling me, "One Shot Charlie."

The pilot assignments are the first thing to go right that morning. Our pilots are Warrant Officer Warren and Chief Warrant Officer Snow. As fitting their rank, we addressed them as mister. Mr. Snow was a soft-spoken man and all business when in the pilot's seat. He served three tours in Vietnam as an Army pilot and was the war's most decorated black helicopter pilot. Together, they had lots of combat experience and were not stuck on the officer's superiority-over-enlisted-men bullshit.

Seeing Snow, I said, "At the risk of sounding like an ass kisser, I just want to tell you that my Angel is with me today, giving me you as our aircraft commander."

"Thanks for that, but we need your Angel to stay with all of us today. This LZ isn't going to be a walk in the park. Today, we have 32 slicks from two companies and six gunships assigned to the mission."

"I heard and F-4s but no artillery," I said a bit worriedly. "Days like today I feel like the guys driving landing craft at Normandy."

"They could swim their way out of trouble, but we can't fly," he said while grinning. Comforting words they were not.

Warren looks over the gig sheet and asks about the ship discrepancies as Snow does the preflight. I tell Snow, "Don't check the red stabilizer bar damper timing. It will just scare you."

"Why don't we replace it?" he asks. "It only takes a few minutes."

"We don't have any," I answer. "It's not a big deal, and I'll keep an eye on it." I winked.

16

"Okay, button her up," Snow said, meaning it was time for Russ and me to get the bird ready for flight.

The pilots buckled in and started the cockpit checklist. Warren called off items as Snow responded with the appropriate check results. Meanwhile, Russ and I closed the covers and cowling. We were flight-ready 10 minutes before 'crank time.' These minutes did not lack for humor. The pilot uses two control sticks. The "collective" stick he moves with his left hand beside his seat to increase pitch in the blades. The other stick is the "cyclic" stick positioned between his legs that controlled the lateral movement of the Huey.

"Russ," I called out. "Do you know I've heard that those pilot boys practice flying by choking the 'ole chicken at night?" I could hear chuckling from somewhere behind the helicopter.

Just then, the horn sounded that signaled crank time. Russ pulled the rotor blade to 90 degrees to the ship.

Mr. Snow sounded, "Clear." Then Russ and I responded, "Clear," signaling it was safe to start the engine.

Immediately, I heard the expected snap of the fuel igniters. I heard the whine of the 1,300 horsepower Lycoming T53 L-13 engines and caught the first blast burning jet fuel perfume as the Huey's 42-foot rotor blade slowly made the first of what would be millions of revolutions before the day was done. Despite the rat hole we were in, I was somewhat comforted by the Huey, as it was the most dependable aircraft made since the C-47, a World War II transport.

Russ and I assumed the positions required to monitor the engine for leaks or fire. Then came a muffled thud that indicated fuel ignition as the rotor began to accelerate until it reached ground idle. I made a final check around the ship for open panels or any leaks, slid my side's pilot bulletproof protector forward, closed his door, and then climbed into my position behind a pole-mounted M-60 belt-fed machine gun.

It took me a couple of minutes to put on my "Chicken Plate", or body armor, and monkey strap, a harness I wore that attached by a belt to the helicopter's bulkhead. This allowed me to move around the ship but kept me from plummeting to terra firma if I happened to fall out for any reason—like if I got shot. Most crew members took out the backplate from the body armor and sat on it to protect the family jewels from up-and-coming Vietcong rounds.

I sat on the left side. Seat assignments were determined by basic rank. In a crash, the transmission and rotor blades most likely go to the right where I assigned Russ to sit. Being the senior enlisted man on the crew, I invoked RHIP protocols. I was able to choose the left side because rank has its privileges.

As the engine reached ground idle speed, I heard our CO, Burk, check in with the entire flight on the command radio. "Bikini, flight Bikini Six. Report when ready," he commanded.

Sometimes it was confusing to hear the Huey's three different radios going, overriding instructions from the pilots on the intercom. I was able to make out that the CO wanted to know when each bird's crew members were in their position and ready to proceed.

Our platoon leader came on next. "Bikini Red, flight Bikini Red Six. Report ready?"

As the Bikini Reds confirmed their ready status, I keyed the ship's intercom. "We got all the big RLO's with us today. By chance, are they fumigating the HQ?" I asked.

"No, they're here to help their careers by earning medals," Warren said. "Watch what medals they'll get put in for today compared to us."

Russ added, "Yeah, and see what you two up front get compared to us poor folks in the back of the bus."

"So, Russ, you may earn your paycheck today," I teased.

I don't know who said it, but it made me laugh. "Now you understand how shit rolls downhill."

There was a clear-cut line between warrant officers and commissioned ones. A commissioned officer could get us into the shit; a warrant can get us out. Essentially warrants are like vocational officers; they actually do stuff—fly an airship to a military cop. Commissioned officers are more overseers and commanders. By military code, I salute both, but a tad bit more hardily when it's a WO returning.

"No, I owe it to Jess from last week's poker night," Russ sheepishly admitted and added, "so I got nothing left for the hookers."

Snow replied over the intercom, "The only sure thing about hookers is it will make your pee burn like acid coming through it."

"No way," I added. "Ba Muoi Ba can kill any germs interior and exterior."

"That Vietnamese 'Panther Piss' of a beer reminds me of a turpentine and oatmeal mix," Mr. Snow said.

Russ asked, "Mack, why don't you come with me tonight, and I'll show you the best places?"

"How many times do I have to tell you? My standards are much higher than those skanks you frequent," I roared.

"Yes, I freqin'..."

Our banter stopped as soon as we heard the CO's radio command, "Bikini, flight Bikini Six. All flights have checked in ready. Line up on me down runway two-six."

Snow brought the engine to full RPM and directed, "Mack, clear me out."

"No, go. We've still got several in the way," We couldn't lift until a couple of Hueys that were behind us cleared our flight path.

As I waited, I looked at our helicopters running nestled in their revetments, which consisted of two rows of L-shaped structures of perforated steel panels and sandbags. They were placed so there was just enough space for one Huey to park between each other. The theory was when Hueys were under a mortar attack, the shrapnel would be contained within the revetment, and the damage would be limited to one bird. The downside of revetments was that pilots had to back out blind with guidance from the crew.

After what seemed like forever, I opened my intercom with, "Our turn, sir."

"Coming up," Snow responded as he pulled up on the collective stick toward him.

"Clear left," I reported.

"Clear right," Russ followed.

Snow backed out and eased our ship into the line moving towards the runway. I thought it resembled the lineup of commercial aircraft waiting to take off at Boston Logan Airport the day of my departure from what we called the "real world" en route to this hellhole.

He explained, "Each aircraft will be identified today with a letter and the ships in that group with a number. This system is so that the C&C ship can single out which aircraft to bitch at."

We were designated Delta 1, the lead ship in group four, D, of the eight groups in the assault. The last ship in the flight, the "tail-end Charley," had our executive officer Major Parker, whose call sign was Bikini Five. XO Parker was a typical West Point grad, or as we called them—ring knockers, because they all wore their class rings as a sign of importance. He was tall and thin with blond hair and hazel eyes. He had issues with my guy, Major Burk. Parker's West Pointer's pedigree bristled that Officer Candidate School graduate Burk held rank over him.

The radio crackled and proclaimed, "Bikini Six, Bikini Five. Your flight's formed."

"Roger, Bikini, flight Bikini Six. Pull pitch in five, four, three, two, one." And like that, we all were off in a deafening roar to whatever destiny awaited us.

CHAPTER 3:
ANY PIN IN A PINCH

I looked back at our flight line as we departed with the hope I would see it again. I could see our six gunships just getting ready. They would catch up to us on the way to the LZ.

Today, the decision was for the gunships to take on extra fuel and leave later than us since we had to pick up our passengers before going on to the LZ. I remember learning about them in Huey school. They taught us that the gunships were UH-1C models, a retrofit of the original Huey body style. They were shorter than us, but unlike the earlier models, they had a 540-rotor system that gave them better lift speed and maneuverability. Their problem was that they had the T53 L-11 engines that produced 200 less horsepower than our power plant. Worse still, they generally were overloaded with armament, and because of their limited power, they would take on less fuel. Less fuel meant they sometimes needed to break off to refuel before the assault was complete instead of remaining with the slicks.

The lone bird that would be left was Giff, the C&C's queen for a day. He blew us kisses as we departed. I returned the gesture this time with a double-barreled middle-finger salute while thinking, *I wish that was me.*

Past Bikini Beach, I saw the CH-47 heavy-lift Chinook crews readying their massive machines for the day. After we inserted the initial assaults, these heavies would drop in supplies and reinforcements and recover any downed Hueys.

I got to hand it to the Army; they tried to tell us that losing one of the Chinooks was like losing four of us. Ha! I didn't buy it for a second. One of them costs so much more than a Huey. That is the real reason I think they weren't as willing to risk them on initial assaults. With their thirty troops and six crew members on board, that is a lot of coin going in up in those flights.

After takeoff, I almost had time to light a cigarette when the infantry's radio opened with, "Cowboy, this is Bikini Six." Our CO was calling out to the call sign for the infantry battalion's commanding officer on today's mission.

Cowboy responded, and our CO informed him that we were ten minutes out. Cowboy and our CO kept communicating while I requested a gun check from the pilots.

Snow confirmed and warned, "Okay, but, Russ, try not to hit our sister to the right."

"Don't tell him that," I teased. "He hasn't hit what he's aimed at yet. Tell him to try to hit the son of a bitch. They'll be safer." With that, we each fired five rounds to make sure the weapons were correctly reassembled from the previous night's cleaning, since the only place to test fire them is in flight. Russ was one of the best gunners in the company. We both knew damn well that things can go wrong after a long duty day. All guns checked out.

"Cowboy, this is Bikini Six. Identify purple smoke," the radio crackled. Identifying smoke color is asked in the field and is essential to ensure the enemy isn't luring us into a trap. Cowboy confirmed the color, which assured our CO that the enemy wasn't luring us into a trap. It also affirmed for the Old Man, our CO, that we had the correct Pickup Zone so he ordered our approach for the PZ in our groups of four.

I noticed the infantrymen waiting to load, lined up in four groups of twelve on the spots where our ships landed. "Sir, there are 12 grunts lined up to board. If we take all of them, we'll be over grossed.".

Snow responded apologetically, "Yeah, they want to put as many boots on the ground as fast as possible, so every ship gets extra men. The theory is we'll burn off enough fuel by the time we get to the LZ so that we'll be under gross weight."

"But that was already calculated, figuring one extra at nine," I said, confused.

"We'll have to work it out," he said irritably.

"Okay, Okay," I responded easily. "The reason I asked is the seal is off the fuel control setting, and the locknuts are loose on the throttle's linear actuator. Give me two minutes while the grunts are loading, and I'll give you about 100 more horsepower."

He didn't hesitate. "Do it," he instructed.

"Russ, load the troops on your side, and I'll tweak the engine," I heard myself say.

When we landed, I jumped out, shut the cargo door to allow me to open the engine cowling, and went to work. I turned the fuel mixture up on the fuel controller, pulled the cotter pin, removed the attaching bolt, backed off the locking nut, adjusted the actuator rod, and reinstalled all the bolts and nuts. Then, everything turned to shit. The cotter pin broke. *Shit*, I thought. *If I don't pin this nut, the engine's vibration will cause the nut to back off the bolt. If that bolt falls out, the engine will go to idle, and we'll eat jungle.* My mind went crazy. *Where do I get a substitute for that cotter pin?* Then it came to me.

After jumping down from the engine compartment, I plugged into the intercom and said confidently, "The cotter pin broke, but I've got another. Give me two more minutes."

Russ asked, "Where did you find one?"

"From a grenade," I said quickly.

I unplugged before I got an answer, as I knew I had no time to respond. I grabbed one of my grenades from its round cardboard shipping container, took off the top, and slid the dangerous explosive out far enough to pull out the safety pin. I then slid it back to where the container would hold the arming handle in place.

I gave it to Russ and warned, "Don't drop it!" I think Russ swallowed his chew right then and there and began holding the grenade like it was a sore dick as he got back into his seat.

After pinning the nut, I closed the cowling and keyed the mic saying, "Ready."

Snow said, "Just in time. Let's do a power check. Call off the numbers." He pulled in power, and Warren read off the engine's RPM. "Sixty-six, 65, 64-50."

"Beep it up," I instructed, indicating he should increase the electric throttle switch on his collective stick to activate the linear actuator and increase power.

Warren said with amazement, "Sixty-five, back to 66-hundred."

"Just don't take torque off the engine without coming off the power. If you do, it will over-speed the engine," I warned.

"Roger that! Here we go," he signaled, and we took off with the rest of the flight.

Snow gave us the usual final instruction that we should remember to recline the pilots' seats in case we crashed so the pilots would have clear egress if their doors were jammed or we sustained other front-end damage. Then he came to the mission particulars, and that got our attention. "We will land in groups of four. Our bird with ships two and three will land in the LZ front, and ship number four will squeeze in behind us. We need to be in and out in 30 seconds, or the groups behind us will stack up, and they're too heavy to hover. So, get the grunts out fast."

When we got to cruising altitude, I confirmed, "Russ, do you still have the grenade?"

He sheepishly replied, "We're still here, aren't we?"

"Well, throw it out, hillbilly!" I ordered. That was the fastest he ever followed one of my commands. A few seconds later, I heard an explosion below us.

Our number-four ship was quick to report, "Lead, you had an airburst below you."

Snow explained, "Chalk four, it's just a grunt who had a grenade with a pin that looked bad, so we had him dispose of it."

It was about thirty minutes to the LZ. This was the first time I noticed that the grunts were looking at me like I had a third eye. They must have seen the hand grenade trick. I smiled and shrugged my shoulders. A big mountain of a sergeant, who reminded me of Hoss Cartwright from the TV show *Bonanza*, took his pointing finger and circled it around his ear. I chuckled at the implication while pointing my finger up and circling it like the rotor.

He gave me the okay signal and a big toothy grin.

Russ pointed and said, "Look, they're sitting on their steel pots."

"They all sit on their helmets; it's the first thing they learn in country. It's for the same reason we're sitting on the chicken plate," I chuckled.

"Protecting their jewels," we said in unison as we nodded knowingly.

When we were five minutes out of the LZ, an F-4 Phantom fighter came alongside us, doing all he could to slow down enough to match our speed. He was so close that I could see the smiles on both the pilots. One pilot saluted, winked, and hit his afterburner, then was gone.

Snow affirmed, "There goes our first calling card on target."

"Show no mercy," Warren barked.

The command frequency broke in with, "Bikini Six, Buccaneer Six. Your guns are with you," the Company Commander acknowledged.

I looked back at the flight and watched as our ship's rotor wash rocked all the ships up and down. The impact of the wind turbulence from our rotors resembled a graceful dance. Watching this airborne ballet gave me a needed moment of peace.

Snow said as he pointed forward with his chin, "Look at that, guys."

I turned to the front and stood to see over the pilots. What I witnessed was an eerie spectacle from 5,000 feet. The sun was breaking over the green jungle as the F-4s released their fury. The morning mist gave the illusion of a larger than usual sun rising with a vibrant mix of orange, reds, and yellows. Below it was the rainbow of colors from exploding napalm and cluster bombs dropped from the F-4s. I thought, *wouldn't it be great if I were an artist able to capture this stunning scene of contrasting beauty and horror?*

Next, it was the gunships' turn. While the fighter jets concentrated on the enemy's encampment along the tree line, the gunships poured their ordinance on the landing zone, hoping to explode as many booby traps and mines as possible before we arrived.

The ground radio woke up with, "Cowboy, this is Green Sword Six." Green Sword Six was the 4th Infantry's Commanding General with Giff. "We're getting secondary explosions in the LZ, so be prepared for mines and booby traps."

Then, our General had to get his two cents in. "Bikini Flight, this is Iron Eagle. Secondary explosions are happening in the LZ, mines or booby traps can be expected. Don't sit down while unloading to avoid setting one of them off."

Now, there were a lot of things wrong with that, I thought. *First, if he was an Iron Eagle, he'd have an iron ass and would be down here with us instead of at 5,000 feet with Giff. Second, he knows we heard the same shit from the Infantry General, and even the dumbest among us know that means—mines. Third, they loaded every aircraft so heavy that the only one that could sustain a hover was us, and I would be in for disciplinary action if they knew what I did to the engine. They call them our superiors. Hell, I don't think they are even our contemporaries.*

"Alpha 1 short final," the CO reported. The bird was on final approach and close to landing.

What seemed like silence for hours suddenly came to an end as the CO continued, "Alpha 1, piece of cake. Boys coming out."

Then Bravo 1 radioed short final. The CO report "piece of cake" was like a thousand pounds lifted off my shoulders.

Snow cut short my moment of contentment by adding, "Don't get comfortable, boys. They just haven't come out of their holes yet."

"You could fuck up a $1,000 piece of ass with that, Mr. Snow," Russ snickered. I thought, *now that's saying something when you could get laid anywhere in this country for three bucks.*

Radio chatter continued, "Bravo 1 coming out."

"Charlie 1 short final."

"Bravo 1 to Charlie 1. Watch that tree line at 10 o'clock. I took several hits on my outbound."

"Buc Three, this is Buc Six. Hit that area Bravo 1 took fire from."

Buc Three responded, "Buc Three with a heavy fire team of guns, rolling in hot."

When Sergeant Jefferson was my gunner, he explained that there are two types of gunship teams: light and heavy. A light team has two gunships, and heavy teams have three to initiate a tactic we call a daisy chain. The theory behind the three ships in the heavy team and the daisy chain tactic is when the first ship attacks the target, the second protects him from behind. When the second one attacks, the third will cover the second. By the time ship three attacks, number one is back from his run to cover three. In this way, each attacking aircraft is covered by the one behind it. This maneuver applies continuous firepower on the target while each ship has suppressive fire from behind.

Snow announced on short final—declaring we were almost at the target. Russ and I opened fire at the tree line.

"Jesus! We're taking a shit load of fire from the left," I called out as I saw a steady stream of green tracers coming up that made me believe I could slide down them. Several thuds were felt, indicating that our aircraft had sustained multiple hits.

"Buc Six. Delta 1 taking heavy fire from our left side," Warren reported.

"Delta 1, this is Buc Six. We're on it," the radio reported.

Snow inquired, "Where did they hit us?"

"Mostly in the tail boom. I hope those bastards never learn how to lead a target," I said as I shook my head in disgust.

Russ said, "Not all went in the tail." I turned and saw a grunt tying a bandanna on another soldier's upper leg flesh wound.

Warren's voice went up three octaves when he announced, "Inbound RPG 11 o'clock." It missed us high but got everyone's attention.

"Bikini Flight Big Brother," the F-4s called in. "Stay clear of the left tree line. We'll give them some 20-millimeter fire that will get their heads down."

As the Jets went past, I heard what sounded like the loudest fart in the world. When the F-4's 20-millimeter Vulcan Cannon opened up with 6,000 rounds per minute, the vegetation above the location of the hostile fire disappeared. The ground fire from that area stopped immediately. I noticed a sulfur-like smell filling the cabin from all the gunfire and the exploding bombs. That let me know we were close to the LZ.

"Bikini Flight, this is Cowboy. We have casualties."

Snow responded instantly, "Cowboy, take them to landing position one, and we'll extract them."

Russ and I turned our attention down to the LZ. Seeing that it was unobstructed, Russ cleared Snow into a hover. A massive explosion went off to our right.

I keyed the mic and said, "Great. Just when I thought things couldn't get worse, now come the mortars."

Russ replied anxiously, "It's not mortars. Our number three bird just hit a mine."

Snow radioed firmly, "Eco Flight, this is Delta 1. Do some S-turns. We need to load the wounded."

I watched as the next group of four ships made turns that resembled the letter "s" to stretch the distance and time to the LZ rather than go straight in.

I looked at the tree line and saw flashes. I thought, "*That looks like fireflies.*" A thud of a bullet hitting behind me brought me back to reality.

Our grunts were out in about ten seconds, even the one who was wounded. I saw him limping off as I thought, *where do we get these men? He could have stayed on the aircraft. We would have lifted him out, and no one would blame him.*

I motioned to the medics to bring the wounded to the ship. We came under fire again, so the grunts helping the wounded were keeping low while they tried to load them into our bird. This action looked like it would take way too long with the next flight coming in on its final approach.

Knowing Snow wouldn't leave until we had the wounded, I jumped out and helped lift the three wounded troopers to Russ in the ship.

The radio came on with, "Bikini Flight, this is Iron Eagle. All number four birds, break off and reform in flights of three behind the Bikini Flight. Delta 3 is clogging up the Eastern landing position."

Next came, "Delta 1, this is Eco 1. We need you out of there!"

Delta 2 and Delta 4 ships pulled pitch and took off as Russ and I were loading the last wounded infantryman. That left us as sitting ducks and the only target in the LZ. The increased volume of bullets whizzed past us as I struggled to get that final wounded soldier to Russ.

I looked up and couldn't believe how the next flight was almost on top of us.

I jumped on the landing skid, and rapidly shouted, "Go, go, go."

Snow pulled in power, and we took off like a homesick angel. As I climbed on board, I noticed the heavy fire from our front and heard the sound of bullets against metal again. Russ was already on his gun, and I got to mine as quickly as I could. As we were clearing the LZ, two explosions from the Buccaneer's rockets hit just below us, so close it rattled the smoke grenades in their rack beside me.

"I've heard of close gun support, but that is a little too close," Warren blurted out.

Snow replied reassuringly, "That may be true, but it gave us enough of a break in the hostile fire that we got out of there without another hit."

I asked with concern, "Russ, how is the ship and crew that hit the mine?"

"The ship is on fire. Billy looks bad, but the rest of the crew are carrying him."

Snow kept all the power he could pull until we cleared the Kill Zone, an area from 100 feet to 500 feet above the jungle where slow-moving aircraft are most vulnerable to ground fire.

Warren warned, "I wasn't going to mention it before, but you over-temped the engine on the way out."

"Who gives a fuck?" I reported nastily. "The only thing that excess heat does is shorten the life of the engine. Every Huey in this rat hole will crash long before its scheduled hour engine replacement time. Heat is one of the side effects of power. I increased the fuel flow to get more heat, and more heat means more power." I took down my anger a notch and confessed, "I should have told you to monitor the engine exhaust temp, but in all the commotion, I forgot."

Snow said easily, "Don't worry; I wouldn't change a thing. When we had to get the hell out of there, we got out quick, and that probably saved our asses."

Russ pointed to the wounded and asked, "What about them?"

"Shit! Someone is bleeding a lot," Warren exclaimed.

Russ replied in amazement, "Fuck! One lost his leg," as we made our way quickly over to him. We started to work on that one first.

He looked down in confusion as he contorted his face. "What do we do for this?"

"How should I know?" I shrugged my shoulders helplessly. "I'm a helicopter doctor, not a physician."

He took a seatbelt and a machine gun barrel to make a tourniquet while I did all I could do to keep him from thrashing around. Russ's fast actions saved the man's life.

I told him flatly, "I wished we had some drugs to give him for the pain." Unfortunately, the commanders had taken our morphine out of the first aid kits because it ended up being used to get our fellow company members high more often than to relieve the pain of wounded soldiers.

Only occasional groans came from the other two injured men, thank God. They were still. We could never have handled two more out-of-control grunts fighting us in pain. On the flight to the hospital, the smell inside the ship was almost unbearable from the mix of the wounded's vomit, blood, and someone's loss of body functions.

After the medics took the wounded troopers at the Pleiku Air Force Base Hospital, Snow took off for Bikini Beach, about two miles away. I asked him to land on the maintenance pad and request a maintenance crew with a fuel truck instead of going to the refueling area.

Snow keyed the microphone and said, "Bikini Operations, this is Bikini Two-Two." When Operations responded, Snow made the request. They confirmed they would comply.

Snow shut down the Huey as I walked around outside it and looked for damage from our morning adventure. There were six small arms bullet holes in the tail, four through the belly, and one on the pilot's floor. I thought, *Mr. Snow was lucky as the bullet couldn't have missed him by more than a few inches. He was so calm when flying through that shit that I didn't notice any deviation from his normal flight. Now that's an Iron Eagle.*

I showed the maintenance crew which inspection panels to remove, revealing the path each bullet took through the ship. I had to make sure we were safe to continue for the rest of the day.

While Russ rearmed the guns and washed the blood and vomit out of the cargo bay, I opened an inspection panel in the tail boom. Inside, I discovered a control tube almost cut in half by a bullet. We replaced the part and temporarily covered the rest of the holes with 100 miles per hour tape, a type we named that sticks to the aircraft up to at least 100 miles per hour. The maintenance crews would make the permanent repairs when we returned that night.

I looked at my watch. It was 7 a.m. I observed the support troopers on their way to duty stations. "Russ, I got to get me one of those jobs."

"You'd go crazy, you restless bastard," he teased. "In a week, you would cry to get back on a crew."

With our temporary repairs completed, we took off to join the rest of the flight. On the way to pick up more troops, Snow relayed what he heard from the command comms, "Billy was medevac'd and is at the Evac Hospital. We're told he will recover. One of our ships had to land at Dak To with low engine oil pressure. Another ship made a running landing at Kan Tum with no tail rotor control. A third went down two clicks (kilometers) from the LZ. The crew was rescued, but the chopper was unsalvageable, so the F-4s bombed it. Jason Diaz, one of the crew chiefs, took two hits in the chicken plate, but other than sore ribs, he's okay. All in all, we were pretty lucky."

The rest of the day, we continued to fly reinforcements and supplies into the LZ. The ground fire was sporadic but nowhere near as bad as we experienced in the morning.

We landed at the Beach around 5 p.m. I completed the scheduled daily maintenance and replaced the pin on the throttle, as Russ took care of the guns. We had just finished when our platoon sergeant told us, "Don't worry about getting the ships ready for morning missions. The company is standing down from combat to allow our maintenance crews time to catch up on repairs."

"I wish you would have said that before we finished getting our ship ready for another mission," I said snidely to him.

He ignored me and continued to announce, "All crewmembers are to go to the Operations Briefing Room."

I got twenty feet from the ship when I remembered something, so I hustled back.

When I entered the room, Russ asked why I went back, I opened my palm and showed him the grenade pin.

"You should wear that sucker around your neck. It's a dang good luck charm there, boy."

I hadn't thought of that. I just didn't want to catch shit and get written up for juicing the engine.

Everyone in the briefing room had a story about the day's events, chattering like kids before homeroom. When the first sergeant came in and yelled for quiet, he told us to take our seats.

He then gave the briefing that would change my life forever.

"Aircraft 66-01200 lost power after dropping off the generals today, and all on board are KIA."

I felt dizzy and short of breath as I told Russ, "Oh my God, that was Giff's Command and Control ship. I was willing to pay him off to trade my assignment for his supposedly safe one."

I thought, *If C&C is supposed to be the safest mission, what the hell am I in for in the 210 days I have left in this adventure of horrors?*

From that moment on, I never thought anyone was luckier than me.

That day in Vietnam reminded me of a story I had heard in history class.

The tale is about a Chinese farmer who used an old horse to till his fields. One day, the horse escaped into the hills. When the farmer's neighbors commiserated with the old man over his bad luck, the farmer replied, "Bad luck? Good luck? Who knows?"

A week later, the horse returned with a herd of horses from the hills. This time, the neighbors congratulated the farmer on his good luck. His reply was, "Good luck? Bad luck? Who knows?"

Then, when the farmer's son was attempting to tame one of the wild horses, he fell off its back and broke his leg. Everyone thought this was very bad luck. Not the farmer, whose only reaction was, "Bad luck? Good luck? Who knows?"

Some weeks later, the Army marched into the village and conscripted every able-bodied youth they found there. When they saw the farmer's son with his broken leg, they let him off. No one returned from the Army. Now, was that good luck or bad luck? Who knows?

Things that seem on the surface to be evil may be good in disguise, and things that seem good on the surface may really be evil. We are wise when we leave it to God to decide what is good fortune and what is bad and thank him that all things turn out for good for those who love him.

CHAPTER 4:
THERE'S GOT TO BE A MORNING AFTER

Day Two LZ Yankee

The CO made good on his promise. An ice-cold trailer of beer was parked at Operations for us, but instead of a celebration, it quickly turned into a wake.

"Giff was one of the nicest guys I ever met," Ron declared in a rare display of seriousness, "He never did nutin' to nobody."

"That's why the CO picked him to fly with all the generals," Russ said. "He knew Giff would be a STRAC soldier and not get the old man in trouble."

STRAC, the Army slang for a well-organized, good performing soldier—I nodded in agreement.

"It's no wonder you flew an assault ship instead of C&C," Ron added. "Your rude actions as a wise-ass hillbilly and all."

I guess his time was up.

"If that's what kept me alive, then I will continue with my habits," Russ responded. "And, aw heck, maybe I can even expand my knowledge and use sophisticated double negatives with words like nutin' to 'nobod'deee' the way you do."

The banter continued and no one heard as I silently toasted my glass to the heavens, "Thanks for being stubborn, Giff." Two other beers managed to infiltrate me. By then I decided to head to the hooch. Surprisingly, the bed felt even more comforting than my mother's arms when I was a child. I was so mentally and physically exhausted that sleep came as soon as my head hit the pillow.

Dreams of my prom night with Susan, this time in the backseat of my dad's old '57 Mercury, were once again rudely ripped from me by that same SOB Charge of Quarters. "Wake up, Mack," the CQ forcefully whispered to not to wake up the others who were sleeping. "Mr. Snow called for you and Russ to get your asses to the flight line now for an emergency mission."

Half-awake, I answered, "Shit, I didn't even get to where she leans over."

"I have no idea what you just said," the CQ responded irritably. "Get your asses to the flight line and make it fast." As the world came into focus, I could smell the odor of stale beer and cigarettes, signs that the wake must have morphed back into a celebratory party, card game, and likely bull session while I was parked on Morningside Cliff.

After I cleared the cobwebs, I woke up Russ.

"Shit. Go away. My head hurts." He clutched the pillow over his head.

"This place smells like shit," I said, as I ripped it away. "What happened after I went to bed?"

"We carried on with the rest of the old man's beer and got into a card game until about one," he grumbled as he rubbed his eyes.

Looking around at beer cans and trash over the floor, I put my hands on my hips as I shook my head, "Mama Son and Baby Son are going to kill you."

"Well, Mama Son and her fat Baby Son take five dollars a month from each of us? Today they'll earn their pay!"

"It's a shame they don't have time to invest it in stocks and bonds while they make up our racks, clean the hooch, do our laundry, clean our boots, and run errands while we are flying missions."

"Damn, stop talking so loud; and your point is?"

"The point," I said loudly, "is that they're like family. Would you leave a room looking like this for your mother?"

As he now sat on the side of the bed, holding his head, he made a peace offering and said, "I'll give them another five bucks this month."

"Where you gonna get an extra 5 bucks? One of your hookers on vacation?" I teased as I handed him his boots.

"I finally pulled a full house on my last hand and got some extra cash." He pulled a five from his pants and stuck it between the wall stud and plywood by his bed.

"Well, pal, you also won all of two hours of sleep."

"We're supposed to fuckin' be off duty today," he groaned as he pulled on his boots.

"You know the Army; they fuck you every chance they get."

Ten minutes after my rude awakening with Susan, we made it to our trusty steed of the sky. I took a deep breath. "It must have rained during the night. This air smells fresh for a change."

Our Huey sported newly acquired fluorescent green patches that covered the bullet holes from the previous day's mission. Since Russ and I must have been the only crew of the group who had finished our daily inspections the night before, it was easy for the maintenance crew to have our ship ready for this mission. *How fucking stupid are we?* I thought.

Lieutenant Rose, the one in charge at night, came out from the aircraft's front to greet us as we approached the ship. Rose always wore freshly starched uniforms and was the only one in the company with spit-shined jump boots. Rose's demeanor was that he was the king of the flight line at night. I guess he had a point since there were no others of his rank on duty in that area. Rose was what we all referred to as an REMF or Rear Echelon Mother Fucker. Everybody knew he was afraid to fly combat missions. That is why Rose volunteered for the worst duty available to an RLO—the Night Maintenance Officer. To make up for his lack of courage, he made it hell on every one of his subordinates.

I looked at Russ and then rolled my eyes as I said, "I'm in no mood for this son of a bitch."

"I'll get the guns," Russ responded in a slow sarcastic way that made it clear how he felt about Rose.

I turned and jeered, "You're a big chicken," and started to cluck like one as he walked toward the armament shed to retrieve our ship's guns.

As I stowed my gear on board, Rose started in, "This ship looks like shit. Don't you lazy ass crew chiefs take pride in the way your assigned aircraft looks?"

"If it bothers you so much, do something about it and stop sitting in your office and acting like a chicken shit to everyone."

"The problem with you, Mack, is you don't respect your superiors."

I turned into his accusing finger and said plainly, "Lieutenant, I don't have any superiors—just equals."

Rose began to shout to the point that the veins on his neck stuck out and his face got redder by the second. "You disrespectful little bastard! I'm going to put you on report."

Things were out of control when Snow walked up and asked, "What's going on?"

Lieutenant Rose grumbled, "Mack is disrespectful, insubordinate, and I am putting him on report."

Mr. Snow knew that if he placed me on report, I would go to the CO for disciplinary action, and that would delay his mission.

Snow motioned to him and said, "Let's take a walk and discuss this."

In a few minutes, I saw Rose storm off, muttering some profanity with his hand in a motion like sweeping a fly away in disgust.

Snow stepped over to me and said, "Let's stop all this bullshit and get on with the business they pay us to do—saving lives."

I asked him, "What happened with Rose?"

"I just told him if he puts you on report, I'll have to ground you, and since this mission has to go out tonight into a shit storm, he was the only other qualified maintenance person available on flight status."

I marveled at Snow's mastery as he shrugged his shoulder and said directly, "Then he would have to fly as crew chief instead of you. I guess he didn't want to be a lowly crew chief."

"No, I guess he did not, sir." Snow joined in on my laughter.

We did one of the quickest preflights that I have ever seen. At the same time, the co-pilot, Wheeler, completed the cockpit checklist. When Snow strapped into his seat, the engine was ready to start. Our preflight and checklist happened so fast that Russ was still working on the guns and ammo. That meant I had to run to untie the rotor blades before Snow gave the command, "Clear," and he engaged the starter. As I approached my seat, one of the maintenance guys came up and surprised me by handing me a precious stabilizer bar damper that needed to be changed soon in this bird. He gave me a thumbs-up, a big smile, and said, "Thank you. You guys made Rose crazy mad; he will be in his office and out of our hair for the rest of the night."

Once the RPMs were up to operational speed, Snow didn't waste any time adhering to established procedures. He took off straight up out of the revetment, past the tower, and over our company's area. There is no doubt we woke up everyone, so we were off to a great start this morning. Rose was crazy mad, and our entire unit's day got off to a lousy and noisy start. We did, however, make the night maintenance crew happy. I thought *one out of three isn't so bad in baseball.*

I keyed the mic and finally had a minute to ask, "What is our mission?"

Snow's voice crackled back, "One of the platoons from the battalion we inserted yesterday morning got cut off from the central unit. They are surrounded and low on ammunition. Our job is to pick up a sling-load of ammo, grenades, mortars, and medical supplies from the 4th Division headquarters and take it to the cut-off unit."

"Let me figure this out," I said, and then slowly stepped through the rest, "We're going into a hot LZ... to sling a load of high explosives... that one tracer round could set off... and blow us out of the sky?"

"Do you have to sugarcoat everything, Mack?" Russ scoffed.

Snow jumped in, "You got part of it right. First, we have to fly up into the mountains in the dark, with sketchy weather, find a spot of about one or two acres, make an approach high enough, so the sling doesn't get caught in the trees, then set it down under fire. Let's see, I think that about sums it up. Oh yes, I forgot one little detail—we do all this with no gunship cover."

"And where are the fucking gunships?" I asked, annoyed.

"Three went to firebase Omega, one's in maintenance for a one-hundred-hour inspection, and two are in for repairs from yesterday's battle," Snow replied.

"Does the unit at least have artillery support?" I asked with concern.

"The NVA are too close to our troops to have artillery support, so, guys, we're on our own tonight."

"Great, and they're regular North Vietnam Army, not shithead Viet Cong," Russ piped in.

Snow radioed the 4th Division tower for instructions. They cleared him to the supply pad and said the ordinance was ready. He brought the aircraft to a hover directly over the sling. One soldier was on top of the load with a nylon donut connected to the 20-foot straps attached to the netting, ready to fasten to our cargo hook. Inside the net was our very volatile sling load. A soldier was positioned fifty feet in front of the load with hand signals. I thought, *when will the Army quit teaching that we need a ground guide?* No pilot ever paid attention to the soldier's hand signals if a crew was on board to give precise directions. In Vietnam, there was always an aircrew onboard.

Once the soldier had hooked up the load and jumped off, I announced, "Load clear."

Hanging over the side, I counted off the feet until the sling harness was tight. At that point, Snow lifted off, and we headed into the cloud-filled night toward our destiny—wherever and whatever that might be!

This mission was nuts. This was not a task for the faint of heart. Warren, our co-pilot, plotted a course and flight time to get us in the general area. From there, we would use the homing needle on the FM radio to zero in on their position. That was the easy part. The hard part was that we were heading into a triple canopy jungle in and out of clouds, with 100- to 200-foot trees surrounding the Landing Zone in a mountainous area, but the comforting news was that the fine print disclaimer on our official U.S. Army map read: ELEVATIONS AS DENOTED MAY BE SUBJECT TO ERROR.

At times, we would fly into clouds and go IFR, meaning clouds obscure any visual references for navigation. While flying blind, instrument flight rules were the only way to stay on our predetermined course and keep the right side up.

I asked during one of those socked-in, IFR moments, "Do we know if the LZ has visibility enough to land?"

"No idea, but we will get this sling in somehow," Snow answered ambivalently. "We have to."

"Okay; just checking," I faltered. The details didn't matter; we had to get these supplies to the distressed men, whatever it took.

The challenge of finding a target reminds me of another incident that was a bit nerve-wracking, to say the least. One time, we had a mission to support a unit that suffered several casualties and was low on ammo. That day, our pilot was Captain Montgomery, our platoon executive officer. He flew us above a low cloud cover to a unit in need of supplies. Air Force ground control got us close to the unit. Montgomery radioed the company as it was a way for us to hone in on their location.

The radio operator started a "long count," so the ground unit began to count from one to ten slowly and then back to one again. Simultaneously, a needle on the gyro-compass points to the signal's source while the frequency is open. When the needle swings from showing toward the station to away from it, you have pinned their location, all the while looking for a "sucker hole" that would get us under the clouds. A sucker hole gets its name from cases where a ship descends through a hole in the overcast then finds itself trapped in zero visibility when the gap closes, making "suckers" out of the ship's occupants. If the crew happens to have God on their side, they may have time to climb out to try again.

That day, we found no holes, sucker or otherwise, but radio contact with the unit on the ground told Montgomery that we had a "sizeable distance" between the clouds and the trees. I had never heard the term "sizeable distance" before. I didn't think it was a real aviation term. I had no idea what we were in for. Montgomery didn't seem the least bit fazed. He established a set of vectors and said he had figured out an instrument approach to the LZ based on our homing unit and flying time.

"I've never heard of anything like this attempted," I murmured, thinking I had released the mic button. "I hope you know what the hell you're doing, Captain."

"Me too," was his response.

Then, from just above the clouds with the homing needle centered, he descended into the abyss. All the while, Copilot, Mr. JD kept calling out altitude and time. When JD reported one minute and 1,500 feet, he turned his reporting to AGL.

When JD called out that we were 600 feet 'above ground level,' Montgomery said, "Shit. We should be out of the soup by now."

JD kept announcing the descending altitude as we were getting closer and closer to land. Just after he called out 450 feet, we finally broke out of the clouds. At that point, we were only 150 feet above the trees.

I remember a chorus of "Amens" in our headsets.

After we dropped our supplies and loaded the wounded for the flight to the evac hospital, I asked Captain Montgomery how much further he would have descended if we hadn't gotten out of the clouds when we did.

His reply gave me goosebumps. "My arm was spring-loaded toward the up position on the collective stick," he explained. "At first sight of trees, I was going to climb out—if it wasn't too late."

"Descending at 500 feet per minute through clouds, it almost certainly would have been too late," I mumbled.

I remembered the captain just smiled.

My thoughts of that day were interrupted by Mr. Warren announcing, "The LZ is a little over 2,900 feet, and the tallest mountain in the area is just under 4,000 feet. I have no reports on what the cloud cover is there."

I punched the side of the bulkhead, "Shit. Deja Vu, all over again."

CHAPTER 5:
NO SHELTER FROM HALF A TENT

Cloud cover is a double-edged sword. We couldn't see down, but the NVA couldn't see up, so, for the moment, we were flying lead-free.

"I'll stay at 5,000 feet until we are over the site and then descend in a left-hand spiral until we get to 3,500 feet," Snow reported. "That will give us a little over 500 feet to clear the trees with the 20-foot sling below us."

"Yeah, if the maps are correct," I said without confidence. "You know, a ship from the 189th smacked into a hill out here one night, and the unit safety officer found the maps were off by 1,000 feet."

Russ joked, "There you go being Mr. Sunshine again."

Flying in the dark of night using questionable information on outdated maps made the 45-minute flight to the platoon seem like hours. Each time the engine's whine changed as the pilot asked for more or less power, my heart almost stopped. A phantom noise in the transmission located directly behind me made me think of everything that could go wrong there. As I looked down at my gifted stabilizer bar damper, I started to imagine the potential disaster if, as the name implies, it let go in flight, then the aircraft would become—unstable. I heard Warren say, "We are in the general vicinity of the LZ."

I thanked God we were flying through only cotton candy-type unorganized clouds and remained in them only momentarily.

Snow radioed, "Two Charlie Foxtrot, this is Bikini Two-Two."

It was instantly acknowledged, "Bikini Two-Two, this is Two Charlie Foxtrot."

Snow responded, "Two Charlie Foxtrot, inbound with groceries."

"Bikini Two-Two, you are the answer to our prayers," the beleaguered unit radioed back. "We are low on ammo and in constant contact with the NVA."

Snow radioed, "Two Charlie Foxtrot, Bikini Two-Two. What is the weather like at your location?"

Two Charlie Foxtrot responded that they had intermittent light rain, but it had stopped for now. He could see the tops of the trees but couldn't estimate how much higher the clouds were. Snow acknowledged the report and requested a long count.

I felt a little guilty and selfish that I let my imagination run wild with one potential disaster after another while these guys on the ground faced real, multiple dangers.

Two Charley Foxtrot executed a long count, and Snow got a fix on his direction. Snow flew for a few minutes and then asked for a short count but, before the radio responded with 'five', we heard, "Bikini Two-Two, we hear you, we hear you."

Seconds later, I reported, "Red flare at 10 o'clock half a mile away, sir."

Snow put us in a slow, right descending turn to end up 500 feet above the trees, if our maps were correct, but there was no way to tell in the darkness. Turning on the landing lights would make us a great target. At this point, if anyone looked into the aircraft from the outside, they would have seen four Marty Feldman types with bulging eyeballs trying to locate the top of the trees.

Snow radioed, "Two Charlie Foxtrot, Bikini Two-Two, please give suppressive fire while we are in the LZ."

"We'll do what we can, but we don't have much ammo left. We also have wounded. Can you medivac them out?"

Shortly after Snow responded affirmatively, Warren was the first to call out, "I got the trees. We're on a good approach."

'Good' was questionable because we then descended through a cloud that took my breath away.

Finally, when we were out of the bottom side of that cloud in one piece, Snow ordered, "Boys, keep your eyes open. Don't let that sling get caught up in the trees."

Russ and I both acknowledged with "10-4."

We cleared the trees and Snow came to a hover at about 100 feet above their tops. The infantry unit below started their suppressive fire. Russ and I talked Snow down to where the sling rested on the ground. "Release, release," I said as I watched the donut and strap make a slow descent towards the care package like a snake falling and twisting.

The NVA now had us as a target, but Russ and I couldn't return suppressive fire from our guns as our immediate task was to ensure the ship's rotor blades missed the fallen trees. Their branches still reached almost 50 feet and filled the LZ. We now had to make a quick landing to pick up the injured. Keeping our heads down, Russ and I loaded three wounded. One of the grunts who was right next to me, handing up a litter—or stretcher, caught a round in his shoulder. His blood splattered on me, and he collapsed. I hefted him into the aircraft as well. As the grunts scrambled back to their cover, I yelled, "Go, go, go!" With instructions to avoid obstacles, Snow got us out of the LZ as fast as our lady Huey would fly. Departing, I looked back at the load we had just dropped. It resembled an anthill as the soldiers rushed to move the ammo to their comrades.

Snow asked, "How's the wounded?"

"They're in better shape than those we had this morning," Russ responded affirmatively. "Their medic must have stabilized them, all but the fourth one."

"Four? I thought they said three?"

"The fourth bought his ticket at the door. He's blacked out and bleeding bad. Wadding it now," I said as I practiced medicine without the benefit of a license.

Russ put up his gun and took over the bandaging as we cleared 1,000 feet. I went to my seat, sat back, lit a cigarette, which isn't easy with doors open at 90 knots, and took a deep breath. I noticed the cigarette was soaked with the trooper's blood from my fingers. I tossed the butt, wiped my hands on my pant legs, and tried to light another one, this time with a shaky lighter.

At times like this, when you come down from the adrenalin rush, your mind remembers what just happened, and you become scared. I think while you are in action, you don't have any free nerve endings to devote to terror. There is just too much happening and too many lives depending on you. I thought, *Now this is stupid. You're scared, now that you're safe.*

The return from the LZ began quietly, as Snow opted to fly through the clouds on instruments.

In our climb out, Snow radioed, "Pleiku Radio, this is Bikini Two-Two, climbing through 5,000 feet approximately 70 miles northwest of Pleiku, requesting clearance direct to 71st Evac Hospital Pleiku Air Force Base."

Pleiku responded, "Bikini Two-Two, Squawk four-two-three-seven." Complying with the "Squawk," Snow entered 4-2-3-7 into our transponder radio to identify us on the air controllers' radar screen.

Pleiku continued, "Bikini Two-Two, got you're 63 miles from Pleiku. Fly heading zero-five-zero degrees and climb to and maintain 6,000 feet."

"Fly five-zero degrees at 6,000 feet," Snow acknowledged.

Russ and I closed the doors, turned the heat on, and tried to make the wounded as comfortable as possible. I couldn't see outside the ship's windows in the clouds except for our red rotating beacon that reflected off the gray every second or two. I didn't have much to do while the pilots were flying on instruments, so I sat in the jump seat to monitor the gauges for abnormalities. Russ checked the patients, settled back in his seat, and fell asleep.

Halfway to Pleiku, I noticed that the EGT gauge started to rise. "Mr. Snow, our Exhaust Gas Temperature is going up," I reported.

"I'm also losing power," Snow responded. "Is this due to your increase in the power settings?"

"No, that would only happen under max power, and we are at cruise," I confirmed.

The words weren't out of my mouth when the master caution light suddenly lit up on the instrument panel. The light was intended to get your attention, and it did. The triggering of that master light indicated that there was another warning light on the pilot's center pedestal called the 'Christmas Tree' that was now illuminated too. The Christmas Tree is composed of two rows of message lights, any one of which can indicate trouble in the aircraft's systems. I looked up and saw a lit EGT light on the panel. "Shit", I cursed out loud because an EGT warning in the engine while flying in the clouds was not a situation you got to brag about later.

To take the edge off, I talked like Porky Pig and squealed, "Dere's somefen verwie screwie going on awound hea." Then I added, "the nose seal isn't leaking, or we'd smell oil burning. The only other thing causing a hotter burn could be a restricted airflow in the inlet— and it's too warm today for ice. I'll take a look to see if something is blocking air to our inlet filters."

Snow slowed the aircraft as much as he dared, and I opened my door to look up at the engine air inlet. I immediately saw what the problem was. A grunt's "shelter half", a part of a two-person tent kit, was blocking the inlet. Each man in the Army was issued one half of a tent, so two men make a full tent for shelter. One half had somehow blown up from the rotor wash in the LZ and now migrated back to block part of my inlet.

"It's a fucking shelter half on the inlet." At times like this you don't think, you just act, or we're all dead. "I'll have to get up there and remove it."

"Whatever you have to do, make it fast," Snow quickly blurted out. "The engine is approaching redline temperature, and I have to struggle to maintain altitude."

I woke up my Sleeping Beauty of a gunner. After a short explanation, we took my gun off its mount. When I unhooked my ammo chute, it slipped out of my hand, and I saw about 50 feet of linked M60 ammo run out of the box and rattle over the side, into the night.

That was a close call. I thanked God we were flying so slow. If not, the ammo line could have easily gotten tangled in our tail rotor.

The next thing I did was shorten my monkey harness to avoid falling too far down if I slipped. Then I stepped on the ammo can, grabbed the air scoop outside the roof over my seat, and up I went. I immediately felt the mist from the clouds and the sting from the raindrops hitting me at 60 miles an hour. The rotating beacon made everything hard to see as it flashed in my eyes.

I dropped back down and shouted into the mic, "Shut off the beacon!"

I looked at Russ, and he shook his head as if to say, 'Good luck.' Then I made my way up again. Now, with the beacon off, the positioning lights gave me enough light to see where I had to go. The entire roof was slippery and wet from the rain, so I took a deep breath and pushed off. The decapitating rotors were less than four feet above me, whipping stinging rain into my eyes and face as I fought the downwash pushing me over the side. I was able to latch on to the transmission cowling in front of the inlet with my left hand. I snagged the shelter half with my right hand and tugged with a quick move to break it away from the suction of the engine inlet gulping for air. Then the airflow caught it, but my hand was tangled, so now I was being dragged off the roof by it. Before I could plummet into the night from the roof, there was the old hillbilly, Russ. He grabbed me as I was about to drop.

Russ pulled me in and closed the door. I immediately sank into my seat in near shock with my heart beating in my ears as rainwater dripped off my chin. I wanted to just sit for a minute. It took Snow informing us that the EGT was dropping and had full power again to wake me from wherever I was. I looked down at one of the wounded as he struggled to raise his thumb and strained out a smile. He couldn't talk, but he mouthed the words, 'thank you.' I finally started to relax.

Thirty minutes later, the radio broke into the horror film playing in my head of what could have been outside the ship, "Bikini Two-Two, this is Pleiku. You're 20 miles from Pleiku. Descend to 5,000 feet. Turn to a heading of one-three-five, expect vectors to runway two-seven. We are presently reporting 1,000-foot ceiling and three-quarters of a mile visibility."

While Pleiku was issuing its heading and altitude instructions, normally good news heralding the end of an extremely tense flight, my mind went into overdrive again. This time I was bothered by the thought that, *we were relying on an air controller in Pleiku who was probably no more than 19-years-old with only six weeks of training. I hope he was a good student.*

The next call worried me more. "Bikini Two-Two, turn to heading one-eight-zero for base to runway two-seven. We are presently at 500-foot ceilings and a quarter-mile visibility."

I exclaimed, "Christ, the landing conditions are half of what they were just ten minutes ago. That puts us at our minimum visibility and ceiling for landing!"

"With what we have in fuel remaining, we can't go to an alternative airport," Snow explained. "And I'm not doing a go-around hoping for an improvement on a second approach, so we'll be okay, as long as the weather doesn't close to zero-zero."

I thought, *wouldn't it be a bitch if, after all we went through in the past two days, it would be the weather or some green Air Force controller screwing up that drove us into the ground?*

Then came, "Bikini Two-Two, on course. Turn to two-seven-zero on glide path. Five miles from touchdown."

After several minor courses and altitude corrections, I could breathe again as Snow radioed back, "Pleiku, we now have the runway in sight."

Pleiku replied, "You're cleared to land, runway two-seven."

CHAPTER 6:
C-RATS IN THE RAT HOLE

After the medics took our wounded, and I cleaned off the blood on me, we received instructions to fly to the 4th Division for standby—better known as "ass and trash", what we called hauling personnel (asses) and supplies (trash) from place to place for various reasons—for the rest of the day.

One of our sister company's CH 54 Chinooks—Big Windy was its call sign—was sitting beside us as we landed. I thought, *this was strange since those birds were never on standby.* After the engine shut down and Russ tied down the blades, I did a detailed post-flight inspection to ensure we didn't miss anything during the hurried preflight check. I also checked the turbine blades to ensure they weren't damaged while the engine's inlet was running with restricted air. When the fuel truck pulled up, Russ topped off our thirsty bird as I finished my checks.

After the checks, the first order of business was to change the stabilizer bar damper and readjust the fuel controller. While I reset the power levels, 'Getthis Jones', as we called him behind his back, walked over from the Chinook parked beside us and smirked, "Uh, oh, fucking with the power, are we?"

That started the friendly bickering that happened between Hueys and Chinook crews like cousins at family reunions.

"Fuck you, Jones," I responded. "If I were a pussy like you guys and had two engines, I wouldn't have to worry about more power."

"So how are you going to hide the broken factory-installed seal, Mr. Master Mechanic, sir?"

I looked right and left to make sure no one was within earshot. Then I said quietly, "I got this all figured out. I stole a seal used on fire extinguishers just for times like this, and nobody will ever know the difference between the factory-installed one and this one. What forced you out of your warm bed this early?"

"We were on a delivery of engineering equipment into LZ Yankee last night and started taking fire," Jones explained. "We all thought they missed us as usual, but get this, we started to lose hydraulic fluid on the final approach to pick up another load. We were lucky to sit down over there before we lost all our controls and went for a thrill ride."

"You mean, they let you go into a hot LZ? How depressing for you guys."

Jones ignored the dig and said, "We had a memorable day yesterday. So get this, they had us transport dead and wounded after we inserted the troops instead of returning empty. Ever hear of Martha Raye?"

I nodded. Of course, I knew Martha Raye, the movie star and well-known supporter of soldiers since World War II.

Just then, Russ joined us, "Hey Jonesy."

"Russ."

"Don't let me interrupt. What about Martha Raye?" he asked as Jones continued.

Jones shakes his head, smiling like he can't believe what he is about to tell us. "So get this, she and her manager and a few green berets show up to hitch a ride, and I see she's got full-bird colonel insignias on her uniform. First time I ever saluted a fucking movie star. So get this, she immediately starts taking care of the wounded in the back on the way to the Pleiku Hospital."

"No shit!"

"And get this, at the hospital pad, a lieutenant tried to tell her she needed to rest up for her show that night for the troops. She ignores him and asked, 'How long has the medical staff been on duty?'

"The lieutenant says, 'Twelve, maybe fourteen hours.' At that, she orders him, 'Take me to the operating room.' The lieutenant then goes, 'Ma'am, er Colonel, sir, er ma'am, I am under orders to escort you to your quarters." Jones then got excited as he got to the 'good part.' "Now get this, she gets all strack and goes off on that son of a bitch. 'Listen, butter bar, I am a qualified emergency room nurse.' Then she lifted the bird on her collar, and says, 'You have to get someone higher than a colonel to stop me from helping out my fellow nurses.'"

"What a great gal, and I'll tell you, she has more balls than most colonels I've run into,"

"Yeah, sounds like nobody is going to fuck with her," Russ added.

As we were shooting the shit, I saw a deuce and a half truck arrive—the Army's 2 ½ ton cargo truck. The load in the back was our first order of business for that day of "ass and trash," namely taking breakfast out to LZ Yankee. Russ and I put up Huey's cargo compartment seats to accommodate the load, as the truck pulled alongside.

When we arrived at LZ Yankee, we unloaded the cans and turned them over to an infantry group who carried them to a makeshift mess hall where a line was already forming for breakfast.

Then it was time for our breakfast. We had C-rations, not the good stuff we brought the troops, but World War II canned goodies. I thought of how Martha Raye probably ate this crap when she was doing her USO shows for guys like me twenty years before.

C-Rats, as they were affectionately known, consisted of a can of starch, package of sugar, salt and pepper, a can of meat, can of fruit, powdered coffee, chewing gum, pack of four cigarettes, a package of toilet tissue, utensils, and matches with a couple of P38 can openers per case. Although the Army now designated them, MCI, for Meal Combat Individual, they were still fuckin' C-Rats.

To heat these meals, we used C4 plastic explosives. One of my brilliant brothers had figured out that if a piece of the explosive is not compressed and simply ignited, it burns a lot like Sterno; but compress it and stick it in a detonator, it will explode. We sometimes would break a piece off for kicks. After we lit it, we would stomp on it, making a bang and knocking our foot in the air. Someone in the 189th used too much C4, and the explosion sent him into a backflip. The rest of the crew gave him a 9.2 combined score. He got a perfect score for style but lost points for being so stupid.

After breakfast, the pilots left for the LZ's headquarters tent while Russ and I explored. As we walked around the firebase, we ran into Two Charley Foxtrot unit members to whom we delivered ammo the night before. One of the sergeants came up to me, and asked, "Aren't you the guys who flew in last night with our ammo?"

"Yes, that was us."

All the members in their entire unit began praising us. They told us how they were almost out of ammo. Their lieutenant had gone to the extent to order 'fix bayonets,' thinking it might come down to hand-to-hand combat.

Then the sergeant said, "Our platoon leader had put you all in for the Bronze Star."

In his usual hillbilly way, Russ sarcastically said, "What the fuck is that good for in the real world?"

After I apologized for Russ, I thanked them. The sergeant got a little misty-eyed. I wasn't sure if he was suffering shell shock, but then he put his hand on my shoulder and said, "You know, when you are desperately waiting for supplies, you strain your ears. Then you hear that sound, you guys coming in, and you get a thrill through your whole body—the only moments of joy in the field. But that sound, after dropping our supplies and taking our wounded, then flying off until you can't hear it anymore, that's the loneliest and scariest silence ever."

Then he patted my shoulder and simply walked off. It was my turn to be shocked. I never thought of us like that, up till that moment. I felt we were more like flying truck drivers, delivering ass and trash, not hope and poetic inspiration.

That warm and fuzzy moment lasted until the pilots returned from HQ and informed us that we would take the men on sick call into the 4th Division base camp. Sick call is not like medivac. It is for colds, sprains, cuts, abrasions, and minor wounds. Russ and I put down the seats and loaded the seven soldiers for their trip. I noticed one was the Hoss Cartwright guy, the sergeant who gave me the crazy sign on the flight yesterday. He was wearing a sling around his butt.

"What happened to you?" I asked as I looked around at his bandages.

"Just a scratch," he replied bluntly.

Another trooper with an immobilized leg blurted out, "Bullshit! He got hit in the ass on your chopper yesterday."

I looked at him this time, making the same crazy sign around my temple, and said, "Man, you're crazy."

He looked at me and replied, "I may be crazy, but you're nuts. You unhinged a grenade in this fucking ship yesterday."

"All right, you got me, but I guess you got to be a little off your rocker to put up with this shit. Would you like a pillow for your ass with a hole in it?"

"Got one?" He grinned.

"Nope. Fresh out." I shrugged.

He made a second gesture with another finger.

Off we were, back to the 4th Infantry Division standby pad. After we left our sicky boys, a bird colonel and his aide walked up to inform us that he had to go to LZ Yankee.

I pointed to the inside of the aircraft and asked with a smirk, "Would you like a window or aisle seat, Colonel?"

The colonel just shook his head and took a seat by the window.

We arrived at LZ Yankee, and the empty marmite cans from our breakfast run were waiting for us. When the colonel left the aircraft, Russ and I put up the seats again, loaded the cans, and headed back to the 4th Division base camp.

When we finished inspecting and fueling our craft, a group of what I would call buck-ass privates, who didn't look like any combat soldiers I had ever seen, came to the ship.

"And where are you guys headed?" I asked.

One young private answered plainly, "We were on KP duty. Some of us peeled potatoes, while others washed pots and pans, cleaned garbage cans, and cared for the dining room area."

I thought, *That explained why their uniforms had a distinct look and smell.*

Then a private got excited and said, "The mess sergeant told us to come to the division helipad for a mission."

"Have you ever been in the field before?" I asked.

They all shook their heads no, so Russ and I put the seats down and loaded our not-so Special Forces.

After getting to LZ Yankee, Snow shut down the bird again and said the colonel wanted to brief him for a mission. He told us not to go far and motioned for the mighty KP fighting force we had just brought out to follow him.

Russ and I walked around and searched for stuff we could pilfer. First, we found a case of hand grenades. Russ thought we could use them in a pinch for extra punch in a hot LZ. Then we decided it was too dangerous to carry live grenades on board where a well-aimed tracer round fired by the enemy could set off the entire case.

Next, we found an NVA soldier who was tied up and being held as a prisoner of war. A Vietnamese soldier was guarding him. The prisoner's personal effects were on the ground next to him. Russ asked the guard what he would take for the prisoner's stuff. Our successful negotiations ended when we handed over two C-ration meals of lima beans and ham, which no one liked anyway. Then we gathered the prisoner's uniform, including his hat, belt buckle, and bayonet. We left him his underwear.

On the way back to the ship, Russ asked, "How much will the REMFs pay for this shit?"

"All we can get," I answered, knowing those Rear Echelon Mother Fuckers liked to buy war souvenirs from us so they could send them home and tell big stories about being war heroes.

CHAPTER 7:
PHANTOM FIGHTERS

As we were returning to our aircraft, we heard the sound of Hueys. As the sound got louder, we could see four slicks from the 189th and two of our gunships on their way.

Looking up as they roared overhead, Russ shouted, "Shit, here we go again!"

We both knew what it meant when guns follow slicks — another combat assault.

Snow returned from his briefing and said, "Let's go, guys."

I asked, "What are we doing?"

"The intel was wrong. The enemy infantry force in the area was a regiment force, not a battalion," Snow continued. "This morning, the NVA have broken off their engagement and are heading for the Laotian border. There are only two mountain passes the bastards can use between us and the border, and it just so happens that a Korean hatchet force with U.S. Special Forces advisors is in one of the passes."

With a wink, Snow said, "So we're going to play a little trick on old Charlie. Our ships are going to insert a phantom unit into the undefended pass. The NVA unit would see this maneuver and hopefully turn them toward the Special Forces trap."

Our not-so-Special Forces were waiting with newly issued combat gear back at our Huey. Other ships were loading clerks, cooks, a generator repairman, and even the colonel's aide. These support troops would constitute the phantom unit on each insertion.

"How are we going to fight with these guys on board?" I asked.

"They will sit in the door as we are going into the LZ and then move to the back of the pilot seats, out of sight, when we take off," explained Snow. "We will fly around for about fifteen to twenty minutes. Our passengers will then sit back down in the door, and we will return to the LZ; then we'll repeat the process. We will do this four times. Hopefully, the NVA will believe a unit is set up in that pass, and they'll take the other way out, right into the ambush."

"The guns are here to prep this bullshit LZ, but they couldn't be with us last night?" Russ sarcastically asked.

"Correct," Snow responded flatly. "These guns are from LZ Omega, so they weren't available for us last night. In the meantime, the 4th's actual infantry units are hot on the trail of the retreating North Vietnamese."

I told Russ, "This tactic reminds me of days back home deer hunting when my Uncle Muna would station me, his brothers, and a few of my cousins in strategic locations around the farm. Muna, being the tracker, would eventually get on the trail of a deer. He would start whooping and hollering to drive the deer toward one of our family members for the kill."

Snow briefed the other pilots while Warren did the preflight.

Looking at the rag-tag team of soft-handed privates in their ill-fitting combat gear, I turned to Russ and told him, "Make sure those nitwits don't have any rounds in their guns. I'd hate for one of them to shoot us accidentally. I'm sure none of them have fired a weapon since basic training."

"Kind of like you and your first gunner, Sergeant Jefferson?"

"Who the fuck asked you," I snickered.

The other ships, with their collection of support personnel, aren't in much better shape. I'm sure these phantom fighters are all very good at their jobs, but this wasn't their job.

Snow was the flight leader for this mission, so the other crews cranked their engines following our lead. We took off in a short time, and the guns were already ahead of us to prep the LZ with rockets and mini-gun fire. To anybody on the ground, this would appear to be a standard operating procedure preceding an attack. On our flights to the LZ, I had to use firm persuasion to get our 'actors' to sit in the doorway with their legs hanging out as the real infantry would have done. Once our decoy troops were seated in the door, I noticed they all had death grips on those tiedown rings Hueys have attached all over the floor to strap down cargo.

We landed with our group as planned. After landing, all four passengers moved behind the pilot's seats, out of sight, and looked like a heavyweight had been lifted off their shoulders. Then we were off again. We flew straight out of the LZ low and slow for about five miles, making sure anyone close could have seen us. After that, we made a right turn back over the LZ Yankee, and then we returned for another dummy landing. We repeated this maneuver four times to simulate the insertion of two platoons of infantry.

After our fourth turn, we headed back to the 4th Division base-camp for fuel and returned our dummy fighting force to their KP duties. This time, we topped off our fuel tanks at the hot refueling area where several helicopters can fuel simultaneously with engines running. That is the reason it was called a "hot" refueling area. The gunner tends to the fuel while the crew chief stands by with a large fire extinguisher.

When all five ships were full of fuel, we headed back to the LZ to return the other mighty fighters to their assigned tasks. On landing, I noticed with the NVA disengaged. The soldiers were already taking down tents while Chinooks were flying out equipment. I wondered how the mothers of the soldiers who perished here yesterday would feel if they knew that their sons died to win this ground. Then we abandoned it less than 36 hours later.

CHAPTER 8:
SCREW YOU, VINCE!

After the other four Hueys dropped off their phantom units at the firebase and continued evacuating the LZ, our mission was to fly eight body bags back to the 4th Division base camp. I never got used to handling the deceased. I couldn't help but think 'there but for the grace of God go I.' Needless to say, it was a grisly task. Fluid would often ooze from the bags, which, combined with the smell, would make the whole crew feel ill.

After delivering the body bags, we headed to Bikini Beach for our aircraft's one-hundred-hour inspection. Normally, Russ and I would do our part of the inspection process by washing the aircraft and removing the cowling so that the maintenance personnel could take it into the shop for their work.

This time, the maintenance sergeant said, "We'll do it all for you."

"What's the deal?" I asked curiously.

He replied, "Mr. Snow told the CO about the confrontation you had with Rose this morning. Hearing this and other complaints, the CO assigned Rose to Firebase Omega to support the Special Forces flying missions into Laos."

"Wow!" I exclaimed, "That's one of the most dangerous missions we fly."

"The CO said he was going to make an example of an officer harassing his men needlessly," added the sergeant.

"Russ and I will still help out so that you guys can get it done sooner," I offered.

I turned to Russ smiling, my esprit'd corps at full throttle, looking for his acknowledgment.

"You fucking asshole, I could have gone to the club for a few beers." He spat on the ground and headed for the tools.

After finishing our work, Russ and I started for the mess hall and saw Snow walking to the officer's quarters. "The Special Forces unit confirmed numerous enemy dead and captured a few NVA soldiers," Snow told us. "Still, most of the unit melted into the jungle and escaped to fight another day."

Then he added, "As for the Bronze Stars, our CO tore up the recommendations and said, 'Nobody gets medals for doing their job.' Even though we did great, it's still your job."

"Really?!" Russ and I blurted out in unison.

Funny what comes into your mind at moments like this. For me, it was Green Bay Coach, Vince Lombardi, who said, 'The price of success is hard work, dedication to the job at hand, and the determination that whether we win or lose, we have applied the best of ourselves to the task at hand.' Well, obviously the officers that were losing this war never heard that from the guy who won the first-ever and the second Superbowl.

CHAPTER 9:
BOYS WILL BE BOYS

Oh, How I Hate to Write

Russ and I were off duty for a few days while our aircraft was in its one-hundred-hour periodical inspection (PI), as were the crews of four other aircraft also in for various maintenance issues. On our first night off, we gathered in our friend Josh's corner of his hooch, since he had the best stereo in camp. His outstanding *Playboy* magazine collection was also a big draw, and, thanks to his serving as a cook, he had numerous snacks that he had confiscated from the mess hall.

Our platoon's resident, gung-ho Ron, asked me, "Why are you such a hippie? You hate this war, so why are you on the slicks?"

I had enough beer in me to speak my mind. At only 21 years old, it didn't take much beer to get me started.

"Fuck you! My grandfather fought in World War I so that he could become an American citizen. My father was wounded in World War II. I also had two uncles in Korea, so can that hippie shit. In Europe, my father and grandfather were greeted as heroes in France. I guess I expected the same reception here, but look at Vietnam's history.

You can't blame the people here because they've been fucked over by everyone, even their own government."

"How so?" The new kid—I couldn't remember his name—asked.

"How so?" I mocked him. Then I held up my finger and counted as a I explained, "First, they had that real bastard, President Diem."

"Yeah, Johnson loved that son of a bitch just because he was an anti-communist fuck, the circle jerk leader that he was to his people," Frank joined in. "Who was the joker they killed?"

"Diem? He was assassinated by a Vietnamese Army General who wanted to run the country."

"Wait! That was Nguyen Cao Ky," Harold blurted.

"…who became Prime Minister." I quickly added, "To make matters worse, Nguyen Van Thieu was made President. That scumbag stole money out of American aid funds and stashed it in Swiss banks."

"Son of a bitch!" exclaimed Josh. "I didn't know that."

"Can we talk about the broads in this month's *Playboy*?" Russ pleaded.

"Hey, this is interesting," Harold said as he waved him off. "Go on, Mack."

"So, these people got a murderer and an embezzler who are running this rat hole. The Vietnamese people can't win. One asshole gets overthrown, and they get two that are worse in return. Can you see why they don't care one way or another about our help?"

"You know, now that you put it that way, they're between a rock and a hard place," Harold said as he shook his head. "Poor bastards."

"So, wait," Hank jumped in. "They persecute the Buddhists, so bad, that a monk sets himself on fire."

"But the communists are even worse." That earned me a look from the kid. "Instead of stealing and murdering opposition politicians like what the leaders in the South do, the commies from the North murder whole families to get what they want."

"This is all well and good, Mack, but for me, it's my country, right or wrong!" said Ron, ever the patriot.

"Even you must see that this is worse than any war my family or yours has ever been in. At least then, one side was trying to stamp out evil," I tried to explain. "I will always give all that I have for my fellow Americans and my country, but my country has made a mistake here. And…"

"I still say, my country, right or wrong," he said.

"So then finish the fucking line, Einstein…" I said and then quoted Civil War Union General Carl Schurz, "It goes, 'My country, right or wrong; if right, to be kept right; and if wrong, to be set right.'"

I stood there while everyone shut up. You could hear the generator half a click away on the other side of the base. Everybody just got up, ready to leave. Boy, could I kill a party. George came over to me. We called him the librarian. He was always reading books.

"Hey, Mack. What you said, just now, about America. I never heard that part, but if this is wrong, why are you here?"

"I can't set America right as a crew chief on a Huey helicopter in Vietnam, so what's left for me but to bitch and protect my fellow Americans? Then, hopefully, I'll get to go home and tell the truth about this fucked up war."

"Hey guys, enough history lesson. I want to get laid. Let's get to the broads," Russ demanded.

"It's after curfew," Josh said, a bit bewildered. "How do you suppose we do that?"

That got crew chief Vincent's attention. He bellowed, "I've been at work on a plan for almost a month."

"And what's this great plan?" I asked sarcastically.

"The only thing that can get off this camp at night is an ambulance, so here's the plan. We take an ambulance to the Arizona Bar downtown and ask for the madam. Her name is Lee. She will make available six of her girls for three hours, which will cost us sixty dollars."

A gunner we named Oklahoma asked tentatively, "And how do you know it will work?"

"The motor sergeant is in on it. We tested it last week," Vincent assured us.

"Let's do it!" Josh said enthusiastically.

A hat was passed around, and sixty dollars was quickly collected. Meanwhile, Vincent snuck the olive drab-painted ambulance out of the motor pool. It wasn't the kind of civilian ambulance you would see in the U.S. It was a three-quarter-ton Army truck with a box behind the engine compartment and stretchers inside. On each side of the vehicle behind the driver and passenger doors was a red cross inside a square white background signifying an emergency vehicle and therefore not a legal target, according to the Geneva Convention, but the enemy would always use ours for target practice. As a result, we blasted the shit out of anything the Northern Army had the nerve to portray with red crosses. Hell, on both sides, the red cross became a sign indicating, "Aim Here."

I was appointed the bag man, and off we were on another foolish quest. At the front gate, the Military Police opened the barrier and waved us through. At the Arizona Bar, money changed hands, and the girls got into the back. Since we were in an ambulance, we had no problem getting back through the front gate waved on by the MPs.

As appointed as Josh's room was, it was too close to officer country for certain operations of a social nature, so we fashioned a hangout in one of the freshly-built bunkers on the edge of the base's new expansion. That new part will eventually house another unit en route from the States. In the meantime, we furnished it with a stereo, coolers, tables, and chairs, so that is where we headed with the girls.

There was no war for the next few hours; no flying in bad weather, no bullets flying, and no aircraft maintenance. We replaced that with dancing, lots of laughter, countless bad sing-alongs to "We Gotta Get Out of This Place" by The Animals, and the casual company of what some referred to as the fairer sex. Our little club had only one room, so no sex was on the program. Everyone just hung out and had the best time in recent memory.

Like all good things, it had to come to an end. We loaded up the girls and stationed Oklahoma with them to keep them quiet while we made our way back off the base. Big mistake!

Oklahoma started one of his Okie routines with our passengers and got them all laughing as we were leaving.

"Oklahoma. Keep those girls quiet," I ordered.

Just as we got motioned through at the gate, the girls started giggling. The MPs yelled, "Stop right there!" …but it was too late. Vincent put the pedal to the metal, and we were gone. Instinctually, after having to hightail it out of LZs under fire, I half-expected to hear the thud, thud, thud of the MP's round bouncing off the box.

The girls got out where we picked them up. Oklahoma wanted us to hang around to get a sample of their trade as evening escorts, but I reminded him and Vincent, "I have always told you guys, I have higher standards than that at home."

When we arrived at the gate, the MPs stopped us. One said, "This is the second trip you've had tonight. What's up?"

"There was an accident. We picked up the injured soldier on the first run," Vincent explained. "We took him to the medics where they stabilized him, and then we just took him to the 71st Evac Hospital at the airbase."

"I heard what sounded like girls giggling when you left the last time," the MP said sternly.

Vincent then impressed the shit out of me by saying, "No, sir, that was our patient whining like a little girl. You know those Marines. They act tough, but they're pussies when it comes down to it." Vincent knew that bashing Marines in front of MPs was always a good thing.

"How come I smell perfume?" the curious MP asked.

I whispered to Vincent, "I got this one."

"When we unloaded our patient, there were two female nurses. You must smell the perfume they had on, sir."

"I'm going to check this out tomorrow," the MP informed us.

"Yes, sir."

As we returned the ambulance to the motor pool, the sun was inching over the horizon. I asked Vincent, "What now? The MPs will find out from the medics that there was no accident."

"Relax. The medics are in on this because I get them war souvenirs. How do you think I get the ambulance?"

CHAPTER 10:
NO SECRETS IN THE ARMY

It took two days to finish our periodic inspection because of the maintenance backlog resulting from the battle damage the company's aircraft received during the assault at LZ Yankee. When Russ and I showed up to retrieve our bird, we noticed that the tail boom lettering of "U.S. Army" had been patched and painted over, so it now read, "U.S. Amy."

I heard the maintenance team that had praised us earlier, laughing it up. One said, "Is Amy one of your sweeties from the other night?"

Russ and I ignored them and went to the paint shop to have the problem corrected. On the way, I asked Russ, "How damned many know about Vincent's deal?"

"I heard that he is making reservations for nightly deals at two hundred bucks per person," Russ said.

"Shit! With so many involved, the command will find out, and we'll all be fucked."

"You worry too much, Nervous Nancy," Russ told me.

Once we were back in the 'ARMY' with our tail boom re-lettered. Our mission for the next three weeks was 'ass and trash.' Although not our favorite assignment, it was a welcome break from the two days of too much stimulation at LZ Yankee.

'Ass and trash days' started with 'pitch pull' between 6 and 7 a.m., so that meant out of the rack at zero dark thirty, between 4 and 5 a.m. That gave us time for the five Ss. That is, we had an hour to shit, shower, shave, slop, and shove off to the flight line before the day's flight on the Huey. The hour of preflight checks consisted of making sure the fuel crew had topped off the bird during the night and verifying that any work done by the night maintenance crew was completed and done correctly. Next, I made a trip to Supply to see if any ordered parts had come in. In the meantime, Russ mounted the guns, filled the ammo cans, and cleaned the windows.

Simultaneously, the pilots were in the flight operations briefing, getting the mission for the day. Their briefs contained information on weather and combat activity in the area we will be working in that day. Combat information would consist of where field units were experiencing contact with the enemy and planned bombing missions or artillery fire. Information about artillery fire is the most important. I don't want to take up the same airspace as one of our artillery shells. After their briefings, the pilots would come to the aircraft for their preflight checks.

Missions usually would end at 6 or 7 p.m. but could go late into the night. On returning to Bikini Beach, we all had at least an hour of post-flight duties. My primary responsibility was to inspect the aircraft to make sure it was ready for the next day's mission. If I found anything significantly wrong, I would submit a maintenance work order to resolve the problem. The minor repairs were my responsibility, or if maintenance got swamped, I would have to repair all of the issues myself. Russ's post-flight duties consisted of cleaning and checking the guns. Then he would clean the aircraft.

For the first few days of 'ass and trash,' things were pretty routine. On the 'ass' side, we did sick calls. From time to time, our 'ass' duty included taking commanders to the field to check on their troops.

We would also take men out to the field to replace others who were designated, DEROS; Army alpha code for Date Estimated Return from Overseas Duty or simply, 'going home'. We would pick up others who earned R&R. Rest and Recuperation was the Army's version of a one-week vacation in some exotic spot. I put in for Bangkok, Thailand.

On the 'trash' side, we routinely hauled meals, ammunition, and even beer. One mission was to take an air conditioner to a Special Forces camp. On another, we delivered a canine to a unit that was clearing tunnels. We even had a mission to provide a large bell to a Buddhist monastery.

On our third day of 'ass and trash,' things started to get interesting. We were resupplying a 4th Infantry company that had been having sporadic contact with an NVA unit.

On the first load in, Russ reported, "Taking fire; taking fire."

The pilot quickly instructed him, "We don't know where the friendlies are, so don't return any fire on that side."

During the next load, Russ reported the same, "Taking fire; taking fire."

The pilot was a little putout and sternly said, "What did I tell you? We don't know where the friendlies are."

Russ's reply was, "No, sir, I don't want to return fire. But next trip, can we come in from the opposite direction, so they're shooting at Mack and not me?"

"Very funny," was my reply.

On another day, we were leaving Camp Holloway, our base camp, to haul loads to the 179th Airborne Brigade. En route between pick-ups and drop-offs, we listened to Radio Vietnam. On one trip, our company radio frequency came to life with chatter, and that pissed me off because it interrupted a Rolling Stone's song, "Let's Spend the Night Together." The transmission was between two aircraft looking for a ground unit to deliver supplies.

The first transmission was, "Hey, where the fuck is that LZ?"

"I don't know. It's gotta be here somewhere."

The original speaker then chimed in, "Man, we are fucked up."

Just then, a senior officer—probably our CO—came on with, "Aircraft using profanity say ID."

After a pause, the radio came to life again with, "We may be fucked up, but we ain't that fucked up."

Back at the mess hall later that night, Russ colorfully retold this story. It was rightly voted the number one story of the day.

After a tough day of flying resupplies from the coast to Kontum, Russ and I were exhausted after our post-flight duties. I saw Oklahoma and Ron exchanging money two ships down from us on the flight line.

"What are you guys doing?" Russ asked with a puzzled stare. "Paying off gambling debts?"

Oklahoma's answer made Russ and me worry about their sanity. He said, "Kinda. We played rotor blade roulette."

"What's that?" we asked in unison.

"When flying, you take your pistols. On the first two trips, each has a turn to fire a shot at the rotor blades. The one who gets a hit wins!"

Alarmed, I said, "Did you know there's such a thing as blade separation which you could cause by doing that?"

"What's that do?" the dumb Okie asked.

"Well, if you're lucky," Russ answered, "it would give you a bad vibration. If you're not lucky, the rotor blade could come apart, and you'd be like Robert E. Lee—history!"

"Man, remind me not to fly with you two assholes," was my answer as we left them while I wondered if they would try it again.

We finished dumping our last load to a little firebase on top of some give-a-shit hill. Once again in the air, I leaned back in my seat, lit a cigarette, and admired the setting sun painting the clouds orange with pink edges on a blue palette. The squelch broke, and I was rudely interrupted by a radio transmission from our operations. We were directed to refuel and report to a master sergeant, code-named Viking, arriving on a Star Lifter C-140 at the Pleiku Air Force Base.

We did as instructed and ended up waiting for about forty-five minutes at the Air Base before Russ informed us that the C-140 had landed. It took several more minutes for the big bird to taxi to our location and shut down. The crew lowered the back ramp, and seven men dressed in civilian clothes carrying huge black duffel bags walked out. I had never seen anything like this before. The pilots met them, and, oddly, a jeep drove up with Sergeant Jefferson. It took about thirty minutes for the group to study maps and a notebook.

The group approached the helicopter, and Mr. Tuttle, our pilot, said, "Let's crank."

The seven men boarded the bird after we were up to operating RPM. The one who was obviously in charge was equipped with a headset to communicate with the crew.

After leaving the Pleiku traffic pattern, I asked, "What is our mission?

The stranger answered, "That's classified. Just get us into our LZ with no shooting, and then forget about us. Got it, cowboys?"

"What if we receive fire," I asked.

I got a short answer, "You won't."

We flew for about forty minutes southwest, judging by the position of the moon. Our LZ was four or five miles outside some city. Our secret passengers were gone in a flash as we touched down. We were on the ground no more than twenty seconds when both Russ and I reported clear, and we were off.

I was the first to ask, "What the fuck was that?"

Tuttle replied, "The only thing we know is that they were CIA and Special Forces out of Fort Bragg and are here for a secret mission. Oh, and they want one of our birds back here when requested to pick them up. The city is Pek Nehi, but other than that, I have not a clue."

The copilot added, "That type of mission is no treat. You can be in the bush for days or months without recognition for medals, injuries, or death. If anything happens to you, they will list them as a training accident. Those guys won't qualify for VA benefits and will get screwed on little things like the ability to join the VFW because they were never officially in combat. Though they may go on numerous missions like this, officially, they were never here."

"What was Sergeant Jones doing there?" I asked.

"I think he knew one of the team members," Tuttle said.

A week later, we heard on Radio Vietnam that a province leader was missing from his plantation near Pek Nehi. Province leaders are known for all kinds of criminal activities and for playing both sides in the war. Our strange passengers' secret mission was no longer a secret to our crew.

CHAPTER 11:
HOOKERS IN THE COCKPIT

In the third week of 'ass and trash days' missions, our pilots were 21-year-old Mr. Smith and Mr. JD, who wasn't much older than Russ and me. Both aviators had reputations for flying way outside the norm. Our mission was to take a colonel to a remote Special Forces camp located in an isolated area controlled by the VC.

The Green Berets' mission was to organize and assist the local Vietnamese defense and strike forces to stop the VC from controlling the area. These Green Berets worked with indigenous Montagnard villagers to fortify their village. The indigenous strike forces could defend other local villages and simultaneously attack and harass the enemy.

While we were waiting for the colonel, one of the Americans from the base approached us. "Hey guys, do you want to make $1,000?"

"Sure, who'd we have to shoot?" JD answered.

"All you need to do is to go to Cam Ranh Bay Air Force Base and return with six hookers from the red-light zone near the base."

We all echoed, "No sweat, GI."

After taking the colonel back to his headquarters, we raced to Cam Ranh Bay to pick up our extraordinary load.

We arrived at the Air Force base. After the pilots shut down the aircraft, a sergeant drove up in a jeep and asked, "Who are you waiting for?"

"A couple of civilian Vietnamese that are going to visit their Province Chief Uncle," Smith said quickly.

"You're going to have to wait a while as the base is on lockdown for a security drill; won't open for another two hours," called out the sergeant as he then drove off, not waiting for a response.

Russ and the two pilots decided to go to the PX.

"While you're at the Post Exchange, I'll be at the C-130s," I said. "There is a guy over there I grew up with. I wrote and told him if I make it to Cam Ranh Bay, I'd look him up."

"Ok, let's meet back here in two hours," Smith said.

As I walked into the massive hanger that housed the C-130 cargo planes, I was awe-struck by the size of the huge structure. I was greeted by the high pitch sound of pneumatic air drills and the percussion bonding of a rivet being installed. It took me a few minutes to find an airman who was not buried halfway into an aircraft. "Where can I find Alfred Stark?" I asked.

"Al, there's a dog face here to see you," the airman yelled out.

"We may be dog faces," I said with a big smile, "but we don't hide behind a guarded base, eating three hots and got a cot every night."

After I said that, I realized how I wasn't making my case of being in the Air Force was somehow stupid. The airman laughed at that insane statement and went back to work.

Behind me, I heard, "Hey Mack."

Turning, I saw my old high school basketball forward, Al, and teased, "Have you learned how to hit a jump shot yet?"

"Nope, but have you finally figured out how to take the ball up the court without dribbling it off your foot?" he jeered back.

"Give me a break. That only happened once," I said as I waved him away.

"Yeah, but that once cost us the division title," he mocked.

"Aw, I am touched you remembered." I said as I put my hand on my heart and feigned a smile.

Al grabbed my hand for a shake, then pulled me in for a hug and asked, "What brings you to this tropical paradise?"

After I explained what we were up to, he rolled his eyes and told me his horror story about when he and his C-130 transport crew attempted a similar mission.

"We loaded the hookers from here and headed north to the remote base that hired us to bring them back," he said. "On the way, operations diverted us to the Philippines to pick up a load going to Korea. Once there, they gave us a trip to Thailand to get another load coming back here to Cam Ranh Bay. All the way, those hookers were driving us crazy, saying things like, 'You promised we make boo koo money, but all we do is fly everywhere—and we make no money,' so we wound up paying for them."

"So you were the ones who got fucked." I chuckled.

"It gets worse. Then we had to pay off one of the loading crews to keep our secret. We even tried to hide the hookers at each fuel stop, but trying to keep them quiet and not offer their services to the fuelers was a trip. Other times we would load them into the cockpit to hide them."

"Pretty funny. Hookers in the cockpit," I added with a laugh.

"It wasn't funny," he quipped. "Instead of splitting $1,000, it cost us $1,500."

"I bet you got to join the the-mile-high club during those long trips," I said with a big grin.

"Yeah, I guess I got my money's worth in the back of an M113 that we were hauling from Soul, South Korea to Udorn, Thailand," he nodded in the affirmative.

I resisted the urge to say, 'So, you got personal with a hooker in the back of a personnel carrier?' but instead said confidently, "We don't have to worry about a deviation to Korea or another country. Our range is about 200 miles, and that will barely get us to Laos from here."

The lockdown ended, and the girls eventually arrived crammed into the back of a Vespa. Not a scooter, but the three-wheeler kind with a canvas-covered box on the back, Saigon's version of a taxicab. We finally got the 'ladies' seated and cleared to take off, except for one of the girls who got airsick. She had never been higher than the second floor of a whorehouse. The rest of the mission went as planned, and we arrived back at Bikini Beach early. I finished my post-flight duties and raced out to spend my share of the "Hooker Express" to buy my Susan a silk robe embroidered with images of colorful dragons. There was a small image on the front and a large one covering the back. I had had my eye on that item for a while but never thought I would have the money to buy it. When I got back to the hooch, the guys were leaving for the Arizona Bar to sample the wares of our new friends from the party night in the bunker. They invited me along, but I gave them my usual answer in such situations: "My standards are higher than that, boys."

That gave Russ the cue to start his normal razzing. "If you think that little cutie of yours isn't getting hit on by every Jody in town back home, you're nuts."

Several days later, we had Smith and JD as our pilots again. The first thing Smith said was, "Come here, boys. We're going to have some fun today." I thought, *Fuck. Here we go again.*

He briefed us on our mission for the day, explaining that we were going to Firebase Omega to act as standby. FireBase Omega was a base that Special Forces used to launch teams into Laos for intelligence gathering. Aircraft had to be ready to extract the men if they got in trouble. That is why the mission was called 'standby.' Our ship was being sent to the firebase because one of the assigned aircraft had a mechanical problem. While their crew fixed it, we had to fill in for them. "That doesn't sound like fun to me," I remarked.

"Why not? Russ said.

"Don't you remember? That's where they sent Rose, and I'm fucked because I'm the reasons he's there."

Smith got all excited, saying, "Let me finish, Mack. Here's the fun part. My roommate just came back from Omega and told me that Rose is still a chickenshit. Being a lieutenant, he was the senior airman there. He assigned himself flare ship standby every night."

What an asshole, I thought as I shook my head, thinking about how his crew would be kept on duty all night if one of our bases or patrols comes under attack. If that happens, the flare ship flies high and out of ground fire range, dropping flares that enable our guys to see the enemy.

"So what?" Russ asked.

Smith laid out his plan. "My roommate said Rose sleeps until noon. When he gets up, he lights the M67 immersible heater on the shower stand. After that, he goes to lunch while the water is heating to have a nice hot shower after lunch. While JD and I keep him busy, you guys will switch the diesel for jet fuel. When Rose lights it, he will get a nice surprise."

I snickered at the plan as I knew that an immersion heater was a simple device that the Army had used for almost a century to warm water. The component creates heat by diesel drips out of a tank located above the unit that burns hot. The trick to safely start the heater is to have only a small amount of fuel poured from the tank into the bottom pan, and then a flame is introduced. By starting with just a limited amount of fuel in the pan, you get a nice flame. Then it is time to add the small stream of diesel drips from the tank. However, too much fuel on startup will get a flash that blows the smokestacks off and scares the shit out of you—and that is when you use the conventional diesel fuel. I was uneasy about what the supercharged jet fuel would do.

After landing, Russ and I went to do our assigned task.

Looking at Omega's field shower, I thought, *What a dump.* I said as I pointed at it, "Look, Russ, it's nothing but a shed with a 50-gallon barrel of water on top. The heater is in the back, out of sight from the rest of the camp."

Russ quipped, "Those damn heaters. I hate them. If you light them too early, you'll get scalded. Start the heater too late, and you will experience extreme shrinkage from the cold water."

"What if someone besides Rose goes to light the heater?" asked Russ.

"I guess we will have to stand guard out of sight to make sure no one else comes to light it. Besides, I'm dying to see what happens when Rose does light 'em," I said with a big grin.

"Once on top, I'll pour the JP-4 fuel to the burner pan but still leave the tank full of diesel as usual. Russ, you stand guard to make sure no one is coming."

Like two little kids, we hid behind the mess tent after our dirty deed was done. Right on cue, Rose came out of his tent and walked toward the shower. At the same time, Smith and JD approached him about twenty feet from the bath. I thought for a minute that the two of them had chickened out and were going to rat on us.

What we heard next reminded me of why Rose deserved what was about to happen to him. Smith greeted Rose with, "Good morning, sir," and saluted.

Rose responded with, "What do you two scum balls want?" There was no return salute, as is customary.

"Nothing, Lieutenant," Smith said. "We're just here on standby and thought we could spend some quality time together."

"What makes you think I want to hang out with a couple of degenerates like you two? I know you fucking warrant officers and those God damned crew chiefs ganged up on me to get me sent to this godforsaken hole," he snapped back at them as he turned to head to his firestorm.

We watched him climb to the shower's top and reach for the petcock on the heater for the starting fuel. He shut it off, lit a piece of paper, and leaned over the heater to guide the flame to its destiny. BOOM! was the sound, as a flash of fire erupted from the fuel port and launched the smokestacks into the air. Rose fell backward and off the shower. As he lay there on the ground, the first thing I thought was, *Shit. We killed him.* My fears got laid to rest when one of the smokestacks came down from its flight path and one landed on Rose. His groan let us know he was at least alive.

It took a few minutes, but he slowly got up off the ground. I noticed that the blast had burned off his eyebrows and singed his hair. Smith and JD came running to him and saw it too. The two started laughing. Smith finally choked out, "Your eyebrows," as he pointed at him.

Rose snapped, "What eyebrows?"

Smith exclaimed, "Exactly! They're gone."

"Don't worry," JD assured him. "Maybelline has a pencil so you can draw them back on. My grandmother does that, but you won't like it because it looks like shit."

This last crack brought out another chorus of laughter. Rose said, "I smelled JP when I lit the heater. I swear, someone sabotaged that goddamn heater."

"Nah," Smith said calmly, "I think they cranked the ailing bird right as that happened, and that's what gave you the jet fuel smell."

"Besides, if there was jet fuel in the heater, it's burned off by now," JD said.

Rose shouted, "I hear your crew chief is that fucking Mack. Where is he and that no-good gunner of his?"

Smith then explained, "Mack and Russ are helping out, so we don't have to spend the night at this dangerous firebase."

Rose said, "I'll check on that. If you're lying, I'll have all of you in front of the Old Man."

Russ and I raced back to the flight line, laughing so hard that we could hardly breathe and run at the same time. When we arrived, the crew was just buttoning up the panels and closing the cowling on their bird. Russ went to talk to the gunner as I explained to the crew chief what had happened and that we needed an alibi.

They got a kick from the story and explained how Rose was on their ass all the time. "Last night, he reamed us out for not having military haircuts," said the crew chief. "Now, where am I going to get a haircut out here? Don't worry. We'll cover for you guys."

Smith came up as we finished our talk with the crew and said, "Good job, boys. Now let's get the fuck out of here and head home before Rose can think of some way to pin that on us."

CHAPTER 12:
DON'T LET THE SMOKE GET IN YOUR EYES

The day started as an unexpected rest day. Our aircraft was grounded while we waited for a needed part. I was taking in some rays outside my hooch when our platoon leader, Captain Patterson, came up and said, "Get your gunner and gear and meet your pilots Montgomery and JD at the smoke shop, ASAP." The naturally joyful captain had a subdued tone today, but I thought nothing of it at the time. I just supposed he was having another bad day. When you are in charge of 40 18- to 25-year-olds flying eight aircraft across three countries, bad days must be a constant visitor.

Smoke ships have a ring around the exhaust that purposely sprays oil into the escaping hot exhaust gas creating smoke. Nobody wanted to be assigned that bird because residue from the smoke left the tail boom, horizontal stabilizers, and vertical fin covered in soot—which required constant cleaning. To spare the smoke ship crew the cleaning duty after every smoke mission, the CO decided to assign flight crews waiting for their aircraft repairs. That means this honor was bestowed on Russ and me that day.

Smoke missions are no basket of cherries. These missions fly low and slow while dispersing smoke to hide our guys from the bad ones. The problem is that while we hide what our guys are doing, we become very visible from the ground. There is a big trail of smoke behind us, making it easy for the enemy to precisely track our position.

Russ and I got to the bird and found our pilots with Captain Patterson talking about the mission.

Captain Paterson then addressed all of us and said, "Good luck, and I want to see the four of you back safe and sound tonight."

We saluted him, he returned it, and then left.

"What's up?" I asked.

"A jet fighter got shot down, and the pilots are behind a dike in a rice paddy," Captain Montgomery said as he began his debriefing. "Artillery fire keeps the NVA at bay, but the Air Force's Jolly Green Giants have aborted their rescue due to the heavy ground and anti-aircraft fire. Our job is to give a smokescreen for the Jolly Greens so that they can pick up their guys."

A duet of "fuuuck" came out of Russ and me.

"You mean they shot down a jet flying at 250 knots, and we're going to fly at maybe 50 nautical miles per hour with a big trail of smoke coming out our ass," I snickered.

"That's about right," the captain said as he was climbing in the pilot's seat.

"Do you have a fucking black cloud following you, Captain?" Russ asked uncomfortably as he untied the rotor blades. "The last time we flew with you, we made a nonstandard made-up approach through the clouds to an LZ and didn't break out until we were just above the trees. That damn near soiled my drawers. This time I'm sure you'll get the job done."

"You got a medal for that, didn't you?" Montgomery asked. "You'll probably get one for this also."

"I hope it's not posthumously," I quipped.

We had already completed the smoke ship's preflight and the pilot's cockpit checklist, before morning. All the pilots would need to do when they arrived is strap in and pull the starter trigger. The aircraft was ready in minutes. Montgomery got clearance for a straight-out departure once we were up to full RPM with the radios on.

"The Air Force base will hold traffic until we clear their airspace," JD said.

"That makes it easy," Montgomery added. "Everyone knows what we're doing and what's at stake, so today, we are a priority."

"Awww, now I feel special," I said.

We flew northwest for about thirty minutes to a spot west of Kontum. Montgomery radioed, "Air Force Jolly Green. This is Bikini Red Five."

Immediately, we heard, "Bikini Red Five, this is Rescue One-Five; how far out are you?"

"We are seven mikes out," he replied.

The Jolly Green came on with what brought knots to my stomach. "Bikini Red Five, we need you to make your smoke run West to East due to current wind conditions."

That made Russ go crazy and say, "That puts me on the hot side. Why do I always get the fucking?"

Montgomery replied, "...because you're so cute, Russ."

"Mack, you wanna switch sides? You're cuter," Russ asked.

"Hey, thanks, but no." I was nervous, being relegated to do nothing but sit and worry, I was actually looking forward to laying down suppressing fire during the run as a distraction. The reality was there was nothing to shoot at on my side.

Even though Montgomery was the aircraft commander, he was flying in the co-pilot's seat, on the ship's left side. He sat there for the same reason I preferred to sit on the left side, and not switch with Russ. The rotor blades go right in a crash. "We'll go in low and slow at 50 knots, 250 feet above the ground," he informed us. "Sorry, Russ, that puts you in the perfect killing zone at that altitude and speed, but that's also the best approach for smoke dispersion."

Russ threw his hands up and said, "At that speed and altitude, why don't I shoot myself right now and get it over with?"

"Quit whining," I said, but I was worried about him.

We started our run, and the smoke came on as planned. The pass probably took less than a minute, but it seemed like it took forever. I heard Russ open fire with his door gun. That sinking feeling hit me again when we heard bullets hit into the cabin above us. That made me say a little prayer for Russ.

I heard JD over the intercom, "Nice shooting, Russ."

After we pulled up and increased speed, Montgomery asked, "Everyone still with us?"

Russ spat, "Those fuckers peppered the ceiling over me, but all I got was a little gash in my cheek."

I think that was the first time I took a breath and said another silent prayer of thanks for him.

"Bikini Red Five, this is Rescue One-Five. We have our guys. Thanks for your help."

Montgomery asked, "What's our damage?"

I made a quick visual inspection and reported, "I see the hits are mostly in the tail boom and whatever is around Russ."

"I have at least three hits around me," Russ confirmed.

"Russ, I saw you got at least five of them," JD said affirmatively.

"All I was doing was trying to keep their heads down and wasn't aiming at nothing special."

"It's a good thing you weren't aiming because if you were, you know you would have missed the whole North Vietnamese Army," I teased him.

"But you stuck it to them good," JD said approvingly. "Russ, you got an extra prize on this trip."

"What?" he asked in disbelief.

"You also earned a Purple Heart," JD added.

Russ responded with his usual attitude and sarcasm, "Oh, be still my beating heart."

Back at Holloway, Captain Paterson was there to greet us, saying, "You guys had me worried. Don't worry about post-flight. I'm sure you need a drink, so go get one."

"All in a day's work, sir," Montgomery said. After nearly getting us killed, that remark made me want to shoot that bastard and rid Russ and me of that walking/flying bad luck charm.

Russ and I got stiff that night. After way too many drinks, I let my guard down and told him how worried I had been and that I had even said a prayer.

That prompted him to ask, "Are you going soft on me?"

"Fuck you, asshole," I said. "Next time, I'll throw you out and let those Communist butchers deal with you."

We got back to the hooch at about midnight. Around 2 a.m., we awoke to someone screaming, "Incoming," and then we heard multiple mortar explosions followed by a big blast. One of the mortars had hit the ammo bunker. It sounded like nothing I had ever heard before. It shook the hooch so hard that dust fell out of our rafters, filling the air with what looked like falling snow. I smelled sulfur.

I took off as fast as I could for the closest door, but when I got there, it wouldn't open. At a full run, I bounced off it and found myself on the floor. The hooch's foundation had shifted from the blast and jammed the exit.

The next thing I heard was Oklahoma calling out from behind me, "This one is free. We need to get to the fraidy hole."

I think I set an Olympic 100-yard dash record to the bunker. Not knowing how bad things were going to get the next day, I prayed, "Lord, what else do we have to put up with today?" Then I asked Oklahoma, "What the fuck is a fraidy hole?"

"At home on the plains when a twister got close, we went down the fraidy hole."

"Do you mean a storm cellar?" I asked.

"That's it," he answered as he pointed at me. "A fraidy hole."

At first light, we surveyed our base. It looked like an Oklahoma twister had hit us head-on. Fortunately, they didn't get the flight line, so our aircraft were safe. Their target was the ammo bunker, and they got it.

I overheard Captain Paterson asking the CO, "What is going on? We're seeing a large increase in frequency, strength, and weaponry in the enemy's activity."

"All along the Laos and Cambodian border, there are reports of some kind of build-up," responded the CO. "It's clear the NVA is on the move. We don't know how many or for what reason yet."

That afternoon, we had our only connection with home—mail call.

That asshole Russ came to me with a letter saying, "By the smell of this, your sweety is sending you a love letter. Does she include nudie pictures too?"

"No, you pervert, and give that to me." I tore the letter open. For the third or fourth or maybe fifth time in two days, I got that knot in my stomach as I read:

> *Dear Mack,*
>
> *I pray this finds you safe. I hope you won't hate me for what I'm going to tell you. I am sorry, but I have been going out with Dennis Friend for the past two months, and I now find myself pregnant. We will be married by the time you read this.*
>
> *Please keep yourself safe.*
> *Susan*

I guess I was standing there with a faraway look on my face because Russ immediately noticed something was wrong. "What's is it now? Someone die or something?" he asked.

Holding the letter up between us, the only words I could croak out were, "Dear John."

He was supportive at first, saying, "Shit, I'm sorry." Then his hillbilly breeding kicked in, and he said, "I think it's time for you to lower your standards, Mack, and do the horizontal mambo at the Arizona Bar."

Trying to catch my breath, all I saw before me was Susan, her smile, her hair. I smelled her perfume and all of it twisted into my stomach like a corkscrew wrenching my insides. I felt alone and scared. I had never felt that way ever since I got to this rathole, but now I was suddenly an alien in an alien world. Abandoned, the one thing that kept me sane through all this unhealthy horse shit and parade of lead was that as long as she was there, at home, waiting for me, I had a shot of getting out of here by divine intervention. After all, why would God punish her with me dying? I guess God let go of the collective, and I crashed and burned. For the first time since I entered this fucking war, I felt as vulnerable as every other poor bastard who bought the farm here. I was no longer protected. I was up on the top KIA candidate list now. Tonight, a mortar round, tomorrow, a hit to the turbine and a short trip to the ground or we will draw that fucker Montgomery on the day he goes so far that we don't come back.

I looked up and saw that hillbilly grin on Russ' face. "C'mon Mack, time to get back on that horse. You've done the boy scout thing, now it's time to fuck that cheatin' bitch out of your system. I'm buying!"

Right then, I decided I wasn't going to die in this shit hole without getting laid, "Why the fuck not!"

I always thought it was a joke that hillbillies said, "Yeee haw!"

On the way into to town, being jostled over the bumpy road, I remembered a quote I had read in J.S.B. Morse's *Now and at the Hour of Our Death* that said, "A broken heart is just the growing pains necessary so that you can love more completely when the real thing comes along."

I was certain it wasn't going to come along that night.

CHAPTER 13

DON'T MESS WITH THE OLD MAN

Our Officers Earned Respect

One sunny morning Russ and I were finishing up our daily preflight when Russ said, "Here comes trouble."

Not too far away, I saw our Commanding Officer, Major Burk, and JD with their flight gear walking towards us. "I think we're going to be Bikini One today," I said.

Russ rolled his eyes and said, "How do you figure that?"

"You know, like how when the president steps on board his Boeing 707, the plane's call sign changes to Air Force One?"

"You are nuts," Russ scoffed. "That ain't the president, and this bird ain't no airliner."

"You're right." After pausing to consider his point, I added, "It's more like Butt Fuck One."

"Hey, boys, how's the bird today?" The CO asked with a big grin.

"Ready to go, sir," I answered.

"Today, you drew the short straw. We're going to take Colonel Lopez to the MACV Command Headquarters in Qui Nhon," said Burk.

"Go get your khakis and money for a night on the town."

"Yes, sir!" I said with a big grin. We were off to get our good 'unies' and a wad of 20s.

Major Burk's cheerful mood made me suspicious. The mission was a routine milk run. We could easily fly to Qui Nhon and return before lunch. Besides, I had never heard of such a short trip requiring an overnight stay. *What's he up to?*

Further piquing my suspicions was that Burk was usually all business, but today he was surprisingly casual. I shrugged it off and thought, *maybe it's because he plans to get laid tonight and knows if he does it around here, it would ruin his reputation as a hard ass and show he actually had some social tendencies.*

Once onboard the chopper, I couldn't help but again notice that Major Burk's demeanor was a bit different; it was weirdly relaxed. A warning light went on while running through his pre-flight checklist, indicating something was wrong with the engine chip plug. Usually, that bright light would trigger a near explosion from Burk with him demanding to know what was wrong and who fucked up. Instead, there was silence from Burk on this day as he patiently waited for me to investigate the issue. It took just a few moments for me to remove the cowling and fix the problem. Evidently, the maintenance crew must have somehow bent the lead to the engine chip plug, which triggered the warning light. Although Burk was unusually calm, I was pissed that the maintenance crew was so sloppy and felt Burk's inner rage when I thought, *God damn idiot. They're going to hear from me when we get back... tomorrow.*

I finally had the aircraft ready for our mission. Russ and I took our positions. I apologized, "Sorry, sir, for delaying your takeoff."

The CO replied, "No problem. We have all day, guys." Our passenger, the colonel, smiled in agreement.

Russ and I eyed each other with a questioning look and mouthed without speaking, 'What's with him?' We both silently answered each other with raised eyebrows as we shrugged our shoulders and tipped our heads to the left, meaning 'I don't know.'

Once we landed at Qui Nhon, and after Russ and I finished our post-flight, another curious thing happened. Instead of walking, a jeep showed up to drive us to our assigned rooms at the Air Force base. Upon entering my room, I looked past the bed and TV… and there it was, a full bathroom with a shower stall. That is where I headed, leaving a trail of clothes along the way. Finally, I got a hot shower in water that didn't have a foul odor. It took great determination to pull myself out of the soothing spray in time to meet our group.

After dressing in what my grandmother would call 'our Sunday go-to-meeting clothes,' we headed for a line of small honkytonks just outside the main gate to the base. The names of the taverns ranged from states to animals. After a short walk, we found the Texas Bar, where JD told us to meet him. When I entered the bar, the smell of cheap perfume tingled my nose, telling me that this was more than just a bar. Looking around, I admired the shelves of several varieties of whiskeys, rums, tequilas, and vodkas. In a bucket of ice was a large selection of beers, all with not a spot of rust anywhere on them. The bartender smiled, revealing a gold tooth, as he said, "They call me Goldie."

I thought, *No Shit.*

"Can I get you somfin?"

"Two Jack and Cokes," I said in awe of the display of abundance of choice.

It sure beat Holloway's, the on-base enlisted men's club back at Pleiku, which was the last stop on the supply line from Quin Nhon.

Somewhere between the supply depot and here, our monthly allocation of beverages got diverted so we were just limited to Ballantine in rusty cans and cognac.

Next, I saw JD dressed in civilian clothes, despite the orders given to Russ and me to wear Class B uniforms.

We joined JD at a table in the back corner. Our Jack and Cokes arrived, with a big smile from Goldie.

I gave Goldie three bucks and said, "Keep the change."

Goldie's shining sun-like smile set and said, "Thank you. I guess all 'mericans no rich."

Russ tossed in another two dollars and nudged me, "Cheap shit!"

I then asked JD, "Why did you want to meet here with us in our Class Bs, and you're in civies?"

"You'll see," was his answer as he chased away three girls trolling for business.

"Why did you do that?" I asked. "Maybe I want a little companionship tonight."

Whispering, he said, "Not tonight, boys. We're on one of the major's special missions."

As Russ ordered the next drink, I saw our commander standing at the door, also in civilian clothes. Again, I wondered why we wore our Class B uniforms, and the officers were in civies.

JD said in a soft voice, "Do not act like he is our CO or even an officer! Got it?"

"Yes, sir." Russ and I looked at each other.

"Didn't I just say act like we aren't officers? So even don't call us, sir. I'm JD, and he's Burk."

The major walked to our table and pulled up a chair, "Evening, boys. Ready for your assignment?"

"Yes, s..." I said, stopping myself just before blurting out, "sir."

"See that table over by the window with four guys dressed in Air Force uniforms?"

I carefully focused on my words so I would not refer to the guy who would otherwise ream me a new ass if I didn't say, "sir" after each answer., "...Yes."

The CO said, "Go over to the table and tell the sergeant that you were talking to Specialist Benson of the First of the Seventh Cavalry in An Khe. He said you could buy a case of Johnny Walker scotch from him for your platoon leader's birthday. The sergeant won't have that much product close, so he'll tell you when and where to pick it up. Here's $200 for the payment. Don't worry if he gives you shit; JD and I are ready." Then he patted a bulge in his beltline and lifted his shirt, exposing the handle of his 45.

"Why are we doing this?" I asked as I pocketed the cash.

The CO came back to his usual demeanor and clarified firmly, "Because I fucking told you to do it. Any more fucking questions?"

"No, sir—I mean, John," I said quickly.

"The next time you call me by my first name will be your fucking last. Got it?" Someone told me when you are in a hole, quit digging, so I nodded in agreement.

I got up and walked toward my assigned mission. Then I remembered hearing about the Seventh Cavalry, known as the Army's bad luck unit. It started with General Custer and carried through every war since up to the disastrous battle two years ago in the Au Shaw Valley. I did not want tonight to continue that legend; I hoped no one scalped me.

I found one older, big, burly sergeant with three younger airmen. All had girls on their laps laughing and acting like they owned the place. The sergeant looked at me with creepy eyes and asked abruptly, "What the Fuck do you want?"

"Specialist Benson tells me I could buy a case of Johnny Walker scotch from you."

"Where'd you talk to Benson?" he grilled me.

"In An Khe," I said. "See, my air crew is in the crapper with our platoon captain, and he's threatening to make us part of the First Cavalry in the infantry. I heard he likes Johnny Walker, and, so, maybe we can get him off his high horse and forget about our little transgression."

"Whatcha do to get him pissed?"

An idiot could determine that this guy was in the black-marketing of military items. I came up with a story that would put him at ease. "We sold an Army air conditioner to a Province leader."

All four started laughing and talked about how stupid we were because Vietnam leaders would do anything to get on the right side of American commands.

He looked at me and said, "So they turn you in for any deviation from regulations to curry favors with the commanders. How stupid can you get, son?"

"I guess real stupid. Can you help a bunch of poor jammed-up soldiers?"

"Two hundred bucks. Meet me at Warehouse Number Eight tomorrow morning at six o'clock. Don't be late because the lieutenant comes in at eight, and he isn't part of our deal."

I gave him the money and said, "I'll be there." Back at the table, I relayed the instructions to the rest of our group. After another round of drinks, we left the bar.

Out on the street, Burk said, "Okay. Don't get distracted. No broads. Get some rack time. I expect to meet you guys at 5:30 tomorrow morning. Have the Huey ready to go. We'll go get our share of this month's allotment of adult beverages and steaks before anyone else for a change."

All I could think of was, *I got all dressed up for this?* What a waste of good cologne.

As planned, we met early and flew our bird to the distribution center before it officially opened. JD landed on their resupply pad.

As I opened the door for Major Burk, he said, "Grab your M16s and an extra magazine of ammo." That command made me shit.

The sergeant from last night came out of the warehouse. "Sir," he said, "you're too early. We don't issue product until eight."

The CO stopped him with a haymaker punch in the mouth. The force of the blow knocked him backward, causing him to fall on his back. Major Burk stepped on his throat and dropped a requisition form on his face and said, "That is my allotment for this month. Put it in that chopper."

His crew of the three airmen, also from the night before, came running out the door and were greeted by our M16s.

"Face the building," I yelled. "Put your hands over your heads. Place them on the building. Now, take two steps back."

Turning to Russ, I added, "See Russ. This is how you do it. They can't make a move towards us without falling flat on their faces."

"Where did you learn that shit?" Russ asked in disbelief.

"A TV show called, *The FBI.*"

With a streak of blood running down his cheek, the sergeant asked, "What is this all about?"

"We're from Pleiku. You've been black marketing our supplies to the local bars, and my men are drinking Vietnamese Coke, cognac, and Ballantine in rusty cans. Now you, and your partners in crime, load that stuff on my ship before I kick your ass so bad, you'll rub shit off your teeth for a week."

After the four completed loading the items on the list, I checked them off. "It's all here, sir."

The major pointed his pistol at the sergeant's head. He said, "The first of every month at this time, a bird with a Little Annie Fanny as nose art will be landing here. I want you to load it with our allotment of not only beverages, but any specialty food items that we're authorized. Don't put on one item more or less than our authorization. Now, if you cause any problems with command or the provost marshal, I have written proof of your black-market scheme from the Texas Bar. Your next girlfriend won't be the whores from last night, but some big-dicked guy named Bubba at the Long Ben Jail. Just for the record, fuck-face, we are doing nothing illegal; we're just picking up our authorized product, which your specialist duly signed off on. Are we clear?"

His, "Yes, sir," was muffled by the bloody rag he was holding over his mouth.

On the flight back to basecamp at Holloway, the CO said, "You three were not picked for this mission randomly. I know what you did to Rose with the exploding shower trick and the misappropriation of government property, flying hookers to an SF camp. Each one of them alone would earn you tough disciplinary action and, coupled together, will be a shit-load worse. If anyone finds out what I just did, I'll show no mercy on you guys. Got it?"

We each responded, "Yes, sir."

The night we returned from the major's secret mission, Russ and I decided to go enjoy the club with friends. As we approached it, we heard an unusually loud sound of what seemed like a giant party going on inside. Inside, we found the entire battalion's enlisted members enjoying their new supply of different beverages.

Ski stopped me and said, "Did you know that we finally got a shipment of the good stuff?"

I shook my head and said, "No, I didn't, but I'm sure going to sample some of it."

Ski raised his glass and said, "It sure beats trying to choke down that stinking cognac or mixing it with ice, coke, water, or even a beer in those awful 'depth charges.'"

"See. Bitching sometimes works."

We found a seat at my friend "Getthis" Jones' table. Jones was the Chinook flight engineer with the company's call sign Big Windy. We got there just in time to hear one of the best stories ever.

He started with, "You know my gunner, Jared?"

Russ affirmed, "Ya, the big guy from Louisiana."

"Correct. Now get this, you know how malaria pills give some of us diarrhea? Today, after Jared took his malaria pill, he soiled his pants. It smelled so bad during our flight that we made him throw them out of the ship. Before I go on, let me tell you about Jared. He once told me that he and his wife grew up together. They were never apart and were in the same schools from the first grade through graduation. Neither had sex until their wedding night, just out of high school."

"Big deal. So?" someone asked.

"To get this in perspective, if Jared dies over here—and remember now, his wife has never been with another man—the poor woman will be bitterly disappointed with the next guy. That is, no one will measure up, if you know what I mean."

"So what? I have no interest to know he's hung like a mule," I blurted out.

"Hold your mules," Jones responded. "I was just setting the stage for the good part of this morning's mission. Now get this, today's assignment was to remove all men and equipment from Fire Base

Charlie. There were about thirty-two grunts left in two lines, ready to get on board on the last load when I lowered the rear ramp. Now here is Jared, the Donkey Dick, walking down the ramp, only wearing a shirt and combat boots, ordering, 'Hurry up, girls. Let's move it. We have a lot of you to load, so to make room for everyone, move close enough to the man in front of you until he smiles.' The look on those grunts' faces was unbelievable. I'm sure some of them was ready to walk the fuck back to Pleiku." That brought on a partially alcohol-induced and uncontrollable fit of laughter from all of us.

CHAPTER 14:
A CHICKEN BECOMES AN EAGLE

Supply convoys were under constant attack between Pleiku to Kontum, so the 4th Division sent a company of grunts to sweep the area. Our assignment to support the 3rd platoon became ordinary. For two days, we flew sick calls, meals, ammo, and supplies of all kinds. On the third day, we picked up the evening meal's empty Miramar cans and were returning home. I was looking forward to a steak and smooth scotch Russ won in a poker game with one of the support guys turned stand-in soldier we flew during 'Mission Improbable.'

Tired from loading ammo, water, and men since six o'clock that morning, I sat back and watched the setting sun cast shadows from palm trees and little hamlets where kids ran out to wave at us as we flew by.

It happens fast. It sounds like a 5-pound hammer being slammed on the roof above our heads; then an immediate coughing and tearing metal sound as the 1,300 horsepower of the engine goes Kamakazi, and it self-destructs.

"Oh shit!" I said as warning lights and sounds lit up the Christmas Tree. The gift under that tree was a brilliant little device that has saved more air crews of rotary-winged aircraft than Sirkowsky could have ever imagined. The freewheel clutch, without it, a helicopter without an engine power would have the aerodynamics of a wall safe. Once that sucker disengages from the main rotor shaft, the blades autorotate and we descend under collective pitch control where the pilot trades off RPMs for lift. The result is the freewheeling rotors act as a defacto parachute.

The sudden descent upset my stomach. As we splashed down in a rice paddy, my seat belt jerked around my waist. I heard Miramar cans smash into the back of the pilot's seat while others flew out the cabin doors, causing mud to fly everywhere.

"One bullet worth about 25 cents just caused a $300,000 helicopter to go down," I muttered in disgust.

"Maybe this is more than just a lucky shot," JD observed, as he pointed to a VC squad at the opposite end of the rice paddy. "I couldn't get anyone on the radio after our engine conked out, and now no one answers on the emergency freq."

"Try the company freq," Montgomery said as Russ racked his M60, waiting for those Cong fuckers to advance.

"Mayday. Mayday. Any aircraft. This is Bikini One-Four-Four."

"One-Four-Four, this is Drydock Five," came an immediate response. "What's up?"

"Shit," I said. "It's Lieutenant Chickenshit Rose."

Montgomery got on and said, "Drydock Five, we are twenty miles northwest of Pleiku, stuck in a rice paddy just west of Route 7 with a squad of VC closing in on us."

"I'm on a test flight with no guns or crew," Rose responded. "I'll try to raise someone in the area."

Rose called for help. A short time later, he informed us the closest helicopter was thirty minutes out.

"Shit, we'll be dead by then" Russ quickly blurted out.

"Where the hell is Rose?" Montgomery questioned.

"Drydock Five, what's your location?" JD inquired.

"I'm within five miles."

Montgomery grabbed the mic and ordered, "Get your ass in here. Now!"

"He's not coming," I said as I watched the edge of the rice paddy for signs of movement or firefly flashes in the weeds over the sights of my M16. "He has an inherent aversion to danger."

"Russ, get the M60s and M16s with all the ammo we can carry and come with me," Montgomery said. "Mack, put the rest of the ammo, guns, and radios in the center of the ship and turn on the fuel drains."

Captain Montgomery's order meant that he was giving up hope that a Chinook could come to our rescue and pull our bird out of the mud. Instead, we not only had to abandon our ship, but we had to destroy it so that it and its contents wouldn't fall into the enemy's hands. I felt a sadness as I had grown attached to this bird. I had spent a lot of harrowing hours in it and countless hours inspecting and cleaning every inch of it, not to mention that she delivered us back to earth without a scratch.

The VC was now halfway across the rice patty and shooting. Montgomery and Russ began to return fire from behind a dike. A noxious smell filled the air as soon as the leaking JP4 jet fuel and oil hit the hot engine surface. All of a sudden, I heard the sound of a Huey.

"Did you get anyone on the radio to rescue us?" I asked JD.

His answer gave me goosebumps all over when he said, "Rose."

I thought, *Shit. Rose is afraid to do an assault under enemy fire with gunship and door gun support. He won't land without it.* I looked up, and to my astonishment, I saw Rose in an approach to land, and so did the VC. Green tracers started to concentrate on the Huey while

Russ and the captain tried to give as much suppressive fire as possible.

"Shit! Rose, is getting pounded," JD exclaimed.

I told JD, "I'm not convinced that he will continue through that much groundfire," but he kept coming.

The aircraft landed. Russ, Montgomery, and JD ran for the Huey. I pulled the pin on two hand grenades, tossed them in my ship, and ran for the rescue bird. A few seconds later, I heard the grenades explode. As I approached Rose's Huey, I felt the heat on my back coming from my beloved bird's demise. As soon as I jumped on board, Rose pulled pitch, and I was pushed to the back of the seat by the acceleration.

I sat there dumbfounded and a bit in shock. Rose saved our asses. I also was amazed at Rose's ability to keep the bird just inches above the paddy's dikes and close to Huey's top speed until we were clear of the VC's range of fire. He then did a cyclic climb out. A cyclic climb is when a chopper is at high speed, and the pilot pulls back on the cyclic stick, sacrificing airspeed for climb rate. That maneuver makes the helicopter soar like a rocket. At 5,000 feet, Rose leveled off and invoked Sir Isaac Newton's first law which states, 'An object in motion stays in motion.' My ass left the seat as we went from climbing at 4,000 feet per minute to level flight. Once the aircraft was at altitude and cruising at 80 knots, Rose asked Captain Montgomery to take control of the aircraft.

Rose lifted his hand and said, "Look, I'm so scared; I'm shaking!"

Montgomery's reply showed us he was a true leader and more than just our bad luck charm. He said, "Courage isn't the absence of fear, just the mastering of it."

After we landed at Holloway, I opened Montgomery's door and pushed back his armored seat plate. I couldn't help but notice that the window above Rose had a bullet hole and the instrument panel had caught three rounds. There was no denying it; Rose was getting hits all around him but kept his approach despite it. I wondered if he realized that he just saved three of the four sons-of-a-bitches who pulled the water-heater-exploding trick on him.

After the rotor blades stopped, Rose took off his helmet. I went to his open door and said, "Thank you, Lieutenant."

He nodded.

I added, "I take back all the bad things I said about you, but only half the bad things I thought about you."

We all laughed at that.

While Rose and Montgomery were leaving, Rose turned and said, "I haven't forgotten about that shower thing."

"What shower thing?"

CHAPTER 15:
GOOD MEAL OR LAST SUPPER

FOB-2

I guess the CO thought Russ and I needed some time off after the crash, so he sent us to Cam Ranh Bay on R&R for three days of sun, beach, bars, and girls. I had been there before and had always demurred from the extracurriculars, but now that I was Susan-free, I hit the place like a horny college student on winter break. I so needed that.

Upon our return, the platoon sergeant had a surprise waiting for us, a new Huey straight out of the factory.

"She's yours," he said, pointing to the new bird. "Try not to wreck this one. Now get your asses ready to be in the field for an undetermined amount of time for SOG missions at FOB-2."

"What is SOG, and where is FOB-2?" Russ asked overwhelmed and bewildered, all at the same time.

"SOG stands for Search and Observation Group," the sergeant said. "It is an Army Special Operations Unit operating at Forward Operations Base Two, just below Kontum."

"Oh, I've seen that," Russ acknowledged. "It's a former French fort located two miles south of Kontum."

As he left, the sergeant shouted over his shoulder, "Yes, it is. Have fun," and laughed.

I wondered what he meant by that manic laugh. I knew the missions were tense, but we hadn't lost a crew there yet. Russ and I spent the rest of the day equipping and arming the new Huey in our unique way.

The next morning, it was time to get back in the air. While the new, spotless, virgin bird was nice to see, my stomach became queasy thinking about what happened in the rice paddy, that hideous laugh, and what that may have foretold of danger ahead.

Still, Montgomery's words came back to me, "Courage isn't the absence of fear, just the mastering of it." I took a deep breath and finished loading my gear.

"Russ, do you feel nervous about saddling up again?" I asked anxiously. "To tell the truth, I gave some thought to joining the maintenance platoon last night."

"I had the same feelings, but they would have sent me to the infantry, so my choice was much easier."

Once in the air, with the wind in my face and the scenery beneath me, my stomach settled, and I knew I could continue slinging supplies for this stupid war.

On the way north to FOB-2, our pilot, Mr. Snow, briefed us on the base. "This camp is unique in several ways. For one, it has a road separating it into two parts. On the west side is the old French fort with a walled-in parade field. We will land and shut down for the night there within the enclosure. Your living quarters will be on the opposite side of the road."

On our first night in camp, we had dinner with some of the Green Berets we would be working with on the missions.

The dining room wasn't up to Howard Johnson's standards, but the food was far superior to Hojo's. It was the first actual good meal I had had since I had left the real world. It was nice to eat like a human being. The dinner consisted of a properly cooked, thick, and tender steak, a fully loaded baked potato, and apple pie for dessert.

These FOB boys ate well. I mean, these steaks were like Kansas City cut, 2-inch prime. We all couldn't wait to dig in. As soon as the plates hit the table, we were fully engaged with knives and forks, but one of the funnier members of our group, a Polish guy whose last name ended in "ski" (and we called him that or "The Pollock"), just sat there staring at it. I looked for bugs crawling on it, but this was one perfectly done cut of meat. "What's wrong, Ski? Turned vegetarian all of a sudden?"

"I can't cut into this marvelous meat; I just want to kiss it! I'm in love." He picked it up off his plate and started kissing it. Everybody howled.

After dinner, it was time for a briefing from the Green Beret first sergeant. First sergeants are the top enlisted men of a company and are referred to primarily as "Top." Every top sergeant I ever met tried to be an example to their men. They all looked like soldiers out of a recruiting ad. That is, they were cleanly shaven with short hair and pressed uniforms.

When it was time for the briefing, I noticed a bearded man walking to the front of the room. He had long hair and wore a multi-colored Hawaiian shirt, Bermuda shorts, and flip-flops. I thought he was a civilian contractor or CIA until he said, "I'm First Sergeant McElroy." That, coupled with the extraordinary meal, made two clues indicating this unit would be different from any company I had flown missions with before.

"Gentlemen, welcome to FOB-2," began McElroy. "In case you haven't heard, everything you hear, see, and do here is top secret. If you reveal anything to anyone, you will be prosecuted and see nothing but the inside of Leavenworth Prison for a long time."

He let that sink in for a while.

"Now that the pleasantries are over, I can get to your part in this operation," McElroy continued. "Our missions are almost all in Laos or Cambodia. A vast majority of the teams will be in contact with highly trained Northern Vietnam regular Army units, not those ragtag Viet Cong militia that is not much more than a pain in the ass that we sweep away like sweat on our balls."

That got a chuckle out of the room. No one asked why there are NVRA units in Laos or Cambodia, nor did anyone point out that this whole clusterfuck was specifically called the Vietnam War, not the Vietnam, Laos, Cambodian War; but then I thought, *Oh, right. Top Secret shit.*

McElroy continued, "As they say, the devil is in the details. SOG is a highly classified Special Operations unit that conducts covert unconventional warfare actions. They perform strategic reconnaissance, as I said, into Laos and Cambodia. We carry out targeting and bomb assessment, capture enemy prisoners, retrieve downed pilots, rescue prisoners of war, and conduct covert activities and psychological warfare operations. We do this with two types of teams. One is recon. Recon or intelligence gathering squads consist of three Americans and three to five Vietnamese, or indigenous people of Vietnam called Montagnards."

Ski, always the clown, was making us believe he was writing all this down. He whispered to me, "Montagnards—is that with one 'g' or two?"

I gave him a light punch in the arm and shushed him, then I whispered back, "Shut the fuck up. The food is good here; don't blow it."

Meanwhile, the sergeant rambled on, "You will support both missions in hostile territory, mainly along the so-called Ho Chi Minh Trail."

I think half the room would have walked out, even if the sarge was a hot chick in a bikini standing there. The guys around the table were rolling their eyes. I was thinking about another piece of apple pie when suddenly, the sarge's words got our attention.

"To give you an idea of how dangerous these missions are, a full 100% of our team members were either wounded, killed, or listed as missing in action over the last twelve months. All you aircrews are hand-selected for your ability to manage under fire, so I expect to see and hear about nothing but the best from your missions."

All of a sudden, the steak dinner felt eerily like our last meal. *Shit.* My stomach suddenly acted up again. *Forget the pie.*

McElroy paused, looked around the room, and made sure everyone was hanging onto his every word. He then changed his tone. His posture and body language were different. He wasn't briefing us anymore; he was sharing something personal as he said, "These SOG men are the best trained, equipped, and bravest souls in the Army, but when they are surrounded and outgunned, who are they gonna call? Barney Fife? It's you guys, and you are the difference between life and death for these teams who are a long way from any other help."

With that, he closed with, "Fly safe. Fight hard and come home."

CHAPTER 16:
MONKEY KILLS

Each morning we would fly seventy miles north to Dak To. We would then be on standby to insert or extract SOG teams from the field. The first few days at Dak To made us think we were in heaven compared to what we experienced hauling ass and trash. We inserted teams and extracted others without a shot fired. For most of the day, we had to be ready for a mission at any time. Sleeping was high on the priority list of activities but sleeping just goes so far when you have men in their late teens and early twenties. We had to find some more exciting ways to spend our downtime.

One afternoon, our resident redneck, Ron, said, "Those gunship rockets look fun," then added, "What does one of the solid fuel propellants in the rockets look like?"

We took one apart and pulled out this greasy white cylinder. Next, I am sure it was Ski who said, "What if we light it? What could happen? C4 burns like Sterno. I bet this does too."

"Let's try it," said one of the fellows who we called "Bone" because he looked like the TV character Wishbone, the cook on the TV show *Rawhide*.

We lit it, and it took off. With nothing to guide it, the propellant started whipping around the Hueys, causing everyone to dive for cover. The real problem was when it headed straight towards the ordinarily even-tempered Captain Montgomery, he managed to hurl himself into a ditch as it went over his head. Once the rocket fuel burned up and stopped, everyone came out of hiding with sheepish looks on all our faces.

Montgomery did not look amused as he came out of the ditch, trying to remove the mud that covered him. He bellowed, "Who lit that god damn rocket?"

To confuse the issue, I blamed Jack, a gunner from Alaska. Jack blamed Ski. Ski blamed the Indian, and we all settled on our California dreamer and said, "It was Vincent," who was sleeping in his ship.

The captain warned, "You guys are way too juvenile to be playing with big boy toys. Next time anything like this happens, you will all lose a stripe."

"Yes, sir," was a chorus line response of crew chiefs and gunners.

Over the next couple of days, we inserted recon teams deep in hostile Laos territory and extracted some still without a shot fired; but like all good things, this had to end. On our third day, the launch commander came out of his tent and said, "Man your ships and get in the air ASAP. Team New Mexico is in a world of shit. Head east to Juliet-Nine and receive your instructions from the forward air controller."

Six slicks and two gunships were airborne within ten minutes. On the way to the LZ, the radio was alive with chatter, "New Mexico Zero-Zero, this is Convey Rider One-One."

The voice of a breathless team member came back, "Convey, this is Zero-Zero. Go."

"Roger Zero-Zero. What is your status?"

"Two wounded and being chased by a squad of NVA."

"Zero-Zero, can you make Juliet-Nine Alpa?"

"Negative LZ Alpha is out of reach with our wounded."

"Zero-Zero, I have two Spads with 500 pounders enroute. They'll blow an LZ."

Hearing about the Spads, with the 500-pound bombs, I asked, "I thought they retired those piston-powered World War II fighter bombers years ago?"

"They decided because the Sky Raider, or Spad, is slower than jets, their bombing runs are more precise," Snow explained.

The Forward Air Controller relayed to the Spads the location to blow us an LZ that we call a hover hole, where you have to vertically descend one hundred and fifty feet while avoiding trees and bullets.

Then came the bad news. "Bikini Flight. New Mexico has two wounded. The LZ is a hover hole, and the greenies will try to clear the debris with their explosive cords; but expect it to be testy with NVA in pursuit."

"Testy?" our co-pilot Warren paused, "I like the way they understate things."

"You want them to say shit storm?" I scoffed.

"Testy is fine," Snow said evenly.

I held my breath as we made a pass over the LZ and said, "I've been in hover holes before, but nothing like this one, sir."

The Spads blew a hole in the jungle with their bombs, and the Green Beret team did use their explosive cords to clear obstructions between trees; but neither of those efforts made us a nice landing strip.

"The LZ is tight, but we can make it," I said.

We were the second ship in to pick up the remainder of the team. When it was our turn, we flew into position over the LZ, and I told Snow, "That's no LZ. It looks like a game of pick-up sticks."

"Stop bitching and clear us in," Warren said.

The Buccaneer gunships resumed cover fire from above, and we started down. During the descent through the triple canopy, Russ and I were to watch the main and tail rotors to make sure they didn't contact a tree. This required constant chatter as we instructed the pilots on how to move the helicopter body or tail—together or separately—to avoid disaster from a blade strike. When we were three or four feet from the ground, team New Mexico began climbing aboard and caused the aircraft to start rocking. The rocking made the pilot's job even more challenging since we were close to the trees. They couldn't let the aircraft move more than a few feet in any direction. I have no idea how they managed to avoid disaster time after time. Now if that wasn't enough excitement, we were continually taking enemy fire and felt like sitting ducks.

While trying to avoid bullets from nearby NVA troops, I remembered that one of the VC strategies was to keep as close as possible to our guys, using them as cover from our gunships and bombers who couldn't hit them without endangering our team or us. Even though the gunships were firing as close to our troops as they could, it didn't stop the total assault on us. At times like that, I sure wished I was up there shooting at the NVA instead of being down here with the North Vietnamese Army shooting at us.

When everyone was finally on board, Russ and I had to clear us on the climb up through the maze of trees. We heard the Special Forces team provide the suppressive fire with their weapons, only after we got out of the trees were Russ and I able to join in defense of our ship by firing our weapons.

As the guns clattered and shell casings dinged as they hit the floor, I thought, *Big deal!* I expect we might have killed a few unarmed monkeys in the trees, but I was sure that the NVA, shooting from protective cover in the rocks and trees, were safe from our fire.

After our first day under fire with an FOB team, I let Russ talk me into going to a little "bar with benefits" outside the base's gate. When we arrived, Captain Montgomery was waiting outside. He stopped me and said, "Let's switch shirts."

I am sure I looked astonished, until I realized the captain's motivation. The ladies charge based on the soldier's rank. It would cost Montgomery four times as much if they thought he was a captain rather than a mere Spec 5. I had no problem with the request as I just wanted a few laughs and a bunch of beers. We quickly exchanged ranks and shirts.

As Montgomery slipped on my shirt, he said, "Don't you ever take a bath? This shirt smells like shit."

"That's the scent of hard work; something a captain wouldn't know."

"I may not strain my body, but it takes straining my brain to keep you assholes out of trouble."

I followed Montgomery into the bar and, in my new role as captain, called, "Attention."

That prompted Russ to say, "Who the hell calls attention in -" he paused as he turned to face me, and his tone dropped as he continued with, "a whorehouse?"

I replied, "A specialist captain." That brought the house down with laughter and got me a stern look from the real captain.

I continued, "You've heard of a sergeant major, so why not a specialist captain?"

"A sergeant major is the top enlisted rank in the Army," Ski said. "What is a specialist captain?"

"Not quite that high." I rubbed my fingers together in the universal sign for cash.

The palace of indulgence we were visiting was called the Goodie, Goodie. A frequent customer named it after a bar in his hometown, and the name fit with the types of activities occurring there. The first thing that struck you at the doorway was the aroma of cheap perfume and sweaty soldiers mixed with stale beer and urine. The urine smell came from the men's room, which has just a five-inch galvanized pipe split in half and hanging on the wall in the pisser. A small stream of water ran to wash the urine down to a tube and into the river because every other building along the waterway had the same septic system that made the river stink like everything else in this country.

At the end of the bar, a middle-aged lady sat dressed in classic Vietnamese attire. She wore a tight silk tunic worn over trousers. That was the madam of the establishment. She always sat at the end of the bar. Along one wall were the doors to the girls' 'workrooms.' The other wall had decorations of military unit patches, cheap colorful paintings on black velvet, and the toilet. In the middle of the room sat eight tables with four chairs. This night, six girls were on duty. They were dressed in the shortest miniskirts you have ever seen, not short enough to reveal their 'Landing Zone' but short enough to signal they were trolling for business. Not girls like the Cherry Ranch in Nevada, but it would suffice for now.

As soon as I sat down, one of the girls sat beside me, and asked, "Buy me Saigon tea?" This approach was the first step in the mating ritual of a Vietnamese call girl. 'Saigon tea' was just plain old tea but would cost the GI twice as much as a beer. I guess that was the price for them to sit with you.

I said, "I'm in here just for the Ba Muoi Ba." She called me something in Vietnamese that I was sure I wasn't, 'You brave American Liberator.'

Since my 'Dear John' letter, I thought my civic duty was to help pull this country out of poverty, so my part was to spend most of my pay on booze and call girls. Then I wasted the rest on essentials.

Ba Muoi Ba means 33 in Vietnamese. It is a rice beer brewed in Vietnam and was the off-base staple among American GIs.

We were all having a good time drinking and joking when Vincent asked, "Request permission from the specialist captain to go on a critical mission to improve my morale."

"Permission granted," I replied.

He took one of the ladies into her room. After a few minutes, we heard, "Insertion completed. Request permission to carry on with the mission." We all got a kick out of Vincent's attempt to mimic our radio calls during a recon mission.

I answered, "The specialist captain grants permission."

After a few more minutes, Vincent shouted, "Ammo expended. Request extraction."

This time, a chorus of Army aviators shouted, "Permission granted."

We continued to raise hell and play silly drinking games as guys left the table for Pleasure Island one by one. After about three hours, Montgomery came to our table and said, "I can't believe I trust my life in aircraft that you knuckleheads keep in the air. Give me my shirt back, you idiot specialist captain."

"You, number ten," the lady at the end of the bar across the room shouted to Montgomery. "You cheater pay tee-tee money, and you owe beaucoup. Di Ra, you number ten GI." We all chuckled that the captain, whom we could never slander to his face, was being derided by the woman for paying so little and being told to leave.

CHAPTER 17:
KILLER THOUGHTS

The next morning, my head said no, but the war said to get to Dak To, where we were to stand by for team Texas's insertion. At about 10 a.m., we got the orders to insert them in an open grassy area called the Golf Course, which consisted of tall elephant grass in Southeast Laos. On landing, the grass bent under us from the rotor wash that created ripples that looked like waves radiating in all directions. As I watched them disappear in the tall blades due to the special tiger striped camo the SOGs and only the SOGs wore, I took a deep breath and realized that the air had a sweet smell, like the recently mowed hayfields back home.

On the way back to Dak To, I commented, "I wish all LZs were like that—no enemy, no trees, just wide open."

Snow said, "That's why they call it the Golf Course. Don't you think the NVA knows that it's a good landing area for us?"

After refueling and checking out the bird, I introduced myself to the new guys that arrived from the second platoon that morning. I had seen their crews around the club but didn't know the other lift group members very well.

One guy named Rodriguez spoke in broken English, so I asked him where he was from. His answer surprised me when he said, "Juarez, Mexico."

I asked him, "Why the hell are you here if you're a Mexican citizen?" His answer made me think about how all our families must have felt except for Chiefs.

"I want to become an American citizen, and the best way to do that was to join the Army. Upon my enlistment completion with an honorable discharge, I will be one of you, a U.S. voter."

It occurred to me that if he thought this was the best way, I would hate to see the worst way. Of course, the irony of all was he was in this shit to get the right to vote for the politicians, politicians who put us in this rathole in the first place. Maybe he would vote smarter than that, and his kids wouldn't have to be hated by the people they are supposedly here to help.

We talked most of the morning. I was curious about Mexico, hearing a lot about the country but growing up thousands of miles away.

Back at my ship, red neck Ron said, "Who is he trying to kid? That wetback will never be one of us. Next, he'll bring his whole family here to be a drag on society."

"Fuck you, Ron," I said angrily. "That's how my grandfather became a citizen after World War I. If it wasn't for that, he never could have passed the citizen's test because he didn't know how to write or read English. At last count, there are seventy-seven children, grandchildren, and great-grandchildren in this family, and none are a drag on society. Eight are here in Vietnam."

Levi, the Indian, overheard Ron and my conversation, and said, "I think immigration has been screwed up since Columbus in 1492, so Ron, go back in that red neck cave you crawled out of."

At about three in the afternoon, we got the order to get into the air as soon as possible and go pick up team Texas. The launch leader explained that they were outnumbered, outgunned, and running for their lives.

We reached the Golf Course just as the team ran out from the tree line, firing over their shoulders while green tracers from the tree line were zipping past them. Green tracers were used only by the NVA. The color told us the enemy was in close pursuit. Moments later, fifteen green uniforms emerged from the tree line running and shooting at our guys.

"Texas, this is Bikini Red Five," Montgomery radioed.

The response was immediate "Bikini, whoever, get your asses down here quick."

The blades of grass hadn't recovered from the first ship rotor wash when Snow brought us to a sliding stop. I saw seven men with anxiety written on their faces waiting in the tall elephant grass. They stopped firing at the enemy and ran for our ship. Climbing on our bird caused the team's backs to be towards the enemy. Three NVA popped out of the undergrowth. I was the only one with a clear shot, and instinctively, took it.

Suddenly, everything seemed in slow motion. My ears started ringing, and I could feel my heart beating under my ribs. I hit the first one with shots from my M60 machine gun. The impact of the bullets knocked him backward, and red blood spewed from his chest onto the green grass. Then the second one's head exploded, and the third jumped back into the blood-stained grass just ahead of my volley. The inertia of our ship's fast acceleration brought me back from my 'fight or flight' mode.

We returned to Kontum with the team. The ride back was uneventful and gave me too much time to evaluate what had just happened. I thought, *I couldn't believe I had just killed two human beings when back at the farm, I couldn't stand to see Grandma when she would kill two chickens for the Sunday family dinner. Those poor bastards weren't unlike me. They are just soldiers doing their job. I'm sure they had mothers, fathers, siblings, and maybe a wife with a child, and I just put a hole in all their lives that will never heal.*

When we got to Kontum, one of the Americans from my ship said, "Come on, killer, I'll buy you a drink and a girl. Your sharp shooting probably saved our lives." I couldn't show my real feelings to these recon guys because their MACVSOG unit's casualty rate was 100%, meaning every one of them was either killed or injured on their missions, so I agreed.

He added, "Don't worry, the first kill is the toughest. It gets easier."

It never did!

Things stayed pretty quiet for the next few days. At night, we would hang out at the Goodie, Goodie and fly routine missions out of Dak To during the day. During this time, I got to know Rodriguez better and liked him. He was quiet and didn't say much, but he enjoyed our antics.

One morning, we headed back to Dak To, thinking we would insert team Nevada. When we got there, the launch leader said, "Refuel. Install McGuire rigs and be ready to fly at a moment's notice."

Rodriguez looked puzzled at the launch leader's request, so I asked, "Have you ever used a McGuire rig before?"

"No."

"Come on. I'll show you."

"Russ," I said. "Install our rig, and I'll help Rodriguez."

"Sure thing, boss."

While we walked to his bird, I explained, "McGuire rigs are a simple, inexpensive, and an effective way to extract soldiers from the jungle when a suitable LZ is not reachable by the teams on the ground."

The first thing I did was hold up the rig's canvas anchor. I grabbed six cords from it and said, "These ropes here are to secure the device. You attach these to the tiedown rings on the floor of your ship. Got it?"

"Si. Seguro."

"Yeah, right. Attached to the anchor are those three one-hundred-foot ropes. There are small seats at the end of each rope, and those loops are for the soldier's hand. Okay. Fill three ammo cans with sand; then tie them below the seats to provide weight so when you send them down to the troops, they go quickly to the ground. Drop the cans when you're over the men."

"What if you hit one with that much weight? It will kill them?" Rodriguez asked.

"They'll know they're coming and will get out of the way. When they're in their seats, the leader will give you a thumbs up. Now, this is the important part. Let the pilots know when they are clear of obstructions, so you don't drag the troopers through the trees. If you don't get this right, you'll have some pissed-off bad mothers when we get on the ground."

"Thanks, man," he said as he took my hand and shook it. "Gracias, Señor."

"One time, just as a joke, I hung out of the aircraft holding a machete close to the ropes." I made like I was holding a rope in one hand and slicing it with a knife. "The rider pointed his weapon at me, and I got the message that the joke wasn't that funny, so don't do that. Okay?"

We laughed, and I returned to Russ and my ship.

The launch leader said, "Team Utah needs help. They set up and camouflaged themselves last night when a company of NVA moved in and camped all around them. So far, the enemy hasn't spotted them, but they have to be extracted soon. The plan is for you guys to be close by when they make a break for it. As soon as they see a spot they can defend, the team leader will pop smoke, and you guys pull them out on the McGuire rigs. Team Utah has eight members. The extraction will require three birds, two taking three at a time, and the third taking two. Snow, you're to fly standby in case something happens. Let's bring our boys home, guys."

At the team Utah's location, we orbited three miles away at 5,000 feet, not to give the NVA a clue what our mission was. The team radiofrequency opened with, "It's showtime."

"Bikini Flight, this is Rider Two-Two. Move into our pre-planned position."

Our plan was for Vincent's ship to be the first to extract the team members, then Jake's, and finally, Rodriguez would get the last two.

Minutes later, Rider Two-Two radioed, "Utah Zero-Zero. Identify purple smoke."

We heard gunshots on Utah's subsequent transmission. "Affirmative purple smoke. Come get us, you flying angels."

I thought, *We're angels now, but tonight they will call us airheads or some other derogatory term to show they are back to their usual antics.*

Vincent's ship hovered over the smoke, and he sent his rigs down. Within minutes, his bird emerged with two Americans and one indigenous. I thought, *This didn't seem right since Americans always came out last.* Then I saw why. One GI was keeping the other in the seat for the reason that he was nearly unconscious. Jake's ship was in with a flash. A minute later, out he came. Then Rodriguez's Mexican express hovered over the spot. He tossed the ammo cans with the McGuire rig, but the ship seemed to be over the site too long. *Why?* Then I saw it. I couldn't believe it, and I thought I was watching a John Wayne movie. Rodriguez got on the skid, grabbed one of the ropes, and slid down it.

Montgomery shouted, "What in the hell is going on over there?"

Rodriguez's pilot reported, "One of the Montagnards had been shot and was hanging upside down from the seat. We can't take off with him like that, so Rodriguez went after him."

About then, the bird started its ascent slowly. As it cleared the trees, Rodriguez was dangling at the end of one rig, holding the wounded Montagnard in his seat. I wondered if he still thought this was an easy way to become a U.S. citizen.

They landed at Ben Hut Special Forces Camp, put all the wounded on with Rodriguez, and headed for the Pleiku Evac Hospital. They kept Rodriquez and the rest of the crew at Holloway and sent a different team to replace them. I guess the Old Man thought that was enough excitement for a while.

Later, I heard that if Rodriquez had rescued an American soldier, the SOG commander would have put him in for the Medal of Honor, but since he saved an indigenous, he would only get the Silver Star. I believe the real reason Rodriguez didn't get the Medal of Honor was that he wasn't an American citizen.

A few days later while we were waiting for the launch leader to tell us if we were picking up or inserting troops, my mind wandered back to the support troops at Holloway who once asked me what it feels like to kill someone in the war.

I answered that it depends.

In some cases, you get word back from the infantry that your service as a door gunner (the crewman tasked with firing a high-powered weapon from the helicopter's open door) killed some of the enemy. It is easy to be detached and lack feeling when this happens, as the violence occurs far in the distance, and you never see the direct result of your action. Works for me. I would prefer to forget the taking of a life, but when Russ learned of a confirmed kill, he stenciled a depiction of a Viet Cong on the ship's side.

Then there are the times when you catch an enemy soldier out in the open and shoot him from five hundred feet up at eighty knots. There is no question in these situations that you just killed a man, but you still can brush it off as if you are in a shooting gallery at the fair with high fives all around…and another stencil goes on the ship.

There is a third type. This is the one that sticks with you for your entire life! It is the one that steals your soul, causes many sleepless nights, namely, the up close and personal killings that cannot merely be called anything but a murder in living color, experiences that are permanently etched into my mind. These are the SOG missions that are forever replayed and revisited in my head, with a repeated intensity that I never wanted to see once, and certainly not over, and over, and over again.

CHAPTER 18:
THE RIGHT WAY

Walking back from breakfast one morning, I was surprised to see our CO land and then rush into the camps ops, leaving the co-pilot to shut down the engine. Soon, the excitement went through the camp like the flu through a grade school's playground.

We all started walking on air because the CIA had spotted a POW camp west of the Laos border, and the SF Command decided FOB-2 had the expertise to be in charge of going and getting our guys.

After his conference with the mission commander, the CO gathered everyone around his aircraft for our instructions. He said, "The CIA has ordered us to fly a 40-man Hatchet Force into a POW camp about 100 miles west of Dak To. All of our ships stationed here are to be involved. Along with the guns, four slicks will take the Hatchet Force to the camp. My ship and two others will fly chase."

One of the gunship pilots from Utah, Frederickson, interrupted, "Christ, that's almost in Thailand. We won't have enough fuel to make it there and back."

That was exactly what I was thinking. Those NVA rat bastards knew the range of our Hueys and had placed their POW camps just far enough from Dak To to be beyond the reach of our point of no return, half the fuel load of our Hueys.

"I'll get to that," the CO responded and continued. "Air Force Jolly Greens with medical personnel will be circling overhead. They will bring out the American POWs after the Hatchet Force secures the prison. Phantom jets will be there for support if needed. After we get our guys, they'll destroy the camp. Now to Mr. Frederikson's issues. Chinooks will fly fuel bladders into the Golf Course, and we will refuel on the way in and out."

The Buccaneer Commander Captain Fisk said, "We were just at the Golf Course, and the NVA have patrols in that area."

"The rest of the Bikinis from Holloway will take all the remaining Hatchet Forces to protect the fueling station," the CO said. "I don't see any problem with this plan for the slicks, but the gunships will have to take on more fuel than usual to make the round trip. I'm concerned because you will have to drag those birds through grassland on takeoff with the extra weight. Getting tangled up in that vegetation could be a problem."

"My guys will take off some armor plating on the pilot's seats and remove other non-essential items. Don't worry, sir. We'll make it work," Fisk said.

Major Burk said, "I believe the CIA has put together a sound plan, but there is no room for error. Okay, let's get to Dak To and be ready when we get the order to launch."

On the way to Dak To, I thought, *Now this is the kind of mission that makes getting up in the morning in this rathole survivable.* I imagined how those men being held by the sadistic NVA will feel when they hear American choppers coming to get them. As I looked out the door at the full team flying in formation all around us, it made me proud. We topped off our tanks on Dak To. As planned the Hatchet Force Hurricane held the Golf Course so we were able to refuel and head west for 45 minutes off to the camp. The trick now was that a ninety-minute round trip meant we would have only a half-hour fuel to stay at the camp's station. That didn't give the Special Forces team much time to clear the camp of NVA and get our guys to a predetermined LZ.

I hope those Hatchet boys are as good as their unit's name, I thought.

A half-hour out from getting fuel, we started receiving 50-caliber machine gunfire. The bastards didn't hit any of us, but they sure got our attention. When you first spot 50-caliber tracers, they look slow and look like they are coming right at your head, but they seem to speed up significantly the closer they get. In this case, they passed over, under, in front, and behind us. I remember the first time I experienced this; it subtly gets your attention...like getting kicked in the balls.

We made it to the POW camp in forty minutes, five minutes less than was calculated. Our flight of four troop-carrying helicopters set down just outside the bamboo-constructed wall that served as the camp's perimeter. Our passengers were off in a matter of seconds, while the Buccaneers blew a hole in the flimsy fence. We took off and circled the camp, watching our guys go door to door and cage to cage. So far, surprisingly, there was no engagement with the enemy. Could it be they saw a far superior force and gave up? Rumors have it that the best of the NVA troops are engaged in combat while the trainees or those too injured to fight any longer guarded the POW camps.

After about twenty minutes, our ground forces' leader radioed, "Rider, this is Apache Six. We have found signs that Americans had been here, but they are gone now. Bikini Flight, pick us up in ten. We're retrieving documents that may be of value."

That is when everybody's heart sank. We thought it would be a joyous day, but it turned out to be just another day in this stinking war. The only high point was seeing the camp go up in flames as the fighters bombed it.

After refueling at the Golf Course, we returned to FOB-2 dejected. The most complicated mission we had yet was executed with great precision, and it had failed.

While I was inspecting my bird, Sergeant Jefferson came to me and asked, "Did any Vietnamese hear Major Burk's pre-mission briefing?"

I pointed to a Vietnamese major and his aid.

"Was he on any of the Hueys during the mission?" Jefferson asked.

"I didn't see him."

"Thanks," Jefferson said while walking away.

I thought, *Now that guy is Combat Investigative Service.*

I turned and asked Russ, "Think Jefferson is CID?"

"Ahh see! and you thought I was a bigot when I told you there is something strange about that guy."

"I think you're right, Russ," I said. "You may not be a bigot, but you're still an idiot. Now let's finish up here and get to the Goodie, Goodie."

CHAPTER 19:
NOW IT'S THE ARMY WAY

The following day after our failed prisoner of war rescue mission, Russ and I were getting our bird ready for the day's mission. Hearing a Huey landing, I looked up to see a red over white painted civilian Air America bird.

One of our ground crew asked, "What's Air America?"

Walking up, Snow said, "It is the CIA's airline."

Two men got out of the back of the Central Intelligence Agency's Huey and went into the base's headquarters. Moments later, they returned with the Vietnamese major I pointed out to Jefferson yesterday and the major's aid. All four boarded the nonmilitary bird and took off.

Major Burk then landed and went into the headquarters building. Hatchet Force Apache members soon started gathering around our birds.

"Something's up," I said quizzically.

Russ said, "No shit, Sherlock," as they got closer to us.

Within twenty minutes, the CIA Huey was back with the Vietnamese major, but not with his aid.

Tom, one of the American Hatchet Forces members hovering around our aircraft, said, "Looks like it's a go."

"What?" I asked.

Tom said, "We're going back after the POWs that we missed yesterday."

"How do you know?" I asked.

"A CIA plan to get someone to talk is to take two up for a helicopter ride. In this case, they ask both, 'Where did they take our prisoners of war? We had hard evidence that they were at the camp just hours before we arrived, so someone told them we were coming.' If they don't answer, they throw one out. Almost always, the second one talks."

"How do you know he talked?" I asked, still not getting it.

"He didn't go flying with his partner," explained Tom. "So, obviously, he's directing us to the new POW camp."

I said, "I killed guys with my M60, but that's the first time I killed a guy with my finger," as I understood what he meant.

Russ joked, "Don't you point that thing at me."

"No, but what about this one?" I said as I held up my middle finger.

A flight of five Hueys with Hatchet Force Hurricane and three Chinooks with fuel blivits underneath flew overhead, interrupting our banter. Tom said, "Back in Nevada, we have truck stop gas stations along our highways for fueling. There goes a Huey stop."

Snow was huddled with the CO and pilots when he yelled to me, "Mack, how much fuel do we have?"

"Seven hundred twenty-five pounds, sir," I said.

"Untie the blades and load the Hatchet Force Apache," ordered Snow.

I watched as the CIA took the North Vietnamese spy to Air America's Huey. I wondered if he was holding the same one-way ticket as his aide.

Snow and Warren got in and started my bird. As soon as we were up to full RPM, the radio chatter started. Over the radio, I heard, "Bikini Flight, Bikini Six, let's go get our boys."

Once airborne, Snow said, "You guys' plan on getting a little wet. As you have probably figured out, we're going after the POWs again. Mack, that major you reported was a spy and radioed soon after we left to move the prisoners of war to a secondary location. To not alert anyone our refueling position has changed, we will use an almost dry riverbed so plan to get a little wet."

The word 'almost', prompted me to say, "So who determined we're not going to be waist-deep in mud or water? Was it those same mission planner geniuses that planned yesterday's fuckups?"

"No, it was our own intellects," Snow answered.

When we arrived at the refueling location, the crews were still rolling out the hoses and starting the pumps. This caused our first screwup.

The radio came on, "Bikini Six, this is Buc Six."

"Buc Six, go."

"The delay on the ground is pushing our fuel envelope. We will be out of fuel before the slicks refuel. If we fuel first, we won't have enough to complete the mission."

"Buc Six, stand by."

"Big Windy Two-One, this is Bikini Six."

"Big Windy, go."

"Big Windy, how much fuel do you have left after what you need for your flight of Hueys and Chinooks?"

"Bikini Six, give me a sec.

"Bikini Six, we can give you about 2,500 gallons."

"Buc Six, Bikini Six, go into the refueling area first and take 25, that's two-five gallons per bird, then get what you need for the mission after the slicks refuel."

"Buc Six, wilco, out."

"Bikini Flight, I'm sure you heard our plan. Don't waste time refueling; we only have 300 gallons to spare over what we calculated for the full mission."

"Yesterday went so smoothly," I murmured. "Now we're already fucked up at our first step, the fueling stop. I can hardly wait to see what it will be like at the POW camp."

"Yesterday's mission was planned over several days," Snow reasoned. "This one was put together in a few hours and keeps changing as we speak."

After all the ships took on fuel, we started towards our destination at fifty feet above the trees. I asked, "How the hell are we going to find a pinprick on the map of this big country when we are flying so low that we can't see any landmarks to guide us?"

"Two Air Force Special Tactics operators are doing a HALO drop and will establish a beacon for a unique radio frequency the Air America ship has," Snow explained. "They will triangulate the signal and guide us in. By flying at just above treetops and taking a different route to the target, we are less likely to give away our objective."

"What is HALO?" Warren asked.

"It stands for High Altitude Low Opening," Snow said. "The guys will jump out at so high of an altitude, they will need oxygen tanks like scuba divers. The team will free-fall until they're 1,000 feet above the ground and then open their chutes, making them hard to detect."

"No shit. They jump out of a plane into thin air?"

"Exactly!"

Forty-five minutes after leaving our fuel stop, we heard on the radio, "Air America, this is Hill Topper Six, turn to heading one-six-four target five miles."

Air America radioed, "Hill Topper, this is Alpha, Alpha Six-Five-One wilco."

After a few minutes, I heard, "Bikini Six, this is Alpha, Alpha Six-Five-One. I am dropping smoke on target now."

"Buc Six, Bikini Six, take the lead for target prep."

"Buc Six on it, Alpha, Alpha, identify red smoke."

"Buc Six, that's a go."

"Bikini Flight, Bikini Six, after your troops disembark, stay on the ground, and go to ground idle to conserve fuel. Gunners and crew chiefs, keep a close watch for targets. Let's not get caught with our pants down."

We landed twenty meters from the hole blown in another flimsy fence. Our force raced through it and immediately started shooting. So, this was the place. Hopefully not just 'a' place.

The first transmission from the Hatchet Force commander call sign Apache made me feel like the old Bible verse, "This is the day the Lord has made. We will rejoice and be glad in it."

"Mercy Flight, this is Apache, be prepared for twenty-six POWs. We are clearing a landing area for you now inside the camp."

As I saw the Air Force Jolly Green Giant helicopter approaching the camp, I heard, "This is Mercy, we see it."

"Rescue Flight, this is Alpha, Alpha, put a move on. You have a Russian-made tank 200 meters west of you coming fast!"

"Sir," I said, "I have two LAWs, but I have never fired one. They are easy to use, but I would hate to waste them."

Snow immediately radioed, "Apache. My crew has two Light Armor Weapons. We need one of your men trained in them here ASAP."

Tom came running towards us. He grabbed the LAWs, smacked, racked, and set the sight like he was shuffling cards in Vegas. Then he took a knee beside our bird, facing where the intended tank would appear.

"This is Buc Six. We've unloaded everything we have on the tank and maybe scratched the paint."

"Buc Six, this is Bikini Six. Get the hell out of here, or you'll run out of fuel."

Captain Fisk, the leader of the Buccaneer gunships, resisted leaving us with no cover fire but gave in and started east.

Air America reported, "We have dropped white phosphorus and smoke grenades on the tank to restrict its vision, but it's now only 100 meters away."

The radio started again, "Apache, this is Bikini Six. Have you heard we have company coming in the form of a Russian tank?"

"Roger that, we're loading our last POW and will be there in ten mikes."

"Apache, make it five, if you please."

It was more like fifteen before our troops came out of the hole in the fence in front of us, running towards the ship, and the tank beside us broke out of the jungle. Tom fired one of the LAWs and hit it dead center, but the tank kept coming. I suddenly realized what a 'light' armor weapon meant. In return, the tank fired a round that landed short of Bikini Six's ship. Tom fired the last LAW, and a massive explosion went off, stopping the tank.

I looked at Tom and screamed, "What the fuck was that?"

I almost didn't get the words out of me when I heard, "Bikini Flight, this is your big brother."

"It's an F-4 fighter," I screamed to Tom as I grabbed his arm and pulled him into the ship. "Get on!"

Big brother continued, "Sorry we're late to the party, but our orders got SNAFU'd. We were at yesterday's camp."

"Big Brother, Bikini Six, it may be Situation Normal All Fucked Up, but as far as I'm concerned, you're right on time." said our commanding officer.

After our close encounter of the worst kind, the flight headed east towards our fueling station.

"Bikini Flight, this is Bikini Six. Does anyone have a fuel issue on reaching the river station?"

All the slicks reported the ability to make the fuel station with less than twenty minutes of flight in reserve.

I got the attention of the master sergeant in charge of the troops and asked, "Where's the enemy guards? I didn't see any come out?"

"They were the bravest fighters I've encountered," he said. "They fought to the last man."

I looked at Tom, my LAW man, who winked. That told me everything. Whether they fought or surrendered, those guards paid dearly for treating our guys worse than animals.

Then came "Bikini Six, this is Buc Six. We will be out of fuel before you guys because that tank attack sucked us dry. Had to tap the reserve."

"Buc Six, you're twenty minutes ahead of us. Do the same plan as this morning. Take on 50 gallons and split what they have left after we're done. Make it fast. We'll be coming in behind you on fumes as well."

After the fueling stop, Snow asked, "Mack, where the hell did you get those LAWs?"

"A grunt had them on one of our missions," I said. "He handed them to me because he was sick of carrying them when there are no tanks in Vietnam.

"An angel was with us the day the grunt gave them to you," Snow said. "It didn't stop the tank, but it took out their machine gun."

"Mr. Snow, as an esteemed and valiant career soldier, maybe you can tell me why yesterday our mission went like clockwork, and we failed; and today, the mission was FUBAR from the first turn of our rotor blade, and yet, we were successful?"

His answer was daft. "That goes back to there are three ways of doing things. The right way, like yesterday: that's not what we usually do, and we failed; the wrong way: we didn't do it that way, you know, because we didn't lose anyone. Now the third way is today's way; The Army way, and we got our guys. Tell me this Army isn't brilliant?"

"Yeah, remind me to run to re-enlist for another four years as soon as we land," I scoffed.

One of the newer Hatchets looked at me and mouthed, 'Fubar?'

"Fucked Up Beyond All Recognition," I said as I pointed to where each capital letter would be if the words were floating right in front of me.

CHAPTER 20

COMING IN WITH A TRANSMISSION AND A PRAYER

The war didn't give us much time to celebrate our great achievement of the POW rescue. The next morning, the camp CO awakened us and said, "Get your birds ready for immediate takeoff for Dak To. Top off your birds and stand by for Team Delaware's emergency extraction."

"We put those jokers in last week," I said as I shook my head.

"Those idiots were going to blow a bridge on the Ho Chi Minh Trail," Jack said.

As I grabbed my M16 and headed to the door, I said, "Sounds like they stepped in a bucket of shit."

We got to Dak To in record time. Upon arrival, the launch leader met us with a worried look during his briefing. He said, "Team Delaware has been ambushed with two wounded, but they have captured an NVA officer," the launch leader said. "Guys, this is the highest-ranking NVA soldier we have ever captured. We need him alive at all costs. The team is now performing basic escape and evasion maneuvers en route to a small LZ with an estimated arrival time of one hour. I will give you a more accurate ETA when I have it. Estimating E&E ploys can't be judged accurately because of their nature of hiding and running when able, so be ready at a moment's notice."

We ran back to our birds and ensured that everything was ready for an immediate takeoff. Then we waited.

During the wait, Vincent came and asked, "Do you know anything about Team Delaware?"

"I've flown two missions with Team Delaware recently," I said. "They know their shit in the field. One of the times we got them out of Cambodia, where they had captured an enemy soldier. That capture, or any capture for that matter, is a big success. The team got a week in Saigon for that one. Hell, in this case, if they make it, they may get to Bangkok."

"If they make it?" he asked.

"You can bet the North Vietnamese will not give up a high-ranking officer without a fight. It's going to be a bitch."

Once the command to launch came, we were in the air in minutes. Our flight consisted of four Hueys and three gunships. Our flight leader, Captain Montgomery, designated us as the first to extract team members and the POW. The captain's Huey would be next. The other two were our backups if a ship was shot down or was unable to make it into the LZ.

"I'm sure glad we're not flying with that lousy luck charm, Captain Montgomery, today," I said to Russ.

"But he is in charge."

"Who asked you?" I jeered.

"Yes, boss, but you know I'm right," Russ added. "He is still with us."

In addition to the gunships and Hueys, we had a forward air controllership that stayed in constant contact with the team. "Delaware, this is Convey Rider One-Five, say status."

"Rider, 1,100 meters to the LZ," the guys on the ground answered.

"Delaware, this is Convey Rider One-Five, that LZ looks pretty tight for the Hueys. I don't want to tip them off to the LZ's location, so radio when you're 50 meters from it. I'll have a spad drop two 500-pound bombs to enlarge the LZ before you and the Bikinis arrive."

"Roger that," replied the team.

Our co-pilot asked, "A spad? What's a World War II fighter bomber doing in a 1967 war?"

"They decided that they are slower than jets so they can give more precise bomb runs," Mr. Snow said with concern.

What seemed like an eternity passed before finally ended when a panting voice, still running said, "Fifty meters."

"Hold your position and hold your ears, Delaware." Convey Rider then radioed the spad to drop their bombs.

We heard the rumble of the ton of explosives that instantly remodeled our LZ. The next transmission was, "Convey, we're at the LZ. It looks good for landing the birds. The rest of the team is setting up claymore mines, and we're taking up defensive positions in the bomb craters."

Russ, being from the infantry, believed he had to explain, "Claymore mines are crescent-shaped directional anti-personnel mines. They fire them by a remote triggering system, and they shoot metal balls into the kill zone like a shotgun."

"No shit," I said. "You think we just got here yesterday."

Warren got irritated and said, "Guys, stop your bickering. I'm having enough trouble focusing on this shit storm."

Montgomery radioed, "Delaware, this is Bikini Red Five. We're running so hard; our tongues are hanging out. Be there in ten."

Snow brought us to a hover over the hole in the jungle. We started down on our first approach and were quickly met with intense ground fire, including RPGs and 50-cal machine guns.

"We can't make it through this much enemy fire," Snow radioed. "We are coming out. Bucs do your thing, and we'll try again."

The gunships and the spads made several runs on the LZ's perimeter.

Montgomery decided to try next. "Bikini Two-Two, I think the gunships and spads did their job, and the ground fire is now minimal. We will continue to the bottom to take on troops." After a few tense minutes, I saw them come up and clear the tree line. "That's the way, fellas."

Then it was our turn to try again. The LZ had lots of trees sticking out of it that kept all our attention maneuvering around to reach the men in the bomb crater. We couldn't sit down but had to stay in a three-foot hover. As I helped load the wounded onto the ship, bullets hit it, sounding like Sammy Davis doing a tap dance on a tin roof. Then I heard a louder noise as pieces of something hit me. I immediately felt something hot and wet on my back. My first thought is *I'm shot*, but I didn't feel any pain. I started to smell hot oil. I wondered what was going on. When I turned to see, it made me wish I was up with the gunships and not here looking at what was in front of me.

"What the hell happened back there?" Snow asked.

I really didn't want to say the words but keyed the mic and sheepishly responded, "It looks like a 50-cal tore through the bulkhead behind me and put a hole in the transmission. It has started to spray oil out of the hole. Christ, I can even see gears turning in there."

"This is bad." Snow said matter-of-factly. "If the transmission seizes from lack of oil, we become a rock and go straight down. Of course, we could stay here and become POWs."

With that, a chorus of, "Let's get the fuck out of here" rose from the crew.

"I hope the name they gave us is right," Snow responded.

"We're the lucky bastards."

Russ responded with, "But our leader today is that bad juju, Captain Montgomery."

I looked up and saw the gunships flying over us, shooting up the LZ. I said again, "I still wish I were up there with the Bucs."

After Russ and I cleared us out of the hover hole, Snow said, "We can't make Dak To, but maybe she'll hold together enough to get us to Ben Hut Special Forces Camp twelve miles away."

I quickly calculated that it would take us about fifteen minutes to get to Ben Hut at 100 knots, including the time it took to get out of the LZ. I prayed our transmission would hold out for just sixteen or seventeen minutes. Soon after we left the LZ, our Christmas tree warning light system started to look like Time Square on a Saturday night. Several chip lights, the transmission, oil pressure, and temperature warning lights were all on. Then the tail rotor 90-degree gearbox chip light came on.

"What's with the tail rotor?" Snow asked.

"There's oil spraying out of that box also," Russ said. "It must have taken a round too."

"Any other encouraging items you boys want to add?" Snow said.

"Yeah, there is a huge hole in the right skid from a 50-cal round," Russ responded. "It looks like it's about half gone."

"Okay," Snow said and summed up our situation. "Let's hope the main transmission doesn't fail. If that happens, we're a rock headed for our maker. If the main transmission holds up, but the tail rotor gearbox fails, I will do a running landing with a skid half gone. Then if that skid fails, we'll be on our side, skidding down the runway. Any other good news you want to share?"

"Well, at least we won't be prisoners of war," I said.

Russ added, "But we might be KIAs."

"Now, who is Mr. Sunshine talking about Killed in Action?" I asked.

The transmission oil was starting to irritate my back. I decided to take off my shirt and threw it out. For some reason, I found relief from the tension of our situation by watching it bounce through the rotor wash.

Snow radioed the flight command ship and communicated our situation and our intentions of landing at Ben Hut.

Immediately, the radio piped up with, "This is Buccaneer Three. We're with you."

Co-Pilot Wagner asked, "What the hell good is that?" If our transmission fails, all he can do is wave to us as we go into the jungle. Being a gunship, he can't even pick up survivors."

Silence. No one responded.

"Where are the fucking chase ships?" Wagner persisted.

"They didn't have enough fuel to stay with us," Snow said.

"Then how are the guns with us?" Warren asked. "Don't they carry less fuel than the chase ships?"

"The plan was always to send the second team of guns from Kontum in case we needed them."

It wasn't long before Snow then reported, "We have no transmission oil pressure, and there are still seven miles to go before we reach Ben Hut."

Ben Hut's radio came alive again with news to throw more shit in the game.

"Bikini, this is Ben Hut. We are under artillery and rocket attack at this time. I suggest you divert to Dak To."

Snow immediately radioed and said, "We are in danger of flying like your overweight ex-mother-in-law. You are our only hope of surviving these extreme mechanical difficulties.

"I just lost tail rotor control," Snow added.

I looked back and said, "The tail rotor is gone, sir."

"I know it's gone," he responded. "I have tail rotor pedals in a free flow. We must have lost a control cable."

My voice went up an octave or two when I reported, "No, sir, it isn't there. It's fucking gone. Left. I mean bye-bye."

"What did it take with it?" Snow asked.

"The 90-degree gearbox, the driveshaft cover, most of the tail fin driveshaft cover is missing, and a small piece of the remaining drive shaft is flailing around at the end of the 42-degree gearbox," I reported.

"Bikini Two-Two, this is Buccaneer Three. We'll give you gun support on your landing," came over the radio. By then, I had lost track of who was talking on what radio. *Big deal*, I thought; *the ground fire is the least of our problems!*

I added up our problems again. Transmission ready to fail; the tail rotor is gone. So now we know we have to do a running landing on a landing skid that was half gone and ready to fail. If that wasn't bad enough, our landing runway was under artillery attack from Laos. It seemed like this was not shaping up as a day for Russ to try his luck at cards.

Snow gave us prelanding instructions and said, "Because fire is always a danger when landing a damaged ship, I'll cut off the engine as soon as we touch down on the runway. Mr. Wagner, you simultaneously turn off the fuel pumps and the master power switch. You guys in the back, tighten your seat belts and remove your monkey straps for a quick exit. Lastly, if you guys get out first, don't forget about us."

"I'll never forget the ones that bring us to the dance alive," I said.

Snow didn't make a fancy approach. His style was at 45 degrees to the airstrip and then lined us up down the center of a wide dirt path they called a runway. We came in at 60 knots, the slowest speed we could set down with no tail rotor. At 60 knots, the air across the airframe offsets the main rotor's torque, which was a job our tail rotor would typically do. That is, if we had one! We landed hard. If I were judging the quality of the runway contact under normal conditions, Snow would have flunked. There is a saying that any landing you can walk away from is a good landing, and this was a perfect landing as far as I was concerned. As the engine wound down, the transmission finally gave up and seized. The inertia from the main rotor blade's sudden stoppage almost tipped us over on the broken skid, but there we were. The best aircraft to ever be built gave us her last gasp to get us safely to Mother Earth.

I heard retching behind me as one of the guys we 'saved' was puking his guts out. "Shit, I forgot for a minute that you guys were back there, along for the ride. Welcome to Ben Hut, where the local time is, get the fuck out, now!" I helped them with the wounded guy, and we scrambled for the bunker. The rocket and artillery fire increased; it was deafening.

We piled into what I would call a bunch of stacked sandbags with a roof, but they called it a bunker. Taking a headcount, I discovered that one of the team members was missing.

Looking back towards our deceased Huey, Russ saw that one of our passengers was lying on the runway. Two of his Special Forces comrades bolted out to retrieve him. When they brought him in, the first thing I saw was his eyes. They were eyes like I had seen before and like I would see several times more. They were blank, like something had left him. I tend to believe it was his soul that went to a better place than this damn war. I thought *he went through all that shit evading the enemy and came out without a scratch. He then flew in a severely damaged Huey, which had a real hard landing, just to get killed on the way to the bunker by a sniper.* That just goes to prove what everyone says, "When it's your turn to go, you can't do anything about it."

Snow said, "Russ, Mack on me. We need to get our guns and ammo from the aircraft and take up positions in a bunker along the camp's perimeter. Let's help defend this place against the coming attack that the base commander assured me is on its way."

The artillery barrage continued, and our team of lucky bastards tested that name again for the next several hours. The artillery and rockets finally stopped at dark. Shortly after that, a bugle sounded, and the jungle began moving like it was a living being. Hundreds of NVA emerged from the tree line, looking like Christmas trees with branches tucked into their helmets, shirts, and pants.

A Special Forces sergeant placed hand grenades in front of Russ and me, "You think you guys can remember from basic training how to use these?"

"Go to hell," Snow responded. "These guys have seen more action than most of your men stationed here."

The sergeant continued apologetically, "I know if you guys get three or four feet off the ground, nobody is better fighters. But down here, how would I know what you're like?"

"Then get us a fucking three-foot ladder, asshole," was my answer.

Three explosions in quick succession startled me, and the sergeant said, "That's the perimeter claymore mines. It looks like it's dance time."

The Special Forces sergeant was right. The attack was on, and every one of our bunkers opened with tracers going everywhere. Enemy bodies started falling fast, but not fast enough as the human wave came closer by the minute. Russ and I just aimed into the mass of men swarming towards us, with no idea if we hit 10, 20, or none. My adrenaline was over the top. I realized I was screaming at those fuckers with every burst of ammo from my gun.

Seeing that the enemy was gaining ground, the camp commander grabbed the radio and called, "Prairie Fire." Prairie Fire is a universal term meaning we were close to being overrun and needed every aircraft in the immediate area to come to our assistance.

Within minutes, we heard over the radio, "Ben Hut, this is Puff the Magic Dragon, ready to bring hell."

The camp commander responded, "Puff, you are an angel! Come as close as you can to the camp's western border. That is where the attack is about to overrun our defenses."

"Roger that," was Puff's reply.

I looked up and saw what looked like a continuous red flame coming out of the three miniguns of Puff's C-47 descending on our unfortunate adversaries. Puff's stream of tracers looked like flames, reminding me of those movies of flying reptiles belching flames. I could see why they called it a dragon.

The sergeant said, "If Puff passed over a football field firing all three guns, the result would be a hole in every square inch of that field." Minutes later, the assault halted. Large areas of the ground in front of us were obscured by mangled bodies and groaning wounded. The smell of gunpowder and gun oil hung in the air. I looked at Russ. We both placed our hands to each other's shoulders and laughed. Funny how not being dead seemed like something to laugh at.

The rest of the night was peaceful, but no one found it restful.

At dawn, we went out to inspect our trusted steed. "She don't look so good for a brand-new bird. Sarge is going to go crazy over us losing a new ship before it reached its first 100 hours," I said with my hands on my hips as I shook my head.

Warner wondered aloud, "I don't know how the hell that broken bucket of bolts stayed in the air."

"I know." I walked over and patted the metal. "For some reason, this Huey knew we were in trouble and needed to make it to this camp. Then, and only then, would it quit."

"I guess we are lucky bastards at that," Russ said.

I nodded to Russ and said, "I think it's time to go on R&R in Bangkok."

"The 170th was involved in the clandestine operations with U.S. Special Forces since its arrival in Vietnam in one capacity or another. By late 1969, they had proven their worth in those dangerous missions and covert operations to a level that had earned them the privilege of becoming one of the only Aviation units to fly full time on these assignments for Special Operations Group out of Pleiku and later Kontum. The crews who flew these missions had an almost fanatical sense of duty and dedication to the SOG ground troops they transported."

~General Seniff, Commanding Officer
1st Aviation Brigade

CHAPTER 21:
ONE WEEK IN BANGKOK IS HEAVEN

Sunday, October 15, 1967—Meeting Bob

The day finally arrived to go on seven days of R & R in Bangkok, Thailand. I was hopping a ride on my fellow crew chief's ship early, which would carry me to Cam Ranh Bay AFB to catch a plane for one week out of this rathole.

When I arrived, our platoon sergeant was chawing with the chief crew Ski and his gunner Oklahoma. Even though I had almost found myself inside of a body bag twice in two weeks, Sarge showed me no mercy.

"I'm sure grateful you're leaving for a week," he quipped with his usual BS. "Maybe we can go a whole week without losing another bird."

"Just because we call them birds don't mean they grow on trees, you know," he added with a big grin.

"Screw you, Sarge. I almost bought the farm on those two experiences. You know, like died!"

"At your pay, I doubt if all of you could have bought a pea patch, if even that," Ski said.

"And don't mix metaphors, bird brain," I shot back.

We had time before the pilots arrived, so I had a cigarette with the guys. Then I saw him approaching the aircraft, our pilot in command, my bad luck charm, Captain Montgomery.

"Could you try to make this a boring flight for a change, sir?" I asked the hotshot who almost killed us on four previous missions.

"Why are you bitching?" Montgomery implored. "Haven't I earned you a chest full of medals?"

"Yeh, and almost died four times. Can we fly at, let's say 10,000 feet, this time?"

"Not a good idea. SAMs can pick us up real easy at that altitude," Montgomery said. "Besides, I get light-headed above 1,000 feet, plus I like the rush of fast and low."

I thought, *you're light-headed just standing on the ground, pal,* but didn't dare say it. Instead, I said, "There are no Surface-to-Air Missiles in South Vietnam."

"Never can be too careful," Montgomery added.

"Yeah, like careful is your middle name," I said as I rolled my eyes.

Two other spec fives from the maintenance platoon joined us for their trip home. I had mixed emotions. Sure, I was happy for them, but at the same time, I sure hated to see two senior, experienced, Huey mechanics leave at the same time.

After leaving Holloway, we picked up two more men from the 4th Infantry Division Base Camp who joined us for rest and recuperation. One was to meet his wife in Hawaii; the other was on his way to Bangkok with me.

Landing at Cam Ranh Bay, Montgomery motioned for me to open his door and said, "Don't let one of those Thai girls spin your head and get you married."

I gave him the finger and boarded a bus to the Cam Ranh's terminal to catch our plane to Bangkok. The terminal looked like three small metal buildings squashed together to make one long one. Over the door was a sign, "Through these doors pass more men who believe in freedom and humanity than any other ariel port in the world." I wondered what the Congressmen, Senators, and President Johnson, men whose brilliance sent us here, thought about that sign when they visited Vietnam. When I flew from Washington's National Airport, the one these dazzling military minds use, the only sign I saw was, "Dignitary Parking Only."

Across the parking lot was a mobile snack bar. Given the lousy mess hall food in Pleiku and C-rats in the field, that snack bar was calling my name. I looked at my companion from the 4th Division and said, "Let's go. We can't pass up this chance for a hot dog and cheeseburger."

His eyes lit up, "And French fries with a Coke!"

An all-American lunch with a real American Coke was a great way to get acquainted between bites.

"My name is Mack and yours?"

"Bob. I'm from Arizona."

"Bob from Arizona? No shit," I said. "My parents just moved there from New Hampshire. My father was disabled from injuries he got in World War II, and they thought the weather in Arizona would be better for his health."

"I bet they didn't move to Heber," Bob said with a smile.

"Where in the world is Heber?"

With a big cowboy grin, he said, "Man, did you sleep during geography class? Heber is halfway between Payson and Holbrook."

"Our family made a trip to Phoenix when I was in high school. I remember driving through Holbrook," I said. "It's a pain in the ass town; you have to get off the interstate and go through downtown, but never saw a Heber. I guess I shouldn't talk. I grew up so far back in the woods, they had to pump in sunlight."

"I don't live in Heber, but on a ranch halfway between Heber and Holbrook. Someone visiting once said we are in the middle of nowhere, but I corrected him and said no, Heber isn't in the middle of nowhere. We're on the other side of nowhere."

"Couple of country bumpkins," I added as I raised my glass of 'Atlanta Boujelay' and he raised his.

"Got a girl waiting for you?" I asked.

"No, just a beautiful Palomino mare named Daisy."

"Really, now ain't that a coincidence? I had a horse's ass named Susan. Known her since before starting school and the only girl I ever dated."

"How's she doing with you here?"

"I was so unforgettable that she got herself pregnant with the bastard who didn't have the balls to enlist. So, it looks like you and I are both free to explore the finer things in life that Bangkok has to offer."

We talked through the rest of our meal. I told Bob how a guy in my unit got a full-time driver when he was here, who doubled as a tour guide.

"We should go in together, hire one, and split the cost. Say, how much money did you bring?"

"I've got $1,500; I've been saving," I said. "It's hard to spend your pay when you're flying missions every day; plus, we make extra cash on unauthorized missions hauling steaks, beer, and broads, charging the guys at remote Special Forces camps for them."

"I just asked because I hope I have enough. Same with me, there are no stores in the bush to spend money. My parents sent me $1,000 for my birthday, so altogether I got about $2,000."

"Did they send them in greenbacks?"

"Yes, good old American 50s, and I had to hide it from the CID," said Bob. "If you're caught with American currency, the provost marshal will recommend disciplinary action."

"Fucking Criminal Intelligent Agency assholes," I said in disgust. "They think they are like the FBI. Do they really believe we're going to sell hard currency to the Viet Cong for them to buy guns to shoot back at us?"

All of us detested the Army's way of paying us. They did not pay us in U.S. dollars. We were issued a paper currency that we referred to as scrips. These Military Payment Certificates ranged in value from five cents to 20 dollars.

"I hate the scrips," I continued to rant. "After a night on the town, your pocket is full of bills. You think you're rich, but most are nickels, dimes, and quarters. Once you count it, you end up with a lousy five bucks. No-siree-bob... Bob, give me good old American cash anytime."

We found a lot we agreed on in a very short time; then we made a pact to do a night on the town in Phoenix after getting out of the Army.

After lunch, we headed back to the terminal. We talked and found more that we had in common, even though we were from different parts of the country. He grew up in a ranching community with a mix of Hispanics and original White settlers. Bob explained how his family came from Mexico more than a hundred years ago and started a ranch. I told him how my family arrived in this country about the same time, also started a farm. We came from Finland.

The PA system squealed and then announced, "All men going to Bangkok, your plane just arrived. After we disembark the men and it's refueled, an airman will direct you to your aircraft."

It took about a half-hour before an airman guided us onto the flight ramp past several planes. We boarded a Convair 440 Metropolitan with Flying Tiger Airlines painted on the side. I have always liked that name. The airline's founders flew for China against Japan before America entered World War II. Their unit was called the Flying Tigers.

Onboard we found fifty-two maroon seats with stained white headrests. The seating arrangement was two seats on each side of the center aisle. Two stewardesses of Oriental descent approaching forty years old greeted us at the cabin door, and I saw two more towards the back. They were older than those found on American Airlines. A musty smell welcomed me, making me feel the plane's cleaning also wasn't up to American standards either. Another thing that struck me as odd was that there were no officers or senior enlisted with us. *They must be on a first-class fight*, I thought.

Bob and I sat over the wing. Through a small window, we could see one of the two turboprop engines. "Bob," I said, "you know we are flying on the lowest bid airline for this government service."

"I already don't like flying," Bob said. "And now you're making me nervous."

"I am uneasy about this airline," I just couldn't hold back. "Last year, a Flying Tiger crashed on landing near Da Nang, killing all four crew and 125 on the board. In 1962, one of their Super Constellations chartered by the United States military also disappeared between Guam and the Philippines. All 107 aboard were declared missing and presumed dead."

"Shut the fuck up already."

The flight lasted about two blessedly uneventful hours. The stewardesses were attentive to our needs. When we landed in Thailand, a master sergeant entered the aircraft. He immediately earned my respect from the glider patch on his hat. That patch signified he was part of the 82nd Airborne glider unit during World War II's invasion of Normandy.

"Men, welcome to Bangkok, home of the Orient's adult Disneyland," he bellowed over the plane's PA system. "We want you to enjoy yourself while here, but there are some things you need to know before we cut you loose. Thailand is a close ally of the United States, and at all times, you are a representative of our country.

"Break any minor military or civilian laws, and you will be sent back to your unit for disciplinary action," he added as his voice became more serious. "If your actions rise to the level of a felony, you will go to LBJ. For you guys from Appalachia, LBJ is not the President but Long Bien Jail."

Holding up several papers, he continued, "If you try to send items on this list home or anywhere outside of Thailand, you're going to LBJ. Bangkok is full of Russian and Chinese spies looking for one of you knuckleheads to tell all you know to a pretty face with a bottle of booze. Be careful. If we catch you giving sensitive information away, it will be like Monopoly. You will not pass go, you will not collect $200, and you will be sent to jail…"

"To LBJ." Some knucklehead upfront parroted.

"No, wise ass, straight to Fort Leavenworth. They got a nicer prison there.

"All the rest of the information you need to know will be in these packets. Take one and read it. Since you all got through basic training, I'm sure you know how to read. Your baggage will be delivered to your hotel later today.

"Specialist Makinen, see me outside," said the master sergeant, as he was about to complete his briefing and disappear down the airstairs. "For the rest of you, your limos await you."

"Sounds like this Makinen guy is in the shit already," the private first class in the seat on the other side of the aisle said.

"I hope not. By the way, nice to meet you. Donald Makinen's the name." We shook hands.

As I approached the aircraft door, I began to understand why there were no officers or senior enlisted with us. Our 'limos' were two cattle cars parked beside the plane. These are the Army's mass transport containers. They were made from modified long-haul trailers pulled by old retired semi-trucks. Inside, we were cramped and crowded, with little ventilation from only a few small windows on the sides. The first men on board get lucky as they get a seat on benches. The rest of them get to stand in the aisle, boxed in on all sides by bodies.

I got to the bottom of the airstairs, where the master sergeant was waiting. "Follow me," he ordered.

Once we were out of hearing range of the rest of the guys, he started, "Specialist, I got the word on you."

"All lies, sir, from jealous co-workers; I assure you. "

"Cut the shit. Headquarters alerted me."

I'm fucked before I get laid, I thought.

"You have to be especially careful because you have been flying secret missions into Laos and Cambodia. Every news person and spy knows we are doing clandestine missions into those countries, but they don't know what it is we're doing there. It would be best if it was kept that way. Be extra careful what you say, especially to the women you'll meet. I'm sure you will be joining them during your stay. You know what we used to say in World War II?"

"Use a rubber?"

He laughed despite himself. "No, loose lips sink ships. But in your case, they can knock the feathers off your whirlybirds. Got it?"

"Yes, Master Sergeant." I turned and headed to one of the cattle cars, saying, "Mooooo."

CHAPTER 22:
MEET JANE

After we checked in, we rummaged through a mountain of bags in the lobby to find ours. Bob and I were on the same floor.

"Meet in the lobby in an hour? "I asked as I opened my door.

"Sounds good."

I found my room appropriately furnished and clean. Not the Ritz, but it was fine by me.

When I met Bob outside the hotel, he had already hired a car with a driver named Po. He informed us he would be available 24 hours a day during our stay for 100 American dollars; then he smiled and added, "And maybe a little tip if you're happy with my service."

It turned out Po always had a smile on his face and called us, "Sir," even after asking him not to.

"I think the first order of business is to get a steak," I declared to Bob as we entered Po's car. "Then girls!"

"No sweat, sir," Po said.

We had an excellent steak with all the sides we could think of for twenty bucks, including several Mai Tais. After our plates were cleared, I motioned Po over. "Next, we want some dessert, and we want it to be women. Not the skanks, like in Vietnam, but good-looking Thai women."

Po walked us three blocks and said, "This will be an excellent place to start, but tomorrow night we will go to Bangkok's best nightclub."

"Why not tonight?" Bob asked.

"It is a nicer place, but they are closed on Sunday," Po explained. "Sirs, that club is owned by a Christian family, so they are closed every Sunday."

I was reminded of that new song by Arlo Guthrie; that this whole country was the Alice's restaurant of perversion and sex. "You can get anything you want at Alice's restaurant" ...except on Sundaaaaaay. I laughed at the irony.

We entered, what according to Po was, the sleazier club and found a room larger than the ones in Vietnamese bars. Colored neon lights around the ceiling lit the room. A Thai band was singing American songs better than those in Vietnam, but still not as good as the USO shows. A maître de met us at the door and guided us to one of the twenty or so tables. The tables were close to being full of Americans. Some we could tell were CIA, Air America, or U.S. Government officials, given that they had long hair, and a few had beards. The rest were soldiers with their short 'high and tight' military haircuts. Girls sat on the side of the room with a number on a badge pinned to their dress.

"Tell me which number you want to talk to, and I'll get her," Po offered as he tried to be helpful

Luckily, Bob and I called out different numbers, and our first argument was avoided. Po went to retrieve them.

Both ladies were in their mid to late twenties, several years older than us. They were somewhat attractive with a nice frame, and each had long black hair. All five of us sat while Bob and I finished our drinks. Then we gave the ladies the requested $20 each and left for the hotel.

By then, it was midnight when Po dropped us off at the front door. We decided to go for a tour in the morning and requested he pick us up at ten the following day.

When we got to the room, I was nervous, not knowing what to expect. The lady said, "My name is Jane." I knew from Vietnam that girls chose names for our benefit. Their Oriental name would be too hard for Americans to pronounce.

Jane noticed my discomfort and then said, "The first thing we'll do is I will give you a bath."

Embarrassed, I replied, "I guess several months of showering in questionable Vietnam water and sometimes not bathing for several days could have given me a certain odor pour ainsi dire." I used a phrase my French-Canadian friends taught me back home, meaning, so to speak.

She startled me with her answer, "Oui, monsieur."

"Okay, now we've used almost all the French I know," I said. "Let's keep it to English."

"Okay, GI," she said as she headed to the bath and closed the door.

A few minutes later, the door opened, and there she was, wearing a sheer nighty with a hotel bathrobe over it, giving me just a teasing glimpse of her bosom. I thought, *she sure is a pro.* I was uncomfortable being bathed by a woman I hadn't known for more than a few hours, should we say, in an enthused way.

After the bath, we retired for the night. The only thing I'll say is, 'Oh, What A Night!'

Monday, October 16, 1967

Jane and I met Bob and his girl for the night at breakfast. The two ladies tried to convince us to agree to have them as escorts for the rest of the week. Bob and I knew Po had a memorable night planned, so I turned to Jane and said, "Au revoir."

After Bob said "Bye-bye" to his overnight friend, the two left with one saying something in Thai that I knew wasn't, 'Those soldiers were great lovers.'

Just as the ladies departed, Po joined us. I asked Po, "Were you hiding somewhere all along, waiting for us to be finished?"

"That's my job to know what you need and when you need me. I have my little tricks of the trade."

Bob asked, "What can we do today?"

"You wanted a tour. I think I should take you to TIM Land or Thailand in Miniature. It is a park that will give you an overview of Thailand and its culture."

"Let's go," I said.

Po explained that first, we needed to get fine clothes for tonight. We signed the bill for breakfast and followed him to a tailor shop next to the hotel. Once in the shop, the tailor took measurements for a suit, shirt, socks, and shoes. I asked, "So Po, you get a commission on our purchases, don't you?"

"No, sir."

I cautioned, "Don't bullshit a bullshitter."

The total for the whole ensemble was only $100, so I said, "No sweat."

After our fitting, off we went to TIM Land. It took about an hour to get there. In route, Po showed off his unique skill of driving in urban

Asian traffic, prompting Bob to say, "This traffic is a goat rope." Cars were everywhere, bumper-to-bumper, and coming at us from multiple directions. Po swerved in and out with a talent that would make Bobby Unser envious.

We spent a relaxed day at TIM Land while drinking Singha beer. The park had several shows and exhibits. We watched traditional Thai dancing, Koi fish ruthlessly fighting over food supplied by, of all things, passive Buddhist monks, and viewed a demonstration of how to grow rice.

As we approached a large tent near an exit, a young man dressed in a white tunic top with white knee-length socks linking black shoes to his yellow nickers stood in front. He sounded like a carnival barker in short broken-English, saying, "Come, come for a few Baht. Get a show you'll never forget. See the tiny mongoose who will bravely take on the mighty king cobra in a fight to the death." We shrugged our shoulders, and said, "What the fuck...." We paid our Bahts and entered the tent.

In the center was a raised green painted three-foot-high wooden structure decorated in dried blood splotches all along the circular pit. It reminds me of my neighbor's illegal structure for cockfights but much bigger. Bleachers surrounded three-quarters of the center arena half-filled with America's and cracked-skin old men, the low hanging fog of cigarette and pot smoke masking the horrific smell.

A large trunk lay on one side of the cement floor. Beside it stood an older gentleman, who could have been the barker's skin-and-bones grandfather, cigarette dangling from his thin lips, holding a metal rod with a hook on one end.

Once the crowd was seated, the PA announcer began, "Welcome to the King Cobra—Mongoose show. First, let me explain that a king cobra's venom is one of the deadliest of all snakes. If bit, it inhibits communication between nerve cells, causing extreme dizziness, blurred vision, and, often, death. Remember that as I introduce our snake-tamer, Kiet. Let's give him a big hand."

Kiet entered from behind a screen and down a ramp into the pit with his right hand raised. An assistant removed the ramp. Kiet was a young man with a slight build who sported long black hair with a red bandana that kept his hair out of his eyes.

The older man used his rod to pull fifteen king cobras out of the trunk. He placed them in a circle around Kiet. Once on the ground, the cobra looks like any other snake, but when they become erect and their head expands, it is known as 'hooded.' This wards off predators by signaling that they are ready to strike. Kiet put his face inches from each hooded cobra and moved just out of the striking snake's range. He then picked one up by the tail and smacked it together with another to irritate them. He kissed each on the head as they stretched themselves upright three feet high and ready to deliver their venom.

After several more tricks with the snakes, all the snakes got picked up and placed back in the box except one. The announcer asked, "How about that, Kiet?" He bowed to the crowd's applause and left the same way he entered the pit as his assistant temporarily replaced the ramp.

"Now it is time to amaze you! To see a mongoose fight the deadly king cobra," the announcer boomed.

A mongoose came through a small door in the side of the pit I hadn't noticed until then. I told Bob, "That mongoose looks like a squirrel with a strange tail. This fight should be over quick."

The mongoose charged the cobra time and time again. As the cobra struck, the mongoose would move side to side, backward, or jump over the cobra's attack and deliver a small bite to the cobra each time. The cobra continued to strike, and the mongoose always moved inches away from it and still managed his small attack. The battle continued for several minutes. Ultimately, the cobra lay dead on the floor.

Suddenly, I got dizzy, my chest became tight, my vision blurred, and I heard my heartbeat in my ears. Inexplicably, I was catapulted back to the time when I climbed across the top of a chopper in flight to pull away the shelter half that was clogging the engine's intake and I almost fell to my death. I told Bob, "I gotta get out of here."

Bob followed me out and asked, "What's up?"

I found a seat and tried to catch my breath. I finally was able to say, "We're going to lose in Vietnam."

"What? Are you crazy?"

"Didn't you see it?" I asked as I tried to catch my breath. "See that squirrel-looking thing? The deadliest snake is larger, many times larger than the mongoose. Did you see how he did it? He did it by repeated deliveries of small bites. Then he jumped, jumped out of the way of the mighty cobra's attack. He was always agile enough to avoid a deadly strike. That's how they'll win. They'll win by knowing that our size makes us slow. Slow to move. Slow to strike. Slow to react. We're powerful, but we're slow to bring our power. Have you ever heard of death by a thousand cuts? That's what that mongoose did to the snake. Our mongoose is the Viet Cong, and they're inflicting a cut a day. We passed a thousand days a long time ago."

"You're nuts." Bob shook his head. "We have never lost a battle and never will."

Po saw me sitting on the curb and came running, asking, "What's wrong?"

I told him, "I need a drink and want to get back to the hotel."

After Po stopped for a bottle of Jim Beam to help relieve my issues, he doubled down on his driving abilities, which was breath-taking, to say the least, as if I wasn't struggling with a tight chest and shortness of breath already. The whiskey helped. When we got to the hotel, I decided to rest until my episode passed.

How odd, I thought. I had been in much tighter squeezes than freeing the tent half since that flight. Why did that come back to me with such devasting clarity? Why now, when we are on R&R a million miles away from that rathole? I drifted off for about an hour.

I awoke feeling better and ordered food from room service.

After eating dinner, I found a perfect-fitting suit hanging in the closet and a shirt with cuff links. I had never used cuff links. They gave me the challenge to get the clasp closed with one hand. My attention then went to that dreaded tie lying on the bed. I said to myself, *you're not getting the best of me this time.* It took several tries, but I finally got the two ends to match.

When Po picked us up at seven, we looked like wealthy Americans. We were on our way to the Peacock Club on Patpong Street.

Po dropped us off at an elaborate building adorned with two large wooden, hand-carved doors. The carvings portrayed elephants lifting logs, a Thai Buddha, and others depicting Thailand's culture. Two doormen dressed in tuxedoes were standing on each side of the doors. The scene made me feel like that new guy in a James Bond movie. To play the part, I lit a cigarette and said, "Good evening, my good fellows." Then I turned to Bob and said, "My name is Bond, James Bond."

When we entered through the large doors, the first thing I noticed was the smell of Jasmine blooming. "Smell that?" I asked Bob. "I have always loved the smell of Jasmine. That is a sign tonight is going to be one to remember."

"Follow me, gentlemen," said one of the two ladies standing at the maître d's station in evening gowns. She led us down three steps to an elegant nightclub with walls that had four-foot teak wood panels starting at the floor. From there to the 20-foot ceiling was white wallpaper with red flocking. Two large chandeliers gave off a soft light. The bar had horizontal red, white, and blue neon lights. Taking up about three-quarters of the room were some 30 semi-circle tables with leather seats. The non-circular side had no seating and faced a stage where an African American lady was singing the latest American songs. A big difference from the Vietnamese groups at our club in Holloway. The remaining part of the room featured a parquet floor that had several couples dancing.

To our left was a separate room with a glass wall. Behind it sat about fifty ladies with numbered badges on their dresses. They were not like the whores from last night's sleaze bar. They were dressed much nicer and looked like debutantes in comparison. As soon as the maître d' seated us, a waiter wearing black pants and a white-collared button-down shirt took our drink order.

I called Po over and said, "I want a gorgeous lady. On a scale from one to ten, I want a ten. Po, not eight or nine. Ten. Got it?"

"Same for me," Bob added.

Po started to bring ladies. After I rejected a couple, I reminded him, "Ten."

During Po's second attempt, I saw one of the most beautiful women in the place. Bob beat me to saying that she was the one for him. She introduced herself as Leah. It was evident that he was smitten at first sight and looked like a kid on Christmas morning. Bob danced every slow dance with Leah, holding her close. She looked like she enjoyed it. I knew she was a social pro who could make you think you were the only man she had ever known, but something told me she was actually into Bob. When they were not on the dance floor, they sat close, and Bob babbled and giggled like a teenager.

When I saw Po heading for our table with his fourth try, I fell in love at first sight, or maybe it was lust. When you are twenty-one, there is no way of telling which it is, but I was impressed. She was my age, five foot tall, with long silky hair, amber-colored skin over a perfect body, and the face of an angel. For the second time that day, my breath was taken away, not like the mongoose revelation at TIM Land. This was pleasant and made me tingle.

Po introduced her to me as Busarakham. He said, "It means yellow sapphire. Doesn't she shine like a precious stone?"

"She sure does!" I exclaimed.

Po guided her to the empty chair next to me, and she said, "Most friends call me Busa."

I asked, "Am I a friend?"

Her answer was electrifying when she said, "I hope so."

I don't dance, so we enjoyed the music and talked for hours about Thailand, the U.S.A., and our homes and families. I found she was from the northeast part of Thailand near Laos. I remembered my near-death experience days before on the top-secret mission in Laos. Without thinking, I told her, "I've been to Laos, and I found the people there aren't too friendly."

She gave me a questioning look and asked, "Why do you say that?"

Remembering what the Master Sergeant said about pretty girls, booze, and secrets, I wondered if I had just crossed the line of secrecy and was going directly to Leavenworth passing Long Bing Jail.

I thought fast and said, "That's a long story about when I was there as a Vista volunteer."

"I had to come to the city because there was no way to make living in my small town," she explained, as she thankfully did not press me. "I am taking classes at night so that someday I can leave the escort business."

I thought, *that's what they all say.* I just said, "Great."

We left the club at midnight. I was ready to jump out of my skin at the thought of getting Busa alone in my room. Po dropped us off at the front of the hotel. I told him we would call in the morning when we wanted to leave for the day.

He gave his familiar big smile and said, "Yes, sir."

My answer was, "My name is Mack; no 'sir!'"

He said, "I know, sir," and with that, he was gone.

Bob and I wished each other goodnight as we left the elevator and retired to our rooms with our dates.

I locked the door after we entered my room and asked Busa, "You want something to drink?"

She shook her head, indicating no. Then she came to me and held my hand. Her touch was warm but tender. It was like a dream for me, very different from the other women I have been close to. We undressed carefully. That night, we made love with our lips. We made love with our hands. We made love with our bodies. We made love! It was 5 a.m. when I finally closed my eyes. It was the sexiest and most memorable night of my short life.

Tuesday, October 17, 1967

At eleven, the phone rang. It woke me from my first uninterrupted sleep from as far back as I could remember. When I picked up the phone, I heard, "Hi, this is Bob."

"No shit," I said. "I thought the King of Thailand was calling."

"Want to join us commoners for breakfast?"

I asked Busa, "Do you want to go to breakfast with Bob and Leah?" She shook her head in approval.

I told Bob, "Give us an hour."

I spotted Bob sitting alone when I entered the hotel café. I joined him near the back of the room and said, "Busa will be down in a little bit. She's still getting ready."

"Leah is doing the same."

"It takes ladies longer to get ready," I marveled.

"But once ready, they look so much better than us," he affirmed.

"Bob, how was your night?" I asked with a smile.

His answer surprised me when he said, "We stayed up all night talking."

"Talking?"

"Yes, talking. When we got back to my room, I suggested we have a nightcap. We sat on the sofa, and it started with questions of where we were from and what it's like to live there. Then for some reason, I looked in Leah's eyes, and I felt safe, so I told her about my dreams, fears, and hopes. I told her things I had never told anyone before. We laughed. I cried. Later, she laid with her head in my lap, and I stroked her cheek and hair. I felt a peacefulness that I haven't felt since I rode my horse Daisy in the mountains of Arizona."

"Am I to believe you spent the night with a gorgeous, willing woman, and there was no bone dancing?"

"Mack, how can you make something so loving and intimate sound so cheap and trashy?"

We both laugh at that.

"Bob, I haven't had a more enjoyable or relaxing night since I was with my long-time sweetheart back home. Busa is gorgeous, funny, smart, and not at all like Jane, who used some basic primal instinct to fuck like something out of one of those triple X-rated magazines. Last night I had to keep reminding myself not to get emotionally involved with Busa. You should struggle to do the same."

"I don't know. Leah is everything I dreamed of in a woman."

"Bob, you know we have been to the gates of hell in that stupid war, and now you think maybe you're seeing an angel?"

"She is an angel."

"You haven't even had sex yet!" I snapped a bit too loud then lowered my voice. "I mean, I could understand if you were a virgin, and she was your first, but that is not the case. Right?"

He shook his head in agreement.

Soft hands covered my eyes. I smelled the sweet smell of Busa. I heard her quiet voice saying, "Guess who?"

"The Queen of Siam," I said.

"Close," she quipped and smiled back.

The ladies sat with Bob and me for breakfast. When we finished our meal, magically, Po appeared. I asked him if he wanted something to eat. He told us he eats early with his family, so he was okay.

After some mindless chatter, I asked, "What should we do today, Po?"

He suggested the Floating Garden that was an hour and a half away. Busa was thrilled about the prospect of going to a place she hadn't seen.

"We're good," Bob said. "I think we'll hang out here by the pool and go for a walk to a special Buddha Leah likes."

CHAPTER 23:
FLOATING WITH BUSA

The Floating Garden was a floating mall. It was aptly named and served as a beautiful backdrop for a great day with Busa. We rented a piloted boat. Our tour guide expertly maneuvered through the different boats that offered their wares in this unique market. The colors, chaos, flavors, and atmosphere gave us a unique experience, and the novelty of buying a snack from a passing boat was enough to flood our senses. We would pull alongside boats with items we wanted to see or buy. Busa and I had a wonderful lunch prepared by an elderly lady cooking in her boat.

As a huge bell rang out, I turned to see a monk ringing it. Busa explained that it signaled the monks for prayer. Flowers were plentiful. Before leaving, I purchased a bouquet for Busa and had our picture taken for her.

Po had beer on ice for the ride home. In a traffic jam outside of Bangkok, a man on an elephant passed us. "I guess you know it's horrible traffic when an elephant passes you," I said to Po.

"This traffic isn't as bad as it is on weekends," he said while waving his hands across the front of the car.

That night Bob and Leah joined us for a dinner show. The waiters gave us as much attention as my mother did at Thanksgiving dinner. They looked for the slightest signal to be at our table to serve our needs.

After dinner, the lights went out, and the curtain lifted to reveal a large, dimly lit turquoise arch. Under the arch, a spotlight suddenly highlighted a beautiful Thai woman in traditional dress. Her two hands were clasped flat against each other and just below her chin. Suddenly, a set of arms came out of her side, then another, and it continued until twelve sets of arms and hands surrounded he, making her look like a peacock in full bloom. All the hands started going from one side to another in a dance to traditional music. After several minutes, a dozen ladies appeared from behind the first one. That prompted an epic theatrical journey into Thailand's rich cultural heritage, traditions, and history. We were dazzled by the entertainment with hundreds of performers, exquisite costumes, music, and drums.

The show ended, and Bob ordered a round of drinks. After smiles and laughs all around, Bob got serious and made a declaration. "Leah and I have decided to get married. We hope that you will join us Thursday for the ceremony."

I was shocked and asked, "Are you both sure? You have only known each other for a little more than a day."

Busa went to Leah, hugging her. She said something in Thai.

"If that's your wish, buddy, yes, of course, we will join you Thursday," Even though I assured Bob, I was still concerned. I figured that when we got back to the hotel, I would ask Bob to have a nightcap so we could have some boy talk.

Once back at the hotel bar, Bob and I sat and ordered our drinks.

"Bob, are you sure you want to marry a girl just one day after meeting her? Plus, remember, you need your commander's permission."

Bob leaned over and said, "I already got it," as he slapped my leg. Then he added, "The company is in garrison at the division's basecamp, so my captain gave me another week for a honeymoon."

"I told you my parents have a ranch in Arizona. It is 40,000 acres between Heber and Holbrook. You don't know where that is, but it's ten miles to my nearest neighbor and twenty-five miles to the school I attended. Christ, it's even five miles off the state highway. I have to go back there to help my father and brother run it. The only woman in my age group within forty miles is either married or left for the city. I like Leah. She is gorgeous and attends to my every wish. What more could I ask for?"

"All I can tell you is that my uncle married a woman from Japan, and he bragged the same as you about attending to his every wish," I said. "But once she had American women friends, they fucked up that 'attends to your every wish' thing, so don't cry to me when that happens." I raised my glass and said, "In the short time we've known each other, I consider you a good friend, and here's to your happiness."

I thought, in combat, your best buddy could be dead before lunch. You wonder if you will see dinner. You make friends fast, like Bob. I have known him thirty-six hours more than he knew Leah; yet, I was chiding him for his feelings for Leah—and here's me calling him a good friend in the same timeframe. Things happen fast in war.

I downed the rest of my drink, threw some bucks on the bar, and said, "Now, I got someone upstairs I want to see. I hope I can keep Busa from spinning my head too." I winked and left him at the bar.

Wednesday, October 18, 1967

The next morning at breakfast, Leah and Bob suggested that we go to the Royal Grand Palace. Busa explained how the royal compound lives up to its name, with spectacular structures that would put the most decadent modern monarchs to shame.

"The Royal Grand Palace is the most important landmark in Bangkok," Leah told us. "It is famous for its impressive architecture and buildings. We must pay homage to the Wat Phra Kaew in the same compound, which houses the most revered Emerald Buddha, carved from a single jade rock. The Grand Palace has numerous buildings, halls, and pavilions set around open lawns, gardens, and courtyards. It has its natural development, with successive kings' making additions for over 200 years."

Po dropped us off a block from the entrance. Bob and I agreed to meet later at the Emerald Buddha.

Busa and I walked hand-in-hand past a white wall until we came to an enormous white gate. Beyond it was a view so filled with splendor that it dazzled my visual senses with the beauty of the colorful buildings, flowering gardens, and enormous statues. Inside the gate, the experience was enhanced by the sweet scent of incense mixed with flowers.

As we walked the grounds, buildings with spirals reaching towards the sky appeared everywhere. There were large murals on the walls decorated with intricate patterns inlaid with gold and colorful stones.

I struggled to focus on all the palace's magnificence because of the grace and beauty walking next to me. Since I made such a big deal of Bob's sudden love for Leah, my brain tried to put up a defense against Busa. *If I didn't enlist in the Army, I could be walking like this in the beautiful Boston Public Gardens with Susan.* Then I chased that thought away. She couldn't be truthful for a few months. On the other hand, maybe she was frightened that a letter could come from the DOD with regrets that there wasn't enough of me to fill a coffin to send home.

At that moment, Busa leaned over and sniffed the reddest flower I had ever seen. Her gentle caressing of the delicate petals softened my mood and my thoughts.

She turned and smiled. Her simple appreciation of a flower and the joy she showed was infectious. I vowed right then and there that I shouldn't waste a single moment more on her thinking about the what ifs.

I bought her a bouquet to pay homage to the Emerald Buddha. She stopped at the bottom of the stairs to the Temple's entrance, guarded by two huge evil-looking statues. "Be conscious of the fact that your back should not face the image of the Lord, and neither should your feet be pointed towards him as that is highly disrespectful."

She spoke like a preacher. I nodded my head to let her know I understood the proper etiquette when we were inside.

The incense smell was the first hint that we were entering a holy place. Inside was a large emerald-colored Buddha adorned with a gold crown atop a golden throne. Gold was the order of the day here, with gold pillars that held up an elaborate ceiling with four gold praying wheels hung over the Buddha. The small wheel was on top, ending with the largest just over the crown. I may be a Christian, but I got a warm feeling that I was standing on holy ground.

After leaving the Temple, Busa took my hand and said, "You have to do one thing," as she led me to the elephant sculptures. As we approached, it was apparent that these elephants' heads were shiny compared to the rest of the statue.

"You need to rub the elephant's head for good luck," she said.

"Where I'm going back to next week, I'll need all the luck I can get," I said as I rubbed, prayed to Jesus and, just to cover my bet, in case she is right, I prayed to the Emerald Buddha as well. "Amazing how the soft touch of repetitive rubbing over the centuries can shine a stone."

"Now, you can understand the basics of Buddhism," she explained. "You can progress on the path to enlightenment if you live a life free from a negative mental state with peacefulness and purity. If you think that is impossible, look at the elephant being shined by the light touch of hands."

I didn't know about the elephant, but her presence was freeing my mind of negativity.

Bob and Leah showed up. "Since you're a grunt," I told Bob as I hitched my thumb over my shoulder, "rub the shit out of those elephants for luck."

"You bet I will," Bob said. "Hey, let's meet in a restaurant across the street in an hour."

As we left the elephants, Busa and I found a bench that overlooked a well-manicured lawn. Trees stood close to the palace on the far side of the property with bare limbs except for leaves shaped like green balls at their tips. A garden of flowers was in bloom under the trees. We sat and, for the first time, I noticed she had bright eyes, not dull like I have seen on the Vietnamese girls. I put my arm around her and pulled her close. As she laid her head on my shoulder, I heard myself say without thinking, "I wish I could stay in peace and tranquility here forever."

She softly kissed my cheek and said, "I wish that too."

Bob and Leah returned, and he said, "You guys look more like lovebirds than we do, and we're getting married."

My answer was, "You sure know how to ruin a tender moment."

Leah then suggested that instead of the roadside restaurant across the way, we go to one that serves cuisine that is like where they are from in Northeast Thailand.

Bob and I said, "Sure. Why not?"

The fact that Po didn't know the place told me this was going to be a genuine experience. He got directions in Thai from the ladies.

When we arrived at the restaurant, it looked different than I expected. The outside appeared understated and was a bit rundown. On both sides of the doors were small bomb-looking black balls with wick lanterns lighting the entrance. It reminded me of what road crews would place around hazards back home.

Inside was a total surprise. The interior had teak wood walls and parquet floors with dark- and light-colored squares. The soft light came from lights inside wooden bird cages that hung from the ceiling. Candles were placed on each table covered with white tablecloths. Each had four captain-style chairs with beige cushions. Tapestry with Thai scenes hung on one wall, and on another hung a stained-glass picture of a peacock in a garden.

Our escorts placed the order in Thai, so we had no idea what we were getting. When asked what they ordered, Busa said, "Don't worry, you'll love it."

The first item brought to our table was a big surprise. I thought I had tried all kinds of drinks, but when I tasted this one called a Chi-Chi, I could tell that it had rum with banana, coconut, and pineapple juice. The mix of flavors went together like nothing I had ever had before.

Bob was laughing at the name and said, "Chi-Chi means tits in Spanish."

Leah let the mild obscenity pass and explained how the food was unique, and said, "Our Northeast Thai cuisine is also called Isaan food. Because it's hot and humid, the food relies heavily on preservation and fermentation with local herbs, vegetables, and spices. Many westerners, when they are trying our dishes, favor them over the traditional Thai food."

My mouth was open. I was getting the feeling these were not just the run-of-the-mill hookers, or even 'escorts,' these girls were humble, knowledgeable, sensitive, and natural nurturers. *What a great country!*

Three waiters brought several family-style dishes to the table. Leah explained the food as she pointed to each item. "Laab – Northeastern Thai cuisine minced meat salad. This red plate is Jaew or Northeastern Thai Nam Prik. Next to it is Om, a delicious curry of Northeastern Thai cuisine. By Busa is my father's favorite Moo Yor or Isaan steamed meat sausage. Then we have Gaeng Nor Mai Bai Yanang. It's an Isaan fresh bamboo shoot curry. And Bob and I got this for you when you told me about your July 4th celebrations back in Arizona, Moo Krata—skillet barbecue, Northeastern Thai style. As my grandmother would say, 'enjoy the blessings before us.'"

While Leah was standing and explaining their traditional food, this was the first time I realized her total beauty. She had a string top silk blouse with apparently no support for her bosom, but her breasts were firm enough to hold the blouse out and show the outline of perfectly sculpted nipples. Her dark brown hair and a smile with teeth as white as new snow on New Hampshire hills accented a beautiful face. She not only smiled with her gorgeous lips but also with her almond-shaped brown eyes. I had been so intrigued by Busa that I missed the beauty of Leah.

I raised my glass of 'tits', "Let's have a toast," they joined me. "Being in the company of two gorgeous females and enjoying great food with incredible drinks. If Thailand is not heaven, it must be on heaven's steps."

Leah said, "At least Bangkok." With that, we drank the sweetest plum wine I had ever tasted.

After our toast, I asked, "What did you mean when you said, 'at least Bangkok?'"

"As you know, our home is in Northeast Thailand," Leah said. "Busa and I met when we were young. Our parents sent us to a Buddhist monastery for education, safety, and to become nuns. We were there for about ten years. That's where we learned English from Mrs. Anderson, an American missionary who fell in love with our country. After finishing what you would call high school, we continued our education and taught classes."

"Why safety?" Bob asked while I was stuck on that they were nuns-in-training.

"In our part of Thailand, being an attractive girl is a curse," Leah said. "There are bandits. They come to villages and give the family money for young girls and good-looking boys for sex slaves. Sometimes they'll just kidnap the teenagers and then steal all the food from the village."

"And you were safe at the monastery?" Bob asked.

"Everyone thought that no one would denigrate a holy place."

Busa interrupted and said, "I'll tell the story of what happened. Leah will be modest and skip the part of how she saved my life. While we were sleeping one night, a bunch of criminals chose to kidnap students at the school. We heard the shooting when they entered the dormitory. She led me to escape out a back window while protecting me from two of the thugs."

"How did you get around two bad guys?" I asked in astonishment.

"I used a trick the monks taught me. Don't ask what because it will take too long to explain," Leah answered.

"We hid in the jungle for a week surviving on Leah's determination and knowledge of edible plants," Busa said.

"I learned that skill from the monks," Leah said. "They taught me to use different plants and herbs for food and medicine."

"Eventually, we found a Royal Thai Army unit," Busa explained. "They were searching for the criminals and students from the monastery attack. The commander told us that all the students were missing, and the monks died trying to protect them. After much discussion, they decided the safest place to take us was Bangkok because the gangs were still in the area. When we got to Bangkok, the Commandant of the Army said, 'The government will provide housing for you for two weeks, but after that, you will be on your own.' Leah had a cousin living just outside the city; she temporarily gave us a place to stay. Then Leah's cousin healed our wounds from our time in the jungle, gave us dresses to use, and talked to the Peacock Club to provide us with jobs."

"The club initially hired us as waitresses," Leah said. "About a month ago, we received notification that the bandits who stole the students came again and took all the villagers' stored food. Our families were hurting, so Busa and I decided to earn more to help our relatives. To do this, we had to become escorts. Being Buddhist, we are not proud of our occupation, but we must not think only of ourselves but also of our loved ones' survival. Soon, our village will harvest a new crop, and the Army has already caught or killed those bandits. In just a month or two, we can find other ways to earn a living."

Busa added, "That's the difference between the sex slaves and the Peacock Room. We can choose not to go with a customer, have Sundays off, health check-ups, and quit when we want."

Bob and I were speechless.

After dinner, Po took us to Thai boxing or better known as Muay Thai boxing. Leah explained how it works, "The fighter will counter his opponent with swift kicks and sweat flies. Usually, one crushing punch lands the other on the mat. When that happens, the crowd will erupt, and with ringside seats, it will feel like we'll be in the middle of it all."

All I could think was, *Swift kicks? Sweat flying? And they were going to be nuns?*

The evening started with amateur matches and ramped up to title fights. In the final bout, Leah indicated they were two of the best boxers in Thailand. Again, I wondered, *how does Leah know so much about boxing?*

The bell rang. I could tell these two were good with their sharp, swift punches and kicks. In the second round, the boxer in red trunks caught the other fighter in the side of the face, causing blood to fly in our direction. Po stepped in to prevent us from the blood splatter.

Watching all this triggered the second strange attack in a week. I got the feeling of floating, ringing in my ears, and I had a hard time breathing. I got up, told Busa, "I need some air," left for the lobby, and headed straight to the bar. I ordered a double shot of whiskey. I downed it and ordered another.

She rushed to my side. She asked, "What's wrong?"

I lied and said, "The heat just got to me, and I needed some air." I could see in her eyes she knew it was more than that.

Po came out of the restroom after cleaning the blood from his arm. She said something in Thai. Po moved his head in agreement and looked concerned. Then I remembered that he had seen the last attack at TIM Land.

Po used his unique driving skills to rush us back to the hotel. In the room, there was no lovemaking that night. I was cold and shivering. Busa took loving care of me. I woke up several times to see her sitting on the bed beside me, holding my hand.

Thursday, October 19, 1967, Wedding Day

When I woke up the next morning, Busa was still sitting beside me.

"Have you been there all night?" I asked.

"Yes, I wanted to make sure you didn't go into another spell and that you kept breathing. What happened to you last night?"

"I don't know. I just felt like I was going to pass out. Then I couldn't breathe. Next thing I knew, I woke up with you beside me in the middle of the night." I smiled unevenly at her.

All four of us were at the pool by mid-morning. I asked what the plans were for this special day.

"Buddhists have no practice like the Christian Sacrament of Marriage," Leah explained. "Our religion includes the right to marry a non-Buddhist, where the law permits."

Bob continued, "So today we'll be married by a chaplain from the Air Force base, and then a Buddhist monk will bless us."

We met the chaplain and monk late that afternoon in a private hotel meeting room. The chaplain said, "Bob, I spoke to your company commander and got permission to marry you two." Then he looked at the monk and asked, "Are you ready?"

He answered with his hands together and a Thai bow.

The chaplain's service was a typical Western ceremony, and, in the end, he pronounced them husband and wife. Then the monk told Leah in Thai to have her and Bob kneel and face each other. The monk chanted words in Thai while he sprinkled some liquid from a wooden ball on the end of a wooden stick.

The monk said in broken English, "You married now." There were hugs all around, and the waiters popped champagne.

It was my turn to give a toast to the bride and groom, so I raised my glass and started. "I want to say, Bob, I have known you less than a week, and I know we'll be friends as long as the sun rises in the East and sets in the West. If you ever need anything, call, and I'll be there. Leah, they say you don't marry the person you can live with. You marry the person you can't live without. I have seen your love for him grow during our time here, and if you ever need me, I'll be there for you too. Now let's raise our glasses and be the first to wish Mr. and Mrs. Bandelier a long and happy life together."

We all drank champagne, except the monk. He had water.

After the toast, the chaplain and monk left, leaving the four of us. We talked for a while, and then I couldn't figure out why things were awkward until Busa whispered, "I think they want to enjoy marital bliss." After her wise advice, we excused ourselves for the evening.

CHAPTER 24:
LAST PARADISICAL DAY

Friday, October 20, 1967

I woke up before Busa but stayed in bed, reflecting on the last four days: the Floating Gardens, Royal Palace, the many Buddhist temples and just staying at the hotel by the pool. The marvelous dinners and shows featured classic Thai costumes.

Most of all, I thought about how she was the perfect escort, explaining the meaning and history behind what we visited. We took walks and laughed at her using the wrong word occasionally or at one of my silly comments. How sweet she was forgoing sleep to watch over me all night with such concern. I thought about how nice it would be to have her with me at home, especially since Bob and Leah seem happy. I had no one there now.

She didn't seem reluctant to be an escort. Quite the opposite, she initiated sex and went after it with abandon. Ironically, Bob described Leah as timid and not comfortable being a soiled dove. Of course, they could both be putting on an act for their customers and be lesbians, for all we knew. Unlike Bob, I didn't feel for Busa what he felt about Leah.

Maybe all that I was feeling was nothing, no more than simple human chemistry.

Then I went dark, imagining how she would probably get pregnant in her line of work, and it would be another heartbreak for me. I didn't need to go through that again; so, like it or not, Vietnam, here I come. I feared betrayal more than a lucky Cong bullet. For a second, I thought, *something is fucked in my brain*, but then dismissed it as bullshit.

Regrettably, this was my last day, and I didn't know what we should do.

Busa had to go home to get her papers for the health department's inspection of sex workers. I asked Po, "Should I go also?"

He said, "If you feel comfortable, go."

Po dropped us off at the head of an alley. Clothes of many colors hung everywhere, and children were playing soccer while a baby was crying somewhere. This alley was better living conditions than Vietnam, but this wasn't like an American middle-class neighborhood either.

We climbed to the second floor and walked down an outside portal that stretched the building's length until Busa stopped and said, "I live with grandmother here, and she knows very little English, so if you need, I'll interpret for you."

She opened the door to the apartment. We entered, and I found a two-room well-kept residence. The front room was the kitchen, dinner table, and four chairs. The other side of the room had a sofa, two stuffed chairs, and a TV sitting on top of an old console model TV. I remember my aunt and uncle did the same thing with their new TV. You would think a table would be better. I guess some things are just universal in working families everywhere.

Busa's grandmother was shorter than she was, and you could tell there were years of hard work painted on her face with wrinkles and hard-calloused hands. She greeted her granddaughter with a big smile and hugged her while she said something in Thai. Busa introduced me, and Grandma put her hands together and bowed deeply. Earlier, I read in the Army briefing papers that in the Thai culture, the lower the bow, the more profound the respect. Then she took my hand with both of hers, using the American way of greeting.

She made us tea. Busa and I sat on the sofa, sipping our tea and enjoying some cookies. Grandma started most thoughts with a few words of English but finished in Thai, that Busa interpreted.

After some chit-chat, she asked, "American?"

I nodded, yes.

"You in Vietnam?"

Again, I gave her an affirmative nod.

"You like Busa?" she asked as she smiled at her and winked.

I finally spoke and said, "Yes, I do."

Then came a question that caused me to sink in my chair and left me speechless when she asked, "You take Busa to America?"

That brought out an obvious scolding in Thai from Busa and no response from me. We had an uncomfortable conversation for the next half hour until Busa told her grandmother we had to leave.

On the way to Po's car, Busa apologized profusely, but I felt a bit set up by the situation.

In the car, we were quiet until I saw an overweight oriental woman that caused me to say, "Po, I thought you said there are no fat Thais."

"No, she is Chinese." Po's comeback got Busa and me to laugh. That broke the ice, and we began talking again.

Saturday, October 21, 1967

I packed my things and felt sad about leaving. Last night, Busa and I talked until midnight, and finally, we were passionate. Not like

Jane but more like Susan, and I thought, *it's a good thing I have to leave today, or I might stay here AWOL.* Absent without leave would get me shipped back to Vietnam once the MPs caught me and probably busted to a PFC and, worse, transferred to the infantry.

We entered the lobby and found Leah and Bob waiting. The rest of the departing soldiers were outside smoking and bullshitting with each other.

"Don't two newlyweds have something better to do early on a Saturday morning?" I asked.

"We couldn't let you leave without saying a final goodbye," Bob said.

"Don't say 'final,'" I said. "Remember, we're getting together in Phoenix when we get out, and you better bring your beautiful bride."

"I don't think I want you two alone in a big city," Leah wisely added. "There's no telling what Bob and you could trip over." Then she kissed me on the cheek and said, "Be safe. We want to see you again." I thought, *how can anyone be safe in a war?*

I heard the roar of an engine downshifting outside and the squeal of breaks announcing the arrival of the cattle car.

Bob hugged me and said, "Maybe we'll meet on that stupid playground they call a police action, and you can give me a ride someday in that airscrew you call a helicopter."

"It will be an honor," I nodded.

A sergeant stood outside and ordered, "Put your bags in the deuce-and-a-half and get onboard."

I looked at teardrops running down Busa's cheeks, leaving a wet trail from the corner of her beautiful eyes, and said, "You little lady, I will never forget."

She grabbed and kissed me more passionately than she had all week, then placed her hands together below her chin, bowed, and said, "May Buddha protect you and bring you back to Thailand someday."

"That would please me," I said as she hugged me.

I ended her embrace and walked to the door. I turned for one last glance at my newfound friends. I waved and turned towards Uncle Sam's Army, waiting to take me back to the nightmare, without Bob and with sweet thoughts of Bangkok.

I don't know why, but unlike most of the guys in high school who read books with sex scenes in them, I read books of quotations, some poetry, and many biographies. As the transport jerked to start the journey, I saw the three of them through the slit in the metal. A line by Azar Nafasi, echoed in my mind, a sentence I didn't truly understand till that moment. "You get a strange feeling when you leave a place, like you'll not only miss the people you love, but you miss the person you are at this time and place because you'll never be this way again."

CHAPTER 25:
TICK DAK TO

Our platoon sergeant awakened us at 3 a.m. on November 10th. He had an edge in his voice when he bellowed, "Get your gear together for an undetermined length of time in the field. Be in Ops in 30."

"What the fuck now?" I scoffed.

"I'm sure it's some second Lewy who got his tit caught in a ringer somewhere," Bone said.

"All I know is that every time they do this, it ain't good," Jim added.

We had to scramble to make it to Operations in thirty minutes. We packed, dumped, and grabbed a breakfast sandwich from the mess hall. At Operations, I was amazed to see more than just the regular flight crews in attendance. Milling around were the cooks, both day and night maintenance crews, and even the headquarters and supply personnel guys showed up.

"This is going to be a monkey fuck," Vincent said to no one in particular.

"Something is going on at Dak To," said the CO's orderly.

"There's nothing there but a small Special Forces camp," Ski said.

The first sergeant entered and barked, "Atten-up."

The CO appeared behind him and ordered, "Stand at ease. Hot intel shows a massive buildup around the Dak To area. Reports have identified four infantry regiments and one artillery regiment of the North Vietnam Army's 1st Division."

Russ said to the crews around us, "That's a shit lot of gooks."

"No shit, Russ," the commander said.

Russ whispered to me, "How did he hear that?"

"I thought the trip to Nha Trang taught you that he knows all and sees all," I hissed at him.

The major continued, "Already there on our side is the 173rd Airborne Brigade and two brigades from the 4th Infantry. The 6th ARVN Battalion is also being moved in for the fight. The 1st Cavalry is in reserve at Ankay. In all, there will be some 16,000 troops in the field. And Russ, that's a whole lot of good guys also." Everybody in the rows in front turned and looked at Russ.

He continued, "This battle will be called 'Operation MacArthur.' We will be providing support where needed. And gentlemen...I know we will be needed."

Jim quietly reinforced, "Didn't I say it ain't gonna be good?"

"Members of our maintenance platoon will be supporting us," the CO nodded to the Maintenance Sargent. "Our mechanics will have their hands full on the big jobs, so crew chiefs, it is your responsibility to keep your aircraft flying. Remember, if you're not flying, men are dying. Crew chiefs and gunners report to your platoon sergeants, and pilots report to your platoon leaders for final instructions."

The CO paused to look around the room at the faces of the men under his command. "May the angels be with you all."

"I never heard him say that angel stuff before," Vincent said.

"I'll say again, this ain't going to be good," Jim repeated.

We huddled around our platoon sergeant, who said he was setting up four teams of four crews with the most senior crewmen. The teams would be led by: Rusty—you can figure out how he got his name; Ski, who is of Polish descent and proved every chance he got that all the Polish jokes had merit; Bone, who got his name because he looked like the character Wishbone on the TV series *Wagon Train*; and finally, Mack, me, yours truly.

After a brief talk by the sergeant about pilot assignments, we readied our aircraft. Again, I got my favorite pilot, Mr. Snow.

Now that we knew our mission, we were in the air by 5 a.m. Approaching Dak To at sunrise, I could see that things had changed since the last time I was there. The little single runway Special Forces outpost now had had a control tower that was busy directing air traffic. While monitoring the radio, I heard several C-130s, Hueys, and Chinooks receiving landing and takeoff instructions.

On landing approach with the full view of the expanding base laid out before us, it was impressive how they had turned one runway next to a small village into a significant military base in just two weeks. It looked like there were close to one hundred tents, with three C-130s unloading, one ready for taking off and another landing. Helicopters were going and coming into a large refueling station on the north side. At the same time, others were in the resupply area where the C-130 cargo planes were unloading.

"Bikini Two-Two, this is Bikini Ops."

"This is Two-Two, go," Snow, our pilot, responded.

"Bikini Two-Two, go to the resupply area, take on ammo and water, and then deliver to Hill 654," came the order. "The unit is engaged with the enemy."

The "654" designation referred to the elevation of a mountain in meters. Using this approach was how we could tell one unnamed peak from another.

On landing, I asked, "How much fuel do we have?"

"Six hundred pounds," Snow replied. "Also, can you do that voodoo magic on our engine?"

"I sure can," I replied. "And this time, I brought cotter pins."

"Great. Do it, Mack."

"First, I need to cipher our load," I instructed.

"You call me a hillbilly, and you use the word 'cipher?'" Russ said.

I ignored him as I gave my report. "We have a little more than 90 gallons at 6.6 pounds per gallon. The aircraft and gear weigh about 2,000 pounds. Russ, you and the grunts load about 3,000 pounds of their trash while I tinker with the engine. That will put us a little over-weight, but my tinkering should make up for it."

"Roger that," Snow responded.

Doing the engine conversion correctly this time took me about fifteen minutes. When I climbed down from the engine and saw the cargo bay loaded with as much water, M16, and M60 ammo as would fit, I was a bit worried.

"Russ, how much weight did you load? It looks way over."

"As much as would fit."

"C'mon, that shit is heavy stuff."

Seeing that the grunts who loaded the aircraft were newbies, I wanted them to know about load limits. Russ and I quickly gave them a crash lesson on aircraft loading, so we wouldn't crash.

"Guys, listen up. The scholarly and by-the-book way to load a Huey is to fill out a form to calculate the load's weight and then to make sure the distribution is within the Huey's center of gravity envelope. We have to know if the CG was within permissible takeoff and landing limits. However, the form we are supposed to use is highly impractical at times like this because it takes too long to calculate."

I heard one grunt say to the other, "Center of gravity—CG, stupid!"

I took a deep breath and forged ahead, "So, to ensure we are not over our limit, the pilots will do a hover check. They will lift off and pause fully stabilized three feet high for several seconds before committing to a full takeoff. This check will indicate whether the ship is 'sort of within limits' and tell us if the load is safe for the task. If not, you'll need to throw shit off from the front first. If you hear nothing else from all this bullshit I tell you, remember this when you take off weight—it comes off from the FRONT of the load."

I looked right at the kid, "Got that, GC?"

"Um huh."

I looked at the pilot and said, "Let's try a hover check." *Damn draftees*, I thought as I shook my head.

It came off the ground fine but was creeping forward.

"Mack, I've run out of aft cyclic," Snow said. "I had the stick pulled to the full backward position, and we still went forward. Boys, better throw some stuff out of the front."

The grunts, Russ, and I threw out several boxes of the most forward ammo. They were complaining a bit, so I let them have it. "You see. You made double work for us because you didn't follow procedure. It ain't a suggestion; it's fucking physics, and you ignore it at your own fucking peril, boys. It will kill us all just as dead as a bullet." God, I felt old all of a sudden.

"Try it again," I suggested.

"It's okay," Mr. Snow informed us. "I can back up now. I'm sure we can stop in the LZ after our in-route fuel burn-off."

The 173rd operated west of Dak To, and the 4th Division began its fighting to the south. Almost immediately, both units engaged in fierce battles with the enemy. We started flying in support of the 4th Division. We would eventually fly support to whoever needed us.

When we got to the LZ for the 1st Brigade A Company, there was a break in the action, so our first resupply task was a milk run hauling water, C-rations, and ammo. We also ferried soldiers who needed transport back to base for various reasons. We completed our last mission at about 6 p.m.

Our platoon sergeant greeted us and said, "All the crews meet at the mess tent."

We had all gotten our meals and found a place to sit when the platoon sergeant said, "Listen up, guys. Benjamin Franklin said almost 200 years ago, 'For want of a nail the shoe was lost, for want of a shoe the horse was lost, for want of a horse a soldier was lost, being overtaken and slain by the enemy, for want of a soldier the battle was lost, all for want of a horseshoe nail.' That Franklin quote is as true today as it was then." He nodded and looked around to make sure we were all paying attention and then continued with, "So pay attention to the little things—like sudden vibrations or unusual noises. Find out what's causing it before it bites you in the ass. Next, everyone needs to move the battery from the nose compartment to the rear battery position."

Robbie interjected and asked, "Why?"

"The battery weighs between 75 and 80 pounds. If any of you guys took physics, you'd know why the move will make a big difference, increase the CG envelope, and allow more weight forward of where you're used to loading. More cargo per load will mean fewer trips out, I hope, but at least you will have far less chance of not stopping when you need to."

"Yeah, we ran out of aft cyclic today, because our load was too far forward," Vincent said. "It's serious, guys. The pilot had to slam us down to stop. Unfortunately, it was on a rock. That means we need to change a damaged landing skid tonight."

"Next, none of us leave the flight line until we're all ready to quit," the sergeant resumed. "If you get your bird ready before the others, you need to help someone else. If you have any questions at all, ask your team leader or me. Remember, no matter how bad it gets, at least we will have cots to sleep on at night with Infantry guarding the perimeter. We won't be bedding down on cold earth with bugs crawling all over us in the boonies thinking every noise could be Charlie trying to kill us. Now let's go get the birds ready for tomorrow."

Since we had fresh birds for the first day of the mission, there wasn't much wrong with them. We finished early, around 9 p.m., but we found that sleep didn't come easy at Dak To. Their 8-inch artillery batteries were so close to our tents. When they gave fire support to units in the south, the shock wave would almost knock us out of bed and the noise was thunderous.

Each of the subsequent days began early, and then we would fly until dark or sometimes late into the night. The only pause in the action was a mandatory shutdown every six flight hours to check our aircraft for airworthiness. Besides that 15-minute required check, we were in constant motion, hot refueling, making an untold number of trips loading and then unloading personnel and supplies, often under enemy fire. We caught catnaps between takeoffs and landings, but exhaustion was our constant companion. We had to manhandle cargo all day while still carrying out hours of post-flight duties at night.

One morning, I saw Levi take out a pipe and fill it with what he said was "tobacco," but it smelled like something more potent. Then he lit it and stood in front of his aircraft, filling the air with smoke. He said something in Apache and pointed the pipe to the sky.

"What in the world are you doing?" I asked.

"Me blessed Sky Horse. He soon carries us into great battle where we kill many VC."

While reciting this declaration, he slowly moved his hands with the pipe across the horizon. He looked like he was playing out a scene in a class B western movie. Others who were watching walked away in disbelief.

"You don't know any of that Apache stuff," I quipped. "You grew up in Denver and went to the University of Colorado. Why do you talk like Tonto from *The Lone Ranger* when you speak better English than I do?"

He laughed and said, "I know this stuff from reading it in a book and seeing it in the movies. I just want to fuck with these guys and make them think I am some kind of medicine man or something. Besides, who knows? It might help."

"Then you ought to also put on war paint," I recommended.

"Good idea. Got any?" he joked.

"Fresh out, Kimosabee." I snickered.

I thought, *Oh shit; here we go. I may have started a new fad with these knuckleheads.*

On another morning, I encountered Ski walking around wearing his flight helmet. In astonishment, I asked, "What's going on, Ski?"

He took off his helmet, and his answer was just as absurd as an urban Indian acting as a medicine man. "I read that when one of the body's senses get deprived, it causes the others to grow stronger."

"Yeah, so?"

"I want to go to pilot training, but my eyesight is too bad to get in so I'm depriving my hearing to improve my eyesight." Then he gave his signature belly laugh.

I had heard somewhere that humor and crazy antics release tension. I thought these two are as tight as a lifting spring on a closed overhead barn door.

The mission dragged on. We fudged the logbooks by entering two hours when we flew six. Keeping bogus flight times allowed us to keep the pilots flying beyond their maximum monthly flight hours. This also reduced the ship's downtime for their scheduled maintenance. *If we ain't flying, men are dying.*

By the second week of the mission, all other crews had at least one crewman wounded or hurt. As soon as the injured men got treated in the aid tent, they returned to their seats. Our ship caught a few bullets, but we took no casualties. The rest of the platoon again started calling us lucky bastards.

The Hueys also took a beating. As soon as a stricken ship got slung loaded below a Chinook, it was a race to see which aviation company's maintenance team would be first to strip it for parts to keep their own ships flying.

One night, a crew chief, Robbie, came to me and said, "My tail rotor's 90-degree gearbox won't hold oil between shutdown checks. I'm afraid it will seize during flight."

"The only reason they want us to use that extremely light turbine oil is because they think we're too stupid to distinguish between different oils for different uses. Let's use some hillbilly ingenuity," I coaxed him.

"Okay, but what?" he asked with confusion.

"You need to trust me with some outlaw maintenance that requires resourcefulness," I said and winked.

"Go on…" he egged me on.

"You know, I grew up on a farm. When it's haying season, you can't stop to replace every little leaking seal. I know from experience that if you got a leak, get thicker oil. Go to the motor pool, get some 90-weight gear oil and put that in and your leak should slow down, if not stop entirely."

"What if I still run out during stops?" he asked.

"Then pack grease into it, and I guarantee that will work."

"How am I going to log this?" he shrugged.

"You don't. Just let your pilots know."

"What if they have an issue?" he asked anxiously.

"If your pilots object to this unauthorized procedure, then have them see me. It just means those pilots don't want to fly in this donkey fuck."

Another time, I walked past as an officer had just finished chewing out a crew chief, Bone.

"What's his beef?" I asked.

"We got three bullet holes in the rotor. He wanted me to fix it. How in the hell am I supposed to change a rotor blade with no maintenance stands or a crane?" he said with his hands up in the air.

"Didn't you go to MIT?" I asked.

"For two years. Then I left to join up," he confirmed.

I shook my head. "We're going have a long talk about that over some cheap beers someday." I turned towards the line of mechanized equipment. "See that self-propelled cannon? Ask one of their grease monkeys to drive it over here, and I'll round up the gang."

I secured two crews that had landed for the day. Much to my surprise, Top, our first sergeant came out of the headquarters tent and asked, "I hear you could use some help with a blade change."

"Top, I didn't know you had a maintenance background," I said.

"Mack, I was fixing aircraft when you were still shitting yellow," he quipped.

"Do you mean you worked on Galileo's helicopter concept?" I asked, just as our banter was interrupted by the arrival of the self-propelled cannon.

"Have the gun tube lift the good blade so we can get the bad one low enough to work on," I told Bone.

"Okay. Will do."

Josh and two other cooks joined us to steady the blade while Top removed the attaching bolts. Then we pulled the old one off its mount and started wrestling the new one in place. The hard part was lining up the blade with the grips so the top sergeant could insert the two bolts.

"Push it in another inch," Top instructed. "I can't get the bolt in yet."

"Put some hair around the hole. It will help," Ron said.

"Is this coming from some guy that has never had a woman that he didn't pay for?" Top replied.

It took seven men and the barrel of the big gun to replace the crane we would normally use to accomplish the job.

Bone came over and asked, "Where did you learn that trick?"

"Good old farmer ingenuity," I quipped as I walked off suddenly remembering, "rotor blade roulette" that Oklahoma used to play with one of his buddies.

"Oklahoma, get over here," I commanded.

I grabbed him by the shirt and asked, "Did you play rotor blade roulette with that bird today?" I continued to interrogate him in a way that would have made the CIA proud.

Finally, after I let him go, he answered, "No, Mack, I haven't played rotor blade roulette since you told us what could happen."

"If I ever find out otherwise, I'll make VC torture look like a game of patty cakes compared to what I'll do to you."

"I promise, Mack. It will never happen."

Whenever we had to do our own repair work, and that was most of the time, we got help from wounded infantrymen and our fellow crewmembers. As soon as these guys were out of the field hospital and patched up, they pitched in. Even off-duty cooks helped, and our first sergeant continued to roll up his sleeves. This team effort allowed us to keep the birds flying.

There was only one group we would not let help—our pilots. If they didn't get some sleep, we all might rest in peace.

After several days of nonstop missions and repairing helicopters, we were walking zombies. What kept us going and men just out of hospitals volunteering were the CO's words, "If they're not flying, men are dying." We understood that the infantry was enduring much worse than we were, so we "soldiered on."

Days later, the flight surgeon called us to his tent and issued us a bottle of pills with instructions. "This will help keep you guys going."

"What is this?" I asked.

"Dexedrine. It's to perk you guys up. It will give you endless energy and may even give you a feeling of invincibility."

"Invincibility We probably need that more than energy," Robbie said.

"If all that's true, should we stay away from Kryptonite?" I joked.

The Doc said, "Get the fuck back to work, you idiots."

We ran numerous sorties resupplying units on the ground and removing Killed in Actions (KIA) for days. The bodies were flown back to Dak To, where they were stacked up at the brigade medical pad waiting for transportation to Pleiku's grave registration. Snow was insistent that we carry as many KIA bodies as we could fly out, saying, "If we can get them back as soon as possible, maybe the family can have comfort with an open casket at the funeral."

We got the message, more than a few times. "All aircraft in the Dak To area. This is Dak To tower. We are presently under mortar attack and will be off the air until further notice." This message usually was spoken faster than I have heard come out of the mouth of a livestock auctioneer. I visualized the tower operators on their way to the bunker, with their mic cord in tow as far as it would reach.

Sometimes, we would hear, "Dak To, this is King Bee. We land now." King Bee is the call sign of Vietnam Air Force CH-34 helicopters.

This message would be followed by, "All aircraft, this is Dak To Tower. We have aircraft in the traffic pattern with no contact in English."

The first time I heard it, we had at least twenty helicopters along with three C-130s in the traffic pattern. "I don't think things could get more screwed up than this," I said and then asked, "and now we have a VNAF pilot flying and trying to communicate with limited English?"

On one of our flights back to Dak To, our operations radioed our call sign, "Bikini Two-Two, proceed to Hill 855, where Bikini Five-Nine-Three is down and one KIA. Proceed to pick up the surviving crew along with the body. You will be flying into a one-ship hover hole LZ with no way to set down and an RPG downed Five-Nine-Three, so stay alert."

That got our attention.

"Another shit storm," I said and shook my head.

"At least this time, I won't be the only one under fire," Russ said.

"That's comforting," I responded sheepishly.

"I hope the title Lucky Bastards holds," Snow said.

We made it in under enemy fire, amazingly, with not a single hit.

In the middle of it all, as I was unloading my gun into the grass from where the fire coming at us was, I asked, "What happened; no RPGs?"

"They must have run out of them," Russ said, just as one then passed over us.

"Don't you ever get sick of being wrong?" I asked.

When we were clear of the LZ, I asked the crew chief we rescued, "What happened? You guys were supposed to be above it all, flying C&C, the safest mission there is?"

"The colonel had us take out the C&C console and fly water out to his men at Hill 855."

"Between what happened to Giff and now you," I said, "I'm not going to ever accept a C&C mission." He had a far-off look in his eye as he shook his head in agreement.

The 173rd Airborne Brigade continued pursuing the 66th NVA Regiment until November 11, when somebody decided to withdraw them. We extracted two companies from an LZ at Hill 821, located on a steep incline covered in elephant grass. Each aircraft taking part in the lift took rounds from ground fire. We were the only crew that a crewman didn't sustain some minor wound.

"Again, we lived up to our name, Lucky Bastards," Snow proudly proclaimed. "I sure hope it continues."

"You know all good things come to an end in this fucking war," Russ added.

"Up pops Mr. Sunshine again," I said.

Amazingly, even with all the wounded and battle-damaged choppers, we had every aircraft ready to fly each morning, and all crew members reported for duty.

CHAPTER 26:
BOB'S FINAL FLIGHT

As we were returning to pick up another load close to the Laotian border, we received a 4th Infantry Unit transmission. "Any aircraft near Hill 764? This is Bravo Alpha Six. We have an emergency."

Snow responded, "Bravo Alpha Six, this is Bikini Two-Two. We're ten minutes away. What's your problem?"

"Bikini Two-Two, we are in contact with an NVA force and have an emergency evacuation needed."

"What ain't a fucking emergency in this fucked up war?" I snickered over the intercom.

Snow got the coordinates, and I felt the chopper bank hard left as we headed for the infantry company's location.

Snow brought us in low and fast over the trees, a lifesaving maneuver to avoid enemy ground fire. He waited to flare the bird until we dropped into the LZ. That flaring maneuver similar to the rearing of a horse used to quickly reduce airspeed didn't make the landing one of his best. We hit the landing zone hard enough that we rocked forward and then back.

I keyed my mic and quipped, "I'd say that landing was a D-minus."

Snow defended himself, saying, "We didn't take any hits, chief, and we're all in one piece, so I'd say it was damn good."

Once I made eye contact with the men kneeling in the grass, I motioned with my hand in a fist and arms bent, pumping it up and down, the universal sign to hurry up. Four men stood up and carried a blood-soaked wounded trooper in a poncho towards us. The wounded man used his arm to motion to a soldier to come to him. When he got there, he bent over the bloodied soldier and then ran back to the tall grass.

A few rounds zipped past us, which quickly got my attention. Russ came from the other side to grab one side of the poncho with the wounded man to help lift him into his last hope: our flight of mercy.

A grunt ran up to us with his helmet and said as he handed it to me, "He insisted I get this to him before you left."

I thought, *why does a man on his way home need this?* My breath got caught in my throat when I looked down and saw it was Bob, my new friend from Bangkok. I glanced down and saw Russ go to work on Bob's bloody lower abdomen.

I spun around the seat's attaching pole and pulled my face up to Bob's. "Bob! Bob! It's Mack!" I screamed above the roar of the rotor blades. He spoke, but it was so soft I couldn't hear, so I put my helmet's microphone close to his lips and opened a continuous com on the hot mic position.

I heard, "Thank God, it's you."

"Don't worry, Bob. We'll be at the aid station in a few minutes. In the meantime, Doc Elliott is taking good care of you," I said, having just given a grunt gunner a degree in medicine.

"Mack, give me my helmet," he requested weakly.

I went back to my seat and retrieved it for him. He took it and grabbed two envelopes out from under the webbing.

Struggling, he said, "Please, Mack, make sure you mail these."

I patted his shoulder, the only part of him that wasn't bloody, and assured him, "Don't worry, Bob. In a few days, you'll mail them yourself."

"Remember what you told Po in Bangkok that night…" he coughed up some blood, "…don't bullshit a bullshitter, so stop the happy talk." He swallowed a mouth full of blood, choked a little, and said, "I've seen enough here to know it's not good."

I looked at Russ. He slowly shook his head, indicating there wasn't much he could do.

Bob's eyes were rolling back in pain as he struggled to say, "When you're home in Phoenix, please go see my parents and let them know how much I loved Leah and to take care of her."

"I promise you anything you need. I'll be there to have your back. Heber ain't that far from Phoenix. I'll tell them about the best love story I have ever witnessed."

Bob looked straight into my eyes and said, "You know I loved Leah like nothing I've ever known before her." He spasmed, his back arched, and then he was gone.

I closed his eyes and said quietly, "I know Bob, I know." I looked at his face. I hadn't known him long but wanted to remember what he looked like for the rest of my life.

As I took his dangling arm and placed it across his chest, I mumbled, "Back in Bangkok, I said that it would be an honor to fly with you someday. I never thought it would be like this. God damn fucking war."

We landed at the aid station. The medics, out of routine, checked Bob's pulse and, of course, found none. They started to take him off the bird when Russ stopped them. Then something odd happened. I heard the engine shut down. It was unusual because we would only shut the engines down to conserve fuel, and I knew we had plenty of flight time left before refueling. Once at rest, it suddenly all hit me. I jumped out, ran back by the tail boom and, holding on with one hand, threw up my guts.

Russ came back, put his hand on my shoulder and consoled me. "I heard everything on the hot mic, Mack, and couldn't let them stack him with the others."

I wiped my mouth on my sleeve and turned to him. I had never seen him soft. He was truly affected by this one death more than the others we were clocking daily.

"Thanks, Russ," I said, patting his hand on my shoulder.

I went back to the front of the ship and found Snow and Major Burke, our CO, talking.

When he saw me, Snow said, "I heard everything over the intercom, so I called our CO to meet us here."

Thanks a lot, I thought. *Now I am going to get my ass chewed out by the doctor of astrology. I braced myself for the shitstorm coming.*

The CO interrupted, "I understand this was a friend of yours?"

"Er...Yes, ah, yes sir. I met him on R&R and was with him the whole stay. I was even the best man at his wedding."

He came close, put a hand on each of my shoulders, and looked me straight in the eyes. "I think you ought to accompany the body back to Pleiku," the CO said in an uncharacteristic compassionate, soft voice. I looked down at Bob's body. He was having an interesting effect on everyone.

"Yes, sir. Thank you." I sniffled and blinked my moist eyes.

I took out the two letters from my side pocket and saw they were bloodstained. When I showed them to the CO, I remarked, "Sir, I can't send these like this."

"Son, if I were you, I'd write another one to each and put them both in a clean envelope. Your crew is to place Bob on aircraft Zero-Two-Zero. It is going back to Pleiku for maintenance. Get on it. Grieve tonight but remember: the other Bobs who are still out there need you back here at 100% tomorrow."

I started to salute him, but he put out his hand and I shook it, man to man. "Thank you, sir."

As I boarded the Huey to Pleiku, I couldn't help but notice that my on-and-off chicken or eagle, Rose, was at the controls. As the maintenance pilot, Rose shuttles aircraft between Dak To and Pleiku for repairs. How fitting, I thought, that he was serving as Bob's and my chauffeur on such a horrible, sad day.

I was in deep thought about Leah, Bob, and what I would say in the letters I had to write when I heard Rose's radio squawk, "Pleiku Tower. Drydock Five requests landing instructions to 71st Evac helipad."

"Drydock Five cleared straight into 71st pad."

"Pleiku, please advise the 71st. We have a VIP, KIA, onboard and request full honors."

"Drydock wilco."

I looked at Rose in amazement over his thoughtful actions and said, "Thank you, sir."

He just looked at me and nodded.

Then I looked down at Bob, "See, they know how special you are, my brother."

We landed on the hospital pad. As I opened the cargo door and stepped out, for the second time today, I heard another unusual flight procedure when the aircraft's engine went to idle. I wondered what

Rose was up to, putting the bird in neutral. Two corpsmen wheeled a gurney out accompanied by a lieutenant in his full-dress uniform.

Rose had idled the bird so he could climb down just to stand by my side. As the corpsmen took Bob out of the helicopter to be placed on the gurney, Rose barked, "Atten-Chun! Preee-sent arms!"

Rose, the Air Force lieutenant, and I came to attention and saluted as the corpsmen gently placed Bob on the gurney.

To end our salute, Rose then hollered, "Orrrr-dah h-arms!"

The corpsmen wheeled Bob's body away with the Air Force lieutenant, informal parade-style, marching behind.

On the short flight back to our base, Camp Holloway, I keyed the mic and said, "I guess now I need to take back all the bad things I thought about you also."

"I guess," was all he said.

That night, I sat alone in my hooch, writing to Leah and Bob's parents.

I wrote Leah first. After several attempts, here is what I came up with:

> *Leah:*
>
> *It is with the most profound grief that I tell you that I was with your love and my dear friend Bob when he passed away today. It saddens me enormously, and I can only imagine how this terrible news affects your young heart. I am sure it is beyond what you think you can stand, so I want to share something with you in this time of your bitterest agony and grief. I hope this brings some comfort to your anguish.*

Leah, Bob's last words were, "I love Leah like nothing I've ever known before her."

Leah, you must now trust that your faith will get you through this. I have experienced enough with death here to know what I say. You need only to believe that Buddha loves you, and so do I.

Your loving friend,
Mack

I struggled more with the letter to Bob's parents but, after several tries, I got one I was satisfied with:

Mr. and Mrs. Bandelier:

I feel I must write to ask you to accept my sincere sympathy on the sad news of the death of your son, Bob. I was with him when we were in Bangkok together, and I was with him today when he passed away.

Hemingway wrote that every man's life ends the same way. Only the details of how he lived and how he died distinguish one man from another. When I was with Bob, he lit up the room with his big smile and loving personality. When he passed today, it was with dignity. I hope I can live up to his example.

Sincerely,

Specialist Donald Makinen

I addressed a new envelope for each letter, placed Bob's with mine, and put them in the outgoing mailbox. As I did so, I said under my breath, "I'll get even with those fuckers, Bob."

CHAPTER 27:
IT'S RAINING HELL

November 16th was one of the few times Russ and I enjoyed shuteye in the daytime. It was rare when we were not busy day and night flying or fixing aircraft. The reason for this slumber time is that we had just ferried a field commander to HQ to get his unit's battle assignment, and thus we had some downtime.

True to Russ's prediction that, "All good things come to an end in this fucking war," I was torn out of my dreams by the NVA starting one of their rocket and mortar attacks.

This time, it got bad in a hurry. In quick succession, two C-130 transport aircraft received direct hits, initially bursting into flames. Then, secondary explosions from their fuel tanks sent pieces of the planes flying in all directions. A part of one plane hit a third C-130 that ignited its fuel and burst into flames. The flames then set off some artillery shells being unloaded and sent more shit everywhere. Then a rocket landed in the ammo dump and started all kinds of things going off and flying up in the air like some immense Fourth of July fireworks show.

The fire spread to the Special Forces camp next to the airfield. As the compound became engulfed in flames, an armored personnel carrier retrieved the Green Berets and their Montagnard fighting team from the camp. Another mortar round hit the petroleum storage station and ignited the aviation fuel stored there. Flames and smoke reached forty feet in the air. We could feel the heat from five hundred feet away. It felt like we were getting a sunburn on some tropical beach.

Another C-130 managed to take off with an unexploded rocket stuck in its wing. Then a rocket struck a propane tank. The explosion sent out shock waves so strong, it almost knocked me over and made a vacuum that sucked the air out of my lungs.

I gulped for air and tried to scream, "We need to find cover."

Russ pointed and choked out, "There's a bunker over there."

Funny how the mind works. As we ran for the bunker, the words of Winston Churchill passed through my head. "When you're going through hell, keep on going." We were going as fast as our legs would carry us.

We hadn't been in the bunker for ten minutes when I heard Snow yelling from outside, "Where is my fucking flight crew?"

Russ answered, "Where the hell do you think we'd be in this hell storm? We're in the bunker next to you."

"Let's get the fuck out of here," was Snow's next command. Mind you, the "F" word wasn't a stranger to our vocabulary, but I had never heard Snow use it before.

I replied, "You got that right." We ran to the aircraft as the mortar shells and rockets were still pounding the camp. JD was already in his seat and hollering, "Clear." The starter began whining just as Russ reached the tie-down for the rotor blade. By the time he undid it from the tail, it was starting to turn so he had to run to get the tie-down unhooked.

The rest of us jumped into our seats. Nobody worried about helmets, seatbelts, shoulder harnesses, or monkey straps; we just all piled into the bird. As our engine was coming up to speed, the field commander and three other grunts jumped on. Snow pulled every bit of horsepower our darling sweet, wonderful chariot of the sky would give him, and we got out of there like a rocket was up our ass.

We flew the commander to his unit. When he got out, the three grunts stayed onboard.

I asked," Where did you think we were taking you guys?"

A corporal answered, "Don't care. We saw you were getting ready to take off, and we knew we wanted out of that firestorm so we jumped on."

My answer to this was, "Well, you bought a round trip ticket, so you're going back."

At that point, we were already twenty feet off the ground. I swear I saw them contemplating if they could survive the jump.

CHAPTER 28:
FROM THE FRYING PAN INTO THE FIRE

Three days later, a battle started that I would classify as catastrophic, disastrous, and controversial or, as Russ put it, "The shit hit the fan."

By mid-November, the 173rd and the 4th Infantry Division inflicted massive losses on the two NVA regiments and forced them toward Laos. A third NVA regiment drew the unlucky straw and was held in reserve, tasked to cover the other two regiments' withdrawal.

Unknown to Army intelligence, prior to the Dak To battle, NVA units secretly prepared Hill 875 by building a complex of bunkers strategically positioned for overlapping fields of fire. The bunkers were covered by logs and four or five feet of earth was moved above that. That kind of construction meant that only a direct hit from artillery or bombs would knock them out. The real strategic advantage they incorporated was the building of tunnels and trenches to connect the bunkers. That allowed for resupply and support under safe conditions, no matter what kind of hell we unleashed above.

When the reserve NVA regiment reached Hill 875, they also activated a predetermined battle plan. Snipers took positions at potential helicopter approaches and in trees. They deployed units at the hill's base below, which was the only LZ location to insert Americans. They could then attack the Americans from the rear after they were in the LZ. That would squeeze our guys between them and the bunker complex, with the snipers screwing them more. All this certainly had the potential to live up to Russ's feces hitting the air circulating device scenario.

We thought the firestorm at the Pleiku airfield was about as bad as it could get, but ….

On November 19th, Snow told us our mission for the day. He said, "Today's task for our entire 52nd Aviation Battalion, which includes us, is to insert three companies of U.S. troops onto Hill 875. Their job is to root out the NVA."

I remarked, "Remember two days ago, we flew a sniffer mission over the terrain of Hill 875?"

Abe, the sniffer operator, said, "Yeah. The sniffer was picking up signs of a heavy concentration of men below us."

"How did you know?" I asked.

Abe explained, "A sniffer works like a bed bug, detecting the carbon dioxide exhaled by living creatures."

"I thought the machine had to be wrong. If you remember, we didn't receive any ground fire. We were flying so slow and low, they could hit us with rocks. If there were heavy concentrations of the enemy, we'd have gotten the shit shot out of us."

"It was probably a bunch of monkeys, fucking carbon dioxide emitting motherfuckers," Russ grumbled.

I feigned tipping my hat to Russ for employing the word 'emitting' in his eloquent alternative theory.

He smiled.

"Let's hope you're right, Russ, and that all we get hit with is flinging monkey shit—and the enemy is not lying in wait." Snow said.

Before loading our troops, the CO had us gather for a short brief of the battle plan. He said, "After all the troopers are on the ground, Companies C and D will move up the hill, followed by two platoons of Company A covering their rear. The weapons platoon of Company A gets to remain behind to cut us out a larger landing zone. If all goes well, this should be over by dark."

We had an unopposed LZ during the insertion of Companies A, C, and D of the 173rd 2nd Battalion. On the way back, I had second thoughts. *This can't be good. I wonder if they were setting us up.*

After getting all our guys on the ground, we returned to Dak To for refueling. Just after landing, we heard on our headsets, "Bikini Flight, this is Bikini Six. Turn your Fox mic radio to the ground troops we just inserted."

We were startled to hear desperate reports from Company A. "We are presently in deep shit, under fire from all sides of the LZ. We'll try to join up with our other platoons. All helicopter companies, bring us everything you can. This is going to be more than anyone planned for."

I pressed my mic button and asked, "Russ, you still think the sniffer was picking up monkeys?"

"He was correct," Snow said. "It's just that they're Ho Chi Minh's monkeys."

We loaded up with ammunition, water and supplies and headed back to the action. By early afternoon, Company A was all but wiped out, and Companies C and D had come under heavy siege near the top of the hill.

All helicopters made repeated runs to the hill with ammunition, food and water, but each time we made an approach, the enemy forced us back before we could reach the Americans. Rusty took a bullet in the leg. In another crew, Captain Boyd got plexiglass in the face from a shot through the windshield. While nicks and near misses had become just another part of a day's work for us, at the same time, the enemy fire was wreaking havoc on our birds. Bikini birds lined up at the Dak To airfield for the overworked and undersupplied maintenance crews to get to them to make whatever repairs were needed so they could get back in the fight. Even the act of refueling became a challenge. It seemed that every time a group of us were at the hot refueling site, a mortar and rocket attack would start. The NVA regulars were executing something rare, a coordinated attack, one that was well-thought out and prepared for. That is why the insertions were so easy and unmolested. They wanted to get our guys in the kill zone.

The shadows were getting long as we got the news that Company A had suffered so many casualties that they had ceased to be a coherent unit. The NVA had encircled Companies C and D along with the remaining fragments of Company A in a small perimeter.

The commander of Company C reported, "We have an undetermined number of NVA surrounding us and are in need of anything you can bring us. We also have numerous casualties for evacuation."

Every available Bikini launched on an emergency resupply mission, making a final effort to resupply the besieged troops. The NVA snipers in the trees and those in fortified positions drove us away with intense small arms and recoilless rifle fire each time we approached. Pilots tried everything they could think of to get the needed supplies to our guys. They tried various approaches, high spirals, and fast low-level approaches up all sides of the hill. Nothing worked. Each time we tried, the intense enemy fire stopped us cold, long before we reached the units. Three birds were hit so badly, they had to return to Pleiku.

Late in the day, Snow ordered, "You and Russ, shorten a sling line to hang below the Huey ten feet instead of the normal twenty feet. I'll try going in fast and so low, we'll almost be in the trees. I'll flair on top of the perimeter and, hopefully, get the sling in. If you want out, let me know now. I can handle the release of the sling from my seat."

I said, "Okay, you haven't let us down yet, and we've been in some pretty tight situations. I'm with you."

Our copilot Warren said, "I'm in."

Russ asked, "Don't I get a vote?"

Snow and I said in stereo, "No!"

"I was going to say yes, anyway so eat shit; all of you. I'm going," Russ answered.

Snow said, "As that new space travel TV show says, let's go 'where no man has gone before.'"

All three of us replied in unison, "Let's do it."

We hooked up the sling and started the flight. True to his word, Snow was getting every bit of airspeed out of our bird. He kept getting lower as we got closer.

I said, "Sir, the sling is almost in the trees."

Snow replied, "We may have to drag it through the trees when we get close."

That was unsettling for us all. If it got hung up bad enough, it could drag us into the ground.

When we finally made it to their location, we knew we had a small window of opportunity to release the load. We had to get it into the perimeter without killing someone with the cargo coming down and hitting them. Snow kept the airspeed as hot as he could and then flared to diminish it. He got so low in his flair that the tail rotor caused the troopers to duck. That is when I told him to jettison the load, but our forward inertia kept it going, tossing it fifty feet past the perimeter.

Sadly, we later learned that snipers cut down a retrieval party sent out for the much-needed supplies.

The CO came on the company frequency and ordered, "Halt all attempts to resupply our guys. All Bikini flights pull back from the hill and circle while the Marine jet bombers from Na Tang come in to drop five-hundred-pound bombs on NVA positions."

We saw the jets fly past the hill and the explosion of their payloads. Immediately after the blast, we listened in horror as a radio operator screamed, "Stop the fucking bombing! You just hit the motherfucking center of our perimeter; there were forty-five men in there. There's another forty or so wounded. You wiped out our command center. Most senior officers and NCOs are dead. We even have casualties at the aid station holding the wounded so whoever you are, go back to the fucking place you came from!"

"Fubar," was all I could say.

Russ echoed, "Yup! Fucked up beyond all recognition."

From dark until dawn that night, artillery flares lit up the countryside and assisted the 173rd in repelling NVA assaults. The dim light allowed us to see the massacre below. Craters were in the center of the perimeter, along with shredded and downed trees. Bodies lay everywhere, distinguishable in the pale light of the flares. We were all tired, frustrated, wounded, and angry as we flew back to Dak To that night knowing that there was nothing we could do but pray for those poor bastards.

Russ and I got tanked that night in an effort to forget about how our misjudging the speed, altitude, and time to hit the ground with the sling had cost lives. In war, the difference between success and deadly failure is often measured in the width of a human hair. You start out to save lives and something random or a consequence of a million little things add up and lead to the opposite result. For those who survive, the only way forward is to not dwell on it. For tomorrow, the hair's width may fall on your side.

The next day, our spirits were lifted as we airlifted the 4th Battalion of the 4th Infantry Division to the south side of the bloody hill. Their mission was to get to the top of Hill 875 and relieve the 1st Battalion remnants who were encircled and fighting just to survive.

All-day, the 4th Battalion was courageously fighting for every foot of the hill, but snipers in the trees made sure no helicopters would make it in to relieve the men under siege. For our boys on the ground, each passing hour brought more pain. The dead bodies lay everywhere with nowhere to stack them out of the way as more continued to pile up.

None of our ships were getting into the hill, but we were paying a high price in our attempts. Six helicopters from different companies were lost. The only chopper to make it in was a medivac ship that touched down just before dark and extracted five wounded. When the aircraft landed at Dak To, it had numerous bullet holes from small arms fire and required a new engine and repairs to the hydraulic and flight controls that were severely damaged.

Finally, just at dark, we heard the 4th Battalion had punched through and were with the remaining men of the 173rd. Their medical staff was tending the wounded as best they could. Whatever rations the 4th Battalion had in their rucksacks were given to the beleaguered men. They have been without food or water for the last fifty hours under the siege. The next morning, they would clear an LZ for our helicopters.

All our crews gathered in anticipation of finally getting to do our job and assist the suffering men. We all quietly dreaded the horror that we knew we were flying into.

One of the horrible situations that haunt me is that the KIA count got so high that the bodies were stacked in piles at the LZ. The only way we could get them out was with a sling load below the birds. By the time they got to Dak To, arms and legs were hanging out of the nets, and there was blood dripping everywhere.

Late the next day, we got orders from Operations to go to the resupply pad to get a unique load. Upon arrival, we found trucks with Miramar cans. It wasn't unusual to take hot chow to field troops, but there were unusual markings on the cans in this case. Cans were labeled turkey, potatoes, vegetables, and desserts.

I asked, "What's going on?"

A chaplain who was going out with us said, "Don't you know? It's Thanksgiving." For the first time in days, smiles broke out on the entire crew when he said, "You're taking the turkey and the rest of the traditional meal out to the troops at Hill 875." He smiled at us and asked, "Can we say a thanksgiving prayer before going out?"

"I think that would be most appropriate," Snow agreed. "Help me out of this tin can." The pilots locked down the controls, and all four of us held hands around the chaplain. I can't remember what he said, but I know how I felt—sorrow for our dead and, at the same time, thankful that we were honored to fly this meal to our brothers.

Build me a son, O Lord, who will be strong enough to know when he is weak and brave enough to face himself when he is afraid; one who will be proud and unbending in honest defeat, and humble and gentle in victory.

~ Douglas MacArthur

CHAPTER 29:
WELCOME TO THE BUCCANEERS

Have (mini)Gun Will Travel
(Anywhere in Laos, Cambodia, Vietnam)

Russ and I returned to Holloway on a Sunday morning from an overnight mission to Saigon. While getting my bag out of the Huey, I was surprised to see our platoon sergeant waiting for us.

I thought, *this can't be good,* but I was wrong.

"Did you get laid in Saigon?" the Sarge asked.

"No, Sarge. I sat in my hotel room all night missing you," I snapped back. "What kind of stupid question is that?"

"I got some good news for you, but bad for the Bell Helicopter company."

"What's the maker of the Huey got to do with me?" I asked.

"Your request for transfer came through. You're going to the gun platoon. That means my two-man wrecking crew won't be losing my helicopters anymore, and Bell won't be selling as many."

"We didn't lose the last one you gave us. Did we Russ?"

"No," the sergeant butted in before Russ could answer. "But the damn thing was in such bad shape after Dak To, our maintenance team couldn't fix it. That bird has been down at the 402nd heavy maintenance company since you left. You also got the 'smoke ship' shot to shit."

"You can't blame us for any of that," Russ protested. "We can't help it if Captain Montgomery flies us into shit or the NVA is trying to kill us."

"Go get your shit out of my platoon's hooch," the sergeant ordered, before getting serious. "You two had always come through for me when I needed help, and I wish you both good luck in the Buccaneers."

I teased, "Don't we even get a kiss goodbye, Sarge?"

Sarge blew us a kiss as he left.

We packed all our shit and were off, six buildings away, to the Buccaneer's hooch.

"Here come the Lucky Bastards," I heard as we arrived.

The Buccaneers broke out into the Vietnam war song that was popular at the time for welcoming new members like us. They sang,

"You're going home in a body bag,
doo dah, doo dah,
You're going home in a body bag,
Oh, dah doo dah day.
(Let's hear it!)
Shot between the eyes,
Shot between the thighs,
You're going home in a body bag,
Oh, dah doo dah day."

The greeting came as no surprise. When I originally went to the first flight platoon, I got razzed. In return, I helped with the newbies' 'initiation' when they arrived.

Another guy said, "You're now with the big boys, and it takes more than luck to survive here."

The platoon sergeant broke in with, "I saw these guys at Dak To, and they had no picnic, so knock it off."

The newest crew gets the oldest ship, so we got a UH-1C model Huey tail number one-four-four.

On my first day on the flight line, the most senior gunship crew chief, Jack Hill, took me under his wing. He spent all morning teaching me the differences between the slick UH-1H and a Charlie model gunship.

"All UH-1C models are underpowered when fully loaded with armament, and the engine has less than the 200 horsepower you're used to in the H model 'slicks,'" Jack explained. "This ship one-four four has a sick engine and has even less horsepower than the typical Charlie. Not only is the power plant old, but it also has the oldest guns."

Other crews walked by us on their way to the day's missions. One of them, Jones, said, "You should make some spitballs before you leave. They'll do as much good getting the gooks off your back as those old broken-down miniguns."

I was encouraged when Jack said, "Never mind them. My tour is up in three weeks. You'll get my aircraft, number one-four-zero, which is newer and has a better engine than this old dog."

Just to put the whammy on it, another guy, Schwartz, made the sign of the cross as he walked by, saying, "Bless you, my son," ...and he was Jewish!

I wondered, *what did I get myself into requesting to be assigned here?*

Jack's brief continued, "To review, they took the old B model and gave it a new rotor system for maneuverability and increased rocket runs stability. They also increased the horsepower, but they didn't put in the more powerful L-13 engine as you had on the H models, so we're underpowered with the L-11 model."

"Why didn't they put the bigger engine in them?" I asked.

"They say, Lycoming, the engine's manufacturer, couldn't produce enough of the larger engines to equip all slicks and guns. They also had a big inventory of the L-11s on hand."

"So, we get screwed because Lycoming has too many under-powered engines," I sadly surmised.

"Looks like it," Jack confirmed. "At least the Army got General Electric designers to scale down the existing 20 mm Vulcan cannon resulting in a weapon called the minigun. These electrically powered six-barrel rotating guns fire up to two thousand rounds per minute or three hundred thirty-three bullets per second. This lighter weight gun elevated the Charlie model to become a lethal assault weapon that can give ground troops closer and more accurate air support than fighters and bombers."

While Jack was with me on the aircraft, Russ took a mandatory course on the miniguns and rockets in the armament shop. Unknown to the armament folks, Russ had taken classes on the minigun system at the General Electric factory. Although he knew more about the guns than the guy conducting the course, he dutifully went along with his orientation. Later, to his credit, he admitted that they did teach him a few things to keep the guns operational long after their recommended retirement time, which unfortunately for us, was several hundred thousand rounds ago.

On my second day with the Buccaneer Gun Platoon, the pilots didn't let up on the harassment about the shit box they had to fly.

"I heard a rumor that you knew a magical way to increase power, and if any ship needed more power, it's this one," pilot McGinnis said.

"I can't turn up the power through the fuel controller because I am sure the engine's hot end has some problem that is reducing the efficiency," I explained. "Adding more heat to get more output could cause catastrophic failure."

"I guess we'll have to drag the ship down the runway until we get fast enough to generate translational lift," McGinnis added.

Mack responded, "Then we only have to worry about the translational lift phenomenon that adds lift to the rotors when flying instead of stationary in a hover."

McGinnis snickered, "Do you have a clue when that happens?"

"I'm no goddamn rookie! It's when the ship reaches sixteen to twenty-four knots, translational lift occurs, and the ship can take off overweight and underpowered," I barked. "Now, do you know the ratio of the reduction from the N2 turbine to the rotor?"

"No. What?" he shot back.

"Go look it up!" I shouted as I walk away.

I pass Russ who has been watching this whole exchange and whispers to me, "Do you know what it is?"

I wink, shake my head, and tell him, "Not a clue, but don't tell him."

When we got back to our hooch that night, we found both of our mattresses rolled up and all our personal items in boxes.

"What the hell is going on here?" Russ demanded.

Eric, a guy from Arizona, said with a straight face, "We didn't expect you guys back tonight after flying in that death trap, so we packed up your stuff, ready to be sent home."

The rest of the crewmen started laughing. I guess that was our final initiation into the Buccaneers.

The actual 'initiation' into the Buccaneers is being the low man on the totem pole in the gun platoon. Along with being assigned to the oldest bucket of bolts ship, the newest men were given the worst jobs; so for the first week, they had us flying in circles, doing convoy cover. That involved flying for hours around and around rows of trucks as they crawled along on narrow crude roads below.

At first, it would seem that the circling maneuver would make us bullet magnets, giving the VC multiple chances to perforate our ship and ourselves with every loop. I even told Russ, "Maybe hauling ass and trash wasn't so bad. At least we had work to do, putting seats up and down and loading and unloading stuff."

Then I noticed the only good part of this current duty is that nobody shot at us. When we circled over the trucks, it probably made the VC think twice about an attack not being worth the risk. It was a tradeoff for the sheer boredom of 'circle-jerking.'

Boredom is not limited to the guys in the back. The pilots would often say, out of the sheer monotony of flying circles, "Hey, Mack, let's change places so I can get some shut-eye, and the co-pilot can teach you how to fly."

"Look, Russ, I've got your future in my hands," I said while I worked the cyclic stick into a hard right turn.

"Shit! Give me a warning, will ya? I was almost asleep, and you scared the shit out of me."

One day we were listening to Radio Vietnam while I was at the controls. The DJ announced, "We just got a new song mailed to us from Cousin Brucie, a disc jockey at WABC New York. It's by The Who and it's called, 'I Can See for Miles.'"

That song seemed to make the world a little friendlier, and the Vietnamese countryside seemed more beautiful as I flew that wonderful bird. "Hey, Russ, with the massive windshields in front, the windows below, and to the side, it gives the feeling of freedom. I can see for miles and miles and miles. I feel free like a bird or Superman. Do you want to try?"

"No thanks. I'd rather sleep so I can rest up for tonight's big card game. I need to be Superman for that," he quipped.

During these monotonous flights, boredom can be a challenge for a fidgety pilot. One such pilot, Franklyn, was inspecting the cockpit and accidentally moved a mechanical lever next to his seat. Unfortunately, this was one of those 'last resort' type handles for emergencies only—it immediately released the rocket pods.

"Shit. I hate these gunships," Franklyn said as he realized he messed with the lever that dumped the left rocket pod into the jungle below.

We even safety-wired the handle so no accidental jettison would occur. Occasionally, a rocket would hang up after being fired. The burning rocket would ignite other rockets that destroyed the ship, or it could start the bullets feeding the miniguns above to cook off which spread to ignite the ammo tray inside the ship. For those reasons, pod jettison like that could be the thin edge between life and death. That mechanical lever next to his seat was to be used as a last resort in case the pilot's electrical release malfunctioned.

"Okay, smart ass," I sneered. "How are you going to write this one up in the logbook and explain to the armament shop why we returned with only one rocket pod?"

His reply was witty. "Easy, the right rocket pod wouldn't jettison."

Back at Holloway, pilots and the armament team teased Franklyn. Sergeant Jefferson, who was my first gunner, asked me, "Where did that tube drop?"

"I don't know; somewhere between here and Kontum."

His next question was further proof of my sneaking suspicion that he was always CID. "Doesn't your gunner have a gambling problem?"

"He likes to play cards," I said.

"Do you know what the VC will pay for one of those tubes?" he asked incredulously.

"No idea," I answered, nonchalantly.

Jefferson walked away and had the armament officer inspect the pod jettison system.

That finally fully convinced me that the old Sarge was Combat Investigation Division, the Army's version of the FBI.

I could tell that Franklyn was humiliated. Just to pile onto his embarrassment, a few days later, when we flew together again, I climbed out on the skid at three thousand feet. I shimmied up to his window and knocked on it, holding on with one hand. I blew him a kiss with the other hand and pointed to the jettison handle as I made a "pull it" gesture. The look on his face was priceless.

Soon after the rocket pod screwed up, we were a single ship flying a convoy cover mission between Pleiku and Kontum. As we approached our destination, the pilot, Mr. France, this time, radioed to the lead truck, "Convoy Leader One-Six this is Buc Three. My Huey is getting thirsty. We are going to Kontum to refuel."

"Roger Buc Three. We're only six miles to go. I'm sure we'll be fine," the leader retorted with the sound of grinding truck gears in the background, making it hard to hear him.

At the Kontum airport, we were half done with the fueling when the pilots motioned us to stop and get in.

When I plugged in my headset, the pilot said, "Our guys in the trucks came under attack with RPGs and small arms fire almost as soon as we'd left."

When we left the airport, there was black smoke from the general area where we had just left the group. We were at the scene in minutes. A squad of Viet Cong was on the west side of the road, and I thought we would finally get into action.

Pilot France said, "Going hot," as he turned on the armament system. Rolling in, he fired two rockets, and then Robinson, our co-pilot and minigun operator, started up the miniguns. All was good for about a minute—until the left minigun jammed.

"Shit. I told those nitwits in armament that the de-linker had too much play," Russ yelled. "Too bad, they told me, 'we ain't got another, so make do.'"

Robinson, our co-pilot, was new. He asked, "What's a de-linker?"

"Later. Right now, it's fucked. Someone has to clear it, and that someone is Mack."

I shot him a look and protested, "Why me? You want me to climb out in the airstream at three thousand feet with less than ninety days left in the country, remove that piece of shit, and give it to you? You will clear it, and I'll have to put it back on and load the gun. Who do you think I am, one of The Flying Wallendas?"

"A. It's on your side. That's why; and B, the official title for crew chief is a flight engineer. We're flying, so engineer the de-linker. Besides, what if I'm disabled or need to work on my side? You need to know how to do it."

"Can't I learn on the ground?" I whined.

"Stop being a pussy. Climb out on the gun pod and get to work."

After removing the piece of shit, I gave it to Russ, and he cleared the jam.

He handed the mechanism back to me and instructed, "After you install it, turn the barrels to load the ammo. Do not put your hand on the business end of the gun! If there's a live round left in there, it will blow your hand off."

"Thanks for the fucking advice."

On this day, despite the jam, we killed four of the Viet Cong as the rest melted into the jungle. When we got to Pleiku that night, still thinking about the jammed guns, Robinson came over to us and again asked, "So, what's a de-linker?"

Russ said with a hint of exasperation, worthy of a kindergarten teacher, "The bullets that get fed to the gun are connected to one another, forming a belt. The metal clips holding the chain of bullets together are called links. The de-linkers pull cartridges out of their clip holders and orient them into the gun's chamber three hundred times a second. Just one of those jams and the gun is fucked."

Russ turned to me and added, "I'll see what gun parts I can to get from an airman at the Pleiku Air Force base who I met at the General Electric minigun school."

The following day, he was off on his mission to restore our guns. About noon, he showed up at our ship and said, "I traded five of his used de-linkers for a ride along on our ship during a fire mission."

"We're already underpowered and overweight," I complained.

"How do you expect to add another two hundred pounds to our load?"

"That's to be worked out later. Now my goal is to take all these de-linkers and make two good ones. I'll have those guns singing like a Black church's choir before you can down two beers."

Days later, we had a fire support mission. We were on cloud nine when our guns worked perfectly, but our aircraft was still under-powered. We always caught shit about it from the pilots. I kept telling them, "There isn't much we can do to increase the power except change the engine, but if it'll make you feel better, maintenance said it passed the power check."

"How can it pass when we can barely take off?" France hissed.

"Because the geniuses do the test at night when it's cool with limited armament," I explained. "When I complain about their test method, they just tell me to bring it in during the day. Now, how can I do that when we fly every day?"

"I guess it's what Joseph Hiller wrote about. It's a catch-22."

I said irritably, "I don't know what that means. All I know is we're fucked."

"That's exactly what he meant," he confirmed.

One particular morning started as good as one could hope. Russ and I got our ship ready for a combat assault, but our spirits were quickly dampened when we saw our pilot in command for the day, Lieutenant Ford. He was always particularly nasty. Using the acronym PIC, for a pilot in command, I would add an 'R' and end with a 'K' because he was a first-class prick.

His greeting was vintage. "You goddam crew chiefs need to go back to the farm since you can't figure out how to maintain a turbine engine."

"Sorry, sir," I quickly responded. "If you want, I'll throw some screws down the inlet on your start. It will suck them in and tear up the compressor blades. Then we'll get a new engine, and you'll get disciplined for telling me to destroy a valuable piece of government equipment."

"Shut the fuck up and let's get going," was his annoyed response.

Our mission that day was to prep an LZ for a Green Beret's Hatchet Force recovery of three POWs captured earlier on a recon mission.

On our way to prep the LZ, we had a slight shower. Ford turned the switch for wipers and asked, "Why don't these goddamn wipers work?"

"I pulled the circuit breakers to give us a moment to decide if they're needed," I explained. "Because if there isn't enough water on the plexiglass, it will scratch the shit out of the windshield. When scratched, it takes us hours of work to polish them out."

"If the Army didn't want us to use the wipers, they wouldn't put them on Hueys," he scoffed. With that, he pushed in the breakers and turned on the wipers to clear just a little moisture.

I sarcastically said, "And a lieutenant knows what the Army wants, sir!"

"A lieutenant knows he outranks a spec five. Something you need to learn."

Okay, I thought, *you asked for it.*

I concocted an evil scheme. Our M-60 machine guns are suspended from the ceiling with bungee cords not mounted to rigid pole, like on slicks. A free gun gave us more range of fire. On my side, the weapon ejected spent rounds towards the front of the aircraft and the pilots. We started our prep of the LZ with Russ and me opening up with our door guns. I concentrated on where the hot spent rounds were going instead of where the bullets were hitting. It took me about fifteen seconds to find my target—Ford's back and down his neck.

He yelped and screamed, "Watch where your shells are going! They're burning the shit out of me."

"Really?" I said as smugly as possible. "I didn't realize where they were going, sir. I'm concentrating on an NVA soldier."

"You did that on purpose," he shouted.

"Prove it," was my reply.

After that, Ford was pissed but didn't dare to give me more shit. The rest of the day turned out good. The Hatchet Forces captured or killed most of an NVA company and rescued our guys.

Back at Holloway, I heard that Ford said he refused to fly with me again, and that was fine with me.

CHAPTER 30:
AND GOD GIVES US HUEYS

Firebase Omega looked more like a shantytown than a base that was the headquarters for Special Forces top-secret missions. Tents and hastily built wooden barracks with tin roofs made up the camp's structures. It is also home to the Lieutenant Rose memorial shower, but it is not the right place to catch up on sleep. On a nightly basis, "Dusters" continuously fired into the hills surrounding it.

"Why are World War II anti-aircraft guns at Omega?" I asked Sergeant Leopard of the camp's security unit.

He explained, "In true Army thinking, they began recalling the obsolete M42-40 mm self-propelled anti-aircraft gun, or "Duster" back into active service for low level anti-aircraft support that the ground-to-air missiles weren't effective for. However, the air threat posed by North Vietnam never materialized. Then, of course, we had to find something for the Duster crews to do, so they came up with using them in ground support missions and here for perimeter defense."

I complained, "Why do they need to fire most nights and interrupt our sleep?"

Sergeant Leopard said with a grin, "There's a battalion of NVA in those hills, and we just want to ruin their sleep by fucking with them using harassing fire."

I responded grumpily, "But Sarge, we can't sleep either."

The sergeant just said, "Too bad, flyboy," as he shrugged.

Later that night, we were awakened by explosions in the camp. As per our standard operating procedures, we scrambled to crew our aircraft. The engine was coming up to full RPM as the mortar rounds got closer, and it appeared that the NVA were trying to zero in on our ships.

When the engine got up to speed, our pilot, Mr. Campbell, said anxiously, "We can't run down the runway to gain translational lift. Let's hope this old bird has one last big lift in her." At that, he pulled in power. Our ship jumped off the ground like it was straight out of the factory.

Some may say that the air that night was cool and moist, which gave us the extra power, but I believe the old bird knew we needed something extra and she gave us all she had to get us out of trouble.

"I couldn't believe it," Campbell said in awe. "We only lost 100 RPMs coming out of there."

I remarked, "It's incredible what these Hueys will do when it's needed and with 86 days to DEROS."

"You think this tin can knows your Date Estimated Return from Overseas?" Russ mocked.

"It does, and it also knows you're an idiot."

An old saying goes, "Out of the frying pan and into the fire," and that's where we went. The pleasant surprise over the Huey's extraordinary power was short-lived as we flew and located the rockets and mortars positions. Buccaneer Three was the first ship to attack the target. As he started in, the whole mountain lit up with muzzle flashes and tracers. The radio crackled, "Buc Two, this is Buc Three receiving heavy 50 caliber and small arms fire. My gunner is hit and my side plate is loose from being struck by a 50-cal round."

Pilot Campbell replied, "Break right, and we'll pour ordinance under you to keep their heads down." We gave him cover with a constant minigun and rocket barrage. Then both ships got up to altitude and called for bomber support.

Buc Three headed to Pleiku to assess his damage and get his gunner looked at by the medics. We circled for a while to observe napalm and cluster bombs light up the jungle. Back at Omega, we refueled and rearmed. Being the only gunship left on the mission made us vulnerable, but the rest of the night was calm; even the Dusters gave us a break.

The memories and surprise over the power we experienced during takeoff and the fact that all armament systems worked made us proud of the hard work we had put into that old lady of the sky, tail number one-four-four. I don't know who the chief designer of the Huey was, but I believe he must have had long hair, a beard, and wore sandals. That night's sleep finally brought back sweet dreams of home.

That wasn't the only time old one-four-four proved Russ wrong, and that she had a heart.

Finally, a USO show with authentic American entertainers and girls was coming to Holloway. The anticipation and excitement were almost unbearable. On the day of the show, we completed our last fire missions and headed home in time to make the event.

In route, the company frequency called, "Buccaneer Four, this is Bikini Ops."

McGuire replied. "Bikini Ops, go."

"Oh shit, here comes a fucking," Russ said.

Then came the bad news, which interrupted him, "Buc Four, this is Bikini Operations. Your team is to refuel and rearm at Kontum, then go to Ben Hut Special Forces Camp. Recon units have located a buildup of NVA close by, and they expect trouble tonight."

"Shit, you're right, Russ," I said with disgust. "The Army even gets to fuck us out of a bit of entertainment. I bet all the REMFs will enjoy it, though."

We all lamented that we wanted to see the only USO show to come to our camp; even the pilot weighed in, "I guess duty calls."

Nobody could believe it when Russ and I showed up at the show.

Our platoon sergeant was the first to quiz us. "I thought you guys got screwed with a mission tonight. How are you here?"

"I swear on everything I hold holy that this is true, Sarg," I said with my hand raised. "Just after McGuire accepted the mission, the EGT gauge started to climb. When it approached the yellow warning line, McGuire reported our situation with the exhaust temperature to base ops and reported we would not accept the mission."

"What did ops tell you?"

"What could they say? We can't fly missions in an unsafe bird, but the operations officer was upset and threatened they will check with maintenance in the morning. If we're goldbricking, we'll fly convoy cover for a month."

Sarge warned, "I hope maintenance finds something, for your sake."

After the show, I went to the maintenance hangar to make sure they found something wrong and wrote the problem up.

I asked the maintenance sergeant on duty, "What did you find the problem is with one-four-four?"

"Let's see," he said as he looked at the work order. "You had a leaking nose seal on the engine. That oil leaked into the inlet and caked on the compressor blades. That restricted airflow caused the EGT problem. We got it fixed and cleaned the engine. Your bird did you a favor."

"Huey's always come through when you need them."

The following day, we were in the air with the engine repairs completed and sweet memories of beautiful women and talented American entertainers. Thanks to chopper one-four-four.

As promised, senior gunship crew chief Ron Hill went home less than a month later, and we got a super bird number one-four-zero.

During the set-up of our new ship, I looked at the logbook and told Russ, "Amazing! This bird has only three hundred hours on it."

"The paint isn't even worn off the ammo cans yet," Russ said as he grinned. "Now we can bring hell on the NVA, which was why we came to the gun platoon."

"And avenge Bob's death," I added.

"If you say so, Mack," he said as he shrugged.

Over the next few weeks, we supported the 4th Infantry. We prepped LZs and drove the enemy off our guys. It was like going from the old farm truck to a Corvette.

In mid-December, Captain Fisk, our platoon leader, came to our ship and said, "Our mission is to fly night hawk tonight."

I asked, "What is night hawk?"

"It is where we fly low and slow with all our lights on after dark around Pleiku. Buc Two will fly high behind us with no lights. We hope to draw fire, and then Buc Two has them."

Russ said hesitantly, "Sounds like we're the bait."

"That's exactly what we are," the captain confirmed.

"When I go fishing in Florida and catch a fish, I often lose the bait," Russ lamented.

"Let's make sure that does not happen tonight," Fisk said.

As we flew around the four bases in Pleiku, we decided to make one last circle around our home Holloway. I was half asleep when I heard a pop, pop, pop. That woke me up. I saw we were 50 meters from the base expansion construction site. A red stream of tracers and the glow of several burning rocket propellants suddenly appeared over us and explosions behind us as our sister ship flying dark unloaded a firestorm on the bastards that shot at us.

I snapped, "They won't make that mistake again. It looks like Buc Two has them headed to gook heaven."

When Russ went on R&R to Thailand, Jeff Gordon was assigned to take his place. Now Jeff was different and was on the express train to Crazy Town. He wore rose-colored glasses, smoked pot every night, painted his living area completely black, and listened to deep, dark, depressing music.

One morning, the CO saw him in his rose-colored glasses and ordered him, "Take the damned things off!"

Jeff complied, looked around without the benefit of a rose-colored world, and said, "Isn't reality a bummer, sir?"

I thought the CO was going to lose his mind, but we were short of gunners and Jeff knew his business around the armament systems, so all he got was a chewing out by a man who had a Ph.D. in ass-chewing. Growing up around farmhands and loggers, I had a pretty good grasp of our language's profanity side, but that CO used phrases I had never heard before. He yelled about jumping mothers, goats, asses of the devil, and many other unforgettable phrases.

One gunship team and a flair ship were always on duty. Crews would rotate for a day on duty every two weeks. At night, we slept in a room at the bottom of the control tower. The ships were always ready to go at a moment's notice.

One night at 10 p.m., Campbell answered the ringing phone and quickly proclaimed, "Let's go." Jeff was late getting to the ship, so I untied the rotor blade, and the engine was already winding up when Jeff got in his seat.

As we cleared our camp, the MPs radioed, "We have VC in control of Sin City."

I immediately started pleading, "We can't wipe out Sin City."

Sin City was built with the Army's approval just north of the 4th Infantry base camp and east of Holloway. It was a place where the troops around Pleiku could "enjoy themselves" safely.

The last thing we wanted was to see Sin City destroyed, so I pressed my mic button and said, "Sir, I'm sure the MPs can handle the situation with our door gun or, at the most, minigun support. We definitely don't need rockets."

The MPs overruled my suggestion when they radioed, "Buc Three, this is Mike Papa One-Two. We need everything you got on the main building. They have us pinned down. We need those fuckers off our back."

"Mike Papa One-Two, we're going hot."

I noticed that Jeff wasn't firing his door gun. When I looked over at him, he was waving his hands in the air and screaming something.

I keyed the mic and asked impatiently, "Are you all right, Jeff?"

"Wow! Man! Look at those beautiful tracers," he replied. "They look like a red snake moving through the grass."

After that declaration, I went over to him, took over his gun, and said, "Jeff, just sit there and enjoy the view, man."

The view, in my opinion, was terrible. When we left Sin City, buildings were either blown up or on fire. I was in mourning for days.

When we landed, Lieutenant Kim, the camp's provost marshal ordered Jeff to follow him, and I never saw poor Jeff again. His room got cleared of personal items before I got back to the hooch in the morning.

CHAPTER 31:
THE AIR SHOW

There was a detachment of MPs stationed at Holloway. They were always on our case, making remarks about what a bunch of pussies we were in our whirlybirds. Of course, they got it back from us in the form of comments about the lack of IQ it takes to guard a gate or drive a jeep in front of a convoy.

When Russ got back from Thailand, I had to know about his experiences in the sex capital of the world. We went to the club for a few drinks and listened to his tales. At about 10:00 that night, some of our fellow company members were leaving.

"Do you guys want to play cards?" Luke asked.

Russ immediately said, "Yes."

About halfway back to the hooch, I heard, "Let's teach those white flyboys what tough guys are like." Almost immediately, a group of black MPs jumped us. When the skirmish was over, I must admit that they had gotten the best of us. One sucker punch caught me in the face and opened a cut below my mouth that required stitches. The others in my group had bumps, bruises, and a black eye or two. I guess I got the worst of it, and I went to the dispensary.

When I got back to our company area after getting my mouth stitched up, the rest of our 'fight club' had assembled in a hooch next to mine. "What happened to you?" Luke asked.

"Just got a few stitches. I'm okay."

Then the conversation turned racial. The N-word freely flowed into the group's angry chatter. Back home, racial division and riots dominated the news, pushing the other war, ours, off the front pages. Race issues were in the air.

After about fifteen minutes, Josh, the cook, a black friend from my hooch, came in and asked, "Have you heard enough of this shit?"

My answer was, "Yes, I sure have," and I left with him.

On our walk home, we stopped, and I said, "You know I hate that kind of talk."

"Yes, I know," he said. "But it always boils down to hate and lumping all us blacks together when a few assholes fuck up, but when a white guy fucks up, he's the only one that's an asshole."

"You know, in New Hampshire, where I'm from, there are very few blacks in the whole state, none in my town or the surrounding area, but still, people needed a group to blame for the ills of society, so the old New Englanders decided to hate Finns, like me."

"That's a new one on me," Josh said with surprise.

I continued to complain, "It's the same old prejudice. They say we are uneducated, lazy, have too many kids, and are just not ready for their society yet." I stopped and turned to Josh, "Sound familiar?"

"Yes, but you don't wear the Finnish flag on you everywhere you go, and it's a sure bet, outside of your town, most guys don't even know what a Finn is," Josh replied.

"True," I agreed.

He touched his fingers to his ebony cheek, "We take this wherever we go."

"You're right," I said as I pointed at him.

"You can relate but you can't equate," he added as he pointed back at me.

"Wow. That was deep," I told him, a bit taken aback by it.

"Ain't it though? I heard some white minister tell us that in church once. It was the first church to have a mixed mass down the delta, where I came from."

"Josh, there's one thing I know, for sure."

"What's that, you lazy, dumb Finn?"

"Very funny. Even though all those white guys in the club who were trying to blame someone other than themselves were being assholes, there is one thing I guarantee you, and I see this all the time. When a black soldier is in a tight spot with the enemy, every one of those assholes will put everything on the line to save him."

Josh thought for a second, "I guess it takes a war to erase hate. Ain't that fucked up?"

"I see it more like families. You can hate and fight amongst each other, but let an outsider fuck with your brother, and there will be trouble."

I turned towards the hooch, "Let's go to my room and get a beer. This shit is getting too deep for a couple of dumb enlisted men."

When we arrived at the flight line the next morning, our pilots had already been there and pre-flighted the ships. Buc platoon leader Captain Fisk said, "We heard what happened, and it's time for a little payback. I have a plan to get even with those MP bastards."

I swear he sounded like General Patton, laying out the battle plan to defeat Romel, as he explained his plan of what we would do. He started with, "I know a convoy left about a half-hour ago, and the MPs from last night are escorting them. It's time that everyone learns that nobody fucks with my men without getting a little payback. Russ, are you still the best shot in the platoon?"

"Yup," we all replied in unison.

"Good," he said. "I'll be with you in Mack's ship. Mr. Evans, you're in the hog. Make sure you have all forty-eight rockets loaded."

After takeoff, we headed towards Kontum. About twenty miles out of Pleiku, we caught up with the convoy. Two MP jeeps were in the lead of a group of trucks and three in the rear.

Fisk radioed, "Okay. Operation Payback is on," as he slowed us down to forty knots. Russ started firing his door gun. Initially, the bullets hit fifty feet from the convoy. Then he carefully walked in the rounds to take out the tires on the lead two jeeps. Simultaneously, Evans fired a salvo consisting of all his forty-eight rockets directly in front of the convoy.

The captain said, "That hole in the road will require the MPs to bust their asses shoveling for hours before they can proceed."

Fisk flew down the other side of the convoy as an encore, firing both rockets and miniguns—leveling a grove of trees. He said, "I guess that will show them who's their momma now."

When we returned to base, the CQ ran up to Captain Fisk and said, "The boss wants all involved in this morning's mission on the military police's convoy in his office—now—and he isn't in a good mood."

When we entered the commanding officer's outer room, I could see two MP sergeants. I thought, *Oh Shit!*, and assumed that they were here to arrest us. Simultaneously, there was one hell of a lot of yelling going on in the CO's office, and our ass-chewer-in-charge was doing all the hollering.

I heard him say, "You lost four tires and a little work, but I've got two men off flight status because of their injuries." That wasn't the whole truth, but it made a good story.

The CO continued, "Do you know how much the Army has invested in those men? Well, I can tell you that it's a hell of a lot more than four goddam tires."

Then came his favorite line. "Do you realize that if those men aren't flying, other men are dying? Not like your Neanderthals who can't keep a fucking VC spy off our camp. Then your men are so fucking blind they can't see them mapping out where to send their mortars so, at night, they blow up our goddam ammo bunker. Captain, you have a detachment of fifty men. I have a company of two hundred and fifty. If your men ever ambush my men again, I will get all my men out of bed and march them into your little fucking area in ranks. Then we'll see how tough your guys are. Oh, and if you report this to higher headquarters, I will fuck you until you fall in love with me. Now, get the fuck out of here."

Then I heard, "Yes, sir."

Next, we heard, "Send my fucking idiots in here."

My stomach was a little queasy as I remembered how the CO chewed out Jeff for just wearing rose-colored glasses. *Christ,* I thought, *what does he have in store for us?* We entered the office and saluted.

Captain Fisk started, "Sir, these men were under my orders, so they have no responsibility for what happened."

The CO shot back, "I don't give a fuck who's responsible or not! The next time someone fucks with our men, I want you to come to me, and we'll do more than put on an airshow for the bastards. Got that?"

Fisk answered, "Yes, sir,

The CO then ordered, "Then get the fuck out of my office."

There is a saying, "What's the difference between the Boy Scouts and the Army?" The answer is, "The Boy Scouts have adult leaders." I think Captains Montgomery, Fisk, and Major Burk have proved in their actions that they're more than Boy Scout leaders.

CHAPTER 32:
RUSS'S TALL TALE

Russ and I were washing our ship one day after a morning mission when Operations told us the 4th Division had a unit requesting support on insertion near a known VC village. We rinsed off what we started and readied the aircraft for the mission. Captain Fisk and our co-pilot Mr. Howell went over the aircraft, performing their prefight.

After rushing to get ready, we did what the Army is famous for, hurry up and wait. Several hours went by, and finally, the CO said, "Slicks will launch in thirty minutes to pick up the infantry unit, and you guys will crank out thirty minutes after them in time to meet the troop carriers on the way to the LZ."

Captain Fisk, our platoon leader that day, made us the lead ship with Buc Three flying as our wingman. We married up with the Bikini Flight about ten minutes from the LZ.

Fisk radioed instructions to Buc Three. "Buc Three, this is lead. I'll hit the Landing Zone, and you take care of the tree line in the left."

"Buc Three, wilco."

As we approached the village, I couldn't see how they needed an infantry platoon and us to subdue a town that small. It was just eight buildings made of bamboo with thatched roofs of clay, straw, and palm leaves. A few farm animals wandered around, and the village sat on the side of rice paddies.

"Captain, why do we need so much firepower for such a small village?" I asked. "Our landing prep is going to destroy their crops."

"I don't know. I'm like you, and I just do as I'm told."

Rockets have fins that open after launch, causing them to spin. This spinning action arms the warhead and stabilizes their flight to the target. Occasionally, the fins got bent, usually from someone dropping the rocket, which caused their flight path to become erratic.

When Captain Fisk fired the first rocket, to clear a landing zone, it came out of the tube, took a sharp right, and headed towards the slicks. In our headsets, I heard all of us say a chorus of, "Shhhhit!"

Fisk radioed, "Heads up Bikini. Errant rocket coming at you."

Midway through Fisk's radio message, the rocket passed in front of the lead slick in the formation.

"Buc Six, this is Bikini Two-Four. Your aim seems a little off this morning. For that, you're paying the laundry bill for our crew's pants and buying tonight's bar bill at the club."

Fisk's response was two numbers: "Ten-Four." What else could he say?

The infantry took an hour to sweep the village, looking for weapons and VC sympathizers. Finding none, they called us back to extract them and bring them back to base camp.

As it looked from the air, the hamlet was a farming community, so we ruined an entire village's yearly income and most likely turned the residents into VC sympathizers for nothing. FUBAR was all I could think of.

Two days later, the 4th Infantry had a different unit under attack, and we were assigned with Buccaneer Three to help them out. We never got to make a gun run. As usual, the NVA decided to leave once we arrived. Southerland was our pilot that day and talked with the infantry platoon leader. We were expecting the standard thanks of, 'We'll call again when we need a little help.'

Instead, we got, "Buccaneer Two, this is Alpha Charlie Six. We have two severely wounded members down here. Can you get them to the evac hospital?"

"As you know, we are a gunship and have a full load of armament and about seven hundred pounds of fuel," Southerland explained. "With that much weight, we wouldn't be able to take off from that small location. I will call for a Medivac."

Southerland radioed the Medivac's unit operations, and they told him it would be at least an hour before they could get a chopper to the ground unit's location. He then called on the emergency frequency, "This is Buccaneer Two, north of the Fire Base Charlie, requesting any aircraft available in the area for an emergency Medivac."

Almost immediately, a Chinook responded, "Buccaneer Two, this is Big Windy Two-One. We're about forty-five minutes away and can handle the job."

That prompted several conversations between Big Windy, Southerland, and Alpha Charlie Six. It was determined that the delay—the time it would take Big Windy to get to the LZ, coupled with the thirty-minute flight to the closest hospital—would result in certain death for the soldiers.

Our company frequency squealed and then said, "Buc Two, this is Buc Three. We've been ordered to Dak To to join Buc Six. He wants us to make a heavy fire team out of his two ships. Good luck."

"Buc Three, thanks. See you at home," Southerland responded. He then asked us, "Any ideas, boys?"

"We now have six hundred and fifty pounds of fuel," I said. "If we dropped the rocket pods and throw out all the ammo, I think we'll be light enough to do a hovering 50-foot vertical takeoff, but that's just Hillbilly ciphering. There are too many goddamn variables to be sure."

"If we can't get out of the LZ, we'll have to sit and burn fuel until we're light enough," Southerland said. "We may have to burn so much that what is left is no guarantee we'll have enough JP4 left to get to a refueling station, or if the engine loses too much power on takeoff, we could end up in the trees, so if anyone has any reservations for trying Mack's stupid plan, let me know now."

He looked at his co-pilot Roberts and said, "You don't get a vote."

Russ and I agreed we had to try.

Southerland radioed, "Alpha Charlie Six, this is Buc Two."

"Go Buc Two."

"Alpha Charlie Six, we're going to try something that's not exactly in our flight manual. We're coming in for your wounded. We're presently too heavy to take off."

"Buc Two, then how the hell is that going to help?"

"We are going to try to get our Huey light enough to get out of that hell hole. I'll jettison our rockets with pods, and the crew will dump out the minigun ammo. There are two things I need from you. First, when we leave, destroy the pods, rockets, and ammo that your men can't use. At all costs, they cannot fall into enemy hands."

"Ten-four. What is the second thing?"

"When we're hovering out of the LZ, stay the fuck out of the way. If we don't have the power to make it, we may come back in a hurry, and a Huey in a crash throws shit everywhere."

"Roger that."

"There is a mathematical equation that all takeoffs have to equal landings," said Roberts. "The only variable is the quality of the landing."

Southerland's reply was a gem. "Do what co-pilots are supposed to do. Sit there and shut the fuck up. When I want your advice," Southerland paused, "... I can't think of a fucking reason for wanting anything from you but to tell me my rotor RPMs when we come out of that piece of shit hole in the trees."

Coming to a hover over the LZ, we started down in a fifty-foot hovering descent.

Roberts asked, "You want me to read Rotor Speed's now?"

"Yes, if you please."

As we descended, Roberts reads, "Sixty-six hundred, sixty-five hundred," and finally, when we landed, he said, "That wasn't a bad drop. The lowest was 64-50."

"How the fuck did you get through flight school?" Southerland barked. "It takes less power to descend than to ascend. Do you understand the word 'ascend'? It means go up."

Through the whole conversation between Southerland and Roberts, I knew to keep my mouth shut, and out of character, so did Russ. Southerland jettisoned the rocket pods while Russ and I stripped all nonessentials out of the ship. We started with ammo from both miniguns and the door guns, smoke grenades, toolbox, two cases of C-rations, even all four sets of chicken plates while the grunts loaded the patients. They were in bad shape but still alert. Russ and the unit's medic talked for a minute or two, and then we were ready.

Southerland announced, "I'm not doing a hover check. It will just scare us." Then he told Roberts, "Give me the rotor speed readouts every ten seconds; less if needed."

Next, he asked us, "Ready, boys?"

"I hope so," I said softly.

We started our fifty-foot climb to clear the trees and debris while the co-pilot called off the RPMs. Roberts started with "sixty-six hundred." When we were only at ten feet, he said, "sixty-five hundred." When we had another fifteen feet to go, I heard "64-50." I knew we couldn't go much lower. When I heard him say "sixty-four hundred," the chopper's nose started to drift right—a sign the tail rotor was losing its tug of war with the main rotor's torque. The treetops were above the main rotor when Southerland nosed it over to get airspeed. The skids got dragged through the trees, but we were flying.

The co-pilot said, "I couldn't believe it before translational lift occurred. Something caused our RPM to come back to sixty-five hundred."

I once saw a picture of a famous painting by Michelangelo of God touching man in the Sistine Chapel, but this one had God's finger touching a Huey. I am a true believer that there was divine intervention in the design of this marvelous helicopter again.

After we were out of danger of crashing, I took my eyes off the engine instruments and saw Russ trying to comfort our patient. One was in bad shape; either a mortar or hand grenade went off close to him. He had multiple wounds all over his body. The unit's medic must have pumped him full of morphine because his eyes were open, but he was not flailing in pain and looked like he was in another world. The other had a bad leg wound, but a tourniquet had stopped the bleeding.

After dropping off our patients, we got a lot of attention back at Holloway. The armament and fueling teams asked why we didn't have rocket pods, saw blood on the floor with no one wounded, and asked us where our chicken plates were.

Now, Russ couldn't miss a chance of making up a good war story, even if the truth was good enough.

He said, "We were coming down the highway between Dak To and the border and caught an NVA truck convoy in the open. After our pilots expended all their rockets and minigun ammo, wiping out four trucks, we didn't stop there. Mr. Southerland used the rocket pods as bombs, dropped them right in the back of one of the trucks and killed about twenty-five NVA."

Dick, the fuel man, asked, "Where're your chicken plates?"

Again, not missing a beat, Russ said, "Not being satisfied, he saw a group of NVA soldiers huddled on the side of the road. Southerland made another low pass, and we dropped our chicken plates right on them, killing a couple more."

Dick said, "Yeah right. Another thing, nobody is wounded, so where did the blood come from?"

Russ was really on his game and explained, "We got so close to one truck. When a pair of rockets hit it, body parts were all over the place. Blood flew up everywhere, and some splashed into the ship. We may get silver stars for this mission. We got over forty confirmed kills with just one gunship."

At that, Southerland added, "Or court-martialed for losing all that equipment we threw out."

In late December, our assignment was Forward Operating Base Two, and things seemed to be heating up. We did insertions and extractions every day. During most extractions, the ground fire was so intense that we needed to call in fighter jets to keep the enemy at bay while the slicks took out the teams. Insertions were also met by heavier than usual resistance. It was so bad that instead of having ten to sixteen teams in the bush, we had only three because of the increase in the enemy's intense ground fire.

On the third day, we were in the launch tent when we heard, "Dak To, this is Buccaneer Two. I am declaring an emergency!"

"Buc Two, what's your emergency?"

"We have taken an incendiary round in the ammo trays, and bullets are cooking off in the cabin. I just had to duck as a red-hot shell hit the windshield and landed in my lap. Fuck!" he yelled. "It's burning the shit out of my leg. Fire extinguishers aren't stopping it. I need to land now. There's no open LZ between us. We are five minutes out!"

"Buc Two, we have no crash rescue here, so we are sending a truck out with the fire extinguishers from the fueling station. Land beside them."

"Wilco, here's hoping we make it," he said calmly as we heard bullet fragments pelting his armored pilot's seat.

On the ground, we gathered the extinguishers and rushed to the runway. The first I saw of Buc Two was a smoke stream about two miles away. At about a mile, I saw what looked like fireworks flying out of the side doors. It didn't look good for their crew chief Schwartz or his gunner stuck in the back amidst that shit. The Huey came in fast and flared hard to stop in front of us. Others used the extinguishers, and I opened the co-pilot's door. To my surprise, I found Schwartz, the gunner, and the second pilot squashed in, shielded by the co-pilot's armor-plated seat. I helped them out and noticed how they could all fit into such a small space—because Schwartz had the brilliant idea to remove the cyclic stick.

After the fire was out, we assessed the crew. All had minor burns, but they were remarkably in good shape—no wounds from shrapnel or fragments.

I looked at Schwartz and said, "Quick thinking, taking out that stick to make room for all three of you."

His answer surprised me. "Fuck you! Fuck that bird and fuck the Army. I'm taking eight days off for Chanukah."

"Eight days off for your Jewish holiday," I said nodding. "And then you'll be off for the Christmas ceasefire because we won't be flying."

"Yes, that's absolutely right. If you don't like it, take it up with God. He's the one who set the holiday calendar."

"Hey, Schwartz," I called out.

"What now?" he asked, unamused.

"How do I become a Jew?" I joked.

Schwartz picked up his knife and said, "Pull your pants down and come here, you fucker."

"No thanks, Schwartz," I chuckled as I shook my head. "I'll see you after Christmas."

Days later, we were sent back to Holloway for the Christmas ceasefire, leaving behind only one fire team from the 189th.

CHAPTER 33:
TET: AMERICA'S MONGOOSE

January 1968

Since Susan had dumped me, Joline, a red-headed neighbor back home, started writing to me several times a week. That brought back beautiful dreams of her and home. Just before I got to the good part of my dream in the early morning of January 30, 1968, I was interrupted again—this time, not by the CQ but by the sound of small arms, fire, and explosions.

"What the fuck is that?" Schwartz shouted. "I thought we had a ceasefire during Tet."

Shaking the cobwebs out, I said, "Schwartz, I guess God thinks you've had enough of a holiday break."

Our Platoon Sergeant Eaton ran into the hooch and ordered everyone, "Get to your ships. Don't bother with pre-flights. Just get in the air ASAP. We're under a human wave attack."

"Fuck me. With thirty-two days left in this stupid war, they have to start this shit," I cursed.

When we arrived at the flight line, we found a total monkey fuck. Nobody knew which pilots got assigned to which aircraft.

Pilot Martinez decided my ship was going to be his. He was already strapping in and shouting, "Untie the damned blades and find me a co-pilot."

I looked around and saw a pilot I didn't know behind the revetment next to us. He looked like he didn't know what to do. I ran up to him and said, "We need a co-pilot, and we're ready to go now."

He started to protest, but I interrupted him and shouted, "Now!"

He reluctantly agreed, and we ran to the ship. I noticed that he looked awkward while getting into the co-pilot's seat. I thought nothing of it because I barely had time to get into my place when Martinez shouted, "Clear me out, guys."

As we backed out, another gunship was hovering towards the runway.

Martinez radioed, "Buccaneer approaching runway, this is Buc Four. We're coming out now, and we'll be your wingman."

"Buc Four, this is Buc Six. Roger. We're to give support to the eastside of the Air Force base that is under a massive attack."

On climb-out, I couldn't believe what I saw. Through the dim light of flares, a wave of over two hundred NVA and Viet Cong forces were attacking the Air Force base with more troops coming about a mile behind.

"Buc Four, this is Buc Six. We're going hot on the front of the line. Clean up after me."

"Buc Four, Roger."

Buc Six had scores of confirmed kills on his pass. Rodriguez went hot with the rockets. our co-pilot finally got his shit together and said, "I am not a gun pilot but am in the second lift platoon."

"Just aim through the sight and pull the trigger," Martinez said. "I'll do the rest."

He soon had reasonable control of the miniguns. Then, Russ and I opened up with our door guns. On our first gun run, enemy troops dropped like the hay falls when we mowed the fields at home.

I said to myself as a dozen or more fell in front of my M60, *That's for Bob, you bastards.*

I told Russ, "If you intend to stencil confirmed kills on the outside of the ship after this engagement, you won't have enough room for them all."

"Then I'll stencil the inside," he quipped.

Flames illuminated the clouds throughout the night, creating an eerie glow. Flares hung in the sky, and helicopter gunships crossed back and forth, firing red streams of tracers into attacking enemies coming from everywhere. The battle was fully engaged. We checked our humanity at the door and killed, killed in wholesale numbers. They kept coming; it was almost like they were offering themselves up to our gunsights. Why would they continue? We had the high ground. We fired down with red hot barrels while they struggled to look up and plink a round or two, and yet they kept coming, feeding our adrenalin, satiating a bloodthirst that arose in us. We had become death.

We rearmed two to three times an hour for the rest of the night and the entire next day. Every available man was helping with the rearming. Mountains of empty rocket boxes and ammo cans started accumulating. At Bikini Beach, two ships could rearm at a time. As one fire team left, another would be waiting its turn to rearm.

We were all exhausted, and the confusion with noise was overwhelming. On one takeoff after rearming and refueling, our pilot, who had only two hours of sleep in a day and a half, keyed his mic and said, "Going hot," meaning he was activating the armament system. As soon as the words were out of his mouth, a rocket fired.

Martinez apologized, "Sorry, guys. My hand had been resting on the launch button and I'm practically brain dead from lack of sleep. I accidentally launched that rocket."

We cringed as it went straight into the 189th's living area and destroyed one of the hooches. Luckily, everyone was on duty that night, and nobody was home. After that incident, we were all given those Superman pills that woke us up but made me jittery.

"In the hippy world, these pills are called black beauties," Russ said.

"How would you know about the hippy world?" I sneered.

"I have a girlfriend who is part of that culture."

"How on God's green earth does a hillbilly like you have a hippy girlfriend?"

Russ answered proudly, "Free love."

The fighting continued and moved into Pleiku City, where the 4th Infantry elements suddenly found themselves fighting house to house as their fathers had done in World War II. During this fighting, our fire team got assigned to support the clearing of the city. It wasn't long before the town was ablaze, and the streets out of town filled with refugees.

One squad got pinned down in a dead-end alley where VC fire was coming from a large, fortified house. As we were heading into town for another run, the pinned-down soldiers radioed for help. Our lead ship that day was a forty-eight-rocket carrier called the hog. On the first gun run, the hog fired all its rockets and destroyed half the house.

I pointed to the house and said, "Look! That house is half gone with just one swipe of the rocket ship."

Martinez said, "Let's take the rest of the bastards out."

Our miniguns and rockets smashed the remainder of the VC stronghold, allowing the men to fight their way out of the encirclement and evacuate their dead and wounded.

All day long, civilians had been darting from their homes and running from the fighting. An alert officer pointed out that there were many young men, all dressed in black pants and white shirts, walking among the refugees. One platoon leader heard this and reported finding discarded AK-47 weapons abandoned as they went house to house. Major Bell, the officer in charge of the units in the city, put the two pieces of information together and ordered all men dressed in black pants and white shirts, detained. Later, we found out that they had captured a record number of VCs traveling with groups of refugees trying to flee the oncoming American troops.

That night, we teamed with a grenade launching gunship called a frog. We were dispatched to Kontum because our troops had been under massive mortar attacks since the offensive started. We refueled and went on a search for the mortar position. Simultaneously, a solid stream of red tracers came from the sky, bringing hell on earth to someone.

"Looks like Puff the Magic Dragon is giving someone hell," Martinez said. He then looked at his co-pilot and said, "Co-pilot, we've been flying together since the start of this shit, and I don't even know your name."

"Nash. Fred Nash, sir," the co-pilot responded. "What is 'Puff the Magic Dragon?'"

"Mr. Nash, Puff the Magic Dragon is our name for the Douglas AC-47 gunships that carry prodigious firepower and are terrifying to the VC."

Martinez asked, "So, what do you think of being a gunship pilot?"

"I don't think I want to leave," Nash said.

"I guess if you're baptized under fire and can take it, you should move into my quarters," added Martinez. "We have a spare bunk."

"What the fuck do I get?" Russ demanded. "I've been baptized so many times, I think I drowned two months ago."

"That's my crybaby gunner, Mr. Nash," I explained. "He's always complaining. First, the weather, then the smoke ship, then a little fight in a rice paddy, and then FOB-2. What next?"

"I'm cool now," Russ said. "Because our bad luck charm, Captain Montgomery, ain't around us today."

By midnight, I had had it and was ready to pass out as soon as we could get to the base. Then I looked out and saw a steady stream of red tracers coming in our direction. I screamed into my mic, "Puffs shooting around us!"

"Looks like Puff is right on top of us," Nash announced.

Martinez immediately radioed, "This is Buccaneer Four on guard attention. Puff operating Northwest of Kontum. Ceasefire, ceasefire. We are in your line of fire."

The tracers stopped, and Puff responded, "Sorry, guys."

"Sorry! What the fuck is that?" I said with disgust. "The fucker could have cut us in half."

"I guess he didn't get the memo of where we were," Martinez replied plainly.

"No shit," Russ added.

Operations radioed, "The mortar attack on Kontum has stopped. We heard about the Puff incident. Go get some sack time."

"Looks like we've been on the clock for almost thirty-six hours," Martinez said. "We need a little break."

We shut down, refueled, and stretched out for a few hours of sleep.

At dawn, the mortar attack started up again. We were in the air in minutes. While still half-asleep, Martinez instructed us to take our Superman pills. Our assignment was to search for the mortar position hitting Kontum.

After about an hour in the air, Russ said as he pointed, "Look. There it is in the middle of that open field at two o'clock."

The lead ship called for a fighter bomber.

Amazingly, within ten minutes, we heard, "Buccaneer Three, this is Chico Two-One. We're a pair of F-4s, ready for business. Please mark the target, and we'll handle the rest."

Our lead ship radioed, "Buc Four, this is Buc Three."

"Buc Three, go."

"Buc Four, we will run from the north to the south and mark the target with smoke grenades. Cover us."

As we began our approach to drop smoke for the fighters, I told Russ, "I can't see the target." Russ kept pointing at where it was, but I couldn't locate it.

When we got to within one mile at an altitude of five hundred feet, I told Russ, "Switch places with me since you know where the target is, and I don't."

As we were switching places, the front windshield exploded. Plexiglass pieces flew everywhere, and the bullet exited just above Russ's head. His eyes were as wide as Marty Feldman's and stared into the 50-caliber hole over him.

"I got pieces of plexiglass in my eyes and can't see," Pilot Martinez yelled out.

"Wash it out with your canteen water," the co-pilot said. "I can take care of the ship."

At the same time, I heard that tap dancing sound as numerous rounds hit our ship. I saw that the lead ship was catching hell and even had its rocket pod shot off. It managed to clear the enemy's position but was still flying. Then the enemy concentrated on us. We started taking the brunt of the fire. As Russ let the smoke canister go, I found my leg on the ceiling. For a split second, I thought, *how odd*, but then the pain started in my upper leg muscle. I grabbed my leg and saw blood coming out of my boot.

I reported, "I'm hit!" By then, we had passed through the ground fire and were in the clear. Russ rushed over to see where they got me.

I told him, "My ankle."

"Then why are you holding your upper leg?"

"Never mind; look at my ankle." The hillbilly Russ pulled out what looked like a bowie knife. "What are you going to do with that? Cut off my leg?" I shouted at him.

"Shut the fuck up," he said irritably.

He cut the boot laces, pulled off the boot, and then the sock. He opened the first aid kit and took out a bandage that could have covered my head.

"Look, you idiot. It's a bullet, not an artillery wound," I yelled.

He bandaged the ankle with gauze and wrapped it.

I told him, "My upper leg hurts worse than the wound. I think the impact of the bullet is what knocked my leg to the ceiling. That got my leg muscles stretched, and it hurts like hell."

"Now, who's the baby?" Russ said.

"Okay," I said. "How are you going to blame this one on Montgomery?"

"I mentioned his name," Russ said. "That is what brought in the bad juju."

On the way back to the 71st evac hospital, I told Russ, "Because we switched places, and I got shot, it means I took a bullet for you, and you owe me."

We landed at the medivac pad at Pleiku Air Force Base. I got out and blew a kiss to Russ and shouted, "You owe me, and don't you forget it."

Then I took a last look at my sweet bird. It was leaking oil and had so many bullet holes in it that a slice of Swiss cheese would have been jealous.

My leg muscles started hurting worse than ever as I limped toward a medical building next to the medivac pad. When I entered the building, I was greeted by an Air Force sergeant dressed in clean-starched fatigues. Quite a contrast to me, who hadn't showered or changed clothes for days.

The sergeant looked at me and scoffed, "What's your problem?"

"I need to see a doctor," I said.

He sarcastically retorted, "Sick call is over. You need to go down two blocks to the hospital."

"So, how am I going to get there?" I asked with frustration.

With a look of disgust, he said, "You got two feet. Walk."

I got within a foot of his face and softly said, "But I have a bullet in one of them."

He immediately picked up the phone and called for a jeep.

While waiting for the jeep, he brought out a chair for me to sit on and inquired, "I guess it's pretty bad out there?"

I immediately got pissed and said, "How would you know in your air-conditioned office, sitting on your fat ass in clean and starched fatigues?"

He didn't say another word until the medical personnel came to get me and then said, "Good luck."

My answer was just, "Thanks."

"From time to time, the tree of liberty must be watered with the blood of tyrants and patriots."

~ Thomas Jefferson

CHAPTER 34:
NO MORE HELL HOLE; HELLO WORLD

February 1968—Operating Room Odyssey

When I arrived at the hospital, I saw a large, boisterous woman giving orders. After looking at my ankle, she said, "Put that one," pointing at me, "in a wheelchair and take him to the waiting room."

I waited for treatment there for what seemed like hours, sitting amongst other injured soldiers.

Finally, an Air Force orderly took me to their operating room, which was more like a large room with eight tables with four against each wall staffed with two doctors and four nurses, all busily going from one patient to the next. I distinctly remember the clanking noise of surgical instruments dropping on metal trays and doctors barking orders.

An orderly helped me onto one of the tables. Next to me, on my right, I could see a nurse busily bandaging an injured soldier's arm. To my left, on the other side, I was surprised to see a Vietnamese woman screaming like a banshee. She had a wound in her boob, and a doctor probed his finger in the hole apparently to make sure he got all the foreign objects out of the laceration.

One of the nurses wheeled up a cart with a white towel over the top tray.

"Your turn," she said. After looking at my ankle, she added, "This doesn't look so bad."

"That is not what hurts. It's the back of my thigh, and it is killing me," I told her without screaming at her with the pain I was in.

She rolled me carefully towards my side to see if there was any blood pooling underneath me. Her forehead wrinkled as she put me back on my back and said, "I don't see any blood there."

"No, ma'am," I told her as I lifted my head slightly. "When I got hit, my leg got pushed over my head. That pulled all the muscles in that area," I explained.

"I'll tell the doctor but, first, let's clean up this wound," she said as she followed her protocol.

"You sure you don't want to look at my muscular upper thighs?" I asked with a grin.

Before she had a chance to respond, I yelled, "Ouch, that hurts!" as a sharp pain hit me when she poured a liquid over the wound.

"Does that answer your question?" she said, striking an innocent pose.

As the doctor approached my table, the nurse removed his blood-stained apron and replaced it with a clean one. I watched as the doctor pulled on a new set of sterile plastic gloves and asked, "What do we have here?"

The nurse pointed at the wings sewn on my uniform and said, "Another one of those prankster helicopter jocks. I think all that light air flying at high altitude does something to their brains."

As he looked at my wound, I said, "Doc, I can wait. It looks like the lady next to me needs you more than I do."

"No, she doesn't," he replied in a stern voice. "She's a VC sympathizer."

He grabbed a syringe and said, "This will sting a bit."

It did.

The nurse startled me by asking, "How long do you have left on your tour?"

"Why? You want a date?" I asked sarcastically.

"Oh, that one is original," she replied as she rolled her eyes. "No, I don't want a date. It's for your chart, dumb ass."

"Thirty-two days," I shot back.

The doctor looked up from his work and said, "Congratulations. You're homeward bound. If you had three months or more, I would send you to Japan to recuperate."

He showed me the bullet and asked, "Do you want a war souvenir?"

I shook my head, signaling no.

"There's a lot of shrapnel in there," he added. "It will have to wait until Clark. They will take the rest out there. As you can see, we're a little busy." He looked around as he said it.

"That shrapnel represents parts of my magnificent bird," I said with a mixture of pride and amazement. "And once again, as the saying goes, 'She took a licking and kept on ticking.'"

"Bandage the wound," the doctor ordered the nurse, "and arrange for transport to Clark."

"What is Clark?" I asked as he walked away to his next table.

"It's an Air Force base in the Philippines with a fully equipped hospital to stabilize patients before shipping them home," the nurse said as she began to wrap my ankle up. "So, you're going home. What do you think of that, hot shot?"

It came to me so quickly; I didn't have time to think and just shrugged my shoulders.

"You lucky bastard!" exclaimed the soldier next to me. "I'm on my way to Japan to recover and then I will be sent back to this goat roping."

I was struck by the two phrases I had heard before: 'lucky bastards' and 'goat roping.' 'Lucky bastards' gave me an adrenaline rush as that was what my buddies called my flight crew and me after our harrowing missions, but that rush turned to numbness when he said, 'goat roping,' which brought back memories from Bangkok. I so vividly remembered how Bob had explained the traffic as a 'goat roping.'

After the nurse finished with her work, she motioned to the airman at the doorway. He brought over a wheelchair and wheeled me to an institutional painted green hospital ward with two windows and twenty beds. The orderly in charge gave me a towel, a package, and a hospital gown—the kind of robe that let my ass hang out. The package was a toiletry kit with a bar of soap, a toothbrush with paste, comb, shaving gear, and cloth booties.

I turned it over to examine it and looked up as he pointed to the shower with one word, "Go!"

That is precisely what I needed. I couldn't remember the last time I bathed and almost couldn't stand my body odor. I let the hot water run over me for several minutes as I thought about the horrors I had experienced—blood dripping off KIAs, legs and arms that stuck out of slings in Dak To. An NVA soldier's head explodes from my gun. Bob, covered in blood and dying in my hands.

As I rinsed off, I saw the filthy bubbles swirling around the drain and thought though it is easy to wash Vietnam off my outside, I wonder what it will take to rinse Vietnam from my brain.

After I dried off and adorned my gown, a Vietnamese worker wheeled me to an assigned bed. At that point, I was so exhausted that

I could have slept on nails. I was given a pill, presumably for the pain, that sent me into dreamland.

Again, it was prom night in my dream. I looked up, *that's odd*, to see the crepe paper streamers on fire. Tracers were lighting it up. Gunfire. A hand grenade went through the basketball hoop. An explosion threw me. A North Vietnam Army unit was attacking. Another explosion sent me up through the roof; I was grabbing the intake cowling of Bikini 22. The rain and the rotor wash were flinging shattered glass that chewed into my face. My skin was peeling back, ripped by a hundred shards. I looked down to see an explosion bring the roof down and leave the gymnasium ablaze. I saw the Cong taking prisoners. I got to my door gun. I aimed, but it jammed. Russ called out, "de-linker." Bob quipped, "It's a goat rope." I screamed, "Bob, Bob!" He shook me with bloody hands...

I awoke to an orderly shaking me and saying, "Be quiet. You're a bother to the rest of the patients."

I woke up wet with sweat as my body stopped wiggling from side to side and asked, "How?"

"You are screaming, 'Bob! Lookout! Get down!'"

"I'm sorry," I said with embarrassment.

"It's okay," he assured me. "You don't get here without living through the nightmare first. It's the quiet, the being safe, so there's nothing to stop your mind from replaying it."

"It was so fucking real...yet it wasn't," I said with confusion. He understood what I was experiencing.

"Here, take these to get some rest, buddy. They'll help." He dropped two green pills in my hand.

I popped them in my mouth and swallowed without any water. They were gone... and so was I.

I had no idea how long I slept when another Air Force orderly woke me. "Wakie, wakie. Time for your flightie," he said in a sing-song voice.

"Where to?" I asked bleary-eyed.

"Cam Ranh Bay," he said as he started to help me out of bed and into a wheelchair.

I shook away his hands and asked irritably, "How would it look for a hardened combat soldier to get helped out of bed?"

"You're not a combat soldier anymore," he softly replied before shouting, "You're my fucking patient!"

He quickly reverted back to his soft voice. "Now, do what the fuck you're told, like a good little boy."

"Don't I get something to eat before the flight?" I asked.

"You slept through breakfast," he replied without any sympathy. "When they brought you a tray, they tried to wake you, but your exact words were, 'Leave me the fuck alone!' You scared the shit out of our Vietnamese server, so she did as instructed and let you sleep. They will have box lunches on the plane." He reached out to again help me out of my bed.

"How come you didn't wake me for breakfast?" I barked at him. "You left that decision up to a server? And now you're waking me for the flight?" I asked with disdain.

"Not my job to babysit everyone's whims," he said, "but it is my job to make sure you don't miss your flight, so let's go!"

I gave up fighting with him. He put me in the wheelchair and rolled me out to a waiting panel ambulance with no windows. I saw the aid that gave me the pills the night before. As I passed him, I just had to ask, "What did you give me?"

He smiled. "A suggestion," was all he said.

I was about to ask what the hell that meant, but I was rolled up into the ambulance. After getting settled in my seat, I took note of the three other passengers, all on stretchers, all in much worse shape than me. I heard the engine start and was almost knocked out of my seat by the way we darted off. I could tell when we entered the flight line by the sound of aircraft engines and the swirling noise of propellers. I knew that sound anywhere. I felt the driver stop and back up our medical limo as it beeped loudly in reverse. The noise stopped and the doors opened. In front of me was a C-130 Hercules with the rear ramp down.

Once on the plane, two crewmen wheeled me down the center aisle past rows of litter—the military's version of stretchers. At the end of the cargo bay, they stopped and placed me in one of the twenty seats in the front.

As he left, he said, "Happy trails, you lucky bastard. I still have ten months left."

There it was again, 'lucky bastard.' This time, I closed my eyes and thanked God for all the luck he gave me for the past eleven months.

CHAPTER 35:
LIKE COPS, NO GUNS WHEN YOU NEED ONE

Two hours later, I was handed another toiletry kit and was lying in a bed in the Cam Ranh Bay's Vietnam evacuation hospital.

As I tried to sleep that evening, I called Arthur, one of the orderlies, over. "Look, at the last place, this guy gave me two green pills and I got the best sleep ever. You wouldn't happen to have any of those, would you?" I asked hopefully.

"Tall guy, red hair?" he asked gruffly.

"Yeah. Nice guy," I confirmed.

He laughed, "That's McCutty. He didn't give you anything."

"Don't tell me that. I held these two pills in my hand, and they were powerful."

"They were sugar pills," he said emphatically. "He does that a lot. He told you they'd put you out, right? He believes in the power of suggestion."

"Son of a bi..." I stopped mid-swear. "Hear that? It's the distinct sound of a Soviet AK47, the VC's choice in weapons."

"You're nuts," he said as he shook his head. "This base is as safe as the U.S.A. It has never had an attack."

His comment did not soothe me. As time wore on, I grew worried. *Did I just hear these sounds inside my head? Or were these real weapons being fired?* I couldn't tell anymore.

I was almost asleep when I heard Arthur yell out, "Incoming!" Immediately, mortars exploded around the base. I jumped up, looked out the window, and saw flairs light up the sky. Red tracers from gunships appeared from the heavens and snaked their way to Earth. I could hardly believe that the Tet Offensive had reached me, even here.

I looked at Arthur and scoffed, "Safe as the U.S.A., huh?"

"I can't believe it," he said as he shook his head and stared out the window. "This has never happened before."

The doctor ordered all the patients to be moved into the latrine, where there were no windows.

A sergeant with blood on his right leg staggered into the ward. Two of the nurses ran to catch him as he collapsed. When they laid him on a bed, he said, "Sappers have penetrated the perimeter and managed to blow up an aircraft refueling station."

"What's a sapper?" Arthur asked.

"Sappers are specially trained VC to infiltrate our perimeters with satchel charges and do as much damage as they can," I explained.

There were eight other patients in the ward of twenty who could still function as soldiers so they stayed in the hospital ward to plan for a way to defend it.

One asked, "Do you have any weapons here?"

The reply came as a surprise. "All weapons are locked in the armory at headquarters."

"Even if we had them," a medic said, "I don't think I remember how to use an M16. We haven't shot a weapon in two years, and that was just for a couple of days in basic training."

The doctor called headquarters, explaining our situation. Minutes later, MPs showed up with three M16s and five 45 pistols with several ammo mags for each. The eight of us who were still ambulatory grabbed the weapons and manned the windows and doors.

Around 2 a.m., there was a brief lull in the sound of fighting. I lit a cigarette that was one of many that night. From the next window over from me, one of the other defenders, a huge mountain-looking man on crutches, came up to me and asked, "Can I get one of those?"

"Sure," I said as I reached into my pocket, grabbed a pack of Marlboros, and tossed them to him.

"How about a light?" he asked.

I handed him my Zippo and noticed an anchor tattooed on his bulging forearm. I asked, "Who are you, Popeye?"

"John Storie. Funny you said that 'cause my shipmates call me 'Popeye.'"

"So, what's your story, Storie?" I couldn't resist.

"Oh, that's original." He rolled his eyes. "I'm in the Coast Guard and…"

I interrupted and asked, "Since when is the U.S. Coast Guard here in Vietnamese waters?"

"Since the beginning of our involvement. We patrol the seacoast and rivers coming in from Laos for contraband."

"What's with the tattoo?" I was curious.

"One night, the guys got on me about looking like Popeye, which prompted me to get his tattoo."

"So what. Were you some kind of exercise nut?" I snickered.

"No, I am from Washington state and was a logger there since junior high. When you use a big chain saw all day, your arms get a workout."

We stood at our post throughout the night, talking about home, girls, and our plans when we got out of the military while always on alert for an attack as we heard firefights that seemed to be coming from all directions, but they never got close to us.

CHAPTER 36:
FIRST CLASS MEDIVAC

By morning, our forces repelled the attack. The critical patients were brought out of the latrine and were put back in their hospital beds.

After lunch, two airmen arrived with a gurney. One asked me, "Can you get on by yourself or do you need help?"

"Sure, I can. What's with the gurney?" I asked. "I can walk," I confirmed.

"This manifest says you're a litter patient to the Philippines, so according to our orders, you're going on your back."

I looked around the ward at the others being prepared to leave. When I saw Popeye in a wheelchair, I pointed at him and argued, "That guy can't walk without crutches, and he isn't on a gurney."

"Look, I do what I'm told, and I'm told you are on a gurney, so get on the gurney," the airman said impatiently.

Understanding that I couldn't win, I stopped protesting and got on the stupid thing, only like I was getting on a motorbike with my legs straddling it. I faked like my hands were on handlebars and joked, "Where's the kickstarter?"

"Look, pal, stop breaking my balls. Will ya?"

I could see he was tired and in no mood for my antics, so I swung around and laid down in the proscribed manner for a patient. "Take me away, James," I ordered as I waved my hand.

After another ride in a military ambulance, an airman wheeled me up the back ramp of a C-141 Starlifter. A nurse with a clipboard who was checking in patients asked, "Last name, please?"

"Makinen," I replied. "And ma'am, I can walk and don't want to take up a space that a more severe patient could use."

"The plane is full, and there are no available seats, so you're getting the VIP treatment and will ride on your back," she said before turning to the orderlies. "Put him in C-two," she ordered.

"C-two. Yes, ma'am," came their quick response.

I got rolled down one of two aisles that went the length of the aircraft. I lost count of the rows of litters I passed. Patients were stacked four high throughout the aircraft. The injured lined each side of the plane, and in the center section, there were two men beside each other. The aisles were unusually wide—big enough for my gurney in addition to the nurses and corpsmen who were caring for the patients.

When I got to my location, two airmen helped transfer me from the gurney to my spot, the second one from the top.

"At last, a thin one," said one of the men as he lifted me. "The last guy was a struggle, over six feet tall and pushing two hundred twenty pounds, and of course, he had to go on the top position." He buckled me in.

Forty-five minutes later, we felt the big bird's wheels lift off the rat hole known as Vietnam to thunderous applause inside the aircraft.

CHAPTER 37:
CLARK, THE WALTER REED OF THE PACIFIC

Day One at Clark

We landed at 5 p.m.

"Welcome to the Clark Air Force Base, Philippines," the head nurse said over the intercom. "The hospital here is known for its exceptional medical services and treatment of soldiers. I'm sure you'll get the best care available and be on your way home soon."

The guy across the aisle from me said, "Who cares? No one at home wants a guy with no legs."

A nurse heard him and rushed to his side.

"You got a brain, don't you?" the nurse asked sternly. "You got hands that can do anything you want them to do. Franklin Roosevelt was in a wheelchair when he was elected President. Now, what if you were on the plane behind us? The one we call the 'flying hearse?' Would the world be better off without you?"

When she turned to look at me, I said, "A little harsh on him, weren't you?"

"If I let a pity party start within him, it will grow like cancer," she said. "Better to rid him of it now before it takes hold and destroys him."

After we unloaded onto buses that transported us to the hospital, staff assigned us to different wards and each to a bed. I watched as doctors and nurses went through the ward and looked at everyone's charts. As the doctor examined the paperwork, he instructed the nurses on the scheduled treatment. Two of the injured left immediately for surgery. The following day, my ankle was x-rayed. I was issued the traditional military class B, khaki uniform and given a pay advance. I was also able to turn in my military payment script for greenbacks.

That afternoon, it was my turn for surgery. The doctor looked like a draftee and not regular Army. His hair was long with sideburns and a Fu Manchu mustache. He wore captain's bars but clearly had no interest in acting like a real officer. As he waited for the local anesthesia to take effect, he asked, "Where you from?"

"New Hampshire."

"I'm from White Plains, New York. Too bad you have to put up with that minor league baseball team, the Red Sox."

"They may suck, but we love them because they don't disappoint us. We'll always know they will be in last place."

"Okay, shall we start?" he asked as he reached for the medical instruments on the cart beside him.

After about a half-hour into his work, I said, "Doc, I need a cigarette."

"Okay, but don't let the nurse see you."

"She's only a lieutenant," I chided him. "You're a captain. Tell her to buzz off."

"Not here," he quickly replied. "She's regular Army. You'll see what I'm talking about."

My ward had ten men. The youngest was eighteen; the oldest was twenty-three, so we called him Pappy. If you get that many young men with nothing to do, bizarre things get thought up for entertainment. It was like when we had standby missions with the Special Forces. Stupid stuff happens.

As guys came back from appointments, we gradually got acquainted. It started with typical questions like, 'Where is your home? Do you have a girl waiting for you? What did you do in Nam?' The next question asked was, 'What are your plans after discharge?'

"Nothing for as long as my money lasts," was my reply.

Todd and Ed said, "Me too."

One guy who was missing a leg said, "Cross-country runner."

We roared in laughter. That one statement brought us together like brothers.

"I'm getting married," Jack said.

"I'll be a bishop in the Mormon church," Sam Smith quickly offered. "And Jack, if you want, I'll marry you."

Gus from Austin, Texas, asked, "So then you're Marrying Sam?"

"Okay, Tex," Sam said as he accepted his nickname graciously, and that started the name game.

The Cowboy got his nickname because his home was in Wyoming. Captain Kid lost an eye and wore a white bandage over it. He got a kick out of lifting the cover to show a bloody hole. This action made me turn my head and almost throw up our lousy hospital lunch. Lefty lost his right arm. We finally gave Hop Along and Stubby their names, as each had lost a leg. My tag was Fly Boy.

We couldn't let the nurses escape our entertaining renaming game. Legs and Jugs were both selected for obvious reasons. Gracie got her name on how she seemed to float with a perfect posture from patient to patient.

"What should we call the head nurse?" I asked, referring to the nurse Doctor Warren warned me about who barked orders.

A bedridden patient, who hadn't said a word since we got there, struggled to sit up and held up a book, *One Flew Over the Cuckoo's Nest* by Ken Kesey. He suggested Ratchet, the evil nurse featured in the book.

"That's perfect," Stumpy said. "And you'll be known as the Professor."

Obviously in pain, the newly christened 'professor' laid back down and smiled over his inclusion in our little game.

Day Two at Clark

There were still two long days before my scheduled flight home. The biggest challenge we all faced was finding something or some way to entertain ourselves.

Stubby and Hop Along got the day started. Unbeknownst to us, the night before, they took two pairs of scrubs and two hospital gowns, and using staples, sutures, and other odds and ends, they created a one-of-a-kind garment. After breakfast, it was fashion show time. The two amputees unveiled their design. As they stepped out of the restroom, they looked like Siamese twins. Each had a leg in one pant leg. The gowns hid their upper bodies. They clumsily approached us as the ward filled with cheers, applause, and laughter.

Nurse Ratchet heard the commotion and stormed into the ward. She didn't notice our Siamese twins and demanded, "What is going on in here?"

"You see," Cowboy paused as he began his creative explanation, "Tex started a game of Texas hold 'em, but Lefty could only sit in for one hand. That meant they needed a fourth person, so I asked Stumpy to hop in the last seat. Captain Kid is keeping an eye out for an available nurse for Fly Boy to get Marrying Sam to hitch them. Are you single?"

"There are serious patients in the next ward," she scolded while wagging her finger, "and they need QUIET!"

We each raised our pointy fingers in front of our lips, turned to each other, and quietly whispered, "Shhh."

Annoyed by our childish mocking of her authority, she turned away in disgust and then, and only then, did she finally see the Siamese twins.

"I ought to send you knuckleheads back to Vietnam." She shook her head in disbelief.

We still don't know to this day whether she cracked a smile as she walked away.

Day Three at Clark

The bedridden guys had been listening to our insanity. They started begging us to get involved in something fun.

"How about wheelchair racing?" Hoppy suggested.

Immediately, all the men begged to participate. I was a little concerned about the lousy shape some of the guys were in, but when I noticed how perked up they became at the thought of some adventure out of bed and involved in the fun, I agreed to participate.

We sent a scouting party of Marrying Sam, Captain Kid, and Lefty to find a place to run the races. In the meantime, another patient took up a collection and got a local worker to buy us some beer. The scouting party returned and led us to a place out of view, in between the main hospital and an outbuilding with a declining 500-foot ramp. I again became worried about some of the participants as they still had IVs attached to their wheelchairs.

Once we were all assembled for the great event, each non-racer had a task. Captain Kid retrieved the beer from under a predetermined group of shrubs. Cowboy announced the rules for the double-elimination tournament. Everyone except the six racing participants was assigned positions along the course as spotters to make sure nothing bad happened to the racers.

It was a glorious afternoon, and everyone got to laugh—some for the first time since they had arrived at Clark. The winner got crowned with a bedpan, and then we headed back to the ward.

Nurse Ratchet met us at the door. We all thought a shitstorm was about to greet us. Instead, it was a smile.

"Who won?" she asked pleasantly.

We pointed at the champion and said, "The Professor."

Nurse Ratchet turned to our victor and said dryly, "Congratulations, Professor." Then she turned to the rest of us and ordered, "Now, get those guys out of their wheelchairs and back to bed."

"Yes, ma'am," Cowboy replied.

Later, Legs was checking my vital signs. Our usual casual chitchat turned into a serious conversation as she began to whisper to me. "For the past several nights, a couple of our patients hadn't slept much and cried most of the time," she said softly, "but those two are now sleeping like babies. They were two of the racers. Don't misunderstand. You guys were reckless. We smelled alcohol on each of you. That alcohol can counter the effect of some of the medication that you guys are taking. That can be dangerous but, I must say, that race brought needed joy to these men."

"How come Nurse Ratchet didn't throw a shit fit?" I asked.

"We have to be careful," she explained. "Some of the boys have gotten mean and out of control. One patient threw a wheelchair out of a window. She noticed some darkness in a few of the guys, and your gang of idiots blew all those clouds away."

I said sarcastically, "Stubby drank a lot of beer. I hope he isn't allergic to... hops."

"That's not nice," she replied with a straight face. "Funny, but still not nice."

Day Four at Clark

On my fourth afternoon at Clark, a corpsman approached my bed. "Pack your shit and get on the bus at the main entrance."

"What shit?" I asked. "My three toiletry kits?"

"Just get down there in thirty minutes if you want to head home today."

"I'm ready." I threw two of the kits in the trash, grabbed the other, and headed toward the door.

"You'll need something to read on the long flight home," the Professor said as he handed me a book of great speeches.

"Thanks, Professor. Take care."

CHAPTER 38:
ISLAND HOPPING ON MY WAY HOME

Two hours later, I was back on a C-141 ready to head for home. The cargo bay of this Starlifter was configured with seats facing the rear of the plane. That meant we were stuck looking at baggage on the rear ramp. I wondered, who had bags? All of us were medevac'd, and all our possessions were a million toiletry kits between us. I didn't care if those bags on the ramp contained dog shit; I was on my way home.

Looking down the center aisle, I saw a friendly face. There was no mistaking those forearms; I would recognize them anywhere. As I walked up to Popeye, I said, "This seat taken?"

"No, sit down, Fly Boy."

I sat content with a new comrade and the knowledge that I would be home soon.

"How long will it take to get to the States?" I asked one of the crewmen.

"We have two stops at Anderson Air Force Base in Guam and Pearl Harbor, Hawaii."

"I was looking at some military literature that said the flight from Clark to Hawaii was about four thousand miles, so why don't we just fly straight to Hawaii?"

"Under ideal conditions, we could make it," he said, "but to be safe, we stop in Guam. You'll like that stop," he quickly added with a grin and went to check something in the cockpit.

I thought about what the Professor told me about Guam. He said it is small, only a little over two hundred square miles. That is like twenty miles by ten miles. How much enjoyment can we get out of a fuel stop there?

We arrived in Guam in the middle of the night. To our surprise, as we departed the plane, the Air Force band was playing small excerpts from all the service songs. When the Coast Guard song started playing, laughter erupted.

"Coast Guard?" Cowboy from the Clark Air Force Base Hospital said with surprise. "There ain't no Coast Guard in Nam!" he exclaimed. "Those shallow-water sailors wouldn't know what to do in real combat."

I hope Popeye didn't hear that and, if he did, he doesn't have his spinach with him today, I thought.

Too late. I heard, "I'm Coast Guard," Popeye said hotly. "Or like you called us, a 'shallow-water sailor.'"

"How did you end up getting medivac'd?" Cowboy asked. "Did you drop an anchor on your foot?"

"I fell on some slippery stairs and broke my leg during a firefight with two river junks on some river deep inside of Laos," he responded. "You want to make something of that?"

Remembering what the Master Sargent warned me about loose lips in Bangkok, I whispered so only Popeye could hear, "Hey man, that's top-secret stuff and punishable if exposed."

Popeye turned and faced me, and said, "What are they going to do? Send me back to Vietnam with a broken leg?"

Cowboy laughed and asked, "Did you get a Purple Heart for that?"

"Knock it off," one of the senior sergeants ordered. "At least he served and fought. That's more than a lot of your friends back home were willing to do. All they want is your girlfriends."

That hit home for me as I thought of Susan. The laughter stopped. Lots of guys patted Popeye on the back as a form of apology. Cowboy even said, "Just yanking your chain, sailor."

As I stepped into the passenger terminal, the first thing I saw was a red, white, and blue sign that read, "Anderson Air Force Base Welcomes our Veterans Back to America." Then I saw tables lined along one side of the room and seventy-five chairs set up in the middle. We found an extensive assortment of cakes, cookies, and fudge with coffee and punch made by the servicemen's wives. As the spouses approached and greeted us, I was taken aback by the delightful air and grace about them. I had been gone so long; it was as though I had forgotten how beautiful U.S. women looked and smelled. I wasn't the only one to notice; not one F-bomb crossed the lips of the one hundred GIs. It was a great experience.

"We meet all medivac planes," one of the older ladies explained. "It is our way of supporting the troops. We are the first place in America to welcome you boys home, and I hope you all see your loved ones soon. We also get enjoyment out of seeing your faces as you come to our little party."

Try as I might to be in the moment, I couldn't help but think, *there must not be much to do in Guam if you like to bake all day to meet a bunch of soldiers in the middle of the night.* Instead, I smiled and said, "I truly appreciate it; it's a wonderful gesture."

After about an hour, the band started playing the "Washington Post March," signaling our departure time. The ladies hugged each of us like we had known them forever, and we boarded our ambulance of the sky for another trip to bring us closer to home.

It took about three hours to get to Hawaii for a quick refueling stop there while some patients left us. The next leg of our odyssey was five hours to Travis Air Force Base, California.

At Travis, they offered us another toiletry bag.

I snapped at the corpsman, "Christ, I like to have the contract to supply those to the military. That's the fourth one offered to me. I think I'm good with just one."

I have no idea why I yelled at him. He was kind and helpful. Losing my temper seems to be happening for no reason lately. I hoped this wasn't battle fatigue.

After a shower, I was assigned a bunk and given a pill.

At eight the following day, I was awakened by what I thought was an angel but, in reality, it was a young woman dressed in a crisp Women in the Air Force (WAF) uniform.

"You got to get going," she said gently. "Your flight leaves at ten this morning."

"I can't remember the last time I slept uninterrupted until eight," I marveled, still a bit groggy and not quite wide awake. "Where am I going?"

"Looks like William Beaumont Hospital in El Paso, Texas," she said as she consulted the clipboard in her hand.

"Isn't that the home of Fort Bliss?" I asked hopefully.

"You're correct. Have fun in Mexico."

With that, she left.

After breakfast, I was off again in a smaller Convair 440 civilian contract plane. After stops in Utah and Denver, we landed in El Paso. I was at the William Beaumont Army Hospital by 6 p.m..

One of the orderlies asked me, "Have you had a chance to call home yet?"

"No," I said with a bit of a surprise. "In all the moving around, I haven't thought about that …until now. Is there a phone available?"

He took me to an area with several phone stations and said, "Take your time. The Army pays for the call."

After dialing my parents' number, I heard the sound of the phone ringing. *I hope they're home.*

After five rings, I was ready to give up and try later when I heard a click, and my mouth went dry as I heard my father say, "Hello."

"Dad, this is Mack."

"Mack, we've been so worried about you!" he exclaimed. "We haven't gotten a letter in over a month. Where are you?" he asked with great concern.

"I'm sorry. Things have been crazy." I didn't know how to explain why I didn't call sooner.

"Yeah, I've been following the Tet Offensive in the news. I hope you weren't involved," he said hesitantly.

"Dad, everyone was involved. That's kind of why I'm in El Paso."

"El Paso?! What are you doing there?"

"I got a little wound in my ankle, so because I didn't have much time left to go until my year is up, they sent me home."

"Are you okay? Can you walk? When can we see you?" he blurted out, one question after the other.

"I'm fine," I assured him. "My doctor is going to do another minor surgery in the morning, and I'll come home after that for thirty days of convalescent leave."

"Your mom isn't here, but as soon as she gets back, we'll leave for El Paso and see you in the morning."

"No need. I'll be there in two days," I said, referring to my upcoming flight to Phoenix, where my parents had recently moved to from New Hampshire for health reasons.

"Okay," he said, "but let us know when and where to pick you up."

"Okay. Love you, Dad. Tell Mom the same." I felt so disconnected.

"I will. I love you, too, son. Thank the Lord, you're home."

Back at my bed, I lifted my book of great speeches off the nightstand. I had been reading it since the Professor gave it to me at Clark. I opened it and came to Bertrand Russell. I had to hide my tears when I read, "War does not determine who is right—only who is left."

CHAPTER 39:
HOME AT LAST

March 1968

My landing at the Phoenix Sky Harbor Airport was hard. The plane bounced several times on the runway. I wondered if this was foreshadowing what my thirty days with my family would be like. I know my family well, of course, but I worried that they might no longer know me since the soldier that would descend from the plane was not the green, wide-eyed country patriot they sent off to fight communism.

I had never flown into Phoenix before and was surprised at the small size of the airport. It had no terminals like the airport in Boston, only long walkways leading to waiting planes. Passengers descended to the tarmac using a set of mobile stairs that were pushed up to the aircraft by a truck. A chain-link fence with gates like the ones we had for the chickens and sheep in New Hampshire separated the flight line from the waiting groups of family and friends. It took several minutes for the ground crew to position our stairs before they knocked on the door to signal the stewardess that it was safe to open it. I was seated across from the door. As soon as it opened, I spotted my mother, father, and younger sister Rosie standing just beyond the four-foot-high gate. I saw my dad holding my mother's hand. My sister was waving at the aircraft like she was hoping that I would see her.

Seeing my father standing there reminded me that he had always been my rock. During the amphibious landing at the Battle of Midway, he was climbing down the ship's side and one of the rope steps on the ladder broke, causing him to fall into the landing craft below. The fall got him out of the battle but plagued him with physical problems for the rest of his life.

When I was young, my father worked around the clock seven days a week. He would leave the house at 4:30 in the morning to pick up milk from farms to take to the Fitchburg Farmers' Co-op. Once he got through with the milk run, he would join his brother processing lumber at their sawmill. On weekends, he was a night watchman at the textile mill down the street. My mother was his loyal partner. She ran errands, kept the books, and would sell gasoline every day out of a skidder tank on the front lawn. Later, part-time gasoline sales evolved into a full-service gas station and garage with a heating oil delivery service.

Like any damaged machine that gets overworked, he finally broke down and spent five years in and out of veterans' hospitals. While I was in Vietnam, the doctors suggested he move to a warmer climate. They decided to move to Phoenix where they had friends who lived there. Mom and Dad made quite a team and worked harder than I would ever be able to match. I really appreciated them.

As soon as I left the plane, I ran to greet my family. There were hugs all around, and then my mother became motherly. She even had a porter with a wheelchair waiting. "How's your ankle?" she asked. She kept looking at me and at my ankle, fawning over me to make sure I could stand on it.

"Fine, Ma, it's hardly more than a scratch," I assured her.

"The classic million-dollar wound," Dad said with relief. "It gets you home, but it's not too serious."

"You know it, Dad," I smiled and nodded.

He turned to Mom and said, "Gloria, get rid of that wheelchair," as he waved the porter away. "You saw him run over here with barely a limp. Let's go home."

My father woke me up at 9 a.m. the next morning and proclaimed, "You need a car. Let's get you one."

We visited three dealerships and found a winner at Courtesy Chevrolet where I bought a badass red 1968 Chevelle Super Sport. It had a black landau top and shiny chrome wheels. Under the hood was a powerful 375 horsepower engine that roared when I revved it up. I thought I would look cool driving such a remarkable piece of American engineering.

After we settled on the price, Dad said, "I'll make a down payment, but you need to establish credit so you can finance the rest." I agreed, and at my father's suggestion, we took the freeway home to see what the car would do. We both were impressed with its performance and headed home to show Mom.

CHAPTER 40:
KEEPING COMMITMENTS

After happily putting up with my mother's hovering for five days, I decided it was time to fulfill my promise to visit Bob's parents. It was a trip I had to make, and what better way to get there than with my new Chevelle. I called their ranch to arrange the visit. A female voice answered the phone on the second ring and said in an accent, "Bandelier residence."

I cleared my throat and said, "Hello, this is Mack Makinen. I served with Bob in Vietnam."

"Un momento, por favor," the woman quickly interrupted me. "I'll get Jefe."

It took a few minutes but, finally, a breathless man's voice said, "Hello, Mack. I'm Bob's father."

"Hello, sir," I responded. "I've returned home and am living in Phoenix with my parents. I'd like to meet you and your wife."

"Donald?" He sounded confused.

When he asked, I realized I had forgotten that I signed the letter to them as Donald. I assured him, "Yes sir, Donald Makinen. I go by Mack."

"Well, Mack, we were hoping you would call us when you returned home as we really want to meet you."

"I would like to drive up to visit tomorrow, if it's convenient?"

"Yes, si segro, please. We will be honored to welcome another of Bob's family from the war to our home for as long as you can stay."

He gave me directions to the ranch. I didn't fully understand the driving instructions, but my pride forced me to assure him that I did.

When I hung up the phone, I wondered, how did he know that I lived close enough to expect a visit? He remembered my name from the letter I wrote to them about Bob's death, but I never said I lived close to his ranch; and what does, 'his family from the war" mean?

I left my parents' house, crossed the city, and drove past the Pima cotton fields to get to the Beeline Scenic Highway. When I turned north on the road, I got my first view of Arizona's desert. Once past Fort McDowell Indian Reservation, I asked my 375 horsepower Chevelle SS for more speed, and she delivered with that roar I loved. The road was flat, straight, and bordered by sand peppered with green scrubs and guarded by tall Saguaro cacti. My senses were ablaze with the smell of a new car mixed with the unique scent of last night's rain on the thirsty Sonoran Desert. A dust devil turned up sand, sticks, and leaves to my right.

In that moment, I looked around and thought, *I am free!* I couldn't remember the last time I wasn't obligated to the military or my family. I put in an eight-track tape of Steppenwolf and cranked the volume up as the song, "Born to Be Wild," came blaring through the speakers.

The road began to roll, and the desert resembled a light tan-colored ocean with sand-filled waves as far as I could see out my open side window. I enjoyed the feeling as my car topped each rise at high-speed, pulling negative 'G's with the inertia lifting my ass slightly off the leather seats, the warm Sonoran wind in my hair, and a big wide grin on my face.

Suddenly, it was as though I had changed the channel on a TV. The landscape drastically changed again as I started into the foothills that preceded the mountains that had been in my front windshield since leaving Phoenix. Skirting around the middle of one of the hills, I noticed impressive-looking boulders as big as my car on either side of the road. The further I drove, the more boulders appeared until they finally covered the entire hillside. Some of them were bigger than my parents' house. The whole countryside seemed to be under the ever-present watch of the Saguaro cacti that looked like soldiers on guard duty.

Overcome by my majestic and unfamiliar surroundings, I pulled off the road by a small stream that swirled between and splashed over red rocks. It was the red rocks that intrigued me. When I lived in the granite state of New Hampshire, all the rocks I had seen were either gray or brown. I leaned against my car and took a snort of Jack Daniels, followed by a Budweiser. Before leaving, I opened my passenger door to hide from passing cars as I relieved myself.

Then I heard a Huey in the distance. I felt something dark starting to build within me. Suddenly, I saw green-garbed soldiers in the hills around me where the cacti had been. I heard bullets zip past, and my breath became labored. At my feet, I saw blood—lots of it! The words of my fellow vets in the hospitals started to come to me. I realized that I was having a flashback. What could I do? I closed my eyes, drank the rest of the whiskey, leaned against the car, and struggled to take deep breaths. After a few minutes, my breathing became more manageable. I opened my eyes and found that the soldiers had turned back into the cacti around me. The sounds of bullets were now just the cars passing on the road at high speed, and the pool of blood was just my pee. I was shaken by the experience. I closed the passenger door, got back in the car, and resolved to fulfill the promise I had made to Bob. I would visit the Bandeliers, no matter how many bad memories it might bring back. The tape player started to annoy me, so I shut it off, content to listen to the roar of my mighty Chevy stallion.

Eventually, I came upon the town of Payson; it was tiny. I remember Bob saying it was one of the big towns closest to his ranch. I thought, Bob's definition of a big town was sure different from mine. I found an A&W root beer stand, got a burger and fries, ate my lunch, and downed my last Budweiser. Before leaving town, the next stop had to be a liquor store for another bottle of Jack and two six-packs of Bud.

As I drove out of town, I was again surprised at how fast vegetation changed in the West. After a short drive, the shrubs were replaced by the smell and view of a pine forest as I drove on. When I wasn't marveling at the scenery, I was in deep thought about Leah, Bob, and what I would say to Bob's parents. As a result, I drove right past the town of Heber—the town Bob said was close to where he lived. After making a U-turn, I re-entered Heber and counted four houses, a cafe, a combination gas station, and a general store where I stopped in front of an old, rusted Phillips 66 gas pump. I turned to get a better look at the store, and to my surprise, a young man dressed in jeans, a western hat, and boots was stepping off the store's porch and heading my way.

"Filler up, sir?" he asked.

"Yes, and do you know where the Bandelier ranch is?" I inquired.

"Yeah. Just up here a spell, you'll come to a fork in the road," he said as he pointed. "One goes to Snowflake and the other to Holbrook. Take the one to Holbrook. Then you'll come to a smaller town than this called Zeniff."

I thought, *how do you get a town smaller than this?*

The young man continued. "Just past Zeniff on the left, you'll see a sign that says the Rollin B Ranch. Take that road. In five or six miles, you'll come to their spread. Did you know their son, Bob?"

It really was a small town where it seemed like everyone knew everybody. "Yes, I was with him in Vietnam," I told him.

"Nice kid. So sorry for the family. That'll be $10 for the gas."

"Yes, he was," I agreed and then asked, "But the pump says $11.34?"

"Yeh. I see that sawbuck in your hand. I don't want to walk in to get change, so ten bucks will do."

I thanked him and started on my way with a beer between my legs, sipping it for comfort. At Zeniff, I did as instructed. The sign said County Road 65, but I thought it was more like what I would call a logging road back home. I couldn't stand the thought of dust rolling in on my new seats, so I rolled the windows up. I also turned on the first auto air conditioner I had ever had in a car I owned.

The gas station attendant's instructions were correct. Five miles past the turnoff, I could see a large house, three smaller ones, and two barns. I drove up the driveway and came upon a teenage boy.

"Is this the Bandelier ranch?" I asked.

"You must be Mack," he said as a big smile came over his face. "I'm Richard but call me Dickie. Bob was my older brother. Come in the house. Everyone is waiting for you."

It was a large stone house with a circular driveway that passed under a twenty-foot-high portal attached to the building on one side. Two large round debarked logs held up the front. The area between the logs had landscaping with small pines and tall grasses inside a stone-lined raised bed.

Dickie ran into the house to announce my arrival.

A middle-aged couple came out of a ten-foot-high entranceway with a hand-carved door. The woman was short and wore a black dress with large multi-colored flowers embroidered on the front and on her sleeves. A turquoise necklace set off her dress perfectly. The gentleman was in a western cut jacket, jeans, and a white shirt. Both had big smiles as they approached and gave me big hugs. As I am of Finnish descent, this made me a little uncomfortable since Finns are not used to hugs from strangers.

"Mack," the man said, "My name is Louie, and this is my wife, Theresa. You already met Dickie. Come in. We have a surprise for you."

We entered a large foyer. It had doors to rooms on each side of a hallway. A large staircase stood in front of me. The walls and stairs were rich-stained pine wood. I turned around to Louie and admired it. "What a magnificent house. I…"

From behind me came a sweet voice I recognized. "Mack!" I turned and couldn't believe my eyes. I lost my breath at the sight of Leah's grace and beauty descending the stairs. I was without words as she rushed to meet me with her arms wide open. She embraced me and started to cry as she thanked me for coming. When she hugged me, I could feel a bump where her once slender midsection had been.

I was so excited to see Leah that I peppered her with questions without waiting for answers. "How long have you been in America? How did you get here? How did the Bandeliers know about you?"

When I finally got over my initial surprise, I slowed down and said, "The reason I'm here is to tell Louie and Theresa about you and Bob. I guess they already know."

Louie interrupted and said, "Bob wrote us all about Leah. We flew to Bangkok after he died. We immediately fell in love with our new daughter. Theresa and I just had to bring her home—where my son's widow belongs."

I pointed to Leah's stomach. She knew what I was asking.

"Yes, and I'm sure it's his," she proudly said. "Bob sent me money every month, so I didn't have to go back to work at the club. After he died, I worked in my aunt's clothing store until the Bandeliers arrived. They know about my past and have accepted it, so don't feel uncomfortable."

They led me to a room with a large table where two housemaids dressed in Mexican style multi-color full skirts and white tops were scurrying around, making sure that all the plates were uncovered. The table was adorned with different Mexican American dishes. I stuffed my plate with food I had never seen before while Dickie explained what the various dishes were and how they should be eaten. After trying several items, I bit into something that seemed to make smoke come out of my ears and tears flowed like a river. Leah saw the look on my face and raced toward me with a glass of water. I beat her to it by downing the rest of the beer I had been sipping.

During dinner, I asked, "How did your family build such a gorgeous ranch?"

Louie explained," This ranch is an American story of imagination and hard work. My great grandfather is Swiss. He was hijacked by the French and sent to fight in the Mexican War of Independence. After the war, he stayed in Mexico and started a family. About 1860, he came here and purchased one hundred acres. Over the years, as ranchers sold out, he bought their land. Today, we have over 40,000 acres deeded and another 30,000 leased from the Forest Service."

"That's a great achievement," I said in awe. "Congratulations!"

After dinner, I told Bob's family about the things Leah, Bob, and I did in Bangkok. I explained about the stone elephants and how rubbing by soft hands over centuries made the stones smooth as glass. I also described the Royal Palace, Emerald Buddha, and all the other sights and food we enjoyed. Then I took a deep breath and explained why Bob wanted me to visit them.

"Louie, Theresa, from the moment they met, Bob and Leah had a special relationship. I never believed in love at first sight till I saw the two of them, so happy, so good with one another. As you know, Bob succumbed to his wounds in my helicopter on the way to the aid station. His last words were for me to promise him I would come here and tell you of his love for Leah."

Everyone remained quiet. Theresa wiped tears from her eyes, and Louie left the room as he pulled a handkerchief out of his pocket.

To give the grieving parents some privacy, Leah dried her tears, grabbed my hand, and tugged gently as she said, "Let me show you around." She led me out of the dining room, down the hall past a full large kitchen, and out the back door to a corral. Behind a wooden fence were a mare and her colt.

"That's my baby boy's horse," Leah said. "The mother is Bob's horse, Daisy."

"My, aren't you getting a bit ahead of yourself? How do you know you're having a boy?" I marveled.

"The Bandeliers took me to Phoenix to have a new procedure performed called an ultrasound. It showed that I'm having a boy. We're going to name him after his dad, but Mr. Bandelier says we should call him Robby."

"Is that what you want?"

"Yes. After you left, Bob was so kind to me that I think it's fitting to give the baby his name. The Bandeliers do treat me like a Lūksāw—I'm sorry, I mean daughter. I'm so lucky."

She gave me another long hug and said, "Thank you. Thank you for bringing Bob to me."

"I think that was Po, but I'll take the hug." I smiled at her.

"Do you ever think of Busa?" she asked.

"Quite often, and seeing you just brings back how special the both of you were to two lonely soldiers," I admitted.

"Do you have someone here—back home?"

"No, I'm afraid I have some demons that I need to work out before I get serious about anyone again." I averted my eyes to hide the pain I felt.

"Oh no, I'm not trying to get you to bring her here. She got a job at a bank, and one of the managers proposed to her. I was just wondering because you two did seem to hit it off."

"I'm happy for her," I assured her. "She is a sweet lady."

When it was time to turn in, Theresa walked me upstairs. She asked if I would mind sleeping in Bob's old room. At first, I felt funny. Then she said, "Leah sleeps in the guest room, and Dickie has his room. The two other bedrooms are full of baby stuff and some of Leah's things."

She had a sweetness that made everything soft and comforting, "Sure." I said, "I'd be honored."

I stepped into the room.

Theresa stopped just inside the door behind me. She admitted softly, "I haven't been in here since we got word he passed." In between short breaths, she continued, "I kept it ...for him ... so that when he came... came home..." She trailed off and started to sob.

I placed my hand on her arm. She dabbed her nose with a hankie she had clutched all night. "The girls did a nice job," she said as she began to compose herself and smiled through her lingering tears. "I asked them to move some of Bob's things to one side of the room and to clear the closet." She pointed to the dresser and indicated, "You can use the top drawer. There are towels in the small closet in the bathroom across the way." She looked around the room with moist eyes. Then she fixated her gaze on me. As she whimpered, she asked, "Did he suffer?"

I wasn't prepared to answer her question with anything other than what happened in the field. I did my best to temper my response, not wanting to add any further injury to the grief she already felt. "The medics gave him something for pain as soon as they found him. It was pretty strong." I paused and then told her a little white lie I prayed I would be forgiven for telling her. "He was given another dose in the chopper when we got him. No, I don't think he was in very much pain at all, ma'am."

She sniffled, held her gaze, and told me, "I'm glad you were with him, and that he didn't die alone. I'll always be grateful to you for that." She dabbed her eyes.

"I was honored to help him leave for a better place. As I wrote in the letter, Bob affected everyone, even as he left this world. Hard-boiled men stopped to pay respect. It was amazing." I remembered it like it was yesterday as I told her about it.

"Leah said at first she thought you were brothers when she met you."

"We were. In a very short time, I grew to love him like a brother..." Then to my surprise, I started to well up and felt a catch in my throat. I looked at her through my tears and couldn't speak. She hugged me. I hugged her back. I cried out, "Oh, God! I miss him." I was blabbering like a little girl.

With her motherly embrace, she comforted me. She said soothingly, "Having you here is like having a little piece of my son back. Thank you for coming and bringing me that."

One final hug and we collected ourselves, "Well, good night, Mack. Sleep tight. Don't let the bedbugs bite. "

As she closed the door, I stood dumbstruck. That is what my mom would say to me at night when I was a kid.

I lay in bed, and God forgive me, all I could think about was Leah. Her beauty, poise, and elegance as she melted my heart with her humility and strength. I finally drifted off and slept well that night, no gymnasium attacks, no hanging off a Huey for dear life.

I awoke to the smell of bacon cooking, which brought me back to early morning breakfasts before missions in Pleiku. As I stood up from the bed, I noticed some of Bob's things were arranged on the top of the dresser. I grabbed my clothes from the top drawer and saw a prom picture of him with a real pretty thing, flip hairdo, blue gown, and Bob in a tux. A medal for track and a box with watches and tie pins were beside it. I looked around and imagined him getting up in the morning in this room and heading off to school—just like me, on the other side of the country, before we went to war as boys.

After a quick shower and shave, I went downstairs. "Come," Theresa said as she grabbed my hand. "Come in and sit." She gave me a gentle tug toward one of the chairs.

I was in the middle of breakfast when Leah entered the room. I got that funny feeling when she appeared, like when I first saw her the day before. I thought, *don't be a dog.* You may like her, but she is the widow of a friend and carrying his baby. I hid my excitement at seeing her.

"Good morning, everyone," she said as she drew nearer, like a breath of fresh air. "And how did you sleep, Mack?"

"Very well, and you?"

"I too slept well." She looked like she had. She smiled and looked refreshed.

I found myself staring at her many times during breakfast. I kept marveling over her beauty, grace, and class. I was smart enough to know I needed to get out of here before I drank too much and screwed up by saying something stupid.

"Can you stay another day?" Dickie asked with enthusiasm. "We got lots of things to see and do on this ranch."

"Unfortunately, no," I responded regretfully. "I need to get back to Phoenix." I felt I needed to give them a reason why I had to go back so I explained, "I have an appointment to have the stitches taken out of my ankle."

"What is wrong with your ankle?" Leah asked with concern.

"I met a bullet, but it's not much."

Louie said, "Esta pinche guerra que chingaos estamos haciendo aqui?" Then he switched to English. "That damn war. Can anyone tell me why we're there? Mack, can you?"

I thought for a minute as they all stared at me, wondering if I would sound like I was saying that Bob died for nothing by telling the truth. I decided on honesty. I looked at Louis and Theresa, and then at Leah. "No, sir," I said as I broke the long silence. "There is nothing I saw worth fighting for in Vietnam; let alone dying for."

"That's what I thought," Louie said. "What's it like being out of there?"

"Like a thousand pounds have been lifted from my shoulders. I honestly believe we went to change Vietnam, but Vietnam changed America."

After breakfast, I packed my bag and waved goodbye to Leah and the Bandeliers. Theresa gave me a tin container filled with cookies.

"A little something for the road," she encouraged me as she placed it in my hand.

I thanked her, almost called her mom, and headed for my car. Leah came over to me and hugged me. She whispered, "Come back after the baby is born. The Bandeliers want him baptized, and I want you to be his godfather."

I was startled by her request. I bowed my head, quietly declined, and explained, "Leah, I am honored, but you need to find someone who's worthy of that title."

"No, Mack," she insisted, "It's got to be you."

I got in my car, started it, and used the oldest copout line in the world as I rolled down my window and told her, "We'll see."

CHAPTER 41:
PARADOXES

I was back in Phoenix by two that afternoon. On the way to the house, I stopped at a small bar on the edge of a canal on Phoenix's north side. When I stepped into the building, I saw three guys at the bar, all in western garb. A barmaid was at the end of the bar shaking a cup. She flipped it upside down with a loud knock, exposing several dice on the bar. She pulled out some of the white cubes, shook the cup, and threw them again.

Then she said, "You win. What do you want?" He ordered a draft.

As I sat down beside him, I looked up at the barmaid and said, "Give me one of those and a shot of whiskey, please."

The man sitting next to me was in his sixties with long gray hair, a mustache, and hands that said, 'I do hard work.'

"I'm Mack," I said, putting out my hand.

"They call me Ed," he said as he gave me a firm handshake.

"What do you do, Ed?"

"I'm into concrete finishing. How about you?"

"Army."

"Did you make it to 'Nam?"

"Yes, just got back," I answered.

"My brother-in-law was a hero in that war," he told me proudly. "He keeps saying how he wants to go back, so he could keep killing gooks. He even has items he took off his kills. Where were you stationed?"

"My base camp was Pleiku," I said.

"No shit. That's where my brother-in-law was. He served in the 170th Assault Helicopter Company."

When I asked his name, he said, "Randel Burtchrum."

I had to bite my tongue. Randel was what we called a REMF—a Rear Echelon Mother Fucker—and he was as big an REMF as there was in our unit, maybe second only to the early version of Lieutenant Rose. At least Rose smartened up, but Randel never did and stayed an REMF his whole tour. He remained in maintenance his entire time in Vietnam, which didn't bother anyone. The longer men stayed in maintenance, the more experience they gained, and the better the aircraft were maintained; but, Randel was a special case.

When one of us would have a close call and have a badly damaged aircraft, Randel would take great pleasure in pointing out damage, laughing, and then proceeding to tell all his pals how stupid we were to risk our lives for a fifty-dollar-a-month flight pay. What upset everyone the most was that he behaved like this even when we lost men. That made him the target of lots of nonlethal harassment. The best prank Russ thought up was when we switched his boots for ones a half size too small, prompting him to complain to the sergeant that there was something wrong with his feet. Finally, his sergeant told him to go on sick call. Everyone got a good laugh when the doctor scolded him for wearing boots that were too small and then sent him to get a new pair. On another occasion, we set his mosquito net on fire while he was sleeping. His fight to escape the flames gave us another reason for joy.

I remembered selling Randel the war souvenirs we took off an NVA soldier at LZ Yankee. At the time, we didn't know what a pariah he was so, unfortunately, I unwittingly helped make him a war hero in the eyes of his family and friends.

I said to the bartender, "Ma'am, I need a double shot of Jack."

I downed it in one swallow and gave Ed my name and contact information. The look on my face made Ed ask, "What's wrong?"

"Nothing. Just give this to your war hero and have him call me."

I paid for my tab and left.

Randel never called.

The morning after my encounter with Ed, I was nursing a hangover by the pool while Dad read the morning newspaper. The only sound was the water sprayers splashing on the pool's surface, cooling the water temperature so it would be less like a bath when I got in to cool off. My father placed the paper on the glass top table between us and asked, "Why don't you go to Glendale Community College and see if you can enroll in this year's summer courses? The campus is about three miles away."

"Okay," I shrugged. "Sounds like a good idea since I don't have any plans yet."

The entrance to the college was at the end of a long driveway with palm trees lining both sides. Nearby was a parking lot full of cars

with no empty spots. After driving around for a few minutes, I followed a student who I hoped was leaving. As she got in her car and pulled away, she gave me a smile and a friendly wave.

So far so good, I thought.

I took her parking place and walked to the Administration Building where a student directed me to the Admissions Office.

As I approached the elderly lady behind the desk, she looked up and asked, "Can I help you?"

"Yes," I said hesitantly, "I'd like to get some information about your summer program."

She took off her glasses, stood up, and pointed to the books and pamphlets that crowded the shelves on the left side of the room behind me.

"You'll find what you need over there," she said with encouragement.

"Thanks." I walked over to the shelves and found several brochures I thought would be helpful. I returned to the counter and asked, "Do I need SAT scores?"

She looked at my crew cut, and asked "Are you prior military?"

"Yes, ma'am," I said with pride.

"Then no, but we recommend that you take refresher courses in English and math. I'd also advise you to check in with the Veterans Assistance Office down the walkway to the right, just after exiting the building."

"Thanks again, ma'am."

Two buildings down the road from the Administration Office, I saw a group of about a dozen students assembled in front of the Veterans Assistance Department. They were dressed like the anti-war demonstrators I had seen on the TV news, and all of them had long hair. One girl was wearing what looked like a bedsheet sewed on the sides with a hole for her head—kind of an awkward poncho. The rest of the girls in the group dressed in colorful wrap-around skirts and tank tops, and none wore bras. My eyes were drawn like a magnet to steel toward that erotic feature. One young boy had a tie-dyed shirt with striped bellbottoms. Others wore t-shirts and blue jeans, and a few wore jeans but no shirts. All had on sandals or flip-flops. In the Army, we called this kind of footwear "Japanese jump boots." The demonstrators held signs bearing messages like "Stop the Killing" and "Impeach Johnson." My favorite, however, was "Make Love, Not War."

As I approached the building, I smiled at the two nipples protruding from the dark green t-shirt as I said as casually as I could, "Good morning."

"Are you a baby-killing veteran?" she sneered.

"I'm a veteran, but I've never killed a baby," I responded peacefully.

"It doesn't matter," came the voice from the bedsheet girl. She sputtered until she managed to get out, "You're a spineless ...soldier --- that makes you part of the war machine." She stopped, took a deep breath, and blurted out at me, "You're as guilty as the rest."

Her assertions stung. My mind was confused; I agreed with her on the war but was angry at her accusations against fellow soldiers and me. I knew I could not let that anger take hold as I did not want to give her any ammunition to confirm that I was capable of what she was alleging.

"In all my time in Vietnam, I never saw a baby killed," I emphasized. "And here is a bit of shocking news: we would fly doctors to remote villages to attend to the health of injured or sick babies. The war does suck, but don't blame the men who fight just to survive." Nipples or not, I was done with her. "Now get out of my fucking way."

"Or what?" came a voice from a guy in a tie dye shirt.

I felt rage again rising within me and had to take a moment to cool down before I did something that would reinforce their opinion of soldiers. Once I felt a bit calmer, I said, "Or I'll walk around you."

That put the dip wad off; he was itching for a fight. *Not today pal, make love, not war.*

Once I got inside the Veterans Assistance Department building, a man who had been watching from the window said, "Those hippies are here every day trying to stop vets from registering for courses. How can I help you?"

"I want to enroll in the first summer session. The lady in the Admissions Office told me you could help."

"I can," he said as he proceeded to walk me through the process and signed me up to receive a $365 monthly check from the GI Bill of Rights. The money would pay for my tuition and subsistence.

After answering a few additional questions about my service, I left the building to face the group outside again. Tie-Dye said, "Don't come back. We don't want warmongers on campus."

Again, I had to reach deep inside not to be drawn into a confrontation. I couldn't just walk away without letting the group know how I felt. When the group started some sort of chant, I smiled at them and walked away, scratching my ass. I guess they got my point because someone said, "That's real classy."

I bought books from the college bookstore to bone up on my math and English skills, and the next several days of my leave consisted of waking up late, having lunch, and studying by the pool. The high point of my days was always the afternoons when I picked my sister up from school. She loved it when I goosed my mighty Chevelle down the streets with the stereo blasting. She was now fifteen. Before going into the Army, I was so much older than her that we never talked much. Now, I was enjoying getting to know her.

Two days after signing up for college and dealing with the protestors, I was on my way to pick up my sister when blue lights appeared in my rearview mirror. I stopped, and a Phoenix City police officer came to my window.

"License and registration, please," he ordered, sounding like a drill sergeant. I reached into the glove box to retrieve the registration, thinking, *this guy sounds like a real hard ass.*

I handed him the registration and said, "I lost my New Hampshire driver's license, sir."

He examined the registration, looked in the back seat where my uniform was still hanging from today's laundry run. He continued to ask sternly, "Why didn't you get a replacement license?"

How can I talk my way out of this one?

I guess the truth is my best defense, and I said, "Sir, I was medivac'd from Vietnam, and I am staying with my parents on convalescent leave. My home is New Hampshire, and I just haven't thought about the driver's license while here in Phoenix."

"Let me see your military ID," he ordered impatiently. After examining it, he asked, "How long will you be here?"

"Another two weeks."

He looked serious and examined my uniform again. "I'm going to give you a warning ticket, which will state you have 30 days to get a license. By then, you'll be gone. I believe anyone who served our country should get a break. If you were anyone else, I would throw the book at you. I could give you tickets for speeding, reckless driving, and no license. This warning is the only "get-out-of-jail-free card" you'll get from me. You better slow down, or I'll give you a speeding ticket next time."

"Yes, sir. Thank you, sir."

Most evenings, I would go to Mr. Lucky's Club with country music on the ground level and rock downstairs. The lower floor walls had kaleidoscope-type images projected on them and music almost as loud as my minigun. I got to know some of the downstairs crowd but having short hair kind of made me stand out. I also just wanted to be left alone. Usually, I was able to find a table in the back of the room where I could drink alone and listen to music.

One night, I was surprised to hear a smooth, soft voice say, "Buy a drink for a lady, soldier?" When I looked up, I saw one of the female protestors from the college. I remembered thinking that she seemed older than the others.

"If you don't call me a warmonger," I answered.

"No problem. I believe in hate the war but love the soldiers."

I stood and pointed to an empty chair. "Then, have a seat, my lady," I said while I got the waitress's attention to bring us drinks. The girl glided around the table into my full view. Her hair was sandy brown and fell over her shoulders. She had gorgeous features and a Roman nose with high cheekbones, her slender figure draped with a white mini dress. An orange knitted scarf hugged her neck, and brown leather boots accented long shapely legs. My feeling that she was more than just a poor hippie student was reinforced not only by her poise but by the fact that she ordered a dry martini.

I started with, "My name is Donald, but everyone calls me Mack."

"How in the world do you get Mack out of Donald?"

"Short for Makinen," I answered.

"I've never heard that one before. I'm Carol, and you can call me Carol," she said with a big smile. "When you saw me at the rally, I was at the college to visit my younger brother. He asked me to go with him to the demonstration, so I did. What's your story?"

"I am getting out of the Army in the next couple of months, and I think I'll move here. When you saw me at the college, I was enrolling in school for the summer session. I believe that will give me a chance to see if Phoenix is for me."

We continued to talk. I found out that Carol was a law student at Arizona State University, and that her family owned a furniture store. I shared the same sort of information about myself.

It was late, and Carol suggested we grab breakfast at Denny's restaurant near her house. After breakfast, I took her home, and she invited me in. I gladly accepted and didn't get to my parent's house until the sun was already up. I was trying to be quiet as I entered the house when, out of the living room, my dad asked, "Attend a pajama party last night?"

"I sure did," was my answer as I went to my room. "Without the PJ's," I said under my breath.

Lying in bed, I thought, *what has this world turned into while I was gone? I get caught in a war protest and hassled because I'm a soldier. Then I get out of a fist full of tickets because I'm a soldier. Now I just had sex with one of the protestors because I'm a soldier.*

I didn't know what was going on, but I think I liked this 'make love, not war' business. It's much better than just making war.

Carol and I saw each other several more evenings before I had to leave for El Paso. The night always ended in what my dad called a pajama party. We both thought our sex was just recreational, but something seemed to be growing stronger between us.

The afternoon before I had to leave, my parents had some friends and neighbors over to meet me. One couple was the Someros from my hometown, the reason my parents knew about this place. The rest were my mom's or dad's new Arizona friends; the others were friends of my sister. I didn't want to be around people, so I downed a couple of stiff whiskeys and chased them with beer. That got me more at ease. I asked Al Somero how the family was doing and if he got to play golf with Dad often. It was primarily mindless chit-chat. When I asked about their son Kirk, Al said, "Kirk is going to enlist in the Army."

"Have him go to Canada," I said. "It's a much better country than Vietnam."

"We all have to pay our way," Al admonished me.

"In the hospitals and during the long flights back across the Pacific, I read a book of great speeches," I said. "Let me offer you my version of a speech, but I will use the cadence of a part of President Kennedy's inaugural address."

I recited...

"I didn't want to kill.

But killing, I did.

I didn't want to lose friends.

But friends, I lost.

I didn't go to lose.

But Vietnam is lost."

Al countered, "But Kennedy also said, 'Ask not what your country can do for you, ask what you can do for your country.'"

I responded, "Which should we ask for—war or peace?"

"Peace, of course," Al said.

"Then have him join the Peace Corps." I continued, "Mrs. Somero, you taught me Sunday school, and you knew I was a devout Christian. From what I saw in Vietnam, I have to conclude that God must be busy fixing the social unrest in the South, because he was AWOL in Vietnam."

My dad walked up and said, "Who's absent without leave? Not you, I hope?"

"No, Dad, I was trying to talk the Someros into getting their son to join the Peace Corps instead of the Army."

Dad motioned to me and said, "Let's go out back for a minute."

We walked out to the backyard and sat on beach chairs beside the pool. Dad started, "I'm worried about your drinking. It's every day."

"I'm fine. I'm just taking it easy during this time of change."

"I never told you about this," my dad continued, "After World War II, I liked to drink, and sometimes I drank too much. What did it get me? For one thing, when I worked for the local power company, I was drinking on the job one day and stupidly drove a pole-climbing spike into my leg."

"So that is where the scar on your leg came from?" I asked in utter amazement.

"Yes, and then when your uncle and I started a sawmill, drinking bit me again." He held up his right hand and drew my attention to the missing finger. He said, "This is a result of drinking. After all those accidents, I still didn't understand that I had a problem."

"I've never seen you even have a beer," I said.

"That's true, and you never will. When I saw you for the first time in the hospital after you were born, I realized that if I was going to be a good father, I needed to quit drinking. You and your sister are the anchors for me. You are what keeps me from drinking. You need to find an anchor of your own, whether it's school, work, or a relationship."

"Thanks, Dad, but I'm fine," I assured him.

I left my dad as he stroked his chin with his four-fingered hand in deep thought. I went off to have another pajama party with Carol and say goodbye.

"Never be bullied into silence. Never allow yourself to be made a victim. Accept no one's definition of your life; define yourself."

~ Harvey Fierstein

CHAPTER 42:
DOWN A RAT HOLE

Bikinis to the Rescue

It took a month, but I finally got my freedom from the Army. When I got to Phoenix, I decided to spend a couple of days with Carol. She met me at the airport, and we sped off to spend three glorious days at the Mountain Shadows Resort. I didn't know what was hotter, the Arizona sun or Carol in a bikini by the pool. I thought about how the helicopter with the nose art showing Little Annie Fanny in a bikini had got me through war. Maybe this woman in a bikini would help me get through peace.

Each night, we would dine like royalty. After dinner, we would go to the Red Dog Saloon in downtown Scottsdale where Carol worked on teaching me how to dance to a group that had a great lead singer and looked like Mr. Clean, and that was the name of the band. The time we spent together was like heaven, but it came down to earth on the third day when it was time to leave. When I pulled out my wallet to pay at checkout, Carol said, "This is my treat," as she placed a hard plastic card on the counter.

Surprised, I asked, "What's that going to do?"

"It's a Diners Club card, silly. I can charge the entire stay with it."

"Won't a bill come sometime? We spent a lot. Let me pay. I can't let a lady treat me. Besides, the Army gave me a large amount of cash for all the leave I didn't use."

Carol's answer was, "I'm not paying for it. My father will send a check when he gets the bill."

"What will he think of me? Spending three days with his daughter, and it's his treat? If I were him, I'd shoot me just for sleeping with you—not to mention the charges."

"I'll tell him it was a girl's weekend." She smiled as if she had resolved it.

I eventually made it to my parents' house. As time went by, my dad's advice and Carol's affection started to help me get my drinking and temper under control; but darkness still occasionally took over my dreamland. One morning, my dad said, "You woke me last night with your screams and cussing. Come with me to the Veterans Hospital and see if they can help with your night terrors."

I said, "Sorry, Dad, I need to check out school today."

"Okay, when?"

"I don't know. Really, what can anyone do? Can they drill into my head and take out those bad images? I'll work it out in my own way."

CHAPTER 43:
BOB'S APPROVAL

In early July, Leah called. "Mack, I had a healthy boy last week, and the second Sunday in August is the baptism in Payson. You promised Bob and me that whatever I need, all I'd have to do is ask."

"Are you okay with your son being baptized Catholic and not raised Buddhist?" I asked.

"I will teach him the four noble truths, and Christianity will teach him more about love and peace. It will be perfect."

"Now, you know I'm not the best choice to be a godfather. I've still got a lot of school and travel to do. I won't have time to spend with Robby. Is that still his name?"

The tone in Leah's voice got serious. "Yes, it's his name." She paused. The silence made me uncomfortable. "Okay," she continued with her campaigning, "if you won't do it for me, do it for Bob's memory, and after the ceremony, we can work out whatever you want."

Once she brought Bob into it, it was hard to say no. I gave in and said, "Okay, I'll do it."

"Make sure you bring your family," Leah insisted and then asked, "and do you have a girlfriend yet?"

I wasn't ready for that. "Yes," I told her and then asked with a laugh, "Are you jealous?"

"Maybe." she teased. "I just need to approve." She didn't miss a beat and continued cheerfully, "Bring her along. It will be a big celebration. You know how the Spanish will throw a party for any reason; like the day in May they call Cinco de Mayo."

Her laughter was contagious. I took down the information and told her we would be there. I thought I had better take Carol with me, figuring that her presence would keep me from forgetting that Leah was Bob's widow.

Dad rented a van. We left early Sunday morning on the drive to Payson and St. Philip the Apostle Parish. I drove with Mom, Dad, Rosie, and Carol, and enjoyed the scenic views. As we headed north, the typically hot Arizona sun was obscured behind thick clouds for the first time in months. On the Beeline Highway, Mom, the world's champion worrywart, kept telling me to slow down, watch out for that guy on the side of the road, and stop following too close. After each of Mom's driving tips, Dad would respond, "He's doing fine, Gloria. Leave him be."

By the time we got to Payson, I needed a drink. While Dad and Mom were checking us into the hotel, I took a bottle of Jack Daniels out of my bag and took a snort. Carol gave me a stern look. I smiled and said, "Mom's backseat driving makes me crazy."

"Your mom is sweet," Carol said. "You need to give her a break."

We entered the church through the narthex—a lobby area at the west end of the building. An usher recognized us and led us through double doors down a center aisle. I noticed that the pews, altar, and wall paneling were all made of dark wood. Images from Bible verses decorated the large multicolored stained-glass windows that lined both sides of the church. The usher seated us in the first row of pews that had a sign, "The Mackinens." The Bandeliers were sitting directly across the aisle. Once I was seated, I looked over at Leah and spotted her sneaking peeks at me. Each time I would catch her, she would turn away quickly.

I must have fallen asleep during the sermon because Mom pinched me as if I was a fidgeting kid. I saw Leah and Carol smirking and tried not to laugh out loud.

Finally, it came to our place in the service. The priest motioned us to approach the front of the church and gather around the baptismal font. A member of the clergy took the wooden lid off the vessel that held the holy water, and then the cleric said, "Blessed be God: Father, Son, and Holy Spirit."

The congregation responded with, "And blessed be his kingdom now and forever."

As soon as they said "Amen," the clouds parted and sent down a beam of bright sunlight that illuminated Leah, Robby, and me. Leah and her baby were dressed in white, and the light made them bloom and appear angelic. At that moment, Leah's and my eyes met. I thought, *it must be some kind of sign. Could it be Bob?*

Outside, the clouds had reformed, and the families were leaving for the reception. I took Carol over to Leah and introduced them.

"What was with that light?" Leah asked, incredulous.

I explained, "My parents said one of the Bandelier's Navajo ranch hands, Big John, just told them that natives believe that deceased family members communicate through signs. He's sure that the light came from Bob. He said that Bob spoke to Leah through Mother Sun. Big John believes that Bob's sign means that the baby's baptism gave him peace and happiness in the afterlife."

Leah nodded and smiled in a knowing way.

I wondered aloud, "But why was I in the light and not the priest?"

Leah snapped, "Because, Mack, you were supposed to be here. That's why."

Leah, Carol, and I had talked longer than I realized when Mrs. Bandelier said, "It's time to go to the American Legion Hall for the reception, Mack. You can follow us. It's five minutes away."

Carol started walking toward the car. As I started to leave, Leah put her hand on my arm, looked at Carol, and whispered to me, "Mack, you did good. I approve."

"Thank God!" I replied. "I would hate to have her sent back on a bus." At that, we had a good laugh.

We migrated to the reception, or what one of Louie Bandelier's brothers called, "La Robby's Fiesta."

Carol and I danced and had several margaritas while Dad and Mom spent time with the Bandelier clan. It turned out that Louie was in World War II, so he and Dad talked about their war experiences.

Leah came to our table to introduce a good-looking young man. "I want you to meet Juan Ortez. He is a deputy sheriff, so Mack, at the speed you drive, I'm sure you will meet each other sooner or later."

I got up from my chair, shook his hand, and chuckled sheepishly, "It's a pleasure. You're the first Deputy Dawg I've met. Glad to meet you here instead of out on the highway."

"That's not funny," Leah said. "Juan has helped me get settled in the community."

As he introduced himself to Carol, I looked at Leah and made my eyebrows go up and down several times as if to ask if they were an item. Leah wrinkled her forehead, made a sour face, and shook her head no.

The four of us had a good time the rest of the afternoon. We told funny stories about our lives, and Deputy Dawg related his adventures in the Sheriff's Department.

He asked me, "What was it like fighting in a war and killing someone?"

My answer was one word, "Hell." Then I stood up and said, "Look at the time, I'd like to stay but gotta go." I kissed Leah on the forehead and said, "Take care, Sweetie."

I took Carol by the hand and we left for the motel.

In the room, after our 'pajama party,' I got up to use the bathroom. When I came back in, Carol was sprawled out on the sheets naked, fast asleep. I stood there and took in her form, her hair, her eyelashes, the cute way her nose made her profile perfect. Leah's words came back to me, *you did good.*

Then I thought, *Carol did well.* She melted into my family like marshmallows on Thanksgiving yams. My mom liked her straight up, my dad's eyebrows and tilt of his head, when she wasn't looking, told me he thought she was a "cute little number". Even the Bandeliers took to her in record time. My sister latched on to her as a connection from her teenage angst to womanhood in a manner not possible with my mom, like a big sister.

I did what I knew how to do best—a preflight check. *Was I selling myself on Carol because Leah was off-limits?* That last thought kept me tossing and turning all night long. Instinct told me to make a move with Carol. My brain was cautioning me against merely using her as a replacement Leah. *Why does this have to be so hard?*

Over the next few weeks, Carol and I got tighter and tighter. My turning point was one night when Carol and I were just going to hang and do nothing special when Leah called. She asked if I was busy. I listened as she told me she wanted me to come out to the ranch to help her organize a scrapbook she was putting together to show Robby who his dad was when he was old enough. In the past, I would have been in the car before she hung up. Any chance to be around Leah was pure gold, and I would have never missed an opportunity. I could go tonight. I knew Carol would be okay with it. She liked Leah a lot and saw only Bob's reflection on my face when the three of us were together at the baptism.

I told her that tonight was not good for me, then asked, "Carol and I can come by on the weekend?"

I don't know if there was any disappointment in Leah's voice, but she said graciously, "Oh, that would be fine. Say hi to Carol and have a good night, Mack."

I hung up. I stood there. My brain, my heart, and my soul had been rewired by the electricity between Carol and me. I vowed right then and there to go to town and look into engagement rings tomorrow.

DEATH AT HOME

Carol and I got married that October and life became somewhat comfortable, with Dad acting as my substitute for Alcoholics Anonymous and Carol's love keeping my demons mostly at bay. Carol graduated from law school and got a job with a big law firm. Meanwhile, I grew restless and bored with college. After receiving an Associate degree in University Studies, which amounted to nothing in terms of leading to employment, I decided to leverage my experience with aircraft. I went to Oklahoma for a two-week quickie course designed to teach me how to pass the exam to get an airplane mechanic's license. Back in Phoenix with a Federal Airframe and Powerplant Mechanic license in hand, I was able to get a job at the local airport as an aircraft mechanic. Things were looking up as Carol and I settled into a suburban lifestyle. The Bandeliers would travel to Phoenix occasionally for business, which would give Leah and Robby time to stop by for a visit.

The following August, early on a Sunday morning, I got a call from my mother. It was not good.

Mom choked back tears.

I was worried. "What is it?" I asked.

Finally, she managed to say, "Daddy passed last night."

The shock of this news brought back a rush of old haunted feelings. At first, I felt dizzy. It took me a minute to catch my breath. All the while, my mother kept asking between sobs, "Mack, Mack, are you there?"

Finally, I could answer, "Yes, I'm here, Mom. I'll be right over."

I woke Carol and said, "My mom just called. My dad died last night."

Still half asleep, she said, "No, it can't be."

Angrily, I retorted, "Like my mother is going to call early and wake me up to play a joke saying that my dad died! Get dressed," I ordered. "My mom needs us now. She's all alone. Rosie is in Colorado."

On the way to my mom's, I said to Carol with exasperation, "How can this be? He was fine yesterday. We played golf in the morning. We went to a Phoenix Giant's baseball game last night, and he was okay when I left him."

Carol just hung her head and shook it. I could see she was crying. My dad called her his daughter too. I guess they were closer than I ever thought. She indeed mourned him as a daughter.

The day of the funeral was one of the worst days of my life. I had no idea what to say. What do you say when everyone you meet gives you the same line, 'So sorry for your loss.' Now, I know that people say things like that when they don't know what else to say. It was an uncomfortable situation to be in. I could only respond, "Thanks."

Up till that point, I had been around death, caused death, and narrowly escaped death, but next to losing Bob, this was the most profound death I had experienced in my life. The abruptness of it all; fine one day, gone the next. That was the most difficult part to understand. In Nam, the goal was to make it home to die in your own bed. My dad went through war, life, and all the battles of life, business, and family, and succeeded in dying in his own bed. For that, I was grateful.

After the funeral service, the minister said, "Everyone is invited to a reception at the Mackinen's house." By the time we got there, the house was crowded with fifty or sixty people. I couldn't take it after a while, so I slipped out to the backyard with my old friend Jack Daniels. I had just finished my second drink when Carol found me. My spirits got a lift when I saw that Leah was with her.

"Mack," Leah said as she came over and hugged me tightly, "I know how close you were to your dad." She paused. "I remember what you told me in the letter you sent when Bob died. I want you to heed your own advice. You wrote, 'You now must realize that your faith will get you through this,' but I'll change the ending. Christ loves you, and so do I."

I struggled in that moment as I heard my own words repeated back to me—and felt nothing. I mumbled, "I think God has been AWOL from my life for a while." My eyes were full of tears as I looked up and saw a stern look on Carol's face.

The three of us visited for a while, and then the girls talked me into returning to the reception in time to say goodbye to almost everyone. I kissed Mom and Leah goodbye, and then Carol and I left. Leah decided to stay with my mother that night before heading back to the ranch.

On the way home, Carol was unusually serious and quiet.

"What's wrong?" I asked.

"Nothing!" she said curtly.

Knowing her, I said, "I can see you're pissed. What did I do this time?"

"What is it between you and Leah?" she blurted out.

"What are you talking about?" I raised my voice in response to her insinuation. "She's the widow of a Vietnam buddy who died in my arms. I'd say there's a connection, a strong one, but it's only through our mutual loss." I tried to cool down.

"Then how come you didn't cry during this whole three days of your father's death and funeral until she showed up?" she accused, "And what's this 'God has been AWOL from your life' crap? What am I? Chopped liver?"

"You're nuts," I scoffed. "Of course, you've been great for me. I was just thinking about the war when I said that, not you. As for Leah, there has never been anything between her and me. I dated her best friend when I was on R&R in Bangkok."

"Dating! I don't think what you guys did with those girls is called a date," she huffed.

That got me angry, and I said, "I'd advise you to stop right now, or one of us will say something we can't take back." I thought, Carol has room to talk. She was a free love hippie when I met her. Leah did what she had to for her and her family's survival. Carol did it for fun.

Not long after Dad's death, black clouds began to form on my outlook on life. After more than four years of marriage, Carol decided that my occasional temper tantrums, binge drinking on weekends, and nightmares that scared her so much she started sleeping in the spare bedroom were too much for her. In February, she filed for divorce. I didn't object, and there wasn't much to fight over or split. She got what she wanted most of all, and that was her freedom from me.

Sadly, I still wasn't free from myself or the ghosts that continued to haunt me.

After the divorce, I decided that I needed to change my life. I applied for a mechanic's job with Trans World Airlines and requested a position at the Boston airport. Two weeks later, a letter arrived telling me to report for work at Logan Airport in Boston. I had three weeks to get there.

It took me less than a week to pack my few things, say goodbye to the dismay of my mother, and head east.

CHAPTER 45:
BACK TO GREEN ACRES

My life in Boston consisted of working forty-five hours a week for TWA and coming home to a small, efficiency apartment each night. To keep from going crazy, I would spend weekends at the family farm in New Hampshire. I stayed in the same very basic guest camp that my cousins and I lived in during the summer when we were tasked to help on the farm. It was just a one-room shack with an outdoor toilet.

My first morning at the farm, I woke to the sound of my two uncles on their way to the morning milking. I groaned as I got out of bed and dressed. On the walk to the barn, I got a whiff of what my uncles called the "smell of money." It might have smelled like money to them, but it was cow shit to me. That smell brought back memories of hundreds of early mornings growing up doing what I was about to do now—milk cows.

I entered the barn through white sliding doors and confronted one hundred cows—fifty on each side facing away from a center aisle. There was my 85-year-old Finnish grandmother, Mummu, hoeing the manure out from under the cows. One of my uncles was behind her, covering the newly cleared concrete with fresh sawdust. At the same time, my other uncle fed the cows into a concrete trough in front. Once the feeding and cleaning were done, the two uncles would start milking while Muumu moved to another barn where she tended the young calves.

I walked over to my grandmother and said, "Mummu, let me do that. You go make the morning coffee."

She chased me off and scolded me. "If you do my vork," she said, "vhere vill I get my exercise? You, go make the coffee."

Those remarks reminded me of what Grandpa told me at my going away party. He had said, "Don't bring back one of those small Asian girls while you're over there. You need to find a good strong Finnish voman. Pull plow." Then he winked, and we touched our glasses as if it was a deal. Unfortunately, he died while I was in Vietnam.

One Saturday night, while I was having dinner at the local Chinese restaurant, Joline, the girl who wrote me in Vietnam, walked in with her younger sister. Joline had been a year behind me in school and lived down the street from the farm. We had hung out together a lot while growing up. She was about my height, with an hourglass figure, and what some would rudely say were huge knockers. That night, her bronze hair with amber streaks was in a ponytail that hung below the top of her blouse. Maybe some would say that she was not a natural beauty—with a long face and pale skin, but I had always found her attractive. I especially appreciated her lips. They had a unique look, not like the Mona Lisa, but more like they were spring-loaded and ready to burst into free laughter, like a flower when it opens. Crow's feet at the edges of her mouth and eyes hinted that her smile was frequently used.

After the two girls were seated, I snuck up behind their table and said in a deep voice, "Hey kid, I've been looking everywhere for a date but haven't found a girl pretty enough until now."

I was sure that at her age, and still living in this small town where the men would rather go hunting than spend a weekend in the arms of a woman, my flirting came as a surprise.

I could see her struggling to ignore the comment, but she couldn't resist a quick glance up from her bird's nest soup. That laugh bloomed like a Roman candle as she said, "Mack, when did you move back in town?"

"I didn't. I live in Boston but come up here weekends to help out at my grandparents' farm."

"Well, Donnie Mack, have the waitress bring your dinner over here and join us," she said. "You must tell me what you've been doing the last ten years."

After settling in next to her, I told her about the job in Boston, Arizona, my parents, and the divorce with no children. I tried to stay away from talking about the Army or Vietnam. When she asked, I gave one of my regular responses, "That's a part of my life I just soon forget. Next time, I'm going to Canada."

"I'm a dental hygienist in Fitchburg, Massachusetts," she said. "And I just ended one of the two relationships I've had since high school."

Ann, Joline's sister, noticed that she was becoming a third wheel and excused herself. "I have an early morning flight back to Buffalo and still need to pack."

I stood up and said, "It was nice seeing you after all these years, Ann."

"Maybe I'll see you on the apron at Logan sometime," she said. "Definitely say hi!"

She looked down. "You two behave yourselves tonight," she said with a smile and left.

The next morning, we woke to the sound of the compressors that run the milking machines.

"What time is it?" Joline asked.

"Five a.m. That is the curse of a dairy farmer. Every day, even on Sunday, they start work at five."

She giggled and said, "I guess we didn't follow my sister's instructions."

"Actually, you behaved very well," I said. "If I'd known you were such a tiger, I would have thrown stones at Susan to drive her away while I ran to your house."

"I hated the way she treated you," Joline said with disdain. "I bet you weren't in Vietnam for a week before she started hanging out at the Legion trolling for men."

"She did make a fool of me," I agreed. "I stayed true to her for months, caught a lot of razzing and ridicule from the other soldiers overseas, abstaining like a boy scout while my buddies were out with the Vietnamese ladies," I said with regret.

"What are your plans?" she asked. "Are you staying here in the East or going back to Arizona?" She searched my eyes. I didn't hesitate to answer.

"The only plan I have right now is to awaken that tiger in you again."

Three months later, Joline and I were married in Las Vegas with only my mother and sister making the trip from Phoenix. During our

Las Vegas honeymoon, I found the first flaw in Joline. She was shitty at blackjack. On the positive side, she hit a $4,000 winning ticket on Keno. I thought, *maybe Joline's good luck is a sign that this marriage is off to a great start.*

With the money I had left in a "Carol don't know" fund and Joline's winnings, we had enough for a down payment on a house in Lexington, Massachusetts. I began commuting to Logan Airport by train, and Joline got a job with a local dentist. I still drank but restricted heavy consumption to weekends. I still had nightmares. Joline found a Vietnam Veterans support group. At first, I refused to go, but like Chinese water torture, I got a constant drip, drip, drip of Joline's "reminders" that I should go to the meetings. She finally wore me down, and I went to the Bedford Veterans Center.

On my first visit, a tall man with a well-trimmed day-old beard and a crew cut greeted me with, "Hello, brother, you must be Mack. I'm John. Your wife called and said you would check us out today."

"She probably told you that I was totally fucked up and listed all the reasons why," I added.

"She did say she was worried about you, and I can tell you that it's a big help having someone who cares. Lots of vets are alone, and it's harder on them. Let's start by me telling you about the program. We have peer groups. One will meet every weeknight at seven. The groups are led by someone like you who has been through the trauma of war. Sharing your story with others may help you feel more comfortable talking about your experiences. Listening to other people talk about their events with similar pain also helps. You can learn to deal with difficult emotions like anger, shame, guilt, and fear if you open up to others who understand."

"I'm not a big talker about my time in 'Nam," I explained.

"That's up to you. There is no pressure here. Joining a peer support group can help you feel better in any number of ways, such as...."

John held up his hand in a fist, and as he listed each item, he extended a finger. One, knowing that others are going through something similar. Two, learning tips on how to handle day-to-day challenges. Three, meeting new friends or connecting with others who understand you. Four, learning how to talk about things that bother you or how to ask for help, and five, learning to trust other people.

When he finished, all five fingers were extended, and I thought, *we're off to a good start. He can count to five.*

I attended a few meetings but thought the vets attending were REMPs just trying to get Post Traumatic Stress Disorder benefits from the Veterans Administration. I came home and told Joline, "That place is just where Rear Echelon Mother Fuckers go to cry and try for PTSD benefits."

We were married for a little over three years before TWA had a big layoff, and I lost my job. As a result, my life abruptly changed and became a routine of applying for work in the mornings and spending my afternoons at O'Malley's Bar in Roxbury. While I was getting hammered at the bar, Joline worked a second job to pay the bills. Finally, I came to a place where I thought that Jack Daniels was now my only friend.

After several months of this, Joline told me she had had enough, and we divorced. The money from selling the house paid all the bills, and she moved back to New Hampshire while I moved into a dump in Roxbury. Facing some semblance of reality, I swallowed my pride and applied for VA benefits. The VA checks and odd jobs I picked up paid for my meager existence.

I had several girlfriends over the next two years, but the problem was that most of them couldn't put up with me, and the ones that could,

I couldn't stand. I was continually getting into fights for reasons I didn't remember the next day. Out of embarrassment, I erased my mother's numerous voicemails. My mindset was that I had enough income to feed my alcohol habit, score a joint of marijuana now and then, and for food and rent. I thought, *what else do I need?* A small part of me knew I was at the bottom of the human food chain, but the larger part of me didn't give a shit.

CHAPTER 46:
SHANGHAI STYLE RESCULE

If I had to select the lowest point in my life, it was one particular day at Roxbury's lowly rat hole O'Malley's Bar when I came in for my daily pick-me-up of shots with beer chasers. Upon seeing me come through the door, the owner Patrick O'Malley tossed a coaster on the bar with the Red Sox logo on it and asked, "The usual?"

"Ya, and keep 'em coming."

Placing a glass with a double shot of Jack Daniels and a 24-ounce Budweiser on the coaster he said, "Some Fed who claimed he was from D.C. was in here wanting to know if I knew you."

"So? What did you tell him?"

"I said I did. Then he asked where he could locate you."

"That you didn't tell him. Did you?"

"And what, lose $600 a month in revenue? Of course not!" As he threw a dirty bar towel in the sink, he continued, "I told him you went to Florida to work on your tan."

"So, my friend, $600 a month buys your silence?" I grinned as I told him, "I knew my drinking would pay off some day."

"Friends don't start trouble in here," he said sternly, and asked "So, what did you do now?"

"Probably about my taxes."

Another customer bellied up to the bar and Pat went to greet him. I looked down at the Sox coaster and heard the warning words of that Master Sergeant the first day he arrived in Bangkok, "Loose lips lead to Leavenworth." Then I thought, *I did talk about Laos and Cambodia in the Veterans group meeting and that's supposed to be top secret. Could it be that?*

I decided they would have to catch me first. "Pat," I called over, tapping my empty glass, "Uno mas."

Five hours later, I staggered out of the bar using the back door... and just in case, I never went back.

I found a new "pharmacy" to fulfill the daily prescription I had carved into my soul. As always, the place was dimly lit, and the only sound was that of pool balls clacking into one another, usually followed by the sound of a cuss word or two. The only brightness came from the sunlight that entered the room through the periodic opening of the front door as people came and left. It was a perfect replacement for Patty O'Malley's.

One day, as I was self-medicating, with no idea as to what time it was, I turned from my beer and became dimly aware of a dark figure silhouetted against the light from the door. When my pupils adjusted to the light, the shadowy figure came into focus. "Fuck, it's Leah," I said under my breath.

As she walked toward me, I recalled a line from an old black and white movie I had recently watched during one of my sleepless nights. I said, "Of all the gin joints, in all the towns, in all the world, she walks into mine. Did I get that right, Leah?"

Leah sat beside me and asked, "What have you done to yourself?"

"Why do you care?" I couldn't look at her.

"Seems like your mother and I are the only ones that care. You don't.

"So that's how you found me." I leaned back on my bar stool, slammed my fist down on the bar, and exclaimed, "My mother!"

"Yes, and I'm here to take you back to the ranch and..." She looked down and read off a piece of paper, enunciating each word, "get your head screwed on straight." She looked up at me from the paper and asked, "Did I get that right, Mack?"

"The hell you are!" I barked at the bar and shook my head. "I've fucked up too many people's lives already. I'm not giving you and the Bandeliers the same opportunity."

She ignored me and said, "If you agree, I'll get you sober. I'll teach you to find a peaceful mind, but don't think this is a free ride. You will work on the ranch during the day and follow my instructions on how to heal yourself."

"What did I say, Leah?" I shouted in exasperation, 'No!'"

One of the degenerates shooting pool asked, "Hey, Mack, who's the gook? Is she here to tell you about your kid in Vietnam?" The other four at the pool table and the bartender thought that was humorous.

"Fuck you, Hollis," I slurred. "She's Thai, not Vietnamese."

He walked over to us, put his arm around Leah, smiled at me, then at her, and said lasciviously, "I'd sure like to get into your pants, little girl."

"Why? Did you shit yours?" I asked him angrily.

Without moving, he looked up at me and replied, "I never had any Thai puss...."

Wham! He never got to finish his thought because he ate my beer bottle. The other four started for me and I threw a napkin holder off the bar at them. It missed. I heard the bartender shout, "Mack, that's it. I'm calling the cops. This time they'll pull your probation."

Hollis' buddies got to me. I hit one of them pretty good, but the others grabbed me. They started working me over with multiple punches. One lifted his head and called out, "Don't bother with the cops. Call the morgue."

In between punches, I saw Leah break a pool cue in half and start toward me and the others. Next, I heard a crack. That was when Leah smacked the guy who was holding onto me. When the stick contacted the side of his head, his arms went limp, and he released his grip. We both fell to the floor. With what seemed like lightning speed, Leah cracked another one of my tormentors—first in the head, then the ribs, and then back to his head. He was out.

I shook the cobwebs off, stood up, and said, "Three down; two to go. I'll take the fat one."

"Good plan," she agreed as she leg-swept her target. Then she hit him in the head with one of the sticks as he was on his way down. I turned to see the fat hero run out the door.

"So, you had the fat one?" She said with hands on her hips, nodding towards the guy waddling out the door. Then she took my arm, tugged it hard, and said, "We go. Now!"

I was dazed from the punches and in awe of her. I asked, "Where did you learn that karate?"

"It's not karate." She straightened up with pride as she tugged my arm again. "It's bōjutsu—stick fighting taught to me by a monk who was a refugee from Tibet."

"So that's your secret," I said conclusively. "You never did tell me how you and Busa escaped the slave traders during the attack on the monastery."

Outside, she motioned to her waiting limo service driver, while she handed me a bar towel she grabbed on the way out to wipe the blood from my face.

As I slid into the black Lincoln, Leah said to the driver, "American Airlines departures, please."

She grabbed me by the shoulders, looked me in the eyes, and said, "Now you have a choice. Go with me to the ranch, or…" Her face was suddenly lit with a flashing red light as the police car pulled up to the bar. "The other option is jail."

"Arizona it is. I always wanted to be a cowboy," I said sheepishly.

She didn't respond. She just looked out the window, her face hardened by serious resolve.

Here was a girl from a million miles away, who I met at what I thought then was the worst time of my life, suddenly appearing at the real worst time in my life. I had turned into a joke, a rummy. The classic cliché, shell-shocked bum. She had come in like a Huey and plucked me out of the shit. I softened. *What was it? Duty? Respect? Love?* I wondered. What motivated her to come all the way across the country and pluck a dirty stinking dreg of humanity out of a slimy bar? Then I thought, *is this Bob protecting me through her?*

She must have sensed me staring at her and said loudly without looking at me, "You need shower!"

But the only person in the depths of despair neglected to look beyond winter to the spring that inevitably followed, bringing back color and life, and hope.

~ Mary Balogh

CHAPTER 47:
OUT OF THE ASHES

March 1985—My Mother, The Co-Conspirator

Stepping off the plane in Phoenix was like entering a blast furnace. I had forgotten how hot Phoenix can be, especially when compared to Boston's March weather. My hangover and the still sore bruises from the fight weren't helping matters either.

I came with only the clothes on my back, and Leah had only a small overnight bag. With no baggage to claim, we went right outside and hailed a cab to my mother's house.

"I'm so glad you're out of that mess in Boston," Mom said as she greeted me with a big hug. "I never liked that town. Leah, thank you for bringing my boy back to me."

"Mom, I am not a boy," I quickly snapped at her, "and your partner in this shanghaied me."

"Hold it right there, Mack," Leah protested. "I did not shanghai you!"

"You picked up English pretty good over the past fifteen years," I said.

"Don't you mean 'well?'" Leah asked as she teased me. She went on to explain, "I have befriended a family from Thailand who now lives in Holbrook and owns the Thai restaurant in town. Their daughter was born here and speaks perfect English. She taught me how to talk without an accent. Although when I get excited or angry, it sometimes comes back."

"She the one who gave you the note to 'get my head on straight?'"

"You bet your bippy," she said with a smile. "That is also one she says much."

"Shanghai schmanghai," Mom said. "I don't care how you got here. I'm just happy to see you out of that horrible life you've been leading."

I was too tired and beat to resist. "Okay, Ma."

"There was a man from Washington D.C. who wanted to know where he could find you," she said inquisitively.

It was like being hit in the back with a bucket of ice water. "What did you tell him?"

"O'Malley's in Roxbury. Brenda Haney's boy, Todd, said he saw you there once."

Safe. I thought, *glad that I had moved from one dark and dank watering hole to another.* "It was just something to do with my taxes."

"Right," Leah scoffed while rolling her eyes.

Mom said, "I have both spare rooms ready with clean sheets, and I opened the air conditioner vents, so it's nice and cool to let you get a good night's sleep."

I took a long hot shower, and as usual, Mom outdid herself with a big dinner consisting of steak, baked potato, corn on the cob, and my favorite—blueberry pie.

Leah was silent. Halfway through dessert, I got out of my own head long enough to ask, "Leah, how's Robby doing?"

"He is doing well in school. He likes math. Makes me very proud. This is the first time I have left him home with Mima and Papi. I will call him after dinner to tell him goodnight." She looked down at the table.

"It's hard when they are that young to leave them." Mom reached across the table and patted Leah's hand. "Thank you for leaving your son to bring mine back."

Normally, a moment like that used to cause me to get all mushy, but that was before the war. Now I just got up and left the table with a terrible need for a drink. I knew Dad was a teetotaler when alive, and I would find nothing left over to ease the pain in the house. My captor, Leah, held all the keys to the cars. To reduce the cravings, I went right up to the bedroom in hopes that sleep would drive my desires away.

Tired from the day's events, I uncharacteristically fell asleep quickly. During the night, I bolted up at the sound of an explosion. I got out of bed, looked around, and saw no signs of a blast. There was no sound of movement in the house either. It was 1:00 a.m., and I was wet with sweat. I then became fully aware that it was my old friend, the night terrors, revisiting me.

I laid back in bed for several hours and thought about how screwed up I have made my life. *It wasn't Carol or Joline, or TWA, not even the war. It was me. I know lots of vets living a decent life with family and friends. Why can't I do that? Why?*

Unable to get back to sleep, I went to sit on the back porch for the rest of the night. From there, I saw the first signs of morning. Hues of bronze, orange, yellow-painted the clouds in front of a pale blue eastern sky, and a dove cooed somewhere behind the house. All signaled the start of another shitty day in a life full of shitty days.

I went back to my room and got dressed. I then knocked on Leah's door and said, "Leah, if we're going to do this transformation thing, let's go."

Behind me, I heard Leah say, "Okay, I'm ready."

My mother came out of her room and asked with misgivings, "Do you have to leave so soon? I was hoping we could spend time together and go get you some new clothes."

"Yeah, Ma. It's a long trip to the ranch, but I promise I'll come to visit you soon," I said, fully knowing it was a lie.

It wasn't that I didn't love my mother, but Dad was the glue that held this family together. His passing changed this previously joy-filled home. I didn't look forward to visiting a cold listless house. It wasn't Mom's fault. She is lost without the rock that grounded her for twenty-six years. I knew I couldn't fill the hole that now exists in her life, so I did what I did best since my Army days. I ran from my responsibilities.

"Then go into your room and get the clothes you left here years ago," Mom chided. "Obviously, you haven't gained any weight. What did that wife of yours feed you? You're so thin. I never liked Joline, even when she was still in school. I don't know what you ever saw in her."

"Ma, let's drop it. It's not her fault we didn't stay together—it was my fault."

I got my old clothes, kissed her goodbye, and again promised her I would be back as soon as I got settled.

Outside, Leah was waiting for me in a new one-ton, Dodge crew cab, dually pick-up with the Bandelier ranch's rocking B brand on the front doors. She looked like a little girl in such a big truck. She had to adjust her seat all the way up to see over the steering wheel. This seat adjustment made her legs just long enough for her feet to work the pedals. I put a garbage bag of my clothes in the back seat and climbed in the front.

"Just to let you know, I could have left last night, and you would never have found me in this big city," I said.

"Then we are off to a good start. You must want to try my program."

I grunted a tacit approval.

Driving through town, Leah said, "You will get paid $80 a week plus room, meals, and the use of ranch vehicles after your probation."

"So, I'm not going to get rich working for you and the Bandeliers."

"No, but I'll get you sober, give you the peaceful mind. Then you can, if you want... leave," she said.

We got to the Beeline Highway by mid-morning. I remembered the first time I drove to Heber, long ago. The beautiful vistas as the flat desert transformed into mountainous terrain made me feel free—free like the deer in an open pasture. Today, I didn't feel anything but the shakes from abstaining from whiskey for a full day.

Finally, in Payson, I told Leah, "I need a drink. Look at my hands." I held them up and showed her they were shaking like a wet dog.

"After lunch, you'll feel better," she said, as she pulled up to a Mexican cantina.

She lied. I didn't, so I leaned back and fell asleep.

CHAPTER 48:
MEET BIG JOHN

I woke up still having withdrawals and had the added discomfort of a dry cough from the county road's dust, which filled my nose and throat. The world came back in focus, and the Bandelier ranch appeared ahead of us. It looked like a landscape by Andrew Wyeth, whose son I knew from playing high school sports. The vast brown high desert landscape ran to the base of ponderosa pine-covered mountains. The high-country forest fed a stream that snaked through the property on its way to the Gulf of California. Around the ranch headquarters in green irrigated fields, colts freely frolicked around their peacefully grazing mothers.

I realized the headquarters had grown from my last visit. The big house and two smaller cabins were still there, but they added two mobile homes and another barn.

"The place is bigger than I remember," I said.

"Yes, we have two new families working here," Leah said. "Both are refugees. One from Eastern Europe, and another from Guatemala."

"What? Are you taking in strays? Am I like one of your refugees?"

"No, they are not strays. The church sponsors refugees and ranchers that need help hire them. You are a particular case. Although you said it was Po, I still have a special place in my heart for you. You're the one who brought Bob into my life. Some think that I am lucky for my lifestyle here, but no one gets it. I'd gladly live in the slums of Bangkok if I could be with Bob. He was and still is my one and only soulmate."

"What happened to Deputy Dawg?" I quipped.

"He comes around, and we occasionally go out, but there is nothing there for me." Her voice was empty.

"It would be a crime for a beautiful woman like you to become a spinster."

Leah ignored the comment and said, "When we get to the ranch, you and Big John will share the cabin. Robby and I live in the house with the Bandeliers. Dickie has the foreman's house, and the refugees each have their trailers." She said as we parked in front of the main house.

Mrs. Bandelier greeted us warmly with, "Bienvenidos! Welcome. Come in. Have you eaten yet?"

"Yes, we ate in Payson, Theresa," Leah said. "I'll help Mack get settled into his new living quarters and then be back to help with dinner."

"Hello, Mrs. Bandelier," I said, doing my best to sound gracious. "Thank you for the opportunity to live and work here. I'm sure Leah told you of my checkered past."

Mrs. Bandelier said, "Jesus tells us not to judge but to give a helping hand wherever we can."

Leah added, "So does Buddha."

"Well, thank you again, Mrs. Bandelier," I said.

"Oh, Mack, please call me, Theresa, por favor."

Leah took me into the house that I would be sharing with Big John. There were two bedrooms, each with its own bathroom on both sides of a common area. A small kitchen table with four chairs took up part of the right hand section. The other side had a couch and two recliners with a TV. On the walls hung Native art. One got my attention—a large wooden hoop with netting in the center and feathers hanging from the bottom.

"What's that?" I asked as I pointed to it.

"It is a dream catcher," Leah said. "It's supposed to catch bad dreams while you sleep."

"That's something I need, but I think all that Indian voodoo is just shit."

Behind us came a deep voice, "I would not be too sure of that, brother."

I looked at Leah and softly asked, "Big John?"

Leah raised her eyebrows and nodded, "Yes, it is."

I turned, saw a gigantic man, and said, "Hi, Big John. We met at Robby's baptism."

He was sitting that day when we met. Now I could fully appreciate why they attach 'Big' on the front of his name. He towered at over six feet five inches tall and had to tip the scales at 300 pounds or more.

"Pleasure mine," Big John said while sticking his enormous hand out to shake. I was hesitant about this handshake. He could and probably would crunch my hand like a vice. I finally gathered the courage to meet his hand. My fears disappeared when all he gave me was a firm one.

Leah said, "I hope this is fine for you. You will work with Big John, and Dickie will run the rest of the ranch hands."

"It's a lot better than where I was in South Boston. I guess part of your plan is for this big guy to keep me on the straight and narrow path you've planned."

Leah got serious and looked straight at me. "There's no alcohol on the ranch. The closest liquor store is forty miles away, and you're not to use any of the ranch vehicles for the first month you are here."

"Well, at least this isn't jail," I snickered.

Leah turned to go out the door and said, "I'll see you at 4 a.m. tomorrow, and we'll start our daily ritual."

I heard 'daily ritual' and wondered, *What did I agree to?*

CHAPTER 49:
NEEDLES AND PINS

Someone shook my leg, waking me.

It was Leah with a stern voice. "Mack, get up. It's time to start our ritual."

"What time is it?" I squinted.

"Four a.m. It's time we get started. Get out of bed and put some clothes on."

I grumbled nothing in particular in protest.

"Let's go," she beckoned. "How did you sleep?"

I turned over and sat up. After rubbing my eyes, I finally said, "I tossed most of the night with bad shaking, sweating, and I could hear my heart beating in my ears."

"That will go away in a few days," she said with a reassuring smile. "I left some tea on the table. Bring it with you. I'll meet you at the Jeep outside. Now, come on. Let's get going. The sun will be up soon."

"Uh huh," was all I could manage to mumble as I got dressed.

We drove to the top of a Mesa. On the way, I drank her so-called tea. I remembered the razzing we gave the cooks in the Army, and asked, "What is this if they ask me at the hospital?"

"Don't be silly," she scoffed. "It's only herbs that the monks taught me to use for healing the body from toxic substances. Big John's grandmother helped me find the Native Southwestern substitutes I needed on the ranch."

When we stopped, I was astonished to see a Buddhist pagoda built with two Thai statues, both sitting with their legs crossed, leading to a raised wooden floor on each side of the steps. One figure played the flute, and the other held on its knee what looked like a bass fiddle but much smaller. Round wooden pillars held up an A-framed metal roof. The sides had four-foot-high walls and were richly finished with a dark stain and a mosaic pattern.

"Follow me," she said as she climbed the stairs. "It's not as elegant as the Wat Phra Kaew, which houses the Emerald Buddha, but it's mine."

Once inside, she lit several incense sticks around a seated Buddha carved out of wood and started a tape player with Buddhist monks chanting.

She had me sit on a rug facing the Buddha with my legs crossed and hands placed in my lap. "Place your right hand gently inside the left, which is a passive position," she instructed.

She inserted acupuncture needles with a round pan on top into the skin between my thumb and the pointy finger. She lit a cube in the pan of something that smelled like pot. While lighting the cubes, she said it is moxa and explained the purpose of moxibustion is to strengthen the blood, stimulate the flow of qi, and maintain general health. Then, without the burning moxa, she inserted more needles in my head, face, and arms.

"Now close your eyes. Start breathing full breaths," she directed. "Concentrate on the breath, in….and out. Whatever thought enters your mind, say okay and dismiss it. Keep the concentration on your breath.

Feel your body. Feel where you're sitting. Feel your hands; feel your arms. Release the tension in your shoulders. Release the tension in your jaw. Just concentrate on your breath and chase any other thoughts away."

A strange feeling of calm washed over me as the ache of the needles, along with the smoke from the moxa and the chants of the monks filled up my senses.

We did this for an hour, and then she said, "Open your eyes slowly and see the sunrise. It's a new day and the start of a new life."

Back at the cottage, Big John had breakfast waiting with coffee. All day I struggled with sweats, shaking, and heart palpitation. Our job assignment was to go to Snowflake for hay and stack it in the hay barn. The day seemed like it would never end, but it finally did, and I was exhausted. That night I went to bed after I ate a Spam sandwich. While I was eating it, I thought of my father, who used Spam as comfort food for lunch. *Dad, if you are there, I need comfort.* Thinking of him brought both consolation along with the sadness that he would not be here with his wisdom and guidance.

The following days were repeats of the day before, each starting at 4 a.m. Leah would come and get me. Every morning I felt a little stronger, and my shakes stopped in the first week. I still craved a drink, yet even that went away slowly in the second week. That is when I started to get a whole night's sleep. I surprised Leah one morning. When she arrived, I was ready to go. I made her Thai tea the way she likes it with cream and sugar.

CHAPTER 50:
EAVES DROPPING

I was at the ranch for two months when Robby came to me and asked if I would help him train for the local rodeo.

"Sure," I said. "I've never been to a rodeo before, but I remember watching them as a kid on TV from Madison Square Garden."

"My event is calf roping. Mom won't let me ride bulls or broncs. All you have to do is put a calf in the loading shoot. I'll be on Diablo beside the pen. When I shake my head, you pull a lever, and Big John will push the animal. The calf will take off like it's shot from a gun, and I'll rope it. Then I need to tie three of its legs together. At the rodeo, the fastest time wins."

"Is Daisy Diablo's mother?" I asked.

Robby said, "Yes, he's 16-years-old, same as me."

I thought so, remembering Leah showing me a colt in the stall with Bob's horse, Daisy, the first time I came to the ranch. Now I see he has turned into a magnificent calf-roping stallion.

I started to take walks around the ranch after dinner. One evening, I heard a noise in the small barn. I looked in the open door and saw two lines of five of our neighbors and some of their children dressed in white karate gis with colored belts across their waists. Most wore white belts, but a few had orange, green, or blue. Leah had a black belt with white stripes.

In a commanding voice, she said, "Hnung." All the students took a sliding step forward and raised their arms in a blocking motion. She then corrected the arm position on two of the younger students.

Then she called out, "Sxng." All took another step, and the block came down to their side, cocked, ready to punch, and the opposite hand raised to the blocking position. She repeated this cadence, with them advancing, snapping between stances with every step until they came close to the barn's wall.

She then called out, "Klap." The students turned and made a down-blocking motion. Then she continued her commands and repeated the process.

She saw me on the third trip the students made across the barn. Her command changed, and she said, "Khwam snci." All students came out of their karate stance and stood at attention. It reminded me of close-order drills in bootcamp. These guys were pretty good. We were sloppy until the D.I.'s beat it into us.

She then called out, "Reg tha serc laew." At that command, they all bowed, gathered their shoes, and bid her goodnight.

As the children departed, I approached her. I looked at her arm, "All that's missing is the tree up two down." She looked at her sleeve thinking there was something on it. Of course, she wouldn't know the rank of my sergeant first-class drill instructor, but I laughed to myself. "I thought you said you didn't know karate when you beat the crap out of those mugs in Boston?"

"I said what I used was bōjutsu stick fighting," she said with a smile. "I know several disciplines in martial arts. Come to our class. It will be fun."

"When will the next class be?"

"We meet Monday, Wednesday, and Friday nights at 6 p.m."

"I'll try it. Sounds like something better than listening to Big John's Navajo radio station."

My days were full, starting with meditation, back for breakfast, out to work, helping Robby with his rodeo training, martial arts training, and dinner. It got so I didn't have time to think about drinking, Vietnam, or my missed opportunities. I discovered I didn't have a night terror or panic attack in weeks. I wondered if Big John's dream catcher had something to do with the lack of nightmares.

After karate classes, I would walk Leah home, talk about the evening class, listen to the coyotes' howls, and stop for a few minutes to feed lumps of sugar to Bob's horse, Daisy. It got so that Daisy heard the class ending and would run to the edge of the fence by the path to wait for her treat.

One night, the moon was exactly right to cause the droplets of water on the field from the day's irrigation to sparkle like diamonds, and the coyotes sang a different, more soothing tone as we stopped for our evening ritual with Daisy. It was a cool night, so I took my coat off to put around Leah's shoulders. As I reached with my arm to place the jacket, she grabbed my hand, bringing it down into a hug. Our eyes met. Then it was like a magnet that drew her head to my shoulder. I had to fight the feelings I had suppressed ever since that first day I saw her at the Bandelier ranch.

"Careful," I softly said. "Daisy will get jealous."

"It's just nice to have someone to lean on. I don't think you're the only one that has benefited from our arrangement. I like our escape from me being a mother, managing the house staff, and walking a narrow path as a surrogate daughter. I have no idea what will happen when Robby leaves for college in two years."

"You know I'm here for you whenever you need me," I reassured her. "The Bandeliers show me all the time they value your living here."

"I know."

We walked to the bottom step of the porch with my arm around her shoulders. There we said our goodnights. As I walked, I was in euphoria. That was the most contact I had had with Leah other than a greeting hug ever. I tried to remember what she said, "not the only one." Just thinking of her admission made me warm like a teenager. I also thought about how God works in strange ways. Lady of the evening escort, fast marriage, death, and sixteen years later, the only thing the Bandeliers have of their son Bob was his child, a gift from heaven, brought on from the hell of war. I started back to my cabin when I tripped over a garden hose.

"Damn kid," I blurted out.

Robby washed his truck and horse trailer earlier in the day. He left all the hoses, buckets, soap, and lots of rags spread across the lawn and driveway. I decided to put everything away so Leah wouldn't need to scold him for the mess. While picking up Robby's stuff, I overheard heard Mrs. Bandelier say, "Mijita, come sit with me. Louis is watching TV, and Robby is doing his homework."

Leah said, "Okay, Theresa. It sounds good to sit and rest after a long day."

"You work so hard starting with Mack before dawn, raising Robby, helping around here, and then teaching karate at night. Why don't you take some time for yourself? You need companionship. I see you and Mack enjoying each other's company over by Daisy at night. I may be an old woman, but you two can't hide that you are both very fond of each other. Why don't you put down your guard and let him in?"

"I'm good. You and Louis treat me like a daughter, and I don't want to disgrace your family."

"Que es esto disgrace stuff? How could you do that?"

"How would you and Louis feel when people start talking about me bringing a damaged veteran here just to have a lover?"

"Mijita, we know that isn't so and who cares what others think. If I had heard of Mack's issues first, we would have sent Big John to get him. When I see him, he reminds me so much of my Bobbie, I can't help but smile."

"That is even a bigger problem," Leah said. "He does remind me of Bob, especially now that he is kind, outgoing, and loving like Bob was. If I drop my guard and get involved with him, is it Mack or the memory of Bob I fall for?"

As I walked back to my place, my head was swimming with different thoughts. What should I do? Make advances to Leah? If she gets insulted, will it ruin our relationship? I do care for her a lot. Then I remembered Bob's last breath was professing his love for Leah. How could I ignore that? What could I do? I remembered my father's advice. He said when faced with a decision that could make your life worse or better, and you don't know which one to pick, play it safe and do nothing. His view was that things will usually work themselves out on their own; so, I decided that was what I would do. Nothing!

CHAPTER 51:
DON'T MESS WITH THE BIG GUY'S HAT

July marked my fourth month on the ranch. Robby was having his sixteenth birthday and now could compete in the adult class in the local rodeo at the county fair.

When the day of the county fair came, Robby repeatedly honked the Dodge truck's horn with Diablo loaded in the horse trailer and the sun barely over the eastern mountains. "Come on, guys! We got to get to registration for my event."

"We're coming! We're coming," Big John hollered as he grabbed what he called his 'go-to-town' hat. That hat was a gorgeous one, a Stetson 10X beaver felt hat. He stuck what he called an 'eagle feather' in the multicolored beaded hatband but I was sure it came from a turkey. In New Hampshire, the turkeys run wild. As a child, I collected turkey feathers, but if all 6-foot 5-inch, 300 pounds of him wanted to call it an eagle feather, I wasn't going to argue.

John claimed he got car sick unless he sat in the front seat. That meant I was to sit in the back. To my surprise, when I opened the door, I found Leah curled up in a blanket on the opposite side.

I asked, "Why are you going so early and not later with Louie and Theresa?"

"I was already up with Robby, so I thought I might as well be one of the boys."

I looked at her and said, "With those good looks, you'll never pass as one of the boys."

As we approached the fairgrounds, we got caught in a line of several dozen trucks, campers, and motorhomes with one thing in common. They were all pulling a horse or stock trailer.

Robby asked with frustration, "Can you believe this traffic?"

"This ain't shit," I called from the back. "You ought to try to get to Cape Cod on a Friday night. It can take three hours to get across the Sagamore Bridge."

Leah added, "Or getting into Bangkok on a Saturday night."

"I trouble over nothing going to Window Rock," Big John declared.

I asked, "What is a Window Rock?"

"Da Capital of the Navajos," Big John sneered.

It took thirty minutes to get into the competitor's gate. Robby and Leah went to registration, showed his birth certificate, and got number 23 in calf roping. Knowing Robby would not compete until early afternoon, the big man and I decided to look around.

Fairgrounds everywhere are the same; just the junk that the hawkers sell is different. We walked through the barns where ranchers and farmers were grooming their animals for show.

Around noon the smell of a barbeque food truck called our name. We each bought turkey legs and large Pepsi's. We ate at the picnic tables beside the food truck while admiring the cowgirls walking away from us in those tight-fitting jeans. I suspect the two women eating at the table across from us were checking out the cowboys in theirs.

After lunch, I said, "Let's go see what they have on the midway."

Big John and I stopped and enjoyed the young ones screaming and laughing as they twirled around on a ride called the Himalaya. Behind the ride, the carnival's diesel generators roared, and their smell reminded me of mornings on Camp Holloway's flight line in Pleiku.

I was standing beside Big John when I saw the signs for the beer garden, and the old feeling of the need for a drink came racing back. Big John must have seen it in my face, so he said, "Let's go to the arena, and I'll explain the different rodeo events and how cowboys get scored."

As we walked towards the arena, I saw something strange.

"John, look at that," I said, pointing towards a green and white motorhome. "A teenage girl is struggling with a guy. It looks like he is taking her through that door. Shall we stroll over there to see if she needs help?"

"Maybe it's just two kids playing around," Big John said at first. "But there have been reports of missing teenage girls north of here, around county fairs. I think we better take a look."

We walked up to the camper and heard a whimpering inside. Big John knocked on the door.

"Is everybody all right in there?" I yelled through the door.

A male voice came back, "Mind your own business. We're just having fun in here. Ain't your mother ever told ya, if the rig's rocking, don't come knocking?"

I still heard whimpering. I asked Big John, "Shouldn't we see what's up in there?"

Big John tried the door and said, "She is locked." He opened his pocketknife and worked at the latch. The door suddenly opened, knocking him back. A man with no shirt jumped him with another close behind. Big John grabbed the first one of them and threw him on the ground. The second one came out with a gun. I grabbed the pry bar sitting on the motorhome's step and knocked the gun out of his hand. Big John hit him once, and down he went. Then Big John kicked the other in the head, knocking him out.

He turned to me and said, "Not much fight in um, is there?" He bent over to pick up his hat and then kicked the shirtless one in the stomach.

"Why did you do that?" I asked.

"He got my hat dirty." He handled his go-to-town hat and looked at it like it was a fine piece of art. He then took his massive hands, bent the hat in a couple of areas, and popped it up in another. He brushed off the dust and kicked the second attacker for good measure. Then he said, "What's in the mobile house?"

We went inside and found three girls handcuffed with duct tape over their mouths. I found the keys for the cuffs hung above the door and tossed them to Big John. He unshackled the girls, and I used the metal bracelets to detain our two attackers to the coach.

I looked toward the midway and saw Leah's deputy friend. I yelled, "Deputy Dawg, come here. We have a surprise for you."

He walked up and said, "How many times do I have to tell you my name is Deputy Juan Ortez. What's your problem?"

"Look," I said as I pointed to the two outlaws now recovered from Big John's abuse and proclaiming their innocence.

One said, "These guys attacked us for no reason."

"Really?" I said as I guided the deputy to the door of the motor-home. He gasped at the sight of the girls.

"Shit! This is big," he blurted. "I need the 'Shariff!' Hell, I need the state police, FBI, and maybe tribal police here too.

He fumbled as he grabbed the radio on his belt, keyed the mic, and said, "Sheriff, Sheriff! I have the 10-78 of the kidnappers from Page."

The radio squawked, "What's your 10-20?"

Another squawk and the deputy answered, "Behind the stock pens at a green over white-colored class A motor home."

"On my way."

Soon it looked like a second midway with scores of police cars, all with their red, yellow, and blue flashing lights bouncing off every building.

Leah came running and said, "What did you do now? I swear the first time I let you off the ranch, and you got the cops after you. And you, John, you're supposed to look after him."

"Slow down," I said. "Big John and I are heroes today."

"Heroes? My ass," she snapped.

"Leah, I think that's the first time I've heard you swear. How about you, Big John?"

"Yep! She never cussed before now."

Deputy Ortez walked up while we were teasing Leah.

"I'm afraid he's right," the deputy said. "Those two nitwits just broke up a sex trafficking gang."

"Nitwits?" I quipped. "Do you want to call my little friend here a nitwit?"

Juan ignored me and said to Leah, "The girls these two found were abducted. Two are from Page, Arizona, and the other is from here."

Leah said, "I got to get Mack home. He has diabetes and needs his insulin. The numskull forgot it at the ranch. If I don't give him his shot soon, he'll go into shock."

"Fine. Take him," Deputy Ortez said. "I can get what I need from Big John."

Robby missed his calf and was out of the competition. That meant Robby, Leah, and I left for the ranch. As we got to the truck, I asked, "What's with that story about me and diabetes?"

"Are you crazy?" Leah said. "You know there is a warrant for you in Boston, and you're talking to Juan."

"I didn't think of that, but what was I supposed to do? Let those girls get kidnapped?"

"Of course not. I'm worried he will find your warrant. Juan is a thorough police officer."

The next day, I was busy cleaning stalls in the new horse barn when Robby came running to me. Breathing heavily, he said, "Deputy Ortiz is at the house, and Mom wants you to join them."

"Well, let's go see what he wants," is what I told Robby, but I was thinking, *I guess it's true. You can run, but you can't hide from your past.*

I saw Leah and Deputy Dawg sitting on the porch with a frosted glass of iced tea.

"Come sit," Leah said to me as she called to the housemaid, "Margarita, please bring Mack a glass of tea also."

I stepped off the top step of the porch, and I used all my better judgment. I greeted him, "Good morning, Deputy."

Deputy Ortez put down his glass and asked, "What happened to Deputy Dawg?"

"Oh, that's a TV cartoon on Saturday mornings," I said as I tried to shrug it off.

Leah said, "Juan is here about your problem in Boston."

"I have a warrant for your arrest from the City of Boston," he said.

"I guess I'm your man," I admitted. "Now what?"

Leah stressed, "Juan, he was protecting me from an assault."

"Is that true, Mack?"

"That's why I started it."

Leah claimed, "I was the one that took out three of the four that fought us, and the fifth ran out in fear. If you arrest Mack, you'll have to arrest me too."

Deputy Ortez surprised both Leah and me when he picked up the warrant and tore it up. He looked at the pieces and threw them on the table.

He looked at Leah and said, "Nobody has seen this warrant but me. Because he's a friend of yours and your deceased husband, I don't think this should go any further."

We all stood up, as I sighed in relief.

Leah hugged the deputy and said, "Thank you, Juan. I'll make sure he stays out of trouble."

I shook his hand and said, "Thank you, sir. I'll leave you two and get back to work."

CHAPTER 52:
PHOENIX BOUND

Weekdays were passing by quickly as my daily schedule remained busy and full, as usual starting at 4 a.m. with Leah and ending with walking her home after martial arts class. I got really good at several self-defense disciplines. Weekends we spent traveling around the southwest for Robby's competitions at rodeos. Robby's skills improved, but it was Diablo who made money. Calf ropers noticed how the horse was fast and followed the calf flawlessly. Robby made money by allowing other ropers to use Diablo in their competition.

After one of the morning rituals as we returned from the pagoda, Leah said, "Robby has entered a rodeo in Phoenix. Why don't you meet some of your Army buddies while we're there?"

The thought of getting together with my old war comrades made me almost giddy, and I could hardly wait to quit work for the day and start calling. First, I called Vincent and told him I was coming to town the last weekend in August. He suggested that he would contact Ski and Rodriguez in San Diego to see if they could make it.

"What about Josh? Where is he?" I asked.

"Yeah, he's here in Phoenix. I'll call him."

"Looks like we have a rainbow coalition."

Vincent laughed and said, "Just like the old times when we would all get together and mooch off of Josh's stash from the mess hall. His cooking has improved. He now owns three restaurants here in town with Jared."

"You mean Francois Jah-red?"

"Yes, Jared, the French Cajun, moved from Louisiana to partner with Josh to open a Cajun restaurant."

"I hope the food is better than that slop in Pleiku."

"Believe me, the food is great."

"Speaking of Josh, make sure that shithead Ron doesn't come," I said.

"He lives in South Carolina, and I don't want that bigot here either."

Russ said he couldn't attend because he was in the middle of supervising a large construction project. I called a friend who still worked for TWA to see if I could wrangle a round-trip ticket for Russ to fly from Orlando to Phoenix. He agreed to help. I then informed Russ that it would cost him nothing to come and reminded him that I once took a bullet for him, and he owed me.

"How long am I going to have to pay for that?" Russ asked.

"Forever!"

"Okay. I'll be there, but please shoot me while I'm there, so we're even."

Levi heard about our get-together and said he would drive down from Denver.

CHAPTER 53:
SADDLE UP

We arrived Friday mid-morning in Phoenix at the Veterans Memorial Coliseum for the Shriner's Rodeo. I helped Robby set up the new Tracer 40-foot horse trailer that Grandfather Bandelier had bought him. It was the best he could find. The back had places for several horses; the front half had a living area that could comfortably sleep four people. The entire unit was air-conditioned and had a generator for power.

After Robby signed in for his event, Leah hailed a cab for Westward Ho, a luxury hotel built in the 1920s, and our temporary home for the weekend. Leah was unusually quiet during the cab ride.

"What's wrong, Leah?" I asked.

She shook her head and mumbled, "I shouldn't have suggested this little reunion of yours."

"Why?" I was confused.

She stared at her hands in her lap as she wrung them right over left. After a moment in silence, she looked up at me and said, "You've worked hard to rid yourself of the demons that haunted you. I'm afraid this little get-together with your Vietnam friends will summon them back."

"I can't stay sheltered at the ranch forever," I smiled softly and continued, "Sooner or later, I need to get out and live again. This is a good weekend to start. Let this be a test," I declared. "If the demons don't come back, you've been a resounding success and together we've managed to slay the dragon. If the demons do come back, all is not lost. That just means I'll need to spend more time at the ranch and more time with you."

She smiled weakly at me.

The cab stopped under the hotel's portico with large white letters spelling out Westward Ho against a bright red background. We were immediately greeted by a bellhop dressed in a blue uniform with gold trim around his collar and sleeves.

"Welcome to the Westward Ho," he said as he opened Leah's door. "May I help you with your luggage?"

I took one look at him and was reminded of a Navy dress uniform as I said, "Yes, thank you. Where is the registration desk, Admiral?"

I was sure that I wasn't the first to reference his dress as he ignored me and said, "The desk is through the lobby past the large white columns. What's the name of the guest for your bags?"

Leah said, "Bandelier."

A doorman opened one of the large glass doors revealing two sets of massive white columns in front of us. The thirty-foot columns were crowned with dark brown Corinthian style tops that held up a tin-paneled copper ceiling. As we walked towards the registration desk, the columns were beautifully reflected on the perfectly shined floor.

Halfway to our destination, I saw an older version of Russ sitting and reading the Arizona Republic newspaper.

"Russ! You old dog!" I yelled out. "You sound the same on the phone but look at you—you're old!"

He jumped up and ran over to greet us. With a slap on the back, he said, "God, you look good for an old crew chief."

"I guess I'm a cowhand now. Flying in Hueys is over for me. Russ, this is Leah, Bob's widow whom I told you about."

Russ took off his hat to reveal a head as bald as the palm of my hand and said, "It's a pleasure to meet you, Leah. I was with Mack when we medevac'd Bob, and all he could talk about was his love for you."

A tear formed at the edge of her eye and her voice quivered as she said, "Thank you for those nice words, Russ. Mack has told me a lot of stories about the adventures you guys had together."

Russ started to blush and said, "I want to let you in on a secret my Daddy taught me: 'Believe nothing of what you are told and only half of what you see.' That's especially true if it's coming from an Army aircrew."

I asked, "What happened to that long blond hair you were so proud of?"

"It just left, like my ex-wife."

"I'll leave you guys to catch up and go register for our rooms," Leah said as she left for the main desk.

After she was out of sight, Russ said, "Man, you're lucky! She is the sweetest thing I've seen in a long time."

"Russ, it ain't like that. Did you hear her say 'rooms' with an 's'? She is the widow of Bob, and I can't bring myself to think of her in your normal perverted way."

"What is it? Is she a bitch? Does she have bad breath or what?"

"No, I actually love her more like a sister."

Russ broke out in a big grin and said, "Then I have a clear path to hit on that little sweety."

I laughed, grabbed him around the neck, and said, "You do, and I'll hit on that big nose of yours." I wasn't laughing on the inside at the thought of someone trying to get together with Leah, not even Russ. I couldn't tell if I felt the need to protect her because I loved her like a sister or out of jealousy.

Leah returned and said, "Our rooms have already been paid." She looked at me and asked, "Did you prepay the bill?"

I looked confused as Russ jumped in and said, "Rodriquez learned something about computers and has some kind of big job with a Portland company working in San Diego. He paid for the entire weekend."

"No shit," I said. "I knew when he repelled down that McGuire rig to save a Montagnard, he was destined for great things."

After we sent our bags to the room, the three of us piled into a cab and headed back to the rodeo grounds to see if Robby would qualify. Russ and I cheered loud enough to embarrass Leah when Robby managed to make it into the top ten, which meant he would compete in that night's show.

That night, after a quick nap back at the hotel, Russ, Leah, and I returned yet again to the Veterans Coliseum. Robby was washing and grooming Diablo for that night's rodeo show. Big John had driven down to give Robby moral support and help him prepare for the evening's event. I introduced Big John and Russ.

"Russ knows nothing about rodeos," I quipped. "I think they wrestle alligators or some other dangerous reptile where he comes from for entertainment."

"Yep, and the winner is determined by who doesn't get eaten," Russ confirmed.

"Calf roping isn't that dangerous," Big John said as he took off Russ's baseball cap and replaced it with a cowboy hat. "Now, you look like you belong here."

Big John stayed with Robby as Leah, Russ, and I toured the vendors and food booths. We first looked at what I referred to as the 'good junk.' That was what you find at every fair, rodeo, or chili cook-off in Arizona. I bought Leah a turquoise squash blossom necklace. Russ got a pair of Tony Lama ostrich skin boots, and I got a Navajo taco.

We got back to Robby and Big John about an hour before the show was to begin, just in time to see Big John open the door to the camper part of the horse trailer and throw a cowboy out on the ground.

"I said no twice," he bellowed, "and now you see what happens the third time you ask."

The young cowboy limped off, as I asked him, "What was that all about?"

"All afternoon, we've had ropers trying to use Diablo for the weekend. Robby has to keep him fresh to compete against these PRCA cowboys instead of the ones at the fairs. Some don't want to take 'no' for an answer, like him," he said as he pointed at the competitor he just removed from his conversation.

"What is the PRCA?" Russ asked.

"It's the Professional Rodeo Cowboys Association," Leah said. "Here, lots of competitors do it for a living, but Robby has been roping, competing against local riders more for fun than anything else. Diablo has a reputation as a fast horse and can stay with a calf whatever way it turns. Robby gets paid when others ride Diablo in the shows. But in this rodeo, it's best to let Diablo rest between go-arounds."

Russ asked, "Does anyone get hurt in roping?"

"Not very often, but sometimes," Robby said.

"I'm going to check out the crowd," Russ said as he headed toward the people standing in the ticket line.

"Why are you going?" I asked.

He looked over his shoulder and said, "I gotta check if that fucking bad luck charm of ours, Captain Montgomery, is around. I don't want to see Robby hurt tonight."

"He lives in Wyoming, you superstitious idiot," I yelled at him.

He said a line I remember Montgomery used about not flying high to avoid the SAMs, "Never can be too sure."

Thankfully, Russ never found Montgomery. Diablo was by far the best horse that night, and Robby's aim was true. Their combination gave Robby the third-best time for the night.

On Saturday, the top ropers showed up and pushed Robby out of the top ten, which meant he could not compete in the Sunday finals. Big John and Robby loaded Diablo and headed for the ranch, leaving Leah and me his 1977 Ford F150 Ranger to use for the ride home Sunday. It also meant we would have time in the morning to swing by my mom's place and spend some quality time with her.

CHAPTER 54:
A THERAPEUTIC REUNION

Leah, Russ and I arrived at Josh's restaurant at about 9 p.m. A big bear hug greeted me as Vincent said, "You old dog, it's great that you got the idea to get us together." He let his death grip go, looked at Leah, and said, "Who is this lotus flower?"

"Leah," I said. "This is Vincent. He is the biggest womanizer you'll ever meet. Be careful. Vincent, this is my friend Leah."

Vincent took her right hand, kissed it, and said, "It's my great honor to meet you finally. Mack has told me how you brought him back from hell. Thank you for that. I was worried about him."

Leah said, "Thank you. Mack always speaks highly of you. When he lived in Phoenix, he told me about the adventures you two undertook."

Vincent smiled and tried to talk, but she interrupted and continued, "I know I don't believe anything I hear and only half of what I see."

"Smart and beauty, what a great combination," he said as he turned to me and smiled.

She blushed and said, "Thank you. I'm going to the hotel. You guys enjoy." She looked at me and mouthed, "Be careful."

Vincent grabbed Russ' hand and said, "Russ, you look good for a backwoods hillbilly."

"Thanks, Vince, great to see you too, city boy," he responded. "Where are the drinks?"

"Right this way, my fellow degenerates," Vincent said.

Russ and I walked into the dining area, and all the guys greeted us.

Before he shook my hand, Ski asked, "What can I get you?"

I guess he heard about my drinking habit. My mind said, *Jack on the rocks,* but I heard my mouth say, "Seltzer with a slice of lime."

"What?" Ski exclaimed. "When did you lose your appetite for the good stuff?"

"I ran out of drink tickets," I answered.

"What tickets?" he asked.

"You know when you're at a reception. You buy tickets from a cashier and pay for drinks with them. Well, I used all of mine."

Wanting to change the topic, I asked, "Where is Josh?"

Vincent said, "He's in the back cooking something special, according to his partner Jared."

"I hope it's not wiener schnitzel," I said. That brought out the laughter I missed from these guys.

"Thinking of fun, Vincent," Ski said, "you sure had a good plan with the ambulance and those girls."

"Yeah, it was also profitable until the motor pool sergeant ended his time in the country and went home."

I turned to Levi and asked, "Do you teach Apache English at the university like when you said, 'Me blessed sky horse. He soon carries us into great battle where we kill many VC?'"

"I sometimes use that vernacular, but mostly teach psychology and work part-time at the VA," Levi answered.

"Someone get a dictionary," Ski said. "The Chief is using big words."

Levi said, "That's Doctor Chief to you, Pollock."

Vincent chimed in and said, "Psychology. I don't know which I fear most. Talking to you as a medicine man or keeping to myself because you're a psychologist. You might figure out how fucked up I am."

Josh and Jared came in with the meals. I said, "Francois, what it is?"

"How's my favorite Finn?" Josh said while grabbing me around the shoulders.

"I'm good, now that the food's here. I hope it's better than what you served us in Pleiku," I quipped.

Josh opened the top of one of the silver chafing dishes. I saw baby lobsters and said, "You know, it's against the law to serve such small lobsters."

"Let me explain something," Josh retorted. "You're an unsophisticated northern Yankee. Those are crawdads."

"They sure look like lobsters to me," I said. *And never call me a Yankee. I'm a Red Sox fan. If you never call me a Yankee, I won't call you a nig....*

"I got it," Josh said as he held out his hand, and we shook on it.

We both laughed and said, "Deal."

That night was a trip back to the good times. The food was great, and the conversation was primarily light about what everyone had done over the past seventeen years. Ski had become an aircraft mechanic for a private jet charter company. Vince was a tennis teacher at the Phoenix Country Club. Russ worked as a superintendent of construction sites but still worried about Montgomery showing up and screwing up the day. All except for Rodriguez had more than one marriage. Vincent was on his fourth. His excuse was the temptation of teaching tennis to ladies with bouncing boobs in short skirts. It constantly led him astray.

The after-dinner drinks were as good as the meal itself. I was pleasantly surprised that the cranberry juice and soda kept me satisfied. Eventually, the conversation turned serious about the effects the war had on each of us.

Ski said, "The VA shrink told me that my crazy antics are covering up my true feelings about the prolonged traumatic experience."

Vincent looked at me and asked, "Do you remember Frank Forge?"

"Yes," I said. "When I lived in Phoenix, you and I got together with him when he was in town. Frank said he got a 100% disability from the VA for PTSD. You reminded me he was only in the flight platoon for a week, and they had a blade strike and crashed. Frank broke his leg and was sent home. After he left, you and I laughed that he has got to be the biggest bullshitter we ever met. Despite never having a bullet fired at him, he was able to convince the VA he had PTSD so bad that he couldn't work."

"We couldn't have been more wrong," said Vincent in a hushed and depressed tone. He paused and shocked us all by adding, "Frank committed suicide last May."

I broke the uncomfortable silence by turning to Levi and asking, "Do you deal with PTSD in your profession?"

"Yes, not only at the VA, but I teach a graduate course at the university. The reason I started in psychology was to deal with my own problems. You guys wonder why Frank took his own life when most of us experienced lots more combat."

"Yeah," said Ski, "What's with that?"

"There are several reasons for a person to do such a traumatic thing. He could have felt guilty that friends died while he came back in relatively good shape. Or maybe he couldn't get over the trauma that he could have died in that crash. It also could have nothing to do with the war. He could have had problems in relationships, legal, or money issues."

"Shit," I said. "This PTSD stuff seems to affect everyone differently. As I sit here and listen, some have problems with drugs and alcohol. Others with nightmares, panic attacks, loss of focus, and divorces. Everyone, that is, except that John Wayne, also known as Juan Rodriguez. You must be made from pig iron. Nothing affects you. Remember that S.O.B. Ron and how he said Rodriguez would be a drag on society?"

"Ron admitted to me that he bullshitted the VA into believing he can't work," Vincent said. "He does odd jobs for cash."

"Now, who's the drag on society?" I asked.

"Don't be too sure I'm not affected," Rodriguez said. "I've been told being a workaholic is also a way of avoiding the past."

"What Ski said tonight makes sense," Vincent said. "The VA told him that the nutty things he does are to hide his real feelings. It could also be my commitment issues."

"You all should come to the ranch with me in Heber and drink Leah's shitty tea, wake up at 4 a.m., have pins stuck in you, and listen to Buddhist monks chant while meditating. I think in three or four months, you'll be as good as new. Trust me, guys, the cuckoo's nest at the VA will be much easier."

"Look, guys, don't freak out," Levi said. "There are ways to help with PTSD. We have drugs to increase serotonin in the brain to help with depression and panic attacks. There are groups so you can talk things out with fellow vets. Both are helpful."

"Done that group shit and found nothing but crybabies," I said.

"You may be misreading those crybabies—it could be their way of crying for help," said Levi. "Your experience with Eastern Buddhist medicine is quite interesting. The Asians have been practicing the natural effect of herbs and acupuncture on the body and mind for thousands of years. Where here in the West, we have only started understanding their relationship. I want to visit Leah someday and get her views on healing."

Russ said, "I still have the sight burned in my brain at Dak To of dead men with legs and arms sticking out of sling loads and blood running on the ground as we set them down. Levi, why did the horror not hit me at that time, even though it's had such a lasting impact on me?"

Rodriguez asked, "How did we not realize what horrors we saw at the time; yet on quiet nights since then, all that shit comes racing back?"

"I believe that we were in fight or flight mode and rightly concentrated on our duty to help the ones still in harm's way," Levi reasoned. "Now we have time to process it. We realize what happened and try to suppress it with drugs, alcohol, or as we discussed, in several other ways."

"I can assure you, though, that nothing works until we get help," Levi concluded.

"I'm just barely getting over my horrors, thanks to Leah and her brand of brainwashing," I admitted.

"With all that perversion that was in your brain, that cleansing of your mind should have been a job for Lestoil, not Leah," Ski chuckled.

"I think it would be more like cleaning out an empty barn," Vince added.

Rodriguez asked, "Do you think Leah could talk to my wife about the tea she gives you?"

"I'm sure she would be honored," I assured him. That request made me believe that there were more issues with him than being an eager beaver.

CHAPTER 55:
ARMY TRAINING TO THE RESCUE

Mr. Bandelier assembled all the ranch hands at the beginning of September. He had a serious look to him, and I could tell he was worried.

"This year has been exceptionally dry," he began. "I want all the livestock moved to the lower pastures out of the mountains. I'll make a fire watch duty list. It will be for twenty-four hours a day, seven days a week. The person on duty must watch for lightning strikes and get the rest of the crew to respond rapidly with Jeeps or three-wheelers. I bought a brush truck—a Ford Ranger 4x6 that carries 1,500 gallons of water and can pump from the water tanks on the range. It will follow you guys if you can't stop the fire with the hoes, shovels, and backpack water cans. The key is to react fast enough before a wildfire gets out of control."

For the next few weeks, we had several fires on the ranch. Fortunately, they were all kept to a small area. A bit west of us in the Sitgreaves National Forest, a big fire did grow and worried us, but it was 75% contained within two weeks. We helped the Forest Service stop it just before it reached the ranch's border.

After we moved the cows out of their summer pastures, Big John and I went to Flagstaff once a week to pick up a load of hay to feed the herd. On the trips, we agreed Big John could listen to his Navajo radio until we got to Winslow, and then we would turn it to a Flagstaff station that I liked. The big Indian won that one because he understood both English and Navajo. The only word I knew in his language was Yah-ta-hey. As far as I could tell, that meant hi, goodbye, or maybe screw you. That issue was confusing because when Big John was with his family, I heard it a lot.

On our last weekly trip that September, as we approached Winslow, I changed the station to KAFF-FM. "Amarillo by Morning" by George Strait was playing. After the song ended, we heard a little jingle, then "KAFF-FM country radio." Then the announcer said, "K-A-F-F country weather on the thirties. Today expect scattered thundershowers with forty miles per hour winds gusting to sixty. That wind is bad news for those firefighters out on the Fox Canyon fire. Stay safe, guys, and here is something for you."

A country song by Waylen Jennings came on, but I didn't pay attention. I gazed over at the smoke from the fire and worried about the wind that could rekindle the flames toward the ranch.

The only interruption in our loading the thirty-foot trailer with hay was the increasing wind that blew Big John's hat and him chasing it.

I teased him and said, "You either need a Red Sox baseball hat like me or tie a string to that kite you're wearing."

"I need a New York Yankees hat," he quickly quipped. "They stay on top."

"That's cold, man."

We finished with the load. I took a towel from the backseat of the truck to wipe the sweat off. Looking South, I noticed the smoke from the fire had mushroomed. It looked like pictures I had seen of an atomic bomb explosion.

Looking at my partner, I said, "We better get back to the ranch fast."

Big John nodded approval.

We set a land speed record on I-40 for a one-ton truck with a severely overloaded trailer. I just prayed that no one would pull out in front of us. That would be like a freight train that takes a mile to stop. It would be about the same for this hay wagon express.

We were twenty miles from Winslow, and the squelch on the ranch radio kept breaking with static. When I read the sign, '10 miles to Winslow,' our radio gave us a garbled transmission. All we could understand was, "Mack, fire," and "Dry Lake." The rest was static. We passed Winslow and headed toward Holbrook. The further we drove, the more of the transmissions we could understand. It was Leah transmitting, and there was a problem with the forest fire. I tried to respond, but my mobile unit in the truck wasn't as strong as the ranch's base radio. Leah couldn't hear me. We could get syllables of additional words as the miles passed but couldn't make out the total message.

Turning south out of Holbrook, I keyed the mic for what seemed to be the hundredth time. "Rolling R headquarters, this is unit six."

The squelch broke, and Leah's voice came on, "Mack, where are you? I've been trying to get you all afternoon."

"South of Holbrook, five miles," I responded. "What's the problem?"

"Robby went up to put out a lightning strike. The wind blew the fire out of control and trapped him in the Big Rock pasture. The Fox Canyon fire has jumped the fire line and is headed towards him.

The whole ranch crew is trying to get to Robby, but the fire is driving them back."

"Where are the Forest Service helicopters?" I asked.

"They're grounded at Dry Lake fire camp because they say the wind is too strong to fly."

"I'll go there, and you can meet me."

She ended with, "I'll leave the ranch now."

Twenty minutes later, we arrived at the Dry Lake firebase. The smell of smoke filled the air, and ash fell like snow around me as I ran to the fire boss's trailer. Inside the trailer, I found a plump, fiftyish-looking man with a big beard talking on the phone to what sounded like a weatherman.

He gruffly said, "Okay," and slammed the phone down on his desk, missing its base. He cussed and then picked it up and stuck it in on the cradle.

Looking cross, he stared at me and barked, "What do you want?"

"We have a boy trapped about ten miles southwest of here and need a chopper to rescue him."

"Impossible. The winds are out of this world, gusting up to sixty miles per hour. They're fanning the flames like it's hell on Earth. No one can fly into that, and I won't let them."

I protested, "But..."

He interrupted me, "No, buts. I'm sorry. It's too dangerous to fly in these winds. All aircraft are grounded. End of story."

As we walked outside, I saw a civilian Huey and its pilot sleeping in the backseat. Big John and I walked up and shook his foot to wake him. On his flight jacket was a 1st Air Brigade patch that indicated he was in Vietnam.

I said, "What will it take for you to fly me ten miles and back?"

The pilot rubbed the sleep out of his eyes and said, "Can't do it. Regulations."

"I'll give you ten-thousand bucks. Look at it this way: nobody will be shooting at you on this flight like in 'Nam."

"No way. That's suicide."

"Okay," I said and motioned to Big John to join me at the front of the bird.

Big John was the first to talk, "What do you want to do, white man?"

"I'm damn sure not letting Robby burn to death," I emphatically declared. "I was unable to save his father's life in 'Nam. I sure as hell am not going to let Bob's son die too. Take care of the pilot, and I'll fly the damn thing."

"Are you a pilot?" he asked with concern.

"No, but I've flown these things a little before in 'Nam when the pilot was hungover."

Big John yanked the pilot out of the seat and firmly persuaded him to go for a walk. I untied the rotor blade and opened the pilot's door. The wind caught it and sprung it open so it wouldn't close. I pulled the emergency jettison handle and watched a gust take the door flying across the field.

I sat in the pilot's seat and saw Big John open the co-pilot's door and climb in.

I asked, "What did you do with the pilot?"

"I put him in the portable toilet and tipped it, so the door is on the bottom."

"Sounds like he's having a shitty day. Surely, you don't want to go on this ride. That pilot wasn't far from wrong in this wind, flying into a fire where any leak on this bird could set us ablaze with a non-rated pilot who has made no more than three or four take-offs and landings. This is close to suicide."

My big friend said, "I was there when Robby was born. If I can't save him, I will gladly go to the afterlife holding his hand."

"Nice words, but it's your life." I added, "I might remember how to start this thing."

Big John said, "That's a good place to begin."

"Starter generator in the start position," I called out. "Battery switch on. Main and start fuel on." I looked at my co-pilot and said, "Here goes nothing."

I pulled the starter trigger. Immediately, the snap of the igniters started. Seconds later, the smell of jet fuel burning was intense since we had no pilot's door. At 15% engine speed, I released the starter, switched the starter switch into the standby generator position, and shut off the start fuel switch. I slowly advanced the throttle to full. We both put on the headsets, and I showed Big John how to use them to talk.

I keyed my mic and said, "Whichever Saint is assigned to me today, I hope he is onboard."

Big John said, "Mother Earth won't hurt us."

"How about Mother Fire?"

"Not sure."

I pulled up on the collective stick to bring us off the ground. The mighty Huey jumped crooked, and the nose pitched to the left. I immediately sat the craft back down. I thought, *Shit! I forgot to hold the cyclic slightly to the rear and add the right pedal to offset the rotor torque. Hovering is too hard. I'll do a running take-off as my gunship did in Vietnam.*

I pulled enough of the lever to get the bird light and pushed the cyclic forward on the next try. We started moving. I pushed the stick further, and we sped up to translational lift.

Big John barked, "Look out in front."

A Forest Service brush truck started coming straight at us. Knowing we had obtained flight speed, I pulled in a lot more power, and the nose went left again. I overcorrected, and it went right too far. At sixty knots, the wind around the tail boom streamlined us straight.

Big John said, "You are shitty pilot."

"You can get out anytime you want," I snapped. "We're only at about 1,500 feet."

He looked down, turned back to me, and said, "I'm good."

I knew how to get to Big Rock Pasture and headed southwest at 3,000 feet above ground level. The wind was bouncing us around like a ride on a bull at the fair. At times, I couldn't maintain altitude. Orange and yellow flames were jumping from treetop to treetop below us, racing towards Robby. A cyclone column of fire rose to our left, and gray smoke was everywhere.

"We can't be sure what direction to land," I told John. "A fire this big sucks air to burn. It can change wind direction at different altitudes It may make it a rough landing."

"Then stop being a shitty pilot."

Finally, I spotted the pasture Robby was supposed to be in, but there was no Robby insight. I set up what a real pilot would call a steep approach into the wind and was turned back due to the fire's wind blowing me offline with the meadow. Aborting that landing, I climbed back to 3,000 feet. I now knew what the wind was like at ground level. Circling the field, I started another approach, this time with the storm's wind at my right side, and at 500 feet, the wind caused by the fire turned to be on my nose.

I decided to do a running landing since, as Big John said, 'I am a shitty pilot,' and hovering in ideal conditions is beyond my capabilities. Hovering in these winds, I wouldn't stand a chance keeping the Huey in one piece. The instant my skids touched the ground, I dumped all the pitch out of the rotor blades and skidded to a stop.

I looked at Big John and said, "We've got to find Robby." The smoke caused my eyes to water, and the heat was intense from the approaching fire. I thought, *I hope that Huey can take this heat without spontaneously combusting.*

Both Big John and I called out loud for Robby. He spotted an area with no grass and yelled, "Over there."

We both ran to the spot. Big John pulled on a poncho covered with dirt. There he was. The intelligent little shit covered himself to give him protection from the fire.

Big John smiled and said, "You listened when Big John said how to save yourself from fire."

The big man picked up Robby like a Raggedy Andy doll, and we raced to the helicopter. Back in the pilot's seat, I could see the flames approaching fast. There would be no room for a running take-off. Big John was tending to Robby in the cargo compartment as I pulled in power. This time, ready for the nose to lurch left, I added more right pedal as the ship came off the ground. Once again, too much pedal. I corrected. I then heard over the intercom, "Robby, Mack is a shitty pilot."

The overcorrections became less as my vertical motion swayed like a pendulum. I eased the cyclic forward to obtain translational lift. At about 500 feet, the wind shifted and pushed us towards a rocky out-cropping. I yanked in all the power this Huey would give me, and like the Army version, it came through. We climbed like a Roman candle, thankfully without the fire.

Back at the fire camp, I did another running landing. When the mighty Huey stopped, I saw Leah run towards us. I thought, *after all we go through, she is the glue that keeps us together. Grandpa would be amazed. Leah may not be Finnish or able to pull a plow, but she is as strong a woman as his wife Mummu.*

Leah ran to the back with Robby as I shut down the engine, took off my headset, and laid my head back on the seat while saying a short prayer of thanks. It took a few minutes to collect my thoughts and get out of the bird. Leah was hugging and kissing Robby. When she saw me, she ran up, threw her arms around me, and kissed me on the lips for the first time. It was like an electric shock went through me. I never felt a kiss like hers before. We immediately knew we had tasted the forbidden fruit and simultaneously pulled back.

"I don't know how I can ever thank you for saving my son," Leah said breathlessly.

"You already have Leah. You saved me." I smiled at her sheepishly.

Big John said, "I'm not flying with him no more. Him shitty pilot."

We all laughed before Big John and I started high-tailing it to the truck.

"There is no rush, boys. You're not in trouble," Leah said. "Mr. B. paid for the rental of the chopper and included a big tip to the dethroned pilot."

CHAPTER 56:
GOOD THINGS COME FROM BAD SITUATIONS

The rains finally came, and the fires came under control. Robby and I were on our way to the house when an Army helicopter circled the ranch and landed in the front pasture. I called Leah, and the three of us rode in the Jeep to see what an Army chopper was doing at the Bandelier Ranch.

A man in a dark suit and sunglasses trotted out from the 'copter. He hustled over to us.

"Chopper problems?" I asked.

Leah said, "You've come to the right place. Mack is a Vietnam vet Huey crew chief."

When he didn't smile, I resigned myself for my fate.

"Are you former Specialist Donald Makinen?"

"Okay. You finally got me. I..." I said as I held my wrists up, awaiting his cuffs.

He looked down at my extended arms with a screwy look. "Wait here, sir," he said as he signaled back to the helicopter.

A man in a suit was helped out of the back of the chopper by the crew chief. He walked towards us, and I noticed that he had a limp. Leah and I walked closer to meet him halfway.

The stranger said, "I'm U.S. Senator Franklyn Montoya from New Mexico, and I have had agents looking for you for quite a while."

I turned, looked at the guy in the sunglasses, and then back to him. I asked, "Okay. What did I do now?"

Leah jumped in, "He didn't steal that Forest Service contract helicopter. We rented it from High Country Aviation for that flight."

"Mack, do you remember picking up two wounded soldiers out of a hover hole LZ in a gunship?"

"Sure, how could I forget? It was one of those ass puckers."

"That's why I'm here. I tracked down your pilot, and he said it was your idea that a gunship could pick up wounded men if you dropped all the armament."

"Yeah, look. I'm really sorry. If you're from the finance committee, I know that stuff was expensive, but..."

"Mack, I'm one of the soldiers you picked up. When you dropped me at the aid station, I was within minutes of dying."

The smile on my face made him laugh. I held out my hand and shook his vigorously as I said, "I am so glad you made it." Then I snapped my fingers as it came back to me. The other soldier was black and covered in wounds, like a grenade had gone off in front of him. "You were the one with the head wound and the right leg bleeding out? Boy, I'm glad something good came out of that nail-bitter, hovering out of that hole in the jungle."

"As I understand, and that's all the more reason why I am here," the Senator said. "I want to thank you for risking your life to save mine and my squad-mate, Marshall Simmons, Mack."

"Sir, it was our job, sir."

426

"Well, I have the opportunity to make an appointment to a U.S. Marshal Service job in New Mexico, and I want you to take it."

The smile washed away from my face. "Er...Senator, I don't want to disappoint you, but not only am I not a law enforcement officer but there is a warrant out for my arrest in Boston."

"First off, it's Frank, to you. Second, thanks to Senator Kennedy, your record in Boston has been expunged," said Senator Montoya. "There's a slot at the Federal Law Enforcement Training Center in Artesia, New Mexico starting in three weeks. I need an answer today. I have been taking a lot of heat for holding up this appointment while I have been looking for you. The only reason I found you now is that crazy flight you made into a forest fire to save a boy. It made national news. So, what is it?"

I looked at Leah and said, "It's a chance for a new beginning. You'd only be a few hours away. Robby and I can visit," she said with a shaky smile.

"Senator, er... Frank, I think I'll accept your offer." We shook hands and then he pulled me in for a bro hug.

He smiled at me and said, "You done good, soldier. See you in Artesia. You've got three weeks."

I smiled at them all, one at a time. Things were looking up.

ACKNOWLEDGEMENTS

Thank You to Joe Badal, an award-winning author who convinced me to write a novel instead of a memoir.

Without Tom Avitabile, an award-winning author and my writing coach, and his teachings, this tale would not be so rich in sight, sound, and smells.

I want to thank Frank Perrin, Stun Nagurka, Bill Haigis, Russel Elliott, Carl Crain, Michael Maki, and all others who helped with my memory, grammar, structure, and input.

Special thank you to Jennifer S. Wilkov and Susie Ward at Your Book Is Your Hook, LLC, my editing, design and production team, and Estina Burgos at e-witched creative for website design.

STAY CONNECTED

To learn more about *Bikini Beach*,
please refer to https://bikinibeach.info

SPEAKING

Butch Maki is available to speak at:

 Book Clubs

 Literary Festivals

 University Visits

 Historical Groups

 Military Groups

NATIONAL VIETNAM WAR VETERANS DAY
MARCH 29

Please remember us on National Vietnam War Veterans Day each and every March 29th.

It was on this day 49 years ago that the last combat troops departed Vietnam. It was also on this day Hanoi freed the remaining prisoners of war the Republic of Vietnam was willing to acknowledge.

It is a day meant to pay tribute to veterans of the Vietnam War, including personnel who were prisoners of war or who were listed as missing in action.

ABOUT THE AUTHOR

At first blush, Walter "Butch" Maki, seems like a typical American success story with many turns in his life, from a decorated war veteran, turned blue-collar worker, turned political mastermind, turned entrepreneurial success story, and now an award-winning author. But for this New Hampshire farm boy who sees all this as "just doing his job," there was a dark side.

The honor and trauma that came from serving with the 170th Assault Helicopter Company in Pleiku, Vietnam, assigned to support the Fourth Infantry Division and the U.S. Special Forces.

For Butch, those minutes of sporadic, intense, and instantly terrifying warfighting followed by the ensuing hours of boredom in which to dwell on it all became a toxic mix that left a deep gash in his psyche.

His Army Commendation Medal, Purple Heart, Bronze Star and numerous Air Medals, including one with a "V" for valor, only tell the outside story of the war. Inside, like many vets, the trauma from the war invaded his life, initially causing rage and depression and relentless panic attacks when he returned.

From a Senior Advisor on a U.S. presidential campaign to building businesses and raising a family, Butch has won many battles since then to overcome the experiences that haunted him and continue his service to his country.

In his debut novel, *Bikini Beach*, love, understanding, and friendship are the special forces that get his main character, Mack, through the war and civilian life that followed it.

It is to those who served and their families that *Bikini Beach* is offered as a hand on the shoulder and a knowing smile.

Made in the USA
Middletown, DE
05 November 2023